THE SOUND OF BOER RIFLES
THE SOLDIER'S SON
BOOK II

MALCOLM ARCHIBALD

Copyright (C) 2024 Malcolm Archibald

Layout design and Copyright (C) 2024 by Next Chapter

Published 2024 by Next Chapter

Cover art by Lordan June Pinote

This book is a work of fiction. Names, characters, places, and incidents are the product of the author's imagination or are used fictitiously. Any resemblance to actual events, locales, or persons, living or dead, is purely coincidental.

All rights reserved. No part of this book may be reproduced or transmitted in any form or by any means, electronic or mechanical, including photocopying, recording, or by any information storage and retrieval system, without the author's permission.

For Cathy

British officers make the grand mistake of thinking their opponents are as stupid as themselves.
General Petrus Jacobus Joubert (attributed)

Only the dead have seen the end of war.
Plato (attributed)

Freedom is a noble thing.
John Barbour

GLOSSARY

Afrikaans: The language of the Boers.
Boer: Farmer; a descendant of the original Dutch settlers in South Africa.
Bok-bok: Child's game where children climb on top of each other until the lowest boy can no longer take the weight and the human structure collapses.
Burgher: For the purposes of this novel, Boer and Burgher are interchangeable.
Commando: A collection of Boers gathered for war. They gather by area and can be of any size from a dozen to thousands.
Donga: Marsh.
Dorp: Village, settlement, town.
Drift: Ford of a river.
Floreat Eton: "May Eton Flourish."
Galekas: A numerous tribe of Southeastern Africa.
Heliograph: Signalling device much used by the British army in the late nineteenth century. It works by reflecting sunlight.
Kopje: Isolated hill that rises from the plateau of the veld; often flat-topped.
Koppie: A small kopje.
Laager: A circle or defensive encampment of wagons.
Landdrost: A local government official.
Mampoer: Home distilled brandy, made from peaches or other fruit.
Mealie: Maize; corn.
Meneer: Mister, sir.
Morgen: A unit of land roughly equivalent to two acres.
Oom: Uncle; a term of respect used for older men.
Public: Public house, a term since shortened to pub.
Rand: Ridge.
Rooineck: Redneck; Boer term of contempt for a British soldier or settler, so-called because of their sunburned features.
Sawnie: Slang word for a Scotsman, particularly a Highlander, from the pronunciation of the common name Sandy or Alexander. By the end of the Nineteenth century, the term Jock had superseded it.
Scoff, Skoff: Food; the term became more popular during the Second Boer War, 1899-1902.
Shave: Nineteenth-century army slang for a rumour.
Slim: Clever, cunning.
Spruit: Water course.
Staatscourant: Boer newspaper.
Stoep: Veranda of a house, often used as a gathering place.

GLOSSARY

Swaddie: Slang term for a British soldier; now more often pronounced squaddie.
Taal: Nineteenth-century word for Afrikaans, the language the Boers spoke.
Taibosch: Tough bush.
Tante: Aunty; a term of respect used for older women.
Tarry-arse: Soldier's slang for a Royal Naval seaman.
Terai hat: A type of slouch hat.
Trek: Journey; the Great Trek was a mass exodus of Boers from British controlled Cape Colony northward into what became the Orange Free State, Transvaal, and Natal.
Veld: The high plateau that makes up much of the landscape of the Transvaal.
Veldcornet: Junior officer of a commando.
Vingertrek: Game of strength where men or boys interlock fingers and pull.
Vrou: Woman or wife.

PRELUDE

CHURCH SQUARE, PRETORIA, TRANSVAAL, SOUTHERN AFRICA.

12TH OF APRIL 1877

A flock of pigeons fluttered over the small crowd in Pretoria's Church Square, circled and split into two groups. The smaller group landed on one of the wilting trees, and the larger landed on the corrugated roofs of the low buildings. A single dominant male perched itself on the bare flagpole above the most prominent building. Busy with their own affairs, the pigeons ignored the people who slouched across the square, talking, smoking, and waiting for events with little apparent emotion. The noise increased when an elegant man alighted from a carriage, stretched his legs, and mounted a raised platform in the flagpole's shadow.

    Twenty yards from the carriage, a man on a slow brown horse entered the square, dismounted, nodded to a friend, and lit a huge pipe. The bandolier across his chest was half empty, although the rifle in its holster beside his saddle was oiled and well cared for.

As the crowd increased, a uniformed man slowly hoisted a flag up the flagpole, with a slight breeze momentarily ruffling the material, revealing the multi-crosses of the United Kingdom. When the breeze died, the flag hung limp, hugging the pole. The pigeon on top preened itself and cooed to attract a mate.

"That's not our flag," the man with the brown horse commented as he joined a small group standing in the shade of a broad *stoep*. He pushed the black hair back from his eyes.

"That's the British flag," a broad-shouldered teenager informed him. He stroked his smooth face, dreaming of the day he would feel a man's beard.

"What's it doing here?" the older man placed his thumbs in his braces and glared upwards. "We are not in Victoria's Britain."

"No," the youth agreed. "We are not."

"I am Theunis Steenekamp," the older man introduced himself.

"Jan van Collier," the younger man lifted his hat politely. "We farm Nuwe Hoop Plaas in the western Transvaal."

"Ja. That is a good name," Theunis said. "A farm of new hope." He nodded. "We all had hope until the British arrived."

Jan did not reply as he turned his attention to the head of the square where twenty-five uniformed police sat their horses. The police watched the gathering nervously, with some fingering the carbines in their bucket holsters. Jan thought they expected an outburst of emotion or perhaps violence from the crowd. He watched as the elegant man cleared his throat before talking.

"Is that Shepstone?" Jan asked, peering over the heads of the crowd.

"Ja," Theunis stuffed more tobacco into his pipe, puffed out smoke, and watched from under the brim of his broad hat. "That's the British diplomat who wants to take our land from us." He shuffled further back into the shade of the *stoep*, folded his arms, and watched through narrowed blue eyes.

PRELUDE

Sir Theophilus Shepstone KCMG had spent fifty-seven of his sixty years living in South Africa and was an acknowledged expert in native affairs. Now he stood before the Free Burghers of Pretoria in the *Zuid-Afrikaanse Republiek*, the South African Republic or the Transvaal, intoning the proclamation that annexed their nation to the British Empire.

The crowd listened, occasionally speaking to one another, many smoking so a thick blue cloud rose from the array of large pipes, bearded faces, and broad hats.

"Why do they want our Republic?" Jan asked as he folded his arms in imitation of the older man.

"The British want everything," Theunis replied, slowly puffing smoke from his pipe. "They think the Lord has given them the right to own the world."

"Listen," a grey-bearded man spoke over his shoulder. "The *Rooineck* is still talking. Let him tell us how they can solve all our problems." He tilted back his terai hat, with the leopard skin band catching the light. Jan wondered how old he was, with his skin tanned mahogany-dark by the sun and a myriad of wrinkles half-hiding his faded eyes.

The crowd subsided into silence as Shepstone lifted his voice. The mounted police stiffened in their saddles, with some still resting their hands on the butts of their carbines. An officer in front scanned the crowd, with his gaze passing over Jan's smooth face before he studied the weather-browned features of Theunis.

Jan could nearly taste the tension in the atmosphere. He glanced up as the male pigeon left its perch on the flagpole and flapped above Shepstone, its slow wings audible in the near silence. Somewhere nearby, a dog barked, high-pitched, with others joining in. The sound died away, leaving only Shepstone's educated voice to fill the square.

"What's the *Rooineck* saying?" Theunis asked, puffing out smoke. He held the police officer's gaze, refusing to drop his eyes.

"He's saying the *Zuid-Afrikaanse Republiek*, the Transvaal, is in

PRELUDE

financial and political chaos, and Great Britain will annex us for our own good," Jan said.

"That's kind of Great Britain," Theunis puffed more smoke. "They are a very charitable nation, annexing half the world for its own good and Britain's profit."

The sun cast a shadow from the flag, which fell on the small group of watchers on the *stoep*. Theunis and Jan were Boers with generations of African-born ancestors. A third man stepped beside them. He was very tall, with the skin peeling from his nose from the unaccustomed strength of the sun. This man stood straight, unlike the farmers, and listened to Theunis and Jan as much as Shepstone's speech.

"Now the *Rooineck* is saying Britain will cure all our ills while also looking after our external affairs," Jan said.

"I thought that's what he said." Theunis continued to puff at his pipe. He eyed the tall, red-faced stranger standing at his side.

"Then Shepstone said the Transvaal needed help because of the threat of the Zulus and other tribes."

Theunis nodded. "The Zulus are a threat," he agreed. "But we have defeated them before and can push them back. When the British come, they think they have the right to all the land we tamed with our blood and our sweat."

The tall man turned around. "Forgive me for interrupting a private conversation," he said, removing his hat to reveal cropped blond hair. Although he spoke in the *Taal*, his accent marked him as foreign. "I am Konrad Bramigan, a visitor to your nation." The broad white scar down his left cheek seemed to glow in the sun.

Theunis replied politely while eyeing Konrad with the suspicion he reserved for any stranger.

Konrad replaced his hat. "Not only the *Zuid-Afrikaanse Republiek* distrusts the British," he said. "You have powerful friends in Europe."

Theunis puffed more smoke from his pipe as he watched Shepstone pack his carefully prepared speech away. "That may be true, *meneer*, but Europe is far from the Transvaal." He removed the pipe from his mouth and surveyed the tall man. "Warm words may look good on paper, but they cannot remove the British. When they stole our lands before, we took to the wagons and trekked into the wilderness. Now, the British have followed us with pretended friendship to grab what the good Lord gave us." He packed more tobacco into his pipe with a calloused thumb. "We shall have to fight them."

Konrad smiled. "We can help," he said.

Theunis struck another match to relight his pipe, dropped the match, and extinguished it under the heel of his boot. "Who do you mean by 'we'? Tell me more, Konrad," he said as Jan listened in the background.

The man with the leopard skin band on his hat patted the breech of his rifle, turned his horse's head, and rode from the square. He did not look back.

CHAPTER 1

FORT AMIEL, NEWCASTLE, NATAL, SOUTHERN AFRICA.

AUGUST 1880

"Where is she?" Andrew demanded.

"Where is who?" The army hospital orderly viewed Andrew with total disinterest.

"I am Lieutenant Andrew Baird of the Natal Dragoons," Andrew introduced himself. "I am looking for Miss Mariana Maxwell. Where is she?"

"Oh, the lunatic," the orderly said. "We got rid of her."

"Lunatic? What? What do you mean, lunatic?" Andrew looked away for a moment to control his temper. "I'll ask again," he said, breathing hard. "Where is Mariana Maxwell? I left her in the garrison's care while I was on duty in Zululand."

The orderly shrugged. "Not in my care, mate. I'm here to look after injured and sick soldiers, not stray lunatics."

Andrew grabbed the orderly by the throat and began to

squeeze. "I've killed Galekas, Zulus, and renegades, my friend. Adding you won't bother my conscience."

When the orderly began to choke and turn red, Andrew released him, straightened his jacket, and smiled. "Where is Miss Maxwell?"

The orderly drew in a ragged breath. "She's locked up. We had to put her in the guardhouse." He rubbed his throat and backed away when Andrew lifted his fists. "It was for her own good, sir! She attacked Corporal Biden and was thrashing about, rambling in her sleep, and disturbing the other patients." He stopped when he realised that he was talking to himself. Andrew had already left.

The red-coated sentry at the guardhouse looked up as Andrew strode toward him. "Where do you think you're going, chum?"

"Inside the guardhouse. Step aside, private," Andrew ordered.

"I don't think so, mate," the private moved to block Andrew's way, hefting his Martini-Henry rifle. "This is a military fort, and civilians don't tell us what to do."

"I am Lieutenant Andrew Baird of the Natal Dragoons."

"Sorry, sir. I didn't realise you were an officer." The private snapped to attention.

"No reason why you should," Andrew glanced down at his civilian clothes. "I believe you have a young woman confined in the guardroom. A Miss Mariana Maxwell."

"Yes, sir, we have a woman. She's a colonial lunatic who attacked a corporal." The private smiled. "Not that I blame her for that, sir."

"Let her out," Andrew ordered. "I'll look after her."

"If you say so, sir," the private said doubtfully. "You should have a letter of authority or some such." He looked around for an NCO or officer for advice.

"If anybody enquires, tell them I have her," Andrew said.

"Yes, sir." The private stepped aside. "This way, sir." He hesitated for a moment. "Be careful, sir. She's a bit erratic. She shouts and screams in her sleep, and we had to restrain her."

Andrew took a deep breath. "Take me to Miss Maxwell, Private."

Knowing her history, Andrew felt responsible for Mariana. Her family had owned a farm on the border with Zululand, and Andrew had intended to marry Mariana's sister, Elaine. However, when the Zulu War started, a group of renegades murdered the Maxwell family and kidnapped Mariana, holding her prisoner for months. Andrew had been part of a mixed rescue party of British, colonists, and Zulus.[1]

"Yes, sir," the private said. "This way, sir."

Major Charles Amiel and the 80th Foot had built Fort Amiel only four years previously, and it still felt raw and unfinished. The guardhouse was solid, dark, and unpretentious, with small cells intended for drunken or insubordinate soldiers rather than traumatised women. Mariana sat hunched on the wooden shelf that served as bed and seat, with heavy handcuffs weighing her slim wrists and a gag in her mouth.

She looked up when the door opened, staring at the incomers through wide, red-rimmed eyes. Tears had streaked grime down her face.

"Good God! What have you done to her?" Andrew pushed past the private. "Mariana! It's me! Andrew!"

Mariana tried to cower away, hugging the cold wall as Andrew stepped closer and gently unfastened the gag.

"Don't touch me!" Mariana held her manacled wrists defensively in front of her.

"It's all right, Mariana," Andrew knelt before the bench. "You remember me. Andrew Baird."

Mariana gasped and tried to fend Andrew off with wild swings of her arms. He inched back to reassure her.

"I won't hurt you," Andrew promised.

"I told you we had to restrain her," the private tried to excuse the manacles. "She scratched the corporal's face. He ordered the restraints, sir, not me."

"Where's the key?" Andrew demanded. He took hold of Mariana's wrists, frowning at the ugly marks where the harsh steel manacles had rubbed off her skin. "Has she not been through enough with the renegades without the British Army treating her as a criminal?"

"I'll get the key, sir," the private said and hastily withdrew.

"It's all right, Mariana. I'm here now." Andrew put a hand on Mariana's shoulder. "You're safe with me. We'll soon have you out of these things."

Mariana's eyes were huge, but she did not resist when Andrew held her.

"Do you recognise me, Mariana?"

She nodded, holding up her hands in supplication.

"We'll have the manacles off you soon," Andrew promised.

The cell was tiny, stinking of urine and stale human sweat. Andrew heard a prisoner in the next cell bawling drunkenly, swearing with a long string of obscene oaths.

"Just a few moments," Andrew said reassuringly.

"What's all this?" A skull-faced corporal banged open the door and appeared in the doorway. "Who gave you authority to come into my guardroom?" He glared at Andrew suspiciously.

"The Queen did," Andrew replied tersely. "I hold Her Majesty's commission. Do you?"

"No, sir," the corporal said, coming to attention.

"Then release this woman." Andrew saw two long scratches on the corporal's left cheek and hoped they stung. "Now!"

"I'll need authority," the corporal said.

"You have mine. Set her free," Andrew demanded, "or I'll have your stripes and ensure you spend the next year cleaning out the latrines. If anybody asks who ordered her release, tell them it was Lieutenant Andrew Baird of the Natal Dragoons."

"Yes, sir!" the corporal reached for the keys at his belt,

unlocked the handcuffs, and stepped back, watching Mariana warily.

Andrew placed an arm around Mariana's thin shoulder. "Come with me, Mariana." He eased her off the bed as she rubbed her weeping wrists.

"It's the moon," the corporal muttered, retaining his distance as if he expected Mariana to lunge at him. "She must have slept under the full moon, and it's sent her mad."

"It's nothing to do with the moon, and she's not mad!" Andrew guided Mariana out of the guardhouse and through the fort, with passing soldiers staring at her.

A heavily moustached officer approached, frowning. "What are you doing with that woman? Who the devil are you?"

"I'm Lieutenant Andrew Baird of the Natal Dragoons, and I'm taking this lady where she can be treated with care and attention, not shackled like a criminal!" Andrew recognised the insignia of a major and added a belated "sir" while lifting his chin challengingly.

"That's Up-and-at-'em!" a private pointed to Andrew. "He fought all through the Zulu War from Isandhlwana to Ulundi!"

A small group of privates joined the speaker, staring at Andrew as though he were an exhibit at a showground. A smooth-faced youngster lifted his hand to wave until an older soldier hissed in his ear.

"That woman is dangerous, Lieutenant," the major nodded to Mariana. "She attacked one of my corporals."

"I'll take care of her, sir," Andrew pulled Mariana closer as she stumbled.

"If it were up to me," the major spoke through his unruly moustache, "I'd send her to Robben Island. They know how to deal with lunatics there."

Robben Island treated people with mental health problems. At one time, conditions on the island had been notoriously poor, and although they had improved significantly, the name still made people shudder.

"That won't be necessary, sir," Andrew said. "She's not a lunatic, just a woman who has been through a terrible experience. Excuse me." He eased Mariana past the sentry at the gate.

"That's Up-and-at-'em, I tell you!" the first private repeated. "He rescued that woman from a thousand Zulus."

Andrew hurried away from the fort before the tales grew even more exaggerated.

Andrew had rented a small house on the outskirts of Newcastle with a surrounding garden and a single soldier-servant. The garden was small, with a lonely Natal Krantz ash tree and a couple of patches of flowers. Andrew had no pretensions of being a gardener, but he did like to see the surroundings tidy, and a splash of green reminded him of growing up in Herefordshire and Berwick-upon-Tweed in the far-off British Isles.

"In you come, Mariana," Andrew opened the front door. "I've got a room ready for you."

The house was basic, for Andrew had few requirements. The bungalow boasted a square hallway with four doors opening off it. One door led to Andrew's living quarters, one to his bedroom, and another to a kitchen. The fourth room had been empty until Andrew converted it into a bedroom for Mariana.

"Go straight in, Mariana," Andrew ushered her inside. "I'll give you a quick tour." He smiled. "It won't take long as there's not much to see."

Andrew had bought a basic bed for Mariana, with a chest of drawers, a stool, a dressing table, and a mirror. When he glanced inside, the room looked spartan. He regretted his lack of experience with women and wondered if she wanted more.

"We can go into Newcastle and see what else you need," Andrew suggested as Mariana stood awkwardly inside the house.

"I get nightmares," Mariana spoke for the first time since leaving Fort Amiel.

"That's not surprising after what you've been through," Andrew told her.

Mariana stood at the open door without entering her room.

"I didn't mean to hurt the corporal. I thought he was attacking me."

"He's a corporal of British infantry," Andrew said. "He'll hardly notice a couple of scratches. Look inside your room and let me know if you need anything."

She'll need more clothes. I didn't think of clothes.

Both looked up as Andrew's soldier-servant appeared. "This lady is Mariana," Andrew said. "She'll be staying in the house for a while. Mariana, this man is Trooper Briggs. He keeps the place clean and tidy and does the cooking."

"Good afternoon, Miss," Briggs was in his late twenties, with quiet eyes. He nodded to Mariana and stood to attention in the hallway.

Mariana said a shy hello and dropped her gaze. She remained within the doorway, her hands twisting together and her head bowed.

"You'll be safe here," Andrew told her. "I'll come home as often as duty permits, and Briggs will ensure you want for nothing."

"I might talk in my sleep," Mariana said.

"Your talking won't bother anybody," Andrew said. "I'm in the room opposite, and Briggs sleeps in the barracks."

Mariana looked at her hands. "I had nice nails," she said. "When I scratched the corporal, some soldiers held me down and cut them."

Andrew lifted her right hand. A careless soldier had crudely hacked Mariana's nails, some into the quick. He drew in his breath. "They'll grow again."

"I might attack you," Mariana said.

Andrew put her hand gently down. "I'll understand," he told her. He gestured for Briggs to move away and guided Mariana into her room, where she sat on the bed.

"You've been through hell," Andrew said. "I am no doctor, but I can imagine how you must be feeling. It will take time, Mariana, but you will get better." He tried to smile. "I promise you will get better."

Mariana nodded, her hands twisting together. "Yes," she said with no feeling in her voice.

"I found you a book," Andrew said. "It's a bit battered, but better than nothing." Reaching across the table, he handed her a book of poetry.

"Tennyson," Mariana said, a flicker of light in her eyes. She leafed through the pages, stopping at her favourite poem.

"A bowshot from her bower-eaves,
He rode between the barley-sheaves,
The sun came dazzling thro' the leaves,
And flamed upon the brazen greaves
Of bold Sir Lancelot."

"The Lady of Shalott," Andrew said. "You always loved that poem." *So did Elaine.*

"Thank you," Mariana held the book to her chest.

"Briggs will make some breakfast for us," Andrew said. He looked up as somebody knocked on the front door.

"It's an officer for you, sir," Briggs reported.

A young subaltern, burned raw by the sun, threw a smart salute. "Lieutenant Baird, sir. I have orders to bring you to General Hook."

"Who?" Andrew asked. The name was vaguely familiar, but he could not recall the context.

"General Hook, sir," the subaltern said. "He's on the staff."

Andrew glanced at Mariana.

"I'll be all right," Mariana intercepted his thoughts.

"I'll look after her, sir," Briggs said. "Unless you want me to accompany you."

"No," Andrew decided. "Stay here with Mariana. Ensure she is safe and feed her well."

"I will, sir," Briggs said. He lowered his voice. "She'll be safe with me, sir."

Andrew nodded. "I know she will, Briggs." He nodded to the waiting subaltern. "Give me a minute to change into my uniform, Lieutenant, and you can take me to this General Hook fellow."

ELDERLY, GREY-HAIRED, AND WITH A NEATLY TRIMMED BEARD, Lieutenant General Hook leaned back in his chair and swirled the contents of his whisky tumbler.

"Tell me what you know about the Boers, Lieutenant Baird."

"I don't know much about them," Andrew admitted. "I fought beside a few in the Frontier War and Zululand, but they kept themselves to themselves."

"Tell me what you *do* know about them," Hook insisted. His eyes were as wise and knowledgeable as time. He poured a generous measure of whisky into another tumbler and pushed it towards Andrew.

"They're tough, hardy, good horsemen and excellent shots," Andrew said, remembering Piet Uys and his commando during the Zulu War. "They're also very religious and family-orientated."

Hook sipped at his whisky without his gaze leaving Andrew's face. "That's the Boers' positive traits. Do they have any weaknesses?"

Andrew cupped his tumbler in his hand. "I found them stubborn," he said slowly. "And a bit moody and argumentative." He recalled Uys's commando leaving the war when the Zulus killed Piet. "They're not very disciplined. They could ride away on a whim if they decided not to fight."

"That's a good start," Hook said, swirling the contents of his glass. "Do you know how the Boers came to be in Africa?"

"No," Andrew shook his head. "I haven't given it a moment's thought. I presume they just settled here, like the Americans in the United States or the Australians in Australia."

"Then sit back and listen," Hook said.

Andrew sat back in his chair, hoping that Mariana was alright and wondering why a general from the staff was questioning him about the Boers.

Hook poured himself another drink. "The Portuguese were the first Europeans to round the Cape of Good Hope, although they called it *Cabo das Tormentas*, the Cape of Storms. The Dutch passed by on their way to the Spice Islands of the East, and in 1652, the Dutch East India Company decided to build a fort at the Cape."

Andrew nodded. "The Dutch have been here for over two hundred years, then, sir."

"They have," Hook said. "With Cape Town fort as a base, the Dutch East India Company allowed discharged employees, soldiers, and sailors to settle. These people were known as Free Burghers and expanded eastward into lands the local tribes, the Khoikhoi, or Hottentots, claimed. It was inevitable that the Dutch and Hottentots would clash, with the first war in 1659. When that trouble ended, the Dutch bought lands from the Hottentots, but despite everything being ship-shape and legal, there was more trouble in 1673 and again from 1674 to 1677."

When Hook paused, Andrew nodded again, tasting his whisky. "I see, sir. So, the Dutch, or the Boers, have had to fight for everything."

"You get my point, Baird," Hook said. "The name Boer only means farmer. The Dutch were always a stubborn people, and they've had to battle for every square mile of land they own, which is one reason why they don't want us to annex their country. While the Boers continued to expand into the interior of Africa, their Dutch homeland also fought a series of wars with England. The constant threat of an English attack on their colony forced them to enlarge the fort at Cape Town."

"The Dutch were fighting on two fronts then," Andrew said.

"That's one of the downfalls of Empire. What you colonise, you must also defend," Hook said. "To return to our Boer friends. Around 1690, three hundred French Huguenots, or Protestants, arrived, including a parcel of women. They merged with the Dutch, adding new vitality and skills in winemaking." Hook smiled. "I find it hard to associate Boers with something as sophisticated and subtle as wine, but they are. South African wine is as good as French, in my opinion."

Andrew smiled. "I've never tried it, sir."

"You should," Hook recommended. "The Dutch colony continued to expand, with the Dutch East India Company very much in command. They rigidly controlled immigration, trade, the law, and what the Boers could grow. The Company could also press any Burgher into their service."

Andrew raised his eyebrows. "That's a bit draconian, isn't it?"

"Some of the settlers thought so, too," Hook agreed. "While most Free Burghers were law-abiding and stolid, others were not. As you'll be aware, every colony and every nation contain a wild element, the frontiersmen, Cossacks, bushrangers, or what have you. These wild men push the boundaries and see what's over the next hill. On the fringes of the South African colony were the Trekboers, the wandering or nomadic farmers. They farmed cattle and sheep, skirmished with the local tribes, and were arguably the toughest, most religious, and most bloody-minded colonists in the world. When they faced danger, they formed groups of fighting men called commandos to retaliate against the tribes or raid their cattle."

"Like the old riding families of the Scottish Borders," Andrew said.

"Very similar," Hook agreed, "except with a deeper religious base. Company restrictions irked the Trekboers, so they pushed further north into the unknown depths of Africa. However, while the Trekboers had been pushing north, the Bantu, another group of people, had been travelling south from Central Africa. Around 1780, the two cultures, or peoples if you will, met at the Great Fish River, to the consternation of both."

"The Bantu?" Andrew repeated. "The Black tribes?"

"You met some of them," Hook said. "The Xhosa, Galeka, Zulu, Matabele and all the rest."

"I met some of them," Andrew agreed soberly.

"In 1795, when Europe was in turmoil with the French Revolutionary War, the Boers kicked out the Dutch East India Company and became even more truculent. They lived according to their version of the Old Testament, put the local Africans into slavery and disliked all forms of authority save their own."

Andrew finished his whisky and placed the tumbler on Hook's desk. "Interesting people, sir," he said.

"They are a race apart," Hook said. "Their attitudes and ideas have barely progressed from the seventeenth century." He smiled at Andrew over the rim of his glass. "I'd say the frontier Boers make the American frontiersmen look like amiable businessmen, but again, they have spent upwards of two centuries dealing with floods, drought, storms, and various warlike tribes."

"And us," Andrew said sagely.

"And us," Hook agreed. "We arrived in 1795, acting for the Prince of Orange, whom the French had forcibly ejected from Holland. We took over South Africa, put down a Boer rising and held the colony until 1802. You'll remember we were at war with Revolutionary France and her satellites at that time. In 1803, we handed control of the Cape back to the Dutch Batavian Republic."

Andrew nodded. He remembered the basics from his school days when his history teacher had lauded Britain's military victories and glossed over the defeats.

"When the Napoleonic War started shortly after, we retook control of the Cape." Hook smiled. "The commanding general was a namesake of yours, General David Baird. Any relation?"

"I don't think so, sir," Andrew said. "Although I don't know much about the Baird side of the family. My mother barely mentions her forbears."

"No? Pity." Hook smiled. "When the Napoleonic Wars ended, Great Britain retained the Cape and imposed decent laws. When we prohibited slavery, thousands of Boers protested

THE SOUND OF BOER RIFLES

by leaving the colony in what is known as the Great Trek. They headed deeper into Africa; some clashed with the Zulus in Natal; others found what they termed the promised land in the high veld, empty of people and suitable for farming."

"Were there no native tribes there, sir?" Andrew asked.

"Not at that time. The rise of King Shaka of the Zulus led to some ugly wars that depopulated much of the veld. The Boers occupied it with little trouble. They formed a couple of republics up there, the Orange Free State and the Transvaal, both beyond British control."

Andrew nodded. "I can't agree with all the Boers believe, certainly not their keeping slaves," he said. "But I can't fault them for wanting independence. Or for their courage and determination."

"Perhaps," Hook said, giving Andrew a look that combined suspicion and doubt. "We had a couple of skirmishes with the Boers in the 1840s, and Sir Harry Smith annexed the lands between the Orange and Vaal rivers, renaming the area the Orange River Colony. With those lands safely under our belt, we signed the Bloemfontein Convention, declaring we had no interest in the Transvaal, the lands beyond the Vaal, which remained under Boer control."

"The Boers do the hard work, and we take over," Andrew murmured, wondering why a general was giving him a history lesson. He hoped that Mariana was all right.

"Careful, Baird, or I'll think you have divided loyalties," Hook warned.

"It's always best to see both sides of the argument, sir," Andrew said. "That way, we can determine what the opposition may do." *That is one lesson my father taught me.*

Hook raised a doubtful eyebrow. "I don't work like that," he said.

"As you wish, sir," Andrew thought it discreet to say no more.

"Naturally, there were complications between the British colonies and the Transvaal Boers," Hook said. "About eight or nine years ago, a prospector found diamonds in Griqualand West, where the Griquas live. They are another unique people with Boer and Khoekhoe ancestry. Harry Smith granted them some autonomy in 1848, but things change."

Andrew nodded. "Yes, sir."

"As Griqualand West is north of the Vaal, the Boers claimed it, but the Griquas sought British protection." Hook's eyes were level as he stared at Andrew. "The Boers' history of slavery and bad treatment of the natives counted against them, you see."

"I see, sir," Andrew thought it diplomatic to agree.

"An arbiter oversaw both positions and agreed with the Griquas, and in 1871, Britain annexed Griqualand West. We made it into a Crown Colony and bought the diamond rights from the Griquas for the princely sum of a thousand pounds a year."

Andrew grunted. "We cheated the Griquas, then." He glanced at the clock on the wall behind Hook's desk. *Mariana has been alone for nearly three hours now.*

"They had our protection against the Boers," Hook reminded him. "Both sides benefitted."

Andrew nodded. "Yes, sir."

"By 1877, the Transvaal was in difficulties," Hook said. "The state was bankrupt, the Boers were already fighting the Pedis and were on the verge of war with the Zulus, the most powerful tribe in South Africa," he looked up, "there's no need to tell you about the Zulus."

"No need at all, sir," Andrew agreed.

"Boers and Zulus argued about a parcel of land on their border," Hook explained. "A British boundary commission agreed with the Zulus, but added they wouldn't get the land back from the Boers until they disbanded their army."

"Yes, sir," Andrew nodded.

"The Zulus refused to lose their army, and the dispute continued. We annexed Transvaal, the so-called *Zuid Afrikaanse Republiek*, to save it from the Zulus and bankruptcy," Hook said.

"Sir Theophilus Shepstone and twenty-five mounted police announced the annexation, and the Boers seemed to accept the fact. As you know, we hope to confederate all the disparate colonies in Southern Africa into one cohesive unit."

"Yes, sir," Andrew said.

"You might not be aware that there is an outside influence," Hook added steel to his voice. "We believe that Prussia, or the German Empire as it is now, is interested in grabbing the Transvaal for itself. The Germans and the Dutch are very similar people in many ways."

"I didn't know the Prussians were involved, sir," Andrew said. "That alters the situation."

"Over the last twenty years, the Prussians have defeated the Danes, the Austrian Empire, and the French," Hook reminded. "They are now the dominant military power in Europe and are looking to expand overseas. They want colonies, a place in the sun, and the only places remaining for them are in the Pacific and Africa."

Andrew nodded. "Their presence in Africa could complicate matters. We already have some friction with the Portuguese in southeast Africa, and God knows what will happen around the Suez Canal."

Hook grunted. "We're keeping a careful eye on Suez, but our attention is now on southern Africa." He poured himself more whisky. "Do you want another?"

"No, thank you," Andrew said.

"Very wise of you. It's a bad habit." Hook placed the decanter on the sideboard. "Now, to return to business. We have not helped our cause in the Transvaal by defeating the Zulus. The Boers needed our protection while the Zulus remained a threat, but now we have removed that menace."

"I see, sir." Andrew wondered where Hook was headed.

Hook's smile lacked humour. "With the Zulu menace gone, I fear the Transvaal Boers are again discussing independence." He swirled the whisky in his glass. "The situation has echoes of

North America after we defeated the French. The colonies there no longer needed British protection and kicked us out."

Andrew nodded. "They did," he agreed. "With French, Dutch, and Spanish help."

"That's right," Hook said. "And Prussia may decide to help the Boers."

"Do you think the Boers will fight for independence?" Andrew asked.

"The Boers have already sent a delegation to London to ask for their lands back."

Andrew nodded. "I can't see the government agreeing to that."

"Nor can I," Hook agreed. "But I have heard the Prussians already have somebody in the Transvaal working with the Afrikander Bond." He waited to see Andrew's reaction.

"I've heard of them, sir," Andrew said. "The Afrikander Bond is a society of extreme Boers across South Africa. They want to unite all the South African colonies and lands under Boer control."

"That's correct," Hook sipped at his whisky. "Now imagine the Afrikander Bond with Prussia pulling the strings, and the diamonds of Griqualand, the gold of the Transvaal, and the strategic position of Cape Town under Bismarck's control." He leaned forward. "I don't care a twopenny damn if the Boers get their independent state on the opposite side of the Vaal. We can monitor them and control the worst of their excesses. I do care if the Prussians get control." He held Andrew's gaze with eyes that were suddenly basilisk-hard. "There's trouble in the wind, my boy, and I want you to tell me in which direction it's blowing."

CHAPTER 2

"Me, sir?" Andrew asked.

"You, sir," Hook said, with his gaze seeming to penetrate Andrew's mind. "You did good work in the Zulu War; you look like a colonial, ride like a colonial, and can talk like a colonial."

When Andrew said nothing, Hook continued. "I've known your father for years and discovered his talent for cloak-and-dagger missions. I hope his son has inherited the same skills."

That's how I recognised General Hook's name. He worked with my father, but I am my own man, not a copy of my father.

"I'm not even a proper soldier, sir," Andrew protested. "I was in the police, remember, and the army dragooned us into becoming soldiers."

"I believe you hold the Queen's Commission," Hook said.

"I do," Andrew agreed cautiously.

"Then you are as much a soldier as Lord Roberts, Sir Garnet Wolseley, or Fighting Jack Windrush."

Andrew grunted at Hook's use of his father's name.

General Hook grinned. "Now that that's cleared up, here's what I want you to do."

Andrew took a deep breath. "Yes, sir."

"I want you to enter the Transvaal as an observer, Captain."

"I'm a lieutenant, sir," Andrew reminded him.

Hook opened the top drawer of his desk, withdrew a thick envelope, and tossed it to Andrew. "Read the contents later. Her Majesty has seen fit to promote you to Captain. Congratulations."

Andrew stared at the envelope. "Thank you, sir." *I am now a captain.*

"No reason to thank me. Redvers Buller recommended your promotion."[1]

Hook continued. "In the Transvaal, you will wear civilian clothes and talk to the Burghers. I want to know how the people feel; I need to understand their mood. You speak the *Taal,* don't you?"

"A little, sir," Andrew admitted, stunned by his unexpected promotion.

"You'll need more than a little. Learn as much as you can." Hook tapped his fingers on his tumbler. "Do you know anybody who is fluent in the language?"

"I am sure someone from the Natal Dragoons will be fluent, sir," Andrew said.

"Find that someone," Hook ordered, "take him with you and bring me back intelligence about the Burghers across the Vaal."

"Yes, sir," Andrew said.

"You leave in two days," Hook said with a sudden grin. "Let's see if you can fill your father's boots, Captain Baird."

Briggs will have to cope with Mariana.

Andrew pulled Lancelot to a halt, removed his hat, and wiped the sweat from his forehead and face.

"Are you all right, Lance?" He patted the horse's neck and gave him a drink of water. He had known Lancelot since his first campaign against the Galekas, and the Kabul pony had never let him down. Lancelot was smaller than most British officers' horses and lacked speed. However, he possessed immense stamina, was as surefooted as a goat, and would continue when more spirited animals had long since given up.

Trooper Mark Kerr halted a respectful distance behind Lancelot.

Andrew looked around at the endless vista of the veld. In the nearly four years since he first arrived in South Africa, he had experienced many landscapes. He had seen the sunlit vineyards of the Cape, the hills of Transkei, the thousand grassy hills of Zululand, and the array of wildflowers of a Great Karoo spring. The austerity of the high veld was unlike any of these places.

Andrew felt a strange fascination for the veld. He found the idea of boundless space liberating, with the vast arc of the sky above and the long bare plateau stretching to a limitless horizon. He and Kerr could see a *kopje* chiselled against the sky in the early morning, ride towards it all day and feel no closer in the evening. The air was so clear it enhanced vision and confused men more accustomed to the misty atmosphere of the British Isles.

Yet Andrew knew there was more to the veld than mere space and freedom. There was some intangible magic in this landscape. Used to the grassy hills of the Borders, Andrew sought the solace of green in the sweeping array of dun, brown, and yellow. He felt relief when he saw the green line of mimosa trees marking a river valley, promising welcome coolness and water for horses and riders.

"How are you, Kerr?" Andrew asked.

"All right, sir, thank you," Kerr replied.

Andrew replaced his hat, lifted his field glasses, and examined the circle of the horizon. "We'll spend the night at that river course," he said. "And reach the next town tomorrow morning."

"Yes, sir," Kerr said.

They moved on, avoiding the conical red ant hills, four feet high and alive with insects. An ant bear watched them for a second from the security of its den and retired to await the cold of the night. A quarter of a mile further, they came to the communal circle of a meerkat family.

"Ride carefully here," Andrew warned, knowing the ground beneath the meerkats would be honeycombed with tunnels which a horse's hooves could easily collapse. Andrew was wary as Lancelot picked his way around the meerkats' domain and breathed more easily when they reached solid ground.

"The veld has hidden hazards, sir," Kerr said as they headed northwest. "Even the most charming animals can prove dangerous, and with *dongas* and *sluits* and stray predators, it's surprising that the Boers ever made this place their home."

They rode on slowly and steadily until Kerr sniffed the air. "I smell people, sir. We must be nearing a settlement."

Andrew nodded. The clear air of the veld had improved their sense of smell, so the distinctive scent of people carried to them on the wind. "Here we go again, Kerr. You know the drill."

"Yes, sir. We're horse traders and itinerant hunters."

Andrew's command of the *Taal* had improved over the last few weeks, but he knew he needed to be fluent. He allowed Kerr to do most of the talking as he listened and took mental notes. As they rode closer, they saw the *dorp* – the town – in the distance, with the details becoming clearer.

Andrew stopped at the outskirts of the *dorp*, allowed the dust to settle, and looked around. Used to the settlements of Cape Colony and Natal, he was no longer surprised by how basic everything looked.

"What's this place called, sir?" Kerr asked. "We've already been to Zwagershoek, Coetzeespos, Honingfontein, and Melkrivier." He reminded Andrew of the towns they had visited.

Andrew consulted his map. "This place is called Vryheidburg," he said. "It doesn't look much different from the others."

"Freedomburgh," Kerr translated. He looked around. "All these high veld towns look the same to me."

To Andrew, it seemed as if a blindfolded politician had jabbed a finger on a blank map and decided to place a village where his nail scored the parchment, for he could think of no other reason for Vryheidburg's existence. The village inhabited a barren stretch of veld no different from any other. The streets were rectangular, without any aspirations of architectural style, beauty, or grace, and held buildings that the owners might have erected in a day or two. The main roadway was broad, lined by small gum trees that wilted under the constant assault of an unrelenting sun, while the houses were single-storied and roofed with corrugated iron.

Andrew compared the settlement with the ancient villages of Northumberland, the Scottish Borders, or Herefordshire with their varied architecture, ancient churches, castles, and cobbled market squares. Vryheidburg did not gain by the comparison, although he admitted the British contrast between rich and poor did not exist in any of the *dorps* he had visited.

"It's easy to forget how new these places are," Andrew said as they rode into the town. "When the Boers rolled their wagons here only forty years ago, they found nothing except the empty veld. No villages, no roads, nothing. Not even a human being."

"No wonder the Boers thought it was the promised land," Kerr said.

Andrew patted Lancelot's neck. "Let's go and see what the people think," he said.

Kerr nodded. "Yes, sir. I doubt they'll be any different to the last lot."

"Nor do I," Andrew agreed with a wry smile. "Try to remember not to call me sir here. We're meant to be civilians."

"Yes, sir," Kerr agreed. "It's not easy calling you Andrew."

"Call me Baird," Andrew advised, "at least until we're back in uniform again."

"Yes, sir," Kerr agreed.

As usual in the Transvaal's *dorps*, Vryheidburg's stores had a stone frontage with the name above the door. The side roads met the central street at right angles, with orange and purple foliage covering the older houses and men lounging on long cane chairs on the *stoeps*, watching the two strangers.

Andrew and Kerr walked their horses slowly along the main street, with the hollow thud of the hoofbeats breaking the pressing silence. A lazy dog lifted its head from its paws, surveyed them briefly, slow-wagged its tail and returned to its daytime slumber.

"Not much happening here, sir," Kerr murmured. "Look, there's the weekly excitement."

An ox-wagon lumbered through the village, with the driver emitting a long, yodelling yell. Andrew watched the driver expertly handle his long whip, listened to him address each of his oxen by name and admired his skill at manoeuvring the wagon and team up one of the side streets.

"Is there any point in stopping here, sir?" Kerr asked.

"We'll talk to these men, Kerr."

Andrew pulled his horse past a couple of men deep in conversation on a shaded *stoep*. "Good evening, *meneers*," he said, lifting his hat.

Both men politely stopped talking to return Andrew's greeting. "Good evening, *meneer*," the older of the two indicated an empty chair on the *stoep*. "Join us." He clapped his hands to summon a servant and asked Andrew what he wanted to drink.

"Coffee, please," Andrew said. He had learned that the Boers were mainly temperate people.

When a servant brought the coffee, they drank silently as the men on the *stoep* appraised Andrew and Kerr. A pair of black-and-white birds flew past, with nothing else disturbing the peace of the *dorp*.

"*En wat over u, meneer?* And what surname do you bear, sir?" The older man eventually asked Kerr, the older of the two strangers.

"I am Mark Kerr, and this gentleman is Andrew Baird," Kerr

introduced them both, and they shook hands, raising their hats politely.

"And your business in the *Zuid-Afrikaanse Republiek*, *meneer?*" the older Boer asked, courteously but with steel behind the words.

"A little bit looking for horses," Kerr said, "and maybe a touch of hunting thrown in."

The Boers glanced at the rifles both men carried beside their saddles. "Hunting?" the younger man smiled. "You're twenty years too late, *meneer*, if you want to hunt here. Maybe try the low veld." He sipped at his coffee, waiting patiently for a response.

"We might do that," Kerr told him solemnly.

Andrew had tried to follow the conversation. "We were a bit worried crossing the Vaal," he said slowly. "We were not sure what kind of reception British settlers would get here."

The older Boer removed his pipe from his mouth and contemplated Andrew before he replied. "That depends on what sort of British settler you are," he said at last. His smile was slow and genuine.

Kerr smiled in return. "This is good coffee, *meneer*. What do you mean?"

The older Boer nodded gravely. "Ja, we make good coffee in our land north of the Vaal. Our land." He paused to allow the words to sink in. "If the British come as friends, then we will be friends, but if they come to tell us what we can and cannot do in our land, then we will not be friends."

"The British come to help you," Andrew said.

"No," the younger Boer shook his head, smiling faintly. "The British come to help themselves." He placed his coffee cup on the faded wood of the *stoep*. "I do not mean you, *meneer*. I mean your government and your officials. Your settlers here are much like us, but your country wants to control everybody and everything. Attitudes like that are not welcome in our land." He glanced meaningfully at the rifle that leaned against the door.

Andrew nodded. He had heard the same sentiment expressed across the scattered *dorps* and farms of the Transvaal. The Boers mixed genuine hospitality with a stubborn refusal to accept British authority. "Thank you, *meneer*," he said. "I have heard others voice the same opinion."

The older Boer smiled again. "Visit Krugersdorp, *meneers*," he said. "You might learn something of interest there." He raised a hand. "Go with God, and I wish you success in buying the horses you have not mentioned again and hunting over land already cleared of much of its game." He raised his hat in a polite dismissal.

"Thank you, *meneer*," Kerr said. "And thank you for the coffee and your advice."

"These people are sharper than we believe," Andrew said as they rode away.

"Yes, sir. That old fellow worked us out in minutes. He told us everything we wanted to know."

Andrew nodded. "He told us the Boers' argument is not with individuals but with the British government trying to control them." He gave a rueful smile. "I would think that many people across the world would echo that."

"Probably, sir, even though we bring civilisation, order, and progress?" Kerr looked across to Andrew as they rode out of the dorp into the vast spaces of the veld.

"Even so," Andrew said. "In my experience, people wish to be left alone with their own culture. What we call progress, they call interference. Maybe we should leave people to their slavery and squalor."

"Maybe so, sir, but the slaves might disagree. Where are we going next?"

"Krugersdorp, as the old fellow suggested," Andrew said. "That seems to be an interesting town."

THE SOUND OF BOER RIFLES

Krugersdorp, Transvaal, eighth of December 1880.

Andrew stood at the fringes of the crowd, trying to count the people. Most were farming men, the ordinarily taciturn, soberly dressed denizens of the veld, together with a scattering of women in their poke bonnets and a few better-dressed townsfolk. Andrew estimated at least eight thousand people were present, with the majority carrying long rifles and bandoliers of ammunition.

"There's an impressive number of people here, sir," Kerr murmured.

"There is," Andrew agreed. "The size of the crowd alone proves the Burghers' strength of feeling. We'd best keep quiet and listen to the Burghers' – the Boers' – point of view."

"Yes, sir," Kerr agreed.

The men gathered around a raised *stoep*, which acted as a stage for a procession of speakers, jostling for space, raising their hats politely yet arguing with fierce intensity. As with any gathering of Burghers, some men made long speeches, while others merely listened.

Most speakers argued for a return to independence, reminding the audience of the Great Trek, their struggles with the Zulus, Basutos, Matabele, and the land itself.

"We lived our choice of life until the British came," a neat-bearded man said. "They imposed their rules and followed us when we trekked away. We only want the British to leave us alone."

Most of the crowd agreed, with some voicing similar sentiments with much more detail. Andrew listened to the Burghers' complaints, and although he could never agree to their acceptance of slavery, he thought the British had been high-handed in incorporating them into the Empire. Man after man gave a passionate speech about returning Boer leadership to the Transvaal. Andrew listened, aware of the desire for independence yet surprised nobody voiced any hatred of the British.

As one passionate speaker followed another, Andrew knew he was witnessing the rebirth of a Boer republic.

"General Hook was correct," Andrew murmured to Kerr. "There is trouble in the wind."

Kerr puffed smoke from his pipe and surveyed the crowd from under the brim of his broad hat. "I can't argue with that, Baird. These men don't look the type to meekly allow us to take over their country."

Andrew ran his gaze over the thousands of men with grim, bearded faces and hard bodies. "No, they don't," he agreed.

A tall man slumped onto the stage, with dark hair spilling from underneath his hat to his neck and shoulders. "My name is Theunis Steenekamp," he thundered. "We need more than the *Zuid-Afrikaanse Republiek*. We should reclaim all the land the British have stolen from us from the Cape to the Limpopo River."

"There's one of the Afrikander Bond Boers now," Kerr said softly.

Andrew nodded. "I can't see even Gladstone agreeing to relinquish such a strategic location as the Cape."

Kerr smiled. "Not even Gladstone," he agreed.

William Gladstone was the British Prime Minister, a man notably averse to imperial adventures and wars.

Some of the gathering cheered at Theunis's words. Others stood in silence, smoking or waiting to hear more, while a few muttered their disagreement. Andrew noted one man standing at the edge of the crowd.

"That fellow there," Andrew murmured to Kerr. "Don't look now. He's a tall man, standing like a soldier. He's no more a Boer than we are, maybe a bit less."

"Less?" Kerr removed his pipe to add tobacco, dropped it, and scrabbled to pick it up, looking sideways at the man Andrew indicated. "I see the fellow you mean."

"What do you think?" Andrew asked while Theunis delivered

a long speech. Andrew could understand about half the words, but the spirit was evident.

"He must be the only Boer in Africa to stand at attention like a Guardsman," Kerr said. "I'm not sure about that scar down his cheek either."

"That's what I thought," Andrew said. "It looks like a duelling scar; the Prussians have a tradition that gives them more honour if they have such a scar. Let's move a little closer."

As they inched through the crowd, Theunis closed his speech with a rousing call for unity. "We are one people!" He announced in language that even Andrew could understand. Theunis lifted his arms in a gesture that Andrew found vaguely disturbing. "First, we shall get freedom for the *Zuid-Afrikaanse Republiek* and then the Orange Free State. We shall unite the Boer people across the whole of Southern Africa!"

The tall, scarred man led the applause, clapping with his hands in the air.

"Speak to the tall fellow," Andrew urged Kerr. "Ask him his name."

Kerr walked towards the sunburned man. "*Meneer*," he said, raising his hat. "I think we share similar views about the unity of southern Africa."

The tall man inclined his head slightly. "Ja," he said. "The Boer people should unite."

"Unity is best," Kerr agreed. "We are from Natal. What surname do you bear?"

The man hesitated before he replied. "I am Konrad Bramigan," he announced. "A recent immigrant from the German Empire."

"I hope you settle well in the Republic," Kerr said solemnly, shaking the man's hand. He noticed Andrew gesturing to him. "Good day to you, *meneer*," Kerr lifted his hat politely and walked away.

"The Burghers are voting for political representatives," Andrew said. "We'd better back off a little, or somebody will count us as part of the Afrikander Bond." They stepped away while Konrad moved further into the crowd.

"The fellow calls himself Konrad Bramigan," Kerr said quietly. "He claims to have immigrated to the Transvaal from Germany."

"Well done, Kerr," Andrew said.

The candidates stood in a row, looking more like farmers at an agricultural fair than men hoping to recreate a nation against the wishes of an expanding empire.

An elderly man invited the people to vote, shouting the candidates' names one by one. Andrew was surprised at how orderly the crowd was as they selected three leaders. One was named Paul Kruger, and the others were Piet Joubert and Marthinus Pretorius.

"That's that, then," Andrew said. "The Transvaal has decided it wants independence."

"Yes, sir," Kerr replied.

"Let's see what Gladstone does next," Andrew said.

As the Burghers cheered, some waving their rifles and others their hats, Andrew decided he would be safer elsewhere and slid away. Two men stopped to shake his hand, smiling as if voting in new leaders had completed the business.

"What will Shepstone say to that?" one man asked as he raised his hat. "What will Shepstone say?"

"I don't know," Andrew replied honestly.

"He will say we are only backveld Boers who know nothing," the man had quiet blue eyes, with three mature sons standing at his back. "Then he will send the *Rooineck* soldiers to bring us back into the Empire." He nodded. "Ya, that is what he will do. And soon after, he will learn how Boers defend their land."

"The British Empire is very powerful, with tens of thousands of soldiers," Kerr reminded.

"Let them come," one of the man's sons said. He touched the rifle slung over his shoulder. "We shall send them back." He smiled as if he liked the sound of his words. "We shall send them back."

"Excuse us, *meneer*." Lifting his hat, Andrew ushered Kerr away.

When they left the crowd to their celebrations, Andrew mounted Lancelot. "Come on, Kerr. We've seen and heard enough to deduce the Boers' mood."

"Yes, sir," Kerr replied. "If we stay much longer, the Burghers will recruit us into a commando or shoot us as British spies."

CHAPTER 3

General Hook placed Andrew's report on the desk. "Were you present at Krugersdorp?"

"Yes, sir," Andrew said.

"What was the mood of the people? Tell me verbally," Hook demanded.

Andrew replied immediately. "Determined, sir. They seemed angry that Britain interfered with their country."

Hook leaned back in his chair. "All the people I sent into the Transvaal found the same thing," he said. "The Transvaal Boers seek independence."

"That seems to be the prevailing mood," Andrew agreed. "Most just wanted us to leave them alone with their farms. A few seem to belong to the Afrikander Bond. The Bond men spoke loudly, but I am not sure they were the majority."

"This Prussian fellow you met, Konrad Bramigan," Hook tapped the paper. "What did you think of him?"

Andrew thought for a minute before replying. "I saw him supporting an Afrikander Bond candidate. He stood like a soldier, and when Kerr shook his hand, his palm was too soft to be a farmer."

"He admitted to being German?" Hook asked.

"He claimed to be a German immigrant," Andrew said. "I would say he emphasised his origins."

Hook grunted and shifted in his seat. "I'll pass his name to my people in the Transvaal. He could be the Prussian spy or a genuine immigrant trying to fit in." Hook's smile lacked humour. "You and I know recent converts are often the most enthusiastic."

Andrew nodded. "That's possible, sir."

"We'll keep an eye open for him," Hook said. "Now get back to your quarters, Baird. I may need you again. Dismissed."

WHEN ANDREW RETURNED TO HIS BUNGALOW, MARIANA WAS sewing the hem on a skirt. She stood up, smiling. "Welcome home," she said. "I'm glad you're back."

"I'm glad to be back," Andrew said, sitting down. "I'll have to see how the Dragoons are getting on without me, but they can wait until tomorrow."

"Are you staying here tonight?" Mariana asked.

"Yes," Andrew said. "I'm staying here tonight." The house was familiar, but it was not home. *Maybe a soldier never has a home, only a place to sleep and eat. Perhaps that is why so many army officers retire to little villas in quiet British towns, tend their rose gardens, and sit outside, nodding benignly to everybody who passes. They have no other notion of a home life.*

"Good," Mariana remained on her feet, sewing in her hand.

"Sit down, Mariana," Andrew said. "How are you?" He saw Mariana's eyes were less vacant, with a renewed spark. "You seem a bit better. Has Briggs been looking after you?"

Mariana nodded. "Mr. Briggs is a good man," she said. "But very hard on his socks. I've darned three pairs since you went away." She sat down and recommenced work with her needle.

"He's meant to look after you, not vice versa," Andrew said.

"He does his best," Mariana said, concentrating on her sewing. She looked up suddenly. "Do you want me to go home?"

Andrew thought of Inglenook, the farm where Mariana grew up. "Do you want to go back?" he asked.

Mariana shook her head. "No," she whispered the word. "But I will if you think I'm in the way."

"I don't think you're in the way," Andrew said. "You can stay as long as you like."

"I don't want to return," Mariana admitted. "I get nightmares about Inglenook."

"Then you won't go back," Andrew reassured her. "Do you want to talk about the bad dreams?"

Mariana looked away, shaking her head.

"Can I help?"

"I want to see my parents' graves. And my sisters," Mariana said quickly. "Are they buried at the farm?"

"No," Andrew said. "When you were in hospital, I had them moved to a cemetery in Newcastle. I didn't think you'd want to return to Inglenook." *I think the sight would push you over the edge into total madness.*

Mariana shook her head. "I can't," she said. "I'm sorry, Andrew, but I can't return to Inglenook."

"Nobody will blame you for that," Andrew said. "I'll take you to your parents' graves tomorrow."

"Will you?" Mariana asked. "I thought you wanted to see your Dragoons."

"I doubt they'll miss me," Andrew said dryly. He could imagine his men smiling at their officer taking a young woman to a cemetery. "We'll go to the graveyard first thing tomorrow."

With trees for shade and the high arc of the sky as a canopy, the Maxwell family lay in Newcastle's peaceful cemetery. Andrew had ordered a separate headstone for each, a simple stone cross with their names and dates of their birth and death inscribed. The three crosses stood side by side, austere grey stone protruding from the verdant green of the grass.

Andrew stood back as Mariana stood beside the graves, holding a damp handkerchief. He watched her, wondering if he should place an arm around her shoulder.

"I don't know what to say," Mariana confessed. "There's so much in my head, yet so little in my mouth."

"Don't say anything," Andrew advised. "They'll know you're here." He kept close to Mariana without touching her. *I don't know what to say either, Mariana. I don't know how to help.* He looked at Elaine's grave, remembering their shared laughter and wondering how life would have been if she were still alive.

"Do you think they know I'm here?" Mariana asked.

"I'm sure they do," Andrew reassured her. *I'll look after your sister, Elaine. I promise you I will care for her.*

Mariana nodded. "I hope so. Oh, God, I hope so."

"They will," Andrew said. He stepped further back to allow her space. "Take your time, Mariana."

If Elaine's death still hurt him, how much worse would it be for Mariana, losing both her parents and her sister and then having the murderers kidnap her? Andrew watched as Mariana knelt beside the graves. She never spoke about her time in captivity.

Should I force her to talk? Would that help? Or would it make things worse?

Mariana ran her hand across the surface of her mother's grave as if seeking reassurance. Andrew saw her shoulders shake and yearned to offer comfort.

No. Mariana needs to cry. Crying is a catharsis to help her accept her family's deaths. The only thing I can do is be here if she needs me. Finding the nearest tree, Andrew checked for snakes and insects before settling down with the trunk at his back. He felt the ache of frustration, wishing he could ease Mariana's pain and clear her mind while knowing he could do nothing. He saw her shoulders shaking, half-rose to help, and forced himself back down. Mariana needed time alone with her family. Andrew thought of

Elaine and, for a brief, betraying second, remembered her calm voice.

"I like Tennyson and Scott," Elaine had said. "The Lady of Shalott is my favourite, even though it's a sad story." She smiled and quoted the final stanza.

> "They cross'd themselves, their stars they blest,
> Knight, minstrel, abbot, squire, and guest.
> There lay a parchment on her breast,
> That puzzled more than all the rest,
> The well-fed wits at Camelot.
> 'The web was woven curiously,
> The charm is broken utterly,
> Draw near and fear not, —this is I,
> The Lady of Shalott.'"

The memory made Andrew smile. He knew that however long he lived, that poem would always be Elaine's rather than Mariana's. But Elaine was gone, and only Mariana remained of the pioneering Maxwell family. As he waited, Andrew watched Mariana, and, in his mind, he saw Elaine standing at her side, comforting her sister in her grief.

What should I do, Elaine? How can I help Mariana?

When nobody replied except the singing birds and the faint wind rustling the trees, Andrew knew he would have to find a solution without help.

I won't leave you, Mariana. I won't leave you alone.

It was nearly dusk by the time Mariana stepped away from the graves. Her face was puffy, and her eyes red-rimmed from weeping. She started when she saw Andrew under his tree.

"I'm sorry, Andrew," Mariana glanced at the gathering dark. "I didn't realise the time."

"It's not important," Andrew replied. "Don't leave until you are ready."

"I've said my goodbyes," Mariana said, brushing a tear from her eyes, and forced a smile. "I've cried myself dry."

"Let's get you home," Andrew said. "You'll be hungry."

Mariana looked at him. "Hungry?"

Andrew knew that food was not on Mariana's mind. "Come on, Mariana. You must eat."

They rode side by side, not speaking, with both lost in their thoughts. Andrew wondered anew what life would have been like if Elaine had survived. He would have treated Mariana like a younger sister. *Perhaps I already do*, Andrew told himself. Yet he sensed more within Mariana. He saw something in her eyes when she looked at him.

No, Mariana. I don't think of you that way. I can't think of you that way. You're Elaine's sister.

WHEN THEY ARRIVED AT THE BUNGALOW, BRIGGS GLANCED AT Mariana's tear-stained face and lifted an inquisitive eyebrow at Andrew. "Is Miss Maxwell all right, sir?"

"We've been at her parents' grave," Andrew knew he did not have to explain to a private soldier.

"Ah," Briggs nodded. "I wondered, sir. Shall I make coffee? Or would you prefer something stronger? A touch of brandy may help Miss Maxwell."

"Coffee, please," Andrew said. "And a decent meal." He raised his voice a little. "Bring warm water, soap and a towel to Mariana's room, Briggs. I am sure she wants to freshen up."

"Very good, sir," Briggs said.

Andrew ushered Mariana to the living room and poured them both a brandy.

"I don't drink," Mariana protested, staring at the glass.

"It's a bad habit," Andrew agreed, "but sometimes it helps." He watched as Mariana took a cautious sip of the brandy.

She coughed and screwed up her face. "That's horrible!"

"It is, isn't it?" Andrew agreed, finishing his drink in a single swallow. "And you thought people enjoyed drinking spirits!" He forced a smile, trying to cheer her up.

Mariana shook her head and placed the glass on the table at her side. "That is vile."

"Here comes the coffee," Andrew said as Briggs entered the room. "It will take away the taste."

"Thank you, Mr. Briggs," Marina said.

Briggs favoured her with a smile. "That's my duty, Miss Maxwell," he said.

Marina's smile froze as somebody shouted outside the house. The voice must have reminded her of one of her abductors as she stared into space, with her body present but her mind miles away in distance and months away in time.

"Mariana?" Andrew said gently. He made eye contact. "Are you with us?"

Mariana blinked, clearing the shadows. "Yes, sorry, Andrew. I drifted away for a moment."

"Try to stay with us," Andrew said, smiling.

I wish I were a doctor. Getting Mariana back to normal will take longer than I imagined.

ANDREW WAS IN HIS ROOM WHEN HE HEARD SOMEBODY OPEN the garden gate. He waited for Briggs to answer and looked up as somebody tapped on his door.

"Come in," he called.

"Excuse me, sir," Briggs said. "Lieutenant Fletcher is here for you."

"I'll see him in the living room," Andrew said. Fletcher was second in command of the Natal Dragoons, a young man who had rapidly matured during the Zulu War. He entered the room and snapped to attention.

"Sir," Fletcher threw a sketchy salute. "The Boers have done it, sir!"

"Sit down, Fletcher, and tell me what the Boers have done."

"Yes, sir," Fletcher sat straight-backed at the table. "The triumvirate who rule the Transvaal Boers have declared the Transvaal is a free nation known as the South African Republic, the *Zuid-Afrikaanse Republiek*."

Andrew grunted and poured Fletcher a brandy. "We expected no less," he said. "I'd better get back to the Dragoons and prepare us for war."

"Will there be war, sir?"

"Undoubtedly," Andrew said. "Not even Gladstone can see a British colony trying to break away." He saw Mariana listening at the door. "Tell me what happened, Fletcher."

"Yes, sir. On the 13th of December, sir, the Boers raised the *Vierkleur*; that's their flag, sir. It means 'four colours' because it's got a green vertical bar and red, white, and blue horizontal bars."

"Where did they raise it?" Andrew asked as Mariana sat down, looking pale under her tan. She began to twist her hands together.

"A place called Pardekraal, sir," Fletcher said.

"I don't know it," Andrew said.

"Nor do I, sir. Then, three days later, on Dingaan's Day, the 16th of December, at Heidelberg, the Boers declared a republic. Dingaan's Day is the anniversary of the Battle of Blood River, sir, when the Voortrekkers defeated the Zulu king Dingaan."

Andrew nodded. "Thank you, Fletcher." He wanted to reassure Mariana that everything would be all right.

"The Boers have reinstated the *Volksraad*, the legislative assembly," Fletcher said. "They're pushing on rapidly with their republic."

"I'll return to barracks with you," Andrew said. He raised his voice. "Briggs!"

"Sir!"

"I am going to the barracks."

"Your uniform is ready, sir. Shall I accompany you?"

Andrew shook his head. "No, Briggs. I have a far more important duty for you."

"What's that, sir?" Briggs stood impassive inside the doorway.

"I want you to remain with Miss Maxwell."

"Very good, sir," Briggs replied.

"Whatever happens, Briggs," Andrew said, "I want Miss Maxwell to stay here. Don't let anybody of any rank take her away."

Briggs glanced at Mariana. "I won't, sir."

"If anybody objects, tell them you're acting under my direct orders."

"I will, sir," Briggs said.

Andrew felt Mariana's gaze fixed on him and hoped she understood.

CHAPTER 4

As Newcastle possessed no official barracks, Andrew had based the Natal Dragoons in a group of farm buildings on the outskirts of the town. The farm owner had died at Hlobane in the Zulu War, leaving no heirs, but the buildings were solid and sufficiently spacious to house the entire unit.

Sergeant Meek was supervising the men grooming the horses and snarling good-naturedly at anything that failed to meet his high standards. He stopped at Trooper Ogden's horse and pointed to a single tangled hair. "I want that groomed, Ogden! Look at that! It's like an Irish blanket after a storm! Get that sorted!"

"Yes, sir!" Ogden flicked the hair back into place.

"Do you call that sorted? Groom your horse, Ogden!" Meek looked around as Andrew walked into the stables.

"I see you're busy, Sergeant," Andrew said.

"Welcome back, sir," Meek saluted. "How's Miss Maxwell?" Meek had helped rescue Mariana from the renegades.

"She's doing well, thank you," Andrew said. "How are the men?"

"Same as always, sir, a useless, lazy bunch who only joined for the *scoff*."

"No improvement since I crossed the Vaal then," Andrew said.

"No, sir," Meek said. "There's a message for you, sir. Some peacock left it soon after Mr Fletcher left."

"Thank you, Sergeant. Where is it?"

"In your office, sir."

Andrew could imagine the peacock. He would have been a young staff officer, well connected and just out of Sandhurst, with his boots shined to perfection, a chin smooth enough for a ski slope, and a disdainful attitude toward colonials and rankers.

The message sat on Andrew's desk beside a pile of letters he decided to ignore. He slid a knife under the seal and removed a single sheet of stiff paper.

The name at the top of the page read "General Hook", and the instructions were written in three clear paragraphs.

"Colonel Winsloe of the 21st Foot is constructing a fort at Potchefstroom to control any independence agitation among the local population. One of Winsloe's officers heard Germans among the town's inhabitants.

Report to Colonel Winsloe and see what assistance you can give. You have knowledge of the possible German threat and are the only officer under my command who may have seen the Prussian agent. Watch the inhabitants of the town for the agent. If the man is the individual you saw in Krugersdorp, detain him and hold him for questioning.

Currently, Colonel Winsloe does not need the Natal Dragoons. Inform Lieutenant Fletcher to remain in temporary command and keep them ready in case they are required.

Hook."

Andrew lowered the letter. *Potchefstroom is in the Transvaal; there's no rest for the wicked.*

THE SOUND OF BOER RIFLES

POTCHEFSTROOM WAS LIKE OTHER TRANSVAAL TOWNS, WITH broad streets, solid public buildings, and slightly pretentious stores. A short distance from the settlement and set on rising ground, the unfinished British fort had low walls surrounding a collection of huts and tents.

That's hardly an impressive example of the Empire's might, Andrew thought.

"Halt! Who goes there?"

The sentry at the gate presented his bayonetted rifle as Andrew approached. Andrew saw a small, neatly made man with his cross belt and sun helmet brilliant white against a scarlet tunic.

"Friend!" Andrew announced. "Captain Andrew Baird of the Natal Dragoons!" He had worn his uniform especially for the occasion, for he knew that British infantry could have nervous trigger fingers when on sentry duty.

"Pass, friend," the sentry allowed, slamming to attention as his suspicious eyes watched the tall, sun-browned stranger in the unfamiliar uniform.

Andrew returned the man's salute. He knew the 21st Foot, the Royal Scots Fusiliers, were veterans of the Zulu War and, like all British infantry, could be relied on to fight if required.

When he entered the fort, Andrew was less impressed. The walls were only four and a half feet high, sufficiently thick to stop a rifle bullet, but no defence against artillery. Inside, a company of the 21st acted as the garrison, together with twenty-five mounted infantry and two nine-pounders of the Royal Artillery.

He looked around, noticing the relaxed way the men moved. *These lads don't expect trouble.*

"Sergeant!" Andrew shouted. "I am looking for Colonel Winsloe!"

A young sergeant glanced at Andrew's unfamiliar uniform. "Who are you?"

"Captain Baird of the Natal Dragoons," Andrew said.

"My apologies, sir." The sergeant stiffened to attention and threw a smart salute. "I didn't recognise the uniform. I can't see any badges of rank."

"You lads were at Ulundi, weren't you?" Andrew referred to the final battle of the Zulu War.

"We were, sir," the sergeant confirmed warily.

"So were the Natal Dragoons," Andrew said.

"Yes, sir," the sergeant allowed himself a grudging respect. "If you follow me, sir, I'll take you to the colonel."

Colonel Winsloe sat at his desk within the largest of the tents. He looked up when Andrew announced himself. "Captain Baird, come in."

The tent was stifling under the sun and crammed with Winsloe's furniture.

"General Hook sent me, sir."

"So I believe. Here's the situation, Baird," recently promoted to acting colonel, Winsloe had been wounded at Ulundi when the Zulus charged the 21st. Andrew knew his reputation as a steady regimental officer. "The Burghers of the Transvaal have declared themselves a republic against the wishes of Her Majesty's government."

"Yes, sir," Andrew saw the pain in Winsloe's face as he moved and wondered if he had completely recovered from his injury.

"One of my officers heard one of the Burghers speaking German," Winsloe said. "The man could be an innocent German settler, but with the powers-that-be in a jumpy mood, I thought I'd better pass on the information. The last thing we want is Prussian interference."

Andrew nodded. "Yes, sir. Could I speak to the officer concerned?"

Winsloe called for his servant. "Fetch Lieutenant Burke," he commanded.

Burke was old for a lieutenant, a saturnine man in his mid-thirties with a downward twist to his lips. "You wanted me, sir?"

"This gentleman is Captain Baird of the Natal Dragoons, an expert on the Prussians. Tell him what you heard, Burke."

Before Baird could protest that he was no expert, Burke began to talk. "I didn't hear very much, sir. It was more what I saw and how the fellow acted."

"What did you see, Burke?" Andrew wondered if he had wasted his time.

Burke screwed up his face in concentration. "A man who looked out of place, sir, as if he didn't belong. He spoke Dutch to some Boers, then switched to German when he addressed his horse."

Andrew nodded. "What did he look like?"

"He was well over six feet tall," Burke replied at once, "and he stood erect. The Boers don't often stand upright; they seem more relaxed, slope-shouldered even."

"I've noticed that," Andrew agreed. *The description fits the man I saw, but there could be hundreds of tall men in the Transvaal.*

"He was looking at the fort," Burke continued. "So was half the town's population, but there was something different about this man."

Andrew grunted. "You've had me ride over two hundred miles from Newcastle to tell me you saw a tall man looking at the fort?"

Burke looked uncomfortable. "It was more than that, sir. He just felt wrong. You know that feeling you get when something is not quite what it should be?"

Andrew relented. "I know it," he said.

"It was like that."

"Would you recognise this fellow again?" Andrew asked.

"Yes, sir," Burke replied.

"If Colonel Winsloe agrees, you and I will wander around Potchefstroom and the surrounding area. If we see this man, and I also recognise him, we'll arrest him."

Colonel Winsloe frowned. "On what grounds, Captain? We can't arrest a man simply because we don't like his looks. We're

British, damn it, not some continental autocracy. We have the rule of law, innocent until proven guilty."

"Yes, sir," Andrew agreed. "We may also be at war."

Winsloe slowly shook his head. "We're not at war yet, Baird. So far, it's all been hot air and rhetoric." He stood up. "We're soldiers, not policemen. I will permit Lieutenant Burke to accompany you for two days to try and identify this man. After that, you can return to Newcastle."

"Yes, sir." Andrew recognised that Winsloe was balancing his sense of duty with a lifetime's experience as an honourable British gentleman. "Come on, Burke, if we change into civilian clothes, we'll be less conspicuous."

"You'll be riding away soon." Aletta van Collier spoke without apparent emotion. The Transvaal would soon be at war with the British Empire; therefore, the men would fight. There was neither argument nor question in her mind; the Boer men had always ridden to war when there was a threat from outside and always would. It was as inevitable as the seasons.

"Ja. We are going to war." At thirty-eight years old, Johannes knew the Commando Law. The Republic expected every Burgher between the ages of sixteen and sixty to fight on demand. Most of their wars had been against threatening tribes, although they had faced British redcoats more than once. It made little difference to Johannes if they fought the encroaching British Empire or an African tribe.

Aletta nodded stoically, hiding her anxiety as she continued to make bread. Making bread was her job this morning. The war was her man's business unless it threatened her farm.

When Johannes stepped outside to check his horses, Aletta watched him for a moment, sighed, and left the table with the bread half-made. She followed her husband, carefully readjusted her poke bonnet to shade her face from the sun and swept flour from her skirt. The hem brushed her ankles above many layers of petticoats.

"Are you taking Jan?" She pointed to their elder son, who was shaping a dozen new fenceposts.

Johannes nodded gravely. "Yes. He is seventeen now. Past time to learn the duties of a man," he said. He nodded to their younger son, who was whitewashing the dairy wall. "I will take Mannie as well."

"Mannie's only fourteen," Aletta's face fell at the thought of her baby riding to war. Her eyes softened when she looked at him, remembering the difficulty she had in labour. She would never admit that Mannie was her favourite.

"I was eleven when I first rode on commando," Johannes said. "Jan and I will be with him." He checked his horse's withers and patted its neck. "Mannie will be better learning young than never learning at all."

Aletta looked away briefly. "You are right, Johannes." She looked at her younger son, tall for his age, slim and handsome in her eyes. "You were fourteen when we met. Mannie looks like you at his age."

Johannes placed an empty pipe in his mouth and contemplated Mannie as if he had never seen the boy before. "He is taller and not as handsome."

Aletta smiled at the comparison and folded her arms. "He is taller than you were and more handsome."

"Yes," Johannes nodded. "That is what I said. Taller and more handsome."

They smiled simultaneously. After twenty years of marriage, they understood each other well.

"What will you take with you?" Aletta asked.

Johannes replied immediately. "The Commando Law demands we bring a riding horse, saddle, and bridle with thirty bullets, thirty caps, and half a pound of gunpowder." He looked at his two sons. "That's ninety between us. We will take double that. We must also carry sufficient provisions for eight days."

"A war with the *Rooinecks* will last longer than eight days," Aletta said. Boer women were as practical as their men. "They are not tribesmen on a cattle raid. You'd better bring sufficient provisions for fourteen days."

"Yes," Johannes said. "Fourteen will be better. Biltong, meat cut in strips, salted, peppered, and dried, with Boer biscuits."

Aletta knew Boer biscuits meant small loaves made with flour and fermented raisins rather than yeast, and baked twice. "I am already making the bread," she told him. "Make sure you take care of my sons."

Johannes smiled. "I will. And they will take care of me."

Aletta touched his arm. "I'll look after the farm until you return."

"I know you will," Johannes said. He stepped into the house, closed the door with his foot, and embraced his wife. They did not need words, for both knew the dangers of war and the hazards of leaving a woman alone on a farm in the high veld. Johannes could not rely on the servants to fight if any of the neighbouring tribes raided the farm. He knew he would worry until he returned, but that was the price of farming on the frontier. The alternative was to trek down to the Cape and suffer the oppressive laws of the British Empire.

Johannes shook his head. He could never live under British rule.

The van Collier men left Nuwe Hoop Plaas two days later as dawn coloured the eastern sky red like a harbinger of oncoming bloodshed. Johannes led, grim-faced, as he left his wife and his farm. Jan rode on his right, as eager as any youth when travelling to his first war, sure in his invulnerability and wishing his girl Engela could admire him. On Johannes' left, Mannie strove to emulate his older brother, although twice he looked back over his shoulder to see his mother, who stood outside the door of their house. She lifted a hand in farewell, hiding her fears and tears. Aletta took the part of generations of Boer women who had watched their men leave for war. She knew the truth behind their brave appearance and the reality that they were fragile humans who could return broken in mind or body or not return at all.

"God be with you," Aletta prayed, wringing a cloth between her hands, but she did not allow her men to see any signs of weakness. She knew they would need all their strength, as she knew her sons left her as boys but would return as men in everything but years.

"God be with you." Aletta watched them ride until they were only distant specks in the vastness of the veld, and then she returned inside. She had a farm to run, and the work would not do itself.

CHAPTER 5

POTCHEFSTROOM, ZUID-AFRIKAANSCHE REPUBLIEK

15TH OF DECEMBER 1880

"Dust, sir! Somebody's approaching the fort!" the sentry lifted his Martini-Henry as if readying himself to shoot the oncoming man. The fort's location afforded the sentry an extensive view.

"Keep me posted, McWilliam." Lieutenant Lindsell, the duty officer, ordered.

"Yes, sir," McWilliam replied. He lowered his rifle. "It's Major Thornhill in the postcart, sir, and he's in a hurry."

"Major Thornhill?" Lindsell repeated. "Open the gates! The major wouldn't return unless there was trouble!"

Andrew strode to the gates, more curious than alarmed. He and Burke had been on two abortive tours of Potchefstroom with no sign of Konrad Bramigan.

Major Thornhill, second in command of the fort, came at the

gallop, his horses lathered with sweat and covered in dust. "Boers!" He shouted. "Hundreds of them!"

The postcart hammered inside the gate, turned in a tight circle, and came to a halt within a curtain of rising dust. The driver slid from his perch and looked around the fort's interior, as sweat-soaked as his horses.

"That's put the tabby cat among the pigeons," Lindsell murmured.

Andrew nodded. "It appears so."

"Sound the Assembly!" Colonel Winsloe ordered. "Close the gates! Man the walls!"

When the bugle gave its brassy blare, red-coated infantrymen ran to their posts, carrying their Martini-Henry rifles at the trail. Sergeants added their shouts to the din.

Andrew checked his revolver and strolled to his quarters to retrieve his rifle. *Never looked hurried in front of the men.* With no official duties in the garrison, he could only make himself as useful as possible. He watched the 21st Foot, trying to assess their capabilities. *They seem a handy bunch, with no panic.*

Colonel Winsloe gave rapid orders. "Major Clarke, take twenty men and garrison the Landdrost's office and the courthouse! Lieutenant Dalrymple-Hay, take a section to the flat roof of the jail."

The regulars obeyed without visible emotion, professional soldiers trusting their officers. Andrew joined the men on the wall, holding his Martini-Henry and waiting for an attack. He peered over the town, seeing only the quiet houses, with a few civilians moving around as if nothing unusual was happening.

"What are the Boers thinking of?" Fusilier Tosh asked. "They're a bunch of farmers! They won't have a hope against us!"

"People said that about the Zulus," a dapper corporal reminded, scratching an insect bite on his neck. "A bunch of naked savages, they called them, until they gave us the right about at Sandwala!"[1]

Andrew examined the interior of the fort. With its low walls containing a handful of recently erected huts and the usual bell tents of British infantry, it did not seem sufficiently strong to withstand an attack. The Royal Artillerymen waited at their guns, smart in their blue uniforms and reassuringly calm.

When Andrew returned his attention to the town, he realised that most of the civilians had disappeared. In their place, mounted Boers rode along the streets, holding their rifles ready. Most wore broad-brimmed hats and ordinary working clothes, while others wore suits but still carried a rifle.

We're on the verge of war, Andrew thought. *Let's hope both sides show some restraint and don't start firing.*

"I could knock that fellow off his horse, corporal," Tosh sighted along the barrel of his Martini at a Boer who rode into the open ground between the town and the fort.

"Hold your fire," Andrew pushed Tosh's rifle barrel down. "We don't know what the Boers intend and don't want to instigate any shooting."

Tosh nodded. "If you say so, sir."

"People coming, sir!" McWilliam warned as a rush of refugees headed for the fort. "They're civilians, sir, and they look scared."

Colonel Winsloe mounted the walls to assess any danger. "Open the gates," he ordered. "Let them in!"

When the gates opened, dozens of native drivers and British civilians from the surrounding area crammed into the fort as the Boers established control of Potchefstroom.

"Do you think they'll attack us, sir?" the dapper corporal asked Andrew.

"I couldn't say, Corporal," Andrew replied. He watched the sun swiftly set in an ominous red glow. "If I were the Boer commander, I'd come quickly while we are still disorganised. That's if he wants a fight and is not merely trying to scare us."

Darkness closed on the fort, with men listening for sounds and waiting for a possible attack. The duty officer lit watch lanterns, giving quiet advice to the sentries.

"Don't stand still for long, don't hover near the lights in case a Boer is waiting to shoot, and don't look at the light because that will damage your night vision."

"Yes, sir," the sentries said and continued their beats.

Andrew patrolled the walls, thankful that the defenders were veteran infantry, not young soldiers fresh from Britain's grim industrial streets. He stared at the town, where candles glowed in some windows while others were dark, hiding the secrets within. He heard the whinnying of horses, listened to the drumbeat of hooves on the ground, and, in the distance, he could see the glow of campfires outside the town.

"How many are there, do you reckon, sir?" Andrew asked Major Thornhill.

"Too many," Thornhill replied. "Hundreds if not thousands." He grinned, lighting a long cheroot. "If they'd come at once, they'd have a better chance of victory, though. As it is, we've nearly completed the fort and are ready and waiting. I'd put my money on a hundred British infantry against any number of rustics."

Andrew glanced around the low walls and the fort crowded with refugees. "I hope you're correct, sir."

Thornhill pulled at his cheroot. "You'll see, Baird. We're only facing armed civilians, not trained soldiers. A few volleys from Martini, and they'll run like scared rabbits."

"Yes, sir," Andrew remembered the quiet determination of the Burghers in Krugersdorp and hoped Thornhill was correct. The 21st Foot appeared professional enough as they stood behind the wall, exchanging black humour and grousing like the veterans they were. They remained at the walls all night, awaiting an attack that never came.

A spectacular dawn heralded what Andrew expected to be a dramatic day. He slumped against the parapet, Martini ready, rubbed a hand over his unshaven chin, and listened to the town wake up. Lights flickered in windows, voices sounded, and Andrew saw a small group of armed horsemen trotting close to the fort.

"Shall I fire, sir?" Fusilier Tosh asked.

"No," Thornhill replied. "They may just be curious to see the funny foreign soldiers. We must be a novelty to them."

"Yes, sir," Tosh lowered his rifle.

At nine o'clock that morning, a moustached corporal took over the guard at the gate. He had no sooner posted his section than he shouted, "A party of Boers is coming, sir!"

Colonel Winsloe stepped to the gate and raised his field glasses. He studied the approaching Boers for thirty seconds.

"Lieutenant Lindsell, take the mounted infantry and find out what they're after." He glanced at Andrew. "You go with them, Baird; you're supposed to be an expert on these people."

"Yes, sir." Pleased to be free from the fort's confines, Andrew and the mounted infantry clattered outside. The day was already uncomfortably hot, although Andrew felt a heaviness in the atmosphere as though rain was imminent.

"I know I outrank you, Lindsell," Andrew said, "but these are your men. I won't interfere in your leadership."

"Very good, sir," Lindsell agreed and raised his voice. "Open order," he shouted. "We'll see what these fellows want."

People in the town watched as Lindsell's mounted infantry approached the Boers. Andrew studied the faces, looking for Konrad Bramigan. He recognised the type of man, if not any individuals among the mass. As Major Thornhill had said, the Boers were farmers but also frontiersmen who leaned back in their saddles and carried their rifles as though they were part of their bodies, scrutinising the British as carefully as Andrew studied them.

The last real war we had with frontiersmen was back in the 1770s, Andrew thought. *That began as a civil war over politics and spread across the globe when France, the Netherlands, and Spain got involved. I hope we can contain this dispute in the Transvaal rather than have the German Empire or any other Powers sticking in their long continental noses.*

THE SOUND OF BOER RIFLES

"They're running, sir!" Sergeant Lennox reported calmly as the Boers turned and withdrew. Lennox wore a row of medal ribbons on his chest and had a finger missing from his left hand.

"I thought they might," Lindsell said. "Follow them up, boys, but don't get too close. I don't want them to panic and open fire."

The mounted infantry advanced, with some men smiling as they pushed the Boers back a few hundred yards. Andrew thought he heard a man cheer from the fort.

"And that's the end of the rebellion," Lennox said. "Close it down, get these lads back to their farms, and we can all go home."

As the British began to relax, one of the Boers turned in his saddle, lifted his rifle, and fired, with the muzzle flare distinct and a rush of blue-grey smoke clouding man and horse. The bullet whined well above the heads of the mounted infantry.

That's the first shot in this war, Andrew thought. *War? I hope there is no war.*

When another Boer fired, with the shot also passing high above the British heads, Lieutenant Lindsell frowned.

"The cheeky beggars," he sounded more surprised than alarmed. "Give them a volley, lads! Don't dismount; just show them we mean business."

Before the patrol returned fire, more Boers lifted their rifles with tell-tale jets of smoke and the sharp crack of musketry. The bullets passed overhead or screamed on either side of the mounted infantry. One trooper swore and fought the reins as his horse panicked.

"It's alright, Badger! It's only the Boers. Calm down, you stupid horse!"

Andrew unholstered his Martini and raised it to his shoulder.

"Fire!" Lindsell ordered.

The mounted infantry squeezed their triggers, with Andrew aiming for the Boer who fired the first shot. He saw his man jerk sideways and grab his arm, and then the Boers withdrew at speed.²

"That's enough, lads," Lindsell said cheerfully. "No need to follow. We've sent a message and chased them away. Return to the fort."

Andrew agreed with Lindsell's judgment. If he were the Boer commander, he'd draw the British away from the fort and ambush them inside Potchefstroom or in the countryside beyond.

"Keep the men extended," Andrew advised softly. "We don't want to present the Boers with a tempting target."

"Extended order!" Lindsell roared.

As the mounted infantry approached the fort, they heard more musketry from the Landdrost's office in Potchefstroom.

"Things are hotting up," Andrew observed. "It looks like we have a fight on our hands."

Lindsell nodded. "I hoped we had quelled this republican nonsense. It seems brother Boer needs a sterner lesson than a single volley."

The sound of Boer rifles increased as the mounted infantry neared the fort. The Boers were firing from three places in the town, aiming at the white sun helmets of the infantry at the walls. "Increase the speed," Lindsell ordered, "and let's hope the sentries open the gates for us." He barked a short laugh. "Ready boys! Canter now! I'd be obliged if you'd keep your head down, sir," he said to Andrew. "I can't have the colonel blaming me for losing a visiting officer."

Taking the rear, the post of most danger, Lindsell ushered his men to the fort, which was now the centre of a battle. Bullets were thudding against the wall, each raising a small spurt of dust, while others ripped through the bell tents in the fort's interior. The 21st retaliated with volleys, aiming at the gun smoke or any Boer sufficiently careless to reveal himself.

The gate was open, with a sentry at either side firing towards the Boers.

"Get inside!" Colonel Winsloe ordered as Boer bullets whined overhead. The mounted men ducked as they entered, swearing when some shots came close. "Take your positions on the wall and return fire, but be careful of the civilians!"

Andrew took his place behind the wall as the mounted infantry dismounted and ran to their stations. They slammed into their various positions, loaded, and waited for the officers' orders.

Andrew scanned his surroundings, noting the houses from where the Boers fired. Although the muzzle flares and spurts of smoke came from three directions, most came from a single house.

"Dr Poortman's house appears to be their main centre of resistance," Andrew pointed out when Colonel Winsloe walked around the wall.

"That's what I thought, Captain," Winsloe said. Ignoring the Boer fire, he approached Lieutenant Rundle of the Royal Artillery.

"Could you silence the men in that house, Lieutenant?"

Rundle grinned. "I thought you'd forgotten about us, sir! We'll see what we can do."

Andrew watched as the gunners made their preparations, ignoring the bullets that buzzed and whined overhead.

Rundle laid the nine-pounder himself, checked the aim, and stepped back. "Right, lads," he said. "Fire!"

The nine-pounder roared, and Rundle's first shell smashed through the front window of Dr Poortman's house, exploding inside. The Boer firing ended abruptly.

"That sorted them out!" A Glasgow voice sounded.

The Boer musketry started again, with less intensity. The bullets kicked dust from the walls and perforated the tents, jerking the canvas with every shot.

"Good shooting, Rundle," Winsloe studied Dr Poortman's house through his field glasses. "There are still some inside. Give them another."

"My pleasure, sir," Rundle said as a bullet pinged off the barrel of the nearer nine-pounder.

The Boers are concentrating on the guns. "Protect the gunners, lads," Andrew said, aiming at the smashed window of Dr Poortman's house. "Make the Boers keep their heads down."

"Volley fire!" Lindsell ordered. "Load! Aim! Fire!"

The infantry responded, firing at the doctor's house, so ten Martinis cracked out simultaneously. Andrew saw puffs of dust all around the front of the building, with bullets smashing the remaining glass and thudding on the solid front door.

"Fire!" Rundle ordered, and the nine-pounder roared again. Andrew did not see the arc of the shell, only the explosion at Poortman's front door. The return fire ended as the surviving Boers left hurriedly, spilling out the back to find a safer vantage point.

Rundle stood back to study Dr. Poortman's house through his field glasses.

"Round two to us," Colonel Winsloe said quietly. "Let's see what Brother Boer tries next."

After that flurry of activity, the day quietened down. The Boers and Fusiliers exchanged a few ineffective shots.

"I thought the Boers were all expert marksmen," Lindsell said quietly. "They don't seem any better than our lads."

"Maybe these are town-based Burghers rather than the high veld farmers," Andrew said quietly. "Or maybe they are holding back." He looked up as Colonel Winsloe stepped closer.

"Any casualties?" Winsloe asked.

"No, sir," Lindsell replied.

The colonel nodded. "Good. Did you see your Prussian, Baird?"

"Not yet, sir," Andrew replied.

"Maybe you'd best return to Newcastle and report."

Andrew nodded. "I'd prefer to wait for confirmation, sir."

Winsloe pushed back his sun helmet and studied Andrew's face. "I know your reputation from the Zulu War, Baird. You're a fire-eater, but you have a duty to General Hook. My men can hold this fort against any number of Boers without your help."

"I realise that, sir," Andrew said.

Winsloe scratched his head. "I'll give you one more day, Baird, then return to General Hook with my blessing."

"Yes, sir," Andrew saluted, turned on his heel, and walked to the wall. He lifted his field glasses, hoping for a chance glimpse of Bramigan.

JAN RODE PROUDLY BESIDE HIS FATHER AND YOUNGER BROTHER as they joined the Groenburg Commando, named after the village of Groenburg, where they assembled. The men greeted each other with handshakes and polite raising of hats. Most knew each other from farmers' gatherings, markets, weddings, and funerals, with many having ridden on commando against raiding native tribes.

"What happens now?" Jan asked, looking around for friends and neighbours. He had seldom seen so many men in one place and, suddenly nervous, edged back from the crowd. He had lived on the farm all his life, rarely venturing out of his familiar patch of veld, and knew only a close circle of people.

"Now we wait for Gideon, the area commandant," Johannes said, "and vote for two veldcornets for the commando."

Jan had expected to see some military men in splendid uniforms and cocked hats. Instead, everybody wore ordinary clothes, with bandoliers of ammunition draped across their chests. One man wore a bowler hat, and another a battered British-style sun helmet. Most of the men were talking, giving their views, and explaining how they would defeat the British if they commanded the republic's forces.

Jan waved to a youth from a neighbouring farm. "I'll speak to Abraham," he said, thankful to see his childhood friend.

"Ja," Johannes said. "You speak to Abraham Hertzog. Ask

him how his sister will survive with both her men out on commando." Johannes laughed, for Jan had been courting Engela for two years. "And how you will survive without her."

Jan coloured and guided his horse through the crowd. Abraham greeted him with a grin.

"We're going on commando together, Jan," Abraham said. A freckled youth, he had a broad, cheerful face, long, untidy blond hair, and hands too large for his arms. Abraham was shorter than most Boer men but made up for his lack of inches with an erect stance, a bouncy walk, and a belligerent attitude. "We'll show the *Rooinecks*!"

"We will," Jan agreed with the supreme confidence of youth. "They wear red coats and think they're the lords of creation."

"They haven't met us yet," Abraham said. "Come on, Jan, there's fun over here." He pointed to a crowd of youths gathering a short distance from their elders.

With Jan and Abraham taking the lead, the boys enjoyed a quick game of *bok-bok,* with one reluctant youth standing against the wall of the house and the others jumping on top until the human tower collapsed in a laughing tangle. After they straightened themselves up, the youths played *vingertrek*, where two boys locked the middle fingers of their right hands and strove to break their opponent's grip. It was a trial of strength in which Jan delighted. As he had been engaged in strenuous physical work on the farm since he could walk, he was stronger than most grown men. Jan demolished a series of town-bred boys before realising Abraham was smiling without participating.

"Come on, Abe!" Jan challenged, and the two interlocked their fingers. Immediately, Jan knew the difference between Abraham and the urban boys. Abraham had also lived all his life with hard manual labour and matched Jan strength for strength.

The crowd watched; with the youths Jan had defeated all supporting Abraham.

"Go on, Abe!" one boy shouted. "Break his finger!"

"Beat him, Jan," Mannie countered. "Tear his arm off!"

Jan strained, enjoying the competition, feeling the strength in his finger drain as Abraham proved equally determined to win.

"Engela's not here," Abraham said to break Jan's concentration. "You don't have to show off, Jan!"

"I don't need to show off to defeat you," Jan responded. "You are as weak as a newborn calf!"

Mannie encouraged his brother until Jan and Abraham realised they were evenly matched. They released each other, stepped back, rubbed their aching arms, and smiled in unstated friendship.

"You should have won, Jan," Mannie sounded disappointed.

"I didn't want to embarrass him by showing his weakness," Jan replied.

As the youths played light-heartedly, their elders dismounted and gathered in a noisy group. Every man voiced his choice of veldcornets until an older man with a long beard fired a shot from his rifle.

"Silence!" he said. "You all know me. I am Gideon Coetzee, the commandant of the area. We will elect two veldcornets for the Groenburg Commando."

The men nodded, with Theunis pushing forward as if seeking the position. Johannes stepped back, looked over the crowd to ensure his sons were all right and returned his attention to the discussion.

"Which names are put forward?"

The men argued for a few moments until they chose four names. "Theunis Steenekamp, Johannes van Collier, Karl Cloete, and Hendrik Ackerman," Gideon Coetzee announced solemnly.

The men discussed the merits of the four, with anecdotes of their experience and character freely given. Although the Boers occupied a large area of southern Africa, the population was thinly spread, and everybody knew their neighbours from farmers' gatherings, weddings, and funerals.

"I select Johannes," a stocky man wearing a bowler hat

announced. "He married my cousin Aletta. He is a steady man with a well-run farm."

Others nodded. "Johannes was on commando with me against the Basuto. He fought well."

"I have known the family for thirty years. His grandfather and mine were on the Great Trek together. They are a good family."

"Theunis is also a good man," a blond giant said. "He is of the Afrikander Bond and will stop the *Rooinecks* from taking our land." He nodded as if his opinion settled the matter.

"I know Karl Cloete," an elderly man said quietly. "He married my youngest daughter, thank the Lord. We had no peace in the house until she was gone."

The men laughed, and the conversation shifted from war and politics to wives and women.

"Stop!" Gideon commanded. "It's time to vote for the veld-cornets."

The men quietened and looked to their front, where Gideon raised his hands.

"Who will vote for Hendrik Ackerman?" Gideon asked and counted the raised hands.

"And who for Karl Cloete?" Gideon asked. "He is my wife's nephew."

"Wife's nephew or not," the bowler-hatted man shouted. "I still will not vote for him."

Every Burgher present had the franchise, and when Jan voted for his father, he felt he had crossed a barrier to become a man. He looked at Abraham, knowing the Pedi had killed his father. "You are the man of the house, Abe," Jan said. "You might be the veldcornet in the next war."

Abraham grinned. "I'd do a better job than these old men."

Gideon gave his decision. "Johannes and Theunis are elected as veldcornets," he announced. "They will lead the Groenburg Commando in the republic's war against the British Empire. May the Lord guide them both."

Jan grinned as a dozen men crowded to shake his father's hand. Mannie was laughing while the grim-looking Theunis Steenekamp tried to recruit the Burghers into the Afrikander Bond.

"Good," Johannes said when the initial excitement died away. "Now we can remove the British and return to our farms. I have thirty cows in calf and want to be present when they give birth."

The men nodded in complete understanding. They would defend their land but were not natural soldiers. Their farms and family were more important than fighting, and going on commando was an inconvenient necessity in the business of life.

Jan grinned at Abraham. "We're going to war," he said.

"Ja," Abraham agreed. "And when we return, you still won't get my sister's hand. Engela is far too good for a rough farmer such as you. She will marry a rich man with a big house and ten thousand *morgen* of good pastureland, not the half-sandy desert of Nuwe Hoop Plaas."

Jan laughed. "She will marry me and help me farm Nuwe Hoop Plaas, bear me many sons and be very happy."

They walked off, leaving their elders to decide how a small nation with a scattered population and no army was to defeat the military forces of the largest empire in the world.

CHAPTER 6

Andrew scanned Potchefstroom through his field glasses. "Could I have permission to take another patrol outside the fort, sir? I want to assess the Boer numbers and see if Bramigan is among them."

Winsloe pondered for a moment. "Your chances of finding the German are slim, Captain."

"I realise that, sir, but I have to look."

Winslow gave a reluctant nod. "Only a short patrol, Baird. Take two of the mounted infantry, and don't get my men killed."

"I'll try not to, sir," Andrew promised.

With Fusiliers Mullan and Logan at his back, Andrew swept out of the gate and turned right, away from the town. He half-expected a flurry of shooting from the Boers, but they allowed him to move unmolested as he led his men at a fast trot around the fort.

"Spread out," Andrew said. "We're here to gather intelligence, not to engage in a battle."

The men nodded. Mullan was a broad-faced man with laughing eyes, while Logan was neat and dark-featured with a bitter twist to his mouth.

"We don't know how many Boers there are," Andrew said.

"There might only be a few dozen, or there could be hundreds. Identify any large groups and estimate their numbers."

"If they fire, can we fire back, sir?" Mullan asked.

"Yes," Andrew replied and saw both men's faces brighten.

"Even if you don't give the order, sir?" Logan sought confirmation as he checked the breech of his Martini.

"Don't wait for my order," Andrew confirmed. "But only if the Boers fire first."

"Yes, sir," Logan replied.

"Keep your heads down, boys," Andrew said. "Follow me!"

With one of the spurts of madness that characterised him during the Zulu War, Andrew led his men into the town. He relied on the surprise of their sudden appearance and the speed of their horses to avoid Boer fire. Andrew knew how difficult it was to shoot accurately at a moving man, especially when they appeared unexpectedly.

Mullan gave a high-pitched yell, laughing as he spurred his horse, loosening the rifle in its bucket holster beside his saddle.

Varying his speed, Andrew rode through Potchefstroom, seeing the heads and occasionally startled faces of armed Boers. He kept a mental count as he rode, hoping he would survive to pass on the information, ignoring the occasional challenge and checking his men. Mullan was laughing, waving to both armed Boers and civilians, while Logan looked tense, riding with his carbine balanced over the saddle. The small British garrisons looked around in surprise as Andrew cantered past and burst out of the far side of town.

"Are you still with me, lads?" Andrew asked, looking over his shoulder. He had been so intent on assessing the Boer numbers he had ignored their intermittent musketry.

"Still here, sir," Mullan replied.

"Best not linger, sir," Logan said as a bullet kicked up a fountain of dirt a foot from Andrew's horse. "Brother Boer is awake and angry."

"Good advice, Logan," Andrew said, patting Lancelot and

setting off in a mazy run to confuse the Boer riflemen. He heard the irregular crackle of musketry and the occasional hiss as a bullet whistled past.

Mullan laughed again, twisted in his saddle, and returned fire.

"Be careful, Mullan," Andrew ordered. "Make sure you don't hit a civilian."

"Yes, sir," Mullan said, reloading and placing the carbine on his saddle.

With the town behind them, Andrew pushed into the countryside. *The Boers are country-bred. They are bound to have a camp outside Potchefstroom.*

"Sir!" Logan shouted, spurring his horse to get level with Andrew. "Over there!"

Andrew followed the direction of Logan's pointing rifle. A group of Boer horsemen had emerged from a wooded ridge and headed towards the British patrol. Andrew estimated between twelve and fifteen riders.

Why the sudden interest in three horsemen? They're trying to scare us away from something.

"Split up!" Andrew ordered. "You two lads ride like the devil for the fort. Don't stop for anything and report what you've seen."

"Where are you going, sir?" Logan asked.

"I want to see where these fellows came from," Andrew said. "Go!"

The Boers were closer now, riding in an untidy group with a broad-hatted man a few lengths ahead.

That fellow is their leader.

Confident in his horsemanship, Andrew ducked down and kicked in his spurs. "Come on, Lancelot!" he whispered in his horse's ear. "We'll lead the Boers a dance."

Lancelot responded by lengthening his stride as Andrew slanted past the Boers' left flank. Glancing over his shoulder, he saw the Boers split into smaller parties, most chasing the two mounted infantrymen but three riders following him.

Andrew already knew the Boers were nimble and enduring horsemen, but he was unsure if their ponies were fast.

Now is my opportunity to find out.

Andrew could not restrain his laugh, whether from nerves, excitement, or exhilaration, he did not know. He pushed Lancelot up the crest and stopped. On the opposite side, Andrew saw scores of wagons in laager, with knee-haltered horses and small groups of armed men riding to and fro. As he watched, more wagons appeared, and a small commando of armed men arrived within a curtain of dust.

Dear God, it's an army! Andrew said to himself. *No wonder the Boers tried to chase us away.* With his pursuers still safely distant, Andrew raised his field glasses to scan the encampment.

The Boers have hundreds of men here. No, thousands. Whoever leads this army must want Potchefstroom badly.

Andrew heard the double report of a rifle and glanced at his pursuers. The Boers had spread out to trap him, with one man firing from the saddle.

I've seen enough. Time to run. Andrew had sufficient experience to know a man on a trotting horse had little chance of hitting his target.

"Come on, Lancelot!" Andrew urged, put his head down and headed for the rider at the edge of the Boer flank. The Boer looked up, saw Andrew galloping directly towards him, and unholstered his rifle.

Are you trying to scare me? That won't work, my friend.

"Fire, then!" Andrew shouted, unable to restrain his crazed laughter. He rode directly at the Boer, saw the man aim, and heard the simultaneous crack of the rifle. He had no idea where the bullet went, except it was not near him.

"Missed!" Andrew yelled. "Come on, Lancelot!"

Seeing a yelling British officer charging directly at him, the Boer naturally pulled away. The riders passed within two yards of each other, and Andrew galloped on, leaving the Boer floundering in his wake. By the time the Boers recovered and altered direction, Andrew was fifty yards in front, with the distance increasing with every stride.

A lone house stood directly in Andrew's path. It was no different from a thousand other homes in the Transvaal, with a corrugated iron roof, a shaded *stoep*, a small garden with carefully tended flowers, and a plain gable. An elderly man slowly rose from his seat to close the green Venetian shutters, protecting his property from the flying bullets. By the time the man sat back down, Andrew was level with the house, with Lancelot's hooves kicking up dust and small pebbles. The elderly man scratched a light for his pipe and watched.

With Andrew's pursuers in a long line behind him, the remainder of the Boer riders were scattered between Andrew and the fort. He saw the fort gates open, and Logan and Mullan ride in, with a tall officer leading a substantial body of mounted infantry outside.

That's Lieutenant Lindsell.

Andrew jinked from left to right to put any hopeful Boers off their aim and heard the thrill of a bugle and the sharp barks of musketry. He saw the white sun helmets of men behind the fort wall and Lindsell pushing his mounted infantry towards him.

"Come on, Captain!" Lindsell shouted, leading his mounted infantry forward. "We'll cover you."

Andrew kicked Lancelot into a final effort, and the Boers veered away with some desultory shooting but no casualties on either side.

"In you come, Baird," Lindsell invited, firing his revolver at the withdrawing Boers. "You've had your outing for the day."

Andrew grinned. "Mother always told me to get home before the darkness came down," he said. He looked behind him at the retreating Boers and wondered at his stupidity as the madness drained away.

"That was sheer lunacy," Colonel Winsloe said, shaking his head. "Did you see your Prussian?"

"No, sir," Andrew shook his head.

"You saw a few Boers, though," Colonel Winsloe sat back in his chair. Above his head, Boer bullets had perforated the tent in three places.

"I estimate about five thousand Boers, sir," Andrew said.

"Five thousand!" Winsloe whistled and gave a rueful smile. "They far outnumber my hundred and seventy men."

"Yes, sir. Their main camp is beyond the town, and more were arriving as I watched." Andrew detailed what he had seen as Winsloe dipped his pen in an inkwell and carefully took notes.

"You say the Boers have taken over various houses in the town."

"Yes, sir. They're turning them into strongpoints."

Winsloe pressed a blotter over his notes and replaced his pen in its holder. "I had hoped they were only raiding. We are not in any position to withstand a long siege. However, we must make do with what we have." He looked up. "Thank you, Baird. Your Prussian spy is less important now."

Or, more important. If the Germans learn how few men we have in Transvaal, they may help the Boers. Andrew decided not to argue with his superior officer. "Perhaps so, sir."

"You are dismissed, Baird," Winsloe lifted his notes and reread them as Andrew left the tent.

As the sun dipped to the horizon, half a dozen artillerymen left the fort, looking to water their horses.

"Be careful, lads," Andrew cautioned.

"We will, sir," the leading artilleryman replied. The sentries let them pass and closed the gate.

The Boers must have been waiting for their opportunity, for they opened fire immediately after the gunners left the fort. One man, Driver Ross, fell, seriously wounded, and a bullet killed a horse outright.

"Open the gate!" Andrew roared. "Get these men back inside! Fire at the Boers! Make them keep their heads down!"

Two sentries dragged open the heavy gates while the remainder fired toward the Boer muzzle flashes.

"What's happened, sir?" Lieutenant Rundle asked.

"The Boers have ambushed your men, Lieutenant," Andrew replied. "Close the gate!" He shouted as the gunners drove their horses back inside the fort.

"Open the gate, close the gate," Fusilier McWilliam muttered. "I wish those bloody ossifers would make their minds up."

"That house there, sir," Sergeant Lennox pointed to a thatch-roofed building. "That's where the Boers are!"

As the artillerymen returned at a run, Rundle ordered his gunners to fire at the house Lennox identified.

"Come on, lads! They shot Rossie!"

With one of their own injured, the gunners worked even harder, and a brace of artillery shells blasted the house into rubble. The Boer musketry ended immediately.

"The Boers are tightening the siege," Andrew observed.

"You're correct, Baird," Winsloe agreed quietly. He gestured to Major Thornhill. "In the morning, we'll have the heliograph operator inform the nearest British garrison."

"Yes, sir," Major Thornhill replied. "If we had one."

"If we had one?" Winsloe repeated. "Are you telling me we don't have a heliograph?"

"That's right, sir," Thornhill confirmed. "It's due to arrive sometime next week."

Winsloe frowned. "Brother Boer won't allow that. We'll have to think of something else."

The desultory firing continued all night and into the next day, with the white helmets of the soldiers providing perfect targets for the Boer marksmen. "Dye the helmets brown," Andrew advised. "A darker colour won't show up so much at night."

Thornhill agreed, so the men gleefully rubbed mud on their helmets, much to the disgust of the NCOs.

"Sergeant Lennox doesn't like this much," McWilliam said.

"That's all the more reason to do a good job," Tosh laughed. "Lay it on thick!"

Whenever the Boer musketry became dangerous, the duty officer ordered a section of the defenders to fire a volley, so the noise of rifles kept the town awake. Ignoring the noise, Andrew slept in a borrowed tent for four hours until artillery fire woke him. He rolled over, rose, dressed, and strode to the wall. The defenders were keeping under shelter as Boer bullets hammered at them.

Lieutenant Rundle grinned as Andrew approached. "Welcome back, sir."

"Anything happened while I was gone?"

"Nothing of any moment," Rundle said. "We're inside the fort, the Boers are outside, and the bullets fly each way."

"I noticed that," Andrew said. "I'll have a look at the defences."

The 21st looked unconcerned at the Boer bullets, sitting behind the wall with their rifles held ready to retaliate. Mullan had propped his helmet on top of the wall and greeted Andrew with a grin.

"There you are, sir. Are we off for another wee jaunt around the town?"

"Not yet, Mullan," Andrew said. "Would you not be better wearing your hat?"

"It gives the Boers a mark to aim at," Mullan explained. "When a Boer bullet hits it, we pop up and fire back."

"Aim for the muzzle flare or the smoke," Andrew advised. "And aim low. The Boers are hunters, remember, they're used to lying prone for hours to kill meat for the pot."

"I wish they'd fight fair, like soldiers, or at least like men, not cowards skulking behind cover." Logan used a rag to polish the barrel of his rifle. "When we fought the Zulus, we knew we were facing real warriors."

Andrew remembered the Boers he met during the Zulu War. "The Boers are not cowards," he said quietly. "They don't fight the same way as us, but they're not cowards."

Logan opened his mouth, decided not to speak, and closed it again. A Boer bullet zipped over, whacked into Mullan's helmet, and knocked it off the wall.

Before the helmet hit the ground, Mullan jumped up, aimed at the smoke, fired, and ducked back down as two Boer bullets smashed into the top of the wall.

"They've learned your game, Mullan," Andrew warned. "They had two marksmen ready for you to appear. I'd not try that again."

Mullan gave his habitual wide grin. "I won't, sir!" Lifting his perforated helmet, he jammed it on his head. "I hope I got one of them."

"So do I," Andrew said. Lifting a couple of mealie bags from the ground, he placed them on top of the wall a few inches apart, placed a third on top and stared through the aperture with his field glasses. The town looked quiet except for the occasional spurt of smoke as the Boers fired.

Show yourself, Konrad Bramigan, Andrew thought. *I want confirmation you are here.*

A bullet whacked into the mealie bag above Andrew's head, releasing a small trickle of corn. He focussed on the smoke, hoping to see the face of his attacker. Another bullet followed, thumping into the bag to his right.

Andrew heard the crack of a rifle and Mullan's low chuckle. "I think I got that one!" he said as he ducked away. "They're targeting you now, sir!"

Andrew looked at the last spurt of smoke without seeing any Boer casualties, yet nobody shot at him when he lifted his field glasses.

THE SOUND OF BOER RIFLES

❄

At half past ten on the morning of the 18th of December, smoke rose from the Landdrost's office. Andrew watched orange flames lick along the thatch, and acrid smoke discolour the clear air. He surveyed the rooftops, wondering at the vulnerability of the sun-dried thatch. Andrew was glad the houses were less closely packed as those in Berwick-upon-Tweed or Hereford, or the flames would race across the town.

Lieutenant Rundle shook his head. "The lads will have fun defending the Landdrost's office now."

Andrew grunted. "They'll have to pull out, but I doubt they can withdraw to the fort with thousands of Boers between us and them."

The flames rose, increasing in size and intensity through the morning.

"We could send a relief force to bring Major Clarke and his men back, sir," Rundle suggested to the colonel.

"The Boers would cut them to pieces in the streets," Colonel Winsloe said. "We'd lose more men than we saved. If Clarke wants to fight his way out, we'll help. Otherwise, we'll sit tight."

"Yes, sir," Rundle said, looking longingly over the wall as the flames consumed the thatch roof.

Just before noon that day, one of the sentries called out, "Major Clarke's lowering his flag!"

Andrew swore softly. The Union flag above the Landdrost's office jerked slowly down to the smouldering roof, with a white flag hauled up in its place. He could feel the disbelief inside the fort.

"Major Clarke's surrendering! To a bunch of bloody farmers!"

"They should have fought on," Fusilier McWilliam said.

"They'd have burned alive," Sergeant Lennox reminded.

"Well, have a fighting retreat here, then." McWilliam gripped his rifle, shaking his head. "We'd have supported him."

Andrew said nothing. He wondered if the men would have

held on longer if they had faced Zulus rather than Boers, who took prisoners.

With the white flag hanging limp above the Landdrost's house, all firing ended as the British waited to see what happened next. A lone Boer rode to the fort with a white rag tied to the muzzle of his rifle.

"Let him approach," Colonel Winsloe ordered and strolled to the gate.

"Good afternoon, my man," Winsloe shouted. "Have you come to surrender?"

The Boer lifted his hat politely. "General Cronje asks for a truce until four this afternoon," he said in perfect English. "He wants to finalise the agreement between the general and Major Clarke."

Winsloe pursed his lips. "Tell your General Cronje that we agree," he said. "We'll grant his truce."

"Thank you, *meneer*," the Boer replied, lifted his hat again and withdrew.

Colonel Winsloe stepped back from the parapet. "Raise the walls," he ordered. "I don't care what you use. And how is our water?"

"Not great, sir," Major Thornhill replied. "We've been digging wells since we arrived without any success. Our first well sunk to twenty-four feet and hit rock. We're still hacking with the second."

"Keep digging," Winsloe ordered. "And raise these walls. The Boers can fire right over them."

"Do you know anything about civil engineering, Baird?" Thornhill asked.

"Not a thing, sir."

"As much as me, then," Thornhill said. "Let's get building while the truce lasts. One must make the most of whatever opportunities the Lord of War offers." He raised his voice. "All men not on duty on the well or wall report to me!"

The men ran up, some grumbling, others eager, a few adjusting their belts or helmets.

"I want these walls higher," Thornhill shouted. "Bring me cases of food, sacks of mealies, and anything else you can find. Keep Brother Boer out and us safe!"

Andrew helped Thornhill supervise the Fusiliers in strengthening the fort's defences. Men hurried to and fro with cases of food and bags of mealies, thumping them on top of the baked mud walls.

"Every sack keeps the civilians safe," Sergeant Lennox said. "Your sweat is helping win the war, so I want to see you dripping wet!"

"The lads at Rorke's Drift did the same," McWilliam staggered under the weight of two sacks.

"They were fighting Zulu warriors, not Boers," Tosh reminded him. "Savages with spears, not farmers with rifles."

"When I joined the army," McWilliam said, "I thought I'd be fighting the Russians or the French. Fight for your country, the recruiting sergeant said. Defend Britain from the grey Cossack hordes, he said. He never said I'd be a builder's labourer in the middle of bloody Africa."

Tosh lifted a wooden case and swore. "That proves what I've always said. Never trust a sergeant."

"You're too bloody late now!" Sergeant Lennox roared in Tosh's ear. "I've got you! You're mine! Get that wall built, or you'll feel the toe of my boot!"

"Yes, Sergeant!" Tosh replied, winking at McWilliam.

"Keep moving, lads," Andrew ordered. Although he knew officers should be above manual labour, he led by example, carrying boxes and sacks, knowing that each could stop a bullet and save a man's life.

"Keep one sack in three for supplies," Thornhill reminded. "We don't know how long the siege will last, and we'll have to eat."

Colonel Windroe toured the walls, pointing out weaknesses. "There are holes here and there. Fill them!"

"Spare clothes," Andrew said. "We can stuff them into any gaps in the walls."

"Will cloth stop a bullet?" Thornhill wondered.

"I don't know, sir, but it will stop the Boer marksman from seeing men on the inside," Andrew said.

Winslow rationed each man to one shirt and trousers, with the remainder of their clothes used to strengthen the defences.

"Every little helps," Thornhill said.

"How about a trench, sir," Andrew suggested. "Rather than raising the wall, lower the ground on this side."

"Maybe later," Thornhill said. "The men are already exhausted."

"Yes, sir," Andrew did not press the point.

At four in the evening, the Boer messenger returned to the fort bearing a flag of truce and a copy of Major Clarke's surrender agreement.

Colonel Winsloe met him at the gate. "Have you seen the error of your ways, *meneer?*" Winsloe asked. "We will accept your surrender on easy terms."

"We surround the town and the fort, Colonel," the messenger replied with a wry smile. "You and your men cannot get out, and nobody can relieve you. We will accept your surrender on the same terms as we did for Major Clarke."

Winsloe muttered something that Andrew could not catch before raising his voice. "Tell General Cronje that I have no intention of surrendering, and we can hold out for months as we lack for nothing in the fort."

Except water, food, shelter and ammunition, Andrew thought. He glanced at the civilian refugees crowded in the centre of the fort, listening hopefully to everything Colonel Winsloe said. The women looked nervous. *No wonder. A small fort does not have the facilities to look after women.*

When the official truce ended, the Boers still held their fire, and at nine that night, Colonel Winsloe looked for volunteers to recall the garrison from the town jail.

"Not you, Baird," Winsloe said. "You have other duties and a message to deliver to General Hook."

Andrew nodded. "Yes, sir."

The Boers did not interfere with the jail evacuation, and the garrison returned carrying one dead and two wounded men.

"We're pulling in our horns," Rundle said. "Brother Boer is pushing us back post by post." He lit a cheroot and winked at Andrew through a curtain of blue smoke. "It's not quite Lucknow, but I wonder what the people in Britain are saying about us."[1]

Andrew smiled. "Oh, we'll be pluckily defying the enemy hordes while saluting the flag and preparing to sacrifice our lives for Queen and country. Or some such nonsense."

Rundle drew on his cheroot. "We don't even have a flag," he said. "Major Clarke had our only flag, and it's gone now, probably a trophy in some back veld farm."

"We have to have a flag," Andrew said. "A beleaguered garrison needs a flag. It's a symbol of defiance."

As the fort settled down for another night under siege, Colonel Winsloe called his officers together. They gathered around him, some expecting Boer marksmen to open fire and others standing erect to prove their disdain.

"We're in a bit of a pickle, gentlemen," Winsloe said. "We have a hundred and seventy men in this fort, plus civilians and animals to look after."

The officers nodded in agreement. They knew the figures.

"Our walls are too low, and Captain Baird has estimated around five thousand Boers oppose us." Winsloe continued. "I intend sending a message to Colonel Bellairs in Pretoria, asking him to send a relief column."

The men nodded, some holding cigars and cheroots whose blue smoke coiled lazily into the still air. A subaltern started when a rifle cracked in the distance.

"I'll send two messengers in case the Boers capture or kill one," Winsloe was brutally frank. His mouth twisted into a smile. "Two messengers will double our chances of success. Passing through the Boer lines will be dangerous, so I'll need volunteers with experience in South African conditions."

Andrew lifted a hand. "I'll volunteer, sir," he said. "I'm not from the 21st, so the garrison won't miss me, and I've been upwards of three years in South Africa." He grinned. "I also have a message to pass to General Hook."

Winsloe nodded. "I knew you'd volunteer, Baird. Didn't your men call you Up-and-at-em?"

Andrew felt the blood rush to his face. "Yes, sir," he said.

"I'll go, sir," a tall officer held up his hand.

Andrew nodded to the second messenger, a young subaltern with the face of a schoolboy and the body of an athlete.

"Well done, Cunningham," Winsloe said. "You two volunteers remain here. The others are dismissed."

Andrew and Cunningham waited until the colonel's quarters were empty. They looked each other over, with the subaltern grinning as if everything were a great joke.

"Ride separately," Winsloe ordered. "Find Colonel Bellairs in Pretoria, inform him of our numbers and position, and tell him we are embarrassed by the presence of the ladies here, and we are using up ammunition at an alarming rate."

Andrew nodded as Cunningham jumped up. "Will do, sir!"

"We'll leave at night," Andrew decided. "Twenty minutes apart. Cunningham and I will study the maps and decide if we're going the same or alternate routes."

"One more thing," Winsloe said quietly. "Lt-Colonel Anstruther is also on his way from Middelburg to Pretoria with about two hundred and fifty men of the 94th Foot. If you meet him, let him know our situation. If you ride in uniform, the Boers won't shoot you as a spy, but you'll blend in better if you wear civilian clothes. The choice is yours. Oh, and remember, your duty is to pass your message along. Don't get involved in any situation that endangers you; the message matters above everything else."

Cunningham grinned. "We'll do our duty, sir!"

"I'll leave the fine details to you," Winsloe said. "Good luck, gentlemen."

CHAPTER 7

BRONKHORST SPRUIT, THIRTY-EIGHT MILES FROM PRETORIA

20TH OF DECEMBER 1880

Andrew lifted his head at the sound of jaunty music and recognised the tune "Kiss Me, Mother Darling."
That's a regimental band, not a Boer commando, but why the music? Don't they realise we're at war?

Andrew saw the rising dust next and pushed Lancelot forward, hoping it was Colonel Anstruther's 94th Foot. He felt a surge of reassurance, remembering the steady infantry of the Zulu Wars with their black humour and regular volleys that dissolved the charging impis. *It must be Anstruther. Nobody else would be out here.*

When Andrew heard the distinct jingle of a horse's harness closer at hand, he froze and leaned forward in his saddle. Experience from the Zulu and Frontier Wars made him pull into the shelter of a group of acacia trees. He heard a voice speaking in Afrikaans and the deep rumble of a man laughing.

THE SOUND OF BOER RIFLES

Trouble. Keep still and assess the situation.

Andrew quietly dismounted. Forcing the horse to lie, he sank to the ground and crawled onto a small ridge, hoping not to disturb any snakes. He felt the ground vibrate and heard the regular tramp of boots and the distinctive bark of a sergeant.

"Heads up, boys, not long until we have a break!"

The 94th were marching in a rough column, many with their white sun helmets pushed to the back of their heads in search of a cool breeze. Some had their Martini-Henry rifles held at the trail or balanced on their shoulders, with the senior officers riding in front and the junior officers and NCOs marching with their men. Behind the main body of infantry, a long convoy of thirty-four wagons trundled across the rough track, with the drivers cracking their whips, shouting, and whistling to encourage the oxen. Andrew saw some civilians on the wagons and guessed they were the wives and families of the marching men.

A few mounted infantrymen rode four hundred yards ahead of the column, and Andrew saw one gallop back to speak to Anstruther. The colonel halted his horse and scanned a farmhouse with his field glasses before shaking his head and pushing on.

Listen to your scouts, Anstruther! That's why you have them. We're at war, for God's sake, not marching across Salisbury Plain!

Andrew looked ahead, where a small group of mounted Boers waited behind a rocky outcrop. He saw others, extended in a skirmish line hidden behind a ridge, with a thin screen of thorn bushes for cover.

Are these men watching the 94th? What's happening here?

It's an ambush, Andrew thought as he saw hundreds more Boers hiding among the rocks. *The 94th are in a peacetime formation, marching into a war situation.*

Andrew slowly unholstered his rifle. His orders were to deliver his message and avoid trouble, but the Boers would massacre the British column unless he warned the 94th.

A Boer spoke nearby, the words low but recognisable.

"Shall I fire?"

"Wait until Commandant Joubert gives the order."

Commandant Joubert? That must be Commandant Frans Joubert, who commands the Boers in this area.

Andrew slid further under the shelter of the trees and slid his finger over the trigger. He hoped that a single rifle shot would warn Colonel Anstruther.

Fire a single shot, mount, and ride like the devil.

Andrew tensed himself and stiffened when he felt something hard prod into his spine.

"What are you doing, *meneer*?"

Andrew froze and slowly looked around to see a young, bearded Boer. The Boer lifted his rifle, eyeing Andrew curiously.

"Who are you?" The Boer asked quietly. "I do not know your face." He prodded Andrew's stomach with the rifle.

"Who are you?" Andrew replied in his halting Afrikaans. "I don't know your face either."

"Jacobus Bester," the Boer replied. "Are you a *Rooineck*?"

"Do I look like a *Rooineck*?" Andrew tried to bluff his way free. He indicated his clothes, especially chosen to help him blend with the Burghers.

"You sound like a *Rooineck*," Jacobus sounded puzzled. He lifted his rifle so it pointed at Andrew's chest. "Stay there."

"I'm not going anywhere," Andrew said. He saw a bead of sweat form on Jacobus's forehead and knew the boy was nervous. *Sufficiently nervous to fire on the slightest provocation? I'll play this game by ear.*

A sudden movement from the British column diverted both men as the band stopped playing.

"Boers!" An officer's voice sounded.

Colonel Anstruther returned to the column, shouting orders. "Halt! Close up the wagons! Prepare the men for action!"

Andrew watched the bandsmen run to the wagons to find

their rifles, and other men sought ammunition. In the meantime, a lone Boer rode towards the head of the column.

"That's Paul de Beer," Andrew's captor said, as casually as if discussing a neighbour. "Now we'll see the *Rooinecks* turn tail!"

Two officers accompanied Colonel Anstruther as he walked his horse toward de Beer.

"Colonel Anstruther," de Beer's voice carried clearly to Andrew. "You are in the free *Zuid Afrikaanse Republiek* of Transvaal. I insist that you and your men turn around and return from where you have come." He handed over a folded note. "This letter is from the leaders of the Republic in Heidelberg."

Anstruther opened the message. "This letter tells me to stop where I am," he reported to his officers. "It says that any further movement towards Pretoria will be seen as a declaration of war." He read the letter aloud, closing with "The responsibility whereof we put on your shoulders."

De Beer waited until Anstruther finished the letter, then added. "You have two minutes to respond."

"My orders are to proceed with all possible despatch to Pretoria," Anstruther snapped. "And to Pretoria, I am going, but tell the Commandant I have no wish to meet him in a hostile spirit."

"Do you wish war or peace, Colonel?" De Beer asked.

"I intend to continue my journey, sir," Anstruther replied.

"Is it war or peace, Colonel Anstruther?" De Beer repeated.

"I intend to continue my journey."

As Colonel Anstruther and de Beer spoke, Jacobus divided his attention between Andrew and the drama unfolding below. Despite the ongoing conversation, armed Boers advanced on the scarlet-uniformed officers. Unsuspecting British soldiers waited for the result, with many unarmed and the officers curious to see what transpired.

The Boers were about two hundred yards from the British when an angry Anstruther returned to his men. Andrew noticed an elderly Boer with a long white beard taking his position beneath a thorn bush. He lay on his stomach, loaded a hunting rifle, and pushed it forward, holding the butt against his cheek. For a moment, the sun highlighted the leopard skin band on the man's hat and reflected on his bright, aged eyes.

Andrew realised that Jacobus was watching the encounter. Slowly lifting his rifle, Andrew was about to fire a warning shot when a second Boer took hold of his arm.

"I'll have your Martini," the second Boer ordered in thickly accented English. With grey streaks in his beard and his hat pulled low over his eyes, he pressed his rifle against Andrew's chest. "Give it to me, *Rooineck!*"

Inwardly swearing, Andrew handed over his rifle without a word.

"Thank you, *meneer*," the Boer said. "What name do you have?"

Before Andrew could reply, movement from the British column distracted all three men.

De Beer had ridden back to the commando and searched for Frans Joubert even as Colonel Anstruther spoke to his officers. Only a few minutes had passed when an impatient Boer leader gave the order to attack.

Andrew saw the hundreds of Boers emerge from cover to open fire on the British column. From close range on an exposed enemy in column, the Boer musketry felled scores of the 94th before they knew they were at war. The Boer with the leopard skin band aimed at a tall officer, squeezed the trigger, and immediately reloaded. At such a close range, he did not need to check the result of his shot. The officer crumpled, dead before he hit the ground.

"Skirmish order!" Anstruther shouted as he galloped back to his men. "Open up to skirmish order! For God's sake, move!"

More Boers galloped closer to the column, dismounted, and lay behind every fold of ground, rock, and thorn bush. Andrew did not hear anybody giving orders, only the incessant hammer of musketry as the Burghers fired on the disorganised 94th Foot. Many of the British soldiers were still in columns of four and fell before they could level their rifles. The unarmed bandsmen died still holding their instruments.

It's a massacre. These lads don't know what's happening.

Andrew saw the long-bearded old Boer take careful aim at the officers and fell them, one by one. His leopard skin band hardly moved as he altered aim to Anstruther and fired, hitting the colonel in the left leg. Anstruther staggered but remained on his feet, shouting orders that were lost in the hellish din of musketry and wounded men. The old Boer aimed and fired again, knocking Anstruther to the ground.

Andrew could only watch in horror as the Boers formed a horseshoe around the British column, some firing from horseback but most from the cover of rocks and folds in the ground.

Those of the 94th who could retaliate stood in the open and fired back. Most of the shots flew high, and Andrew swore.

Adjust your sights! The Boers are close, and you're aiming for distance shooting.

Despite Colonel Anstruther falling with multiple wounds and nearly all the other officers being dead or wounded, the surviving 94th stood fast. Caught at a disadvantage in territory the enemy knew well, they refused to break or panic. Although their shooting was inaccurate, Andrew admired their courage.

Further down the column, scores of mounted Boers charged at the supply wagons. Andrew saw them fire from around four hundred yards, gallop through the smoke, shoot at the oxen, civilian drivers, and escort before wheeling their horses and returning. Some native drivers fell, dead or wounded, and the others fled, running before these merciless horsemen of the veld.

"Shoot them!" Jacobus shouted, firing towards the beleaguered British. "Shoot them all!"

With the second Boer holding him at rifle point, Andrew

swore in frustration as the Boers massacred the British infantry. The 94th fired back, aiming at the hiding Boers or the mobile horsemen, but with the officers and non-commissioned officers gone, the men were leaderless and bewildered. Within ten minutes, over a hundred British soldiers had fallen, and five minutes later, Colonel Anstruther, badly wounded, ordered the cease-fire and surrendered.

"We won!" Jacobus began to cheer, with his friend joining in. They shook hands, yelling at their victory and nearly dancing as they watched Joubert approach the shattered British column.[1]

Now! Now's my time!

With his captors distracted, Andrew grabbed back his rifle, crashed the butt into the young Boer's shoulder, pushed his surprised companion away, and ran to his horse.

"Come on, Lancelot!"

Andrew had mounted before the Boers recovered, and spurred towards the south as the first shots screamed past his head.

You're too late, lads! You'll have to catch me now!

Jinking and turning, Andrew galloped away, not heading in any direction but determined to escape from the Boers. He gambled that Francois Joubert would be too busy with his prisoners to be concerned about a lone British horseman. Only a few Boers followed him, four riders on small Boer ponies and one with a larger horse. When Andrew looked over his shoulder, he recognised the horse as a thoroughbred, fine for European conditions but too delicate for the rough veld. Andrew frowned, easing Lancelot into an erratic run to disturb the aim of any potential marksman.

After a quarter of a mile, Lancelot had increased the distance over his pursuers. Andrew allowed him a few moments' rest while he lifted his field glasses to examine the Boers. Riding slightly behind his companions, the man on the thoroughbred was tall and straight. Andrew grunted.

That's Konrad Bramigan. That's the Prussian spy!

THE SOUND OF BOER RIFLES

With Joubert blocking the route to Pretoria and the Boers having declared war on the British Empire, Andrew realised he was deep in a hostile country. Glancing behind him, he saw no signs of pursuit.

Joubert or no Joubert, I'll try to get to Bellairs in Pretoria.

CHAPTER 8

Andrew kicked in his heels, heading north, deeper into the Transvaal, to avoid Joubert's army. Watchful for parties of Boers, hostile or otherwise, he covered five miles before resting Lancelot at a *spruit*. He knew it was about thirty-two miles from Bronkhorst Spruit to Pretoria, a day's ride at most, but Lancelot was tired, and his route must be circuitous.

Twice, Andrew saw small bodies of armed Boers riding towards Pretoria, kicking up dust as they powered forward. He heard an occasional crack as somebody fired a rifle.

Well, Colonel Bellairs, I hope you are ready to launch a relief column. British arms aren't doing very well in this war, but we rarely do at the start of a campaign.

Andrew rode slowly until he realised something significant was happening outside Pretoria. He saw the Union Flag flying above a large walled encampment and dust rising from a concourse of people. Andrew pulled Lancelot to a halt and watched for a few moments. Men, women, and children moved slowly from the town, most on foot, some on horseback and others in wagons.

Exodus. I am watching an exodus of people; the Jews are leaving Egypt, but Bellairs is no Moses. What is happening here?

A group of mounted men escorted the civilians, wearing a uniform that Andrew did not recognise. He watched for a moment, wondering if the Boers had already captured Pretoria, and then rode forward. As he approached the refugees, he heard an officer snapping a command in abrupt English.

"Halloa!" Andrew shouted, keeping one hand on the butt of his rifle. "What's happening here?"

The uniformed officer turned to face Andrew. "Who the devil are you?"

"Captain Andrew Baird of the Natal Dragoons," Andrew introduced himself. "Who are you and what's happening here?"

"Captain? You don't look like a captain."

"What's happening?"

"I am Lieutenant Bryan of the Pretoria Carbineers, and Colonel Bellairs has declared martial law in Pretoria."

"Who are all these people, and where are they going?"

Bryan shouted a string of orders that saw his men urge the civilians to greater speed.

"These are the British citizens of Pretoria," Bryan explained.

"Sir," Andrew prompted, "you say 'sir' to a superior officer. What's happening here?"

Bryan stiffened in the saddle. "Yes, sir. Colonel Bellairs has established a camp half a mile southwest of Pretoria and a defended redoubt, the Convent Redoubt, near the Loreto Convent. We're commandeering all the food and moving the British civilians into the camp, sir."

Andrew saw the refugees hurry past, most carrying bundles of clothes and bedding, some with children in their arms, all confused, a few in tears. "Where's Colonel Bellairs?"

"He's in the camp, sir," Bryan said, pointing in the direction the civilians headed.

"Thank you." Andrew pushed on, watching for Boers as he passed the long column of refugees. It felt like the end of the world, or at least the end of British power in the Transvaal.

Did the British not play 'The World Turned Upside Down' when they surrendered Yorktown to Washington in 1781? This situation feels similar.

A veteran of the Crimean and Xhosa Wars, Colonel William Bellairs was slightly overweight, with a receding hairline and a fine moustache. He greeted Andrew with a nod and listened to his report from Potchefstroom.

"Thank you, Captain," Bellairs replied. "I cannot help Winsloe at present as I expect the Boers to invest me here in Pretoria."

"So I see, sir."

"Lieutenant Cunningham reached here hours ago, and I ordered him to inform Winsloe he'll have to wait for relief from Natal. I cannot afford men to help Potchefstroom when we are also under siege."

Andrew looked around the fortified enclosure with its bell tents and perimeter guards. A scattering of wooden huts and other buildings waited for the Pretoria refugees. "How many people will you have here, sir?"

"Around five thousand, mostly civilians," Bellairs replied. "Our garrison is five companies of infantry from the 21st and 94th Foot, with a troop of mounted infantry, and two nine-pounders of the Royal Artillery, maybe seven hundred regulars including support and medical staff."

"I saw some colonials as well, sir," Andrew said.

"I have over four hundred Pretoria Rifles and a couple of hundred mounted men, Nourse's Horse and the Pretoria Carbineers."

Andrew nodded. "That should be sufficient to stop the Boers," he said.

"I also have a couple of forts in the hills south of the town," Bellairs seemed desperate to detail his defence arrangements. "We'll need every man we can get. You confirmed the details of the dreadful affair at Bronkhorst Spruit, and I expect thousands of Boers to attack us any time."

Andrew looked at the haphazard array of tents, huts, and

buildings within Bellairs' enclosure. "Will you be using this encampment as a base to attack the Boers, sir? The infantry could hold the fort, and the mounted men raid the enemy."

Never give unasked advice to a superior officer.

Bellairs' expression altered. "I'll attend to the strategy later, Captain. In the meantime, we'll hold the fort and await a relief column from Natal."

"I see, sir," Andrew said.

"You have delivered your message, Baird, and I have replied. Cunningham will be halfway back to Potchefstroom by now. You may return to Colonel Winsloe or not, as you please."

Andrew nodded, aware Bellairs had dismissed him. *I have a choice: find one of the British garrisons and sit tight until somebody relieves us, or ride for Natal. Well, I'm not sitting behind a wall to be sniped and starved by Brother Boer.* Andrew felt a surge of relief that he had made the decision.

"I'll ride to Natal, sir, and inform them of your desperate plight."

JOHANNES LOADED HIS RIFLE AND CHECKED HIS SONS. Jan leaned against a tree, cleaning his rifle, while Mannie was pale beneath his tan, licking dry lips as he stared over the battlefield of Bronkhorst Spruit. Busy medical teams tended to the dead and wounded redcoats.

"That was your first battle," Johannes said. "And you both survived." He pushed away his guilt at putting his sons in danger. Jan was nearly a man, and Mannie also had to learn a Burgher's duties.

"Ja," Jan replied. He lifted his rifle and automatically pushed a cartridge into the breech. "We all survived." He looked up briefly and tried to ignore the pitiful groans of a wounded soldier. The smell of gun smoke and raw blood clung to the ground and his clothing. He had not realised that even such a short battle could smell so strongly.

Mannie continued to stare at the field of slaughter. "I killed a *Rooineck*," he said. "One minute, he was standing, and then I shot him, and he fell. He screamed. I heard him scream." Mannie's rifle lay on the ground at his feet.

"If you had not shot him, he would have killed you, Mannie," Johannes said. "That is his job. He is not a farmer like us or a storekeeper or a merchant. His job was to fight and kill for his country." He put a rough hand on his son's shoulder. "You did what you had to do."

"The good Lord said thou shalt not kill." Mannie refused to be consoled. He had only fired two shots. The first had missed, and the second killed the soldier.

"He also said an eye for an eye," Johannes reminded him. "The *Rooinecks* invaded our country."

"Yes," Mannie agreed, fighting the tears that threatened to unman him. "They invaded our land. We had to kill them." He pushed his rifle further away, reliving the instant his bullet hit the soldier, the expression on the man's face, the way his mouth gaped, and his body contorted as the bullet entered his chest. "I had to kill him."

Jan watched without saying anything. He shared some of Mannie's feelings but was older and hid them better. He remembered every detail of the battle, from de Beer challenging the British colonel to the men firing and falling and the final surrender. Although Jan had been on many hunting trips, killing men was different to shooting game. He had seen the bravery of the British soldiers, standing in the open as the Boers shot them down, but he also thought them foolish not to lie on the ground or find cover.

Ja, the Rooinecks are a foolish people to fight like that. The Lord made them act like targets so we could not miss. Jan smiled, trying to convince himself that God was on the Boer's side. He winked at Mannie and tried to forget the men he had shot.

"Engela will be glad you survived," Johannes tried to cheer his sons up. He remembered his first commando when he had ridden against a band of tribesmen who had murdered a neighbour and committed unspeakable atrocities on the man's wife.

When Jan looked up, a new light chased the dark shadows from his eyes. "I wonder if she ever thinks of me."

Johannes began to pack tobacco into the bowl of his pipe. "Ja, she will think of you more often than you think of her." He smiled as Jan coloured. "Why don't you write her, Jan? Tell her what you have been doing and how Abraham has been fighting harder than you."

"He has not!" Jan said.

Johannes scratched a match and applied the flame to his pipe. "I can guarantee he'll tell Engela about his heroic actions and how he defeated the British single-handedly."

"He did not!" Jan raised his voice.

"I know that, and you know that," Johannes said. "But Engela doesn't know. Maybe you'd better write and tell her what you've been doing. Women like men to talk to them." He stepped away and turned around as if to add an afterthought. "Ask how Engela is doing as well. Women also like you to be interested in their lives."

"Where can I find paper and a pen?"

"Didn't I say?" Johannes reached inside his jacket. "I found this in a British officer's saddlebag. He won't need it again." He pulled out a small leather case which contained a writing pad with pens, ink, and blotting paper. When Jan took the case, Johannes winked at Mannie. "Come on, Mannie, Jan will be busy for a while. We can talk in peace and then return to Potchefstroom."

ANDREW SAW THE HUMP OF MAJUBA HILL RISING AHEAD OF him and eased Lancelot to a halt at a cool spring. "Drink your fill, Lance," he said, "we might have a long day tomorrow."

For the previous three days, Andrew had avoided parties of Boers moving towards the border between the Transvaal and Natal. The Boers had ridden singly, in small groups or large commandos with ox-wagons driven by skilled Africans. As he waited beside the spring, Andrew heard the distinct crack of a wagon whip and the discordant rumbling of wheels on the ground.

How many Boers are there, for goodness' sake? The Transvaal seemed to have poured its entire Boer manhood to the border. *Will they invade Natal and invoke the Afrikander Bond to drive the British into the sea?*

Andrew pushed Lancelot harder, aware it would take a flight of imagination for a Boer to recognise him as British, as he wore similar clothes and rode in the same fashion. Wondering where the Boers were headed, Andrew followed one small commando, keeping half a mile in the rear and lifting a hand in acknowledgement when anybody passed nearby.

Within two hours, the commando rode into a large concourse of men and horses, with two large wagon laagers and scores of draft oxen.

That's far enough, Andrew decided. *I've found the Boers' main camp. Now, I must cross the pass into Natal and alert the British authorities.*

POTCHEFSTROOM, DECEMBER AND JANUARY 1881.

Jan loaded his rifle, checked the foresight, and winked at Mannie. "Are you all right, Mannie?"

The youngster nodded, brushed a fly away from his face and nodded. "Ja, I am all right." He forced a smile that lacked any humour.

They sheltered inside a large building with a view of the fort, avoiding the window, for it invited bullets when both sides exchanged gunfire. Hanging limply above the fort, the multi-crossed Union flag proclaimed British control. Other members of the Groenburg Commando occupied the other rooms, having commandeered the building as their base.

"We will soon remove that flag," Johannes joined them, passing out bread. "Keep your strength up, boys."

Lifting his rifle, Jan took a snapshot at a bobbing British helmet. "That made him jump."

"We are not here to make the British jump," Johannes reprimanded his son. "We are here to chase them back across the sea. Don't waste your ammunition."

Jan nodded, shamefaced, and reloaded, pressing home the brass cartridge. Mannie had not moved, holding the bread in his hand.

"Our artillery is arriving tomorrow," Johannes said. "Then we shall see how the British react."

"Artillery?" Mannie showed some interest. "I didn't know we had cannons."

Johannes sat beside his sons, leaned on the wall, and placed his rifle at his side. "We don't have parks of artillery like the *Rooinecks*, but we have a few cannons." Taking his pipe from his pocket, he stuffed tobacco into the bowl, scratched a match and applied it, puffing happily.

All three ducked when the British replied to Jan's single shot with a volley that crashed against the outside wall of the house. One bullet smashed the last remaining glass in the window, sending glittering shards into the room.

"That's another reason for not firing at the British," Johannes told Jan. "It makes them angry." He grinned, drawing on his pipe. "I was telling you about our artillery. When the British annexed our republic in April 1877, we knew their occupation would not last and prepared for war with them."

Jan and Mannie listened, with Karl, Abraham and a few

others inside the house also paying attention. Jan flicked some loose glass from his bread and took a bite as Johannes continued.

"You may remember that when we fought the Zulus at Blood River in 1838, we had an old ship's gun for artillery, and we used another cannon at Boomplats."

Jan nodded, for the battle of Blood River was part of Boer folklore. He knew less about the Battle of Boomplats, probably because the British had won.[1]

"After Shepstone's announcement that the British had annexed our republic," Johannes continued, "we buried the barrels of the old cannon to prevent the *Rooinecks* from taking them." He puffed out smoke, removed the pipe from his mouth and prodded Jan with the stem. "One gun is called *Ou Greif* and comes from Carron in Scotland. It was made over a hundred years ago, in 1762."

"Does it still fire?" Mannie asked.

"We'll make it fire," Johannes replied solemnly. "We'll turn the British gun against them."

All three van Colliers looked over as Karl aimed and fired, with the British retaliating with a surprisingly quick volley. Bullets struck dust from the walls of the house and splintered wood from the window frame. Johannes looked up briefly, brushed dust from his shoulder and continued.

"The British navy used *Ou Greif* in the later eighteenth century," Johannes said. "It's not a big barrel, only twenty-four inches long, and was built for case, that's bags of small balls rather than cannonballs."

"It won't hurt the British fort then," Jan immediately understood. "We need something explosive or a heavy ball for that."

"No," Johannes said. "It won't hurt the walls, only the soldiers."

Mannie ducked as Theunis fired, but the British did not retaliate. "Shoot them!" Theunis shouted. "We won't defeat them by watching from a distance."

"We dug up *Ou Greif* and the other cannon," Johannes

ignored Theunis's outburst. "Marthinus Ras of Bokfontein spent days mounting the barrel on a wagon axle and fitted a pair of wheels. Marthinus is a clever man who will use wagon wheel rims to make more cannon. He will help give the British a warm welcome to our republic."

"Or a hot farewell," Theunis said from the far corner of the room.

Jan wondered how even a skilled mechanic could create a cannon from wheel rims when an outbreak of firing brought all the Groenburg Commando to their stations. Johannes fired one shot, watched his sons, and nodded when he realised they were aiming rather than merely firing blindly.

"That's the way, boys," he encouraged. "Let the British waste their cartridges. Every bullet they fire costs Queen Victoria money and weakens their empire."

Karl fired and swore as a British bullet knocked a piece of stone from the wall against his forehead. He put a hand to the wound. "The damned British are learning how to shoot."

Johannes grunted. "They were probably aiming at the house next door," he said. "Let me see." He examined Karl's injury through critical eyes. "It is not even a scratch. It'll take more than a British bullet to damage your thick skull."

"My wife has done worse when she is in a bad mood," Karl said. "I pity the servants when she doesn't have me to shout at."

Jan laughed too loudly, a young man wishing to appear equal to his elders. He glanced sideways as Mannie coughed. "Are you all right?"

"Yes," Mannie said. "The smoke caught my throat."

Jan saw Johannes watching. "It's only gun smoke," he said. "It's because we're inside a room. You wouldn't even notice it outside." He thumbed a cartridge into the breech of his rifle and searched for a target in the fort. "The redcoats have learned how to take cover. We have taught them well."

"We had better not teach them anymore," Karl grumbled. "Or they will be as good as we are."

"Stop firing," Johannes ordered. "Unless you see a definite target." He thought of their limited supply of ammunition. "Don't waste bullets."

As the firing eased, Johannes heard the drumbeat of horses' hooves and a burst of wild cheers. "What's happening? Go and find out, Jan, but keep out of trouble."

Jan kept low as he left the house in case a British sharpshooter was watching, but soon straightened up and ran towards the sound of horsemen.

"What's all the noise?"

"Over there," an old man gestured with his hand. The leopard skin band on his hat seemed out of place in his drab clothing. "Another commando has just arrived in Potchefstroom."

Jan hurried to see the commando. "What's happened? You seem very excited."

A man of about Jan's age removed his hat and banged it against his leg, releasing clouds of dust. "We've been to Klerksdorp," he shouted, laughing. "We raided Leask's stores and got two thousand pounds of lead for bullets and took all the Martini-Henry cartridges he had."

"We don't have many Martinis," Jan said. "The rest will be useful though."

"We'll take out the lead and powder and make bullets for the rifles and round shot for the cannon," the rider explained.

"Could we have some for the Groenburg Commando?" Jan asked. "We are running short of ammunition."

"We'll distribute it fairly," the man said. "You'll get your due."

When Jan returned to the Groenburg Commando, he passed the news to his father.

"Now, can we fire at the British?" Karl asked.

"Not until we have the ammunition in our hands," Johannes replied. He looked up when a man entered the back of the house.

"Johannes van Collier?" The man glanced around.

"That's me," Johannes confirmed.

"You and Theunis are wanted, Johannes. There is a *kriegsraad* [2] in five minutes."

"I'm coming," Johannes replied. He glanced at his sons. "Keep your heads under cover," he said. "Don't let the British see you. They are terrible shots, but one might get lucky."

"I'll look after them," Karl promised. "I'll care for them like they were my own sons."

Johannes shook his head. "I've seen you with your sons, Karl. I expect better than that."

Jan laughed yet could not avoid his loneliness when his father left the house. He heard Mannie's heavy breathing and punched his arm playfully. "He's gone at last, Mannie! Now we can do as we like." Jan knew Mannie's smile was forced and pressed his last piece of bread into his brother's hand. "I can't eat this, Mannie. You'd better have it."

THE DARK CLOSED IN ON THEM, CRISP AND COLD. JAN HELD HIS rifle close to his cheek, sighted along the barrel, and wondered how his mother was coping at Nuwe Hoop Plaas. He felt Mannie trembling at his side.

"It will be all right, Mannie," Jan said. "The British only shoot when we do, and then they miss."

"It's the cold making me shiver," Mannie said. "I am not afraid."

"You are not afraid?" Karl spoke from across the room. "I am afraid. Your father is afraid; we are all afraid. You must control your fear, boy, and don't let it control you."

"It does not control me," Mannie said stubbornly. "I am not afraid."

"Is it time yet?" Jan diverted attention from his brother.

"Nearly," Johannes replied. "You will hear the signal at four o'clock." He resisted the temptation to put an arm around Mannie, knowing such an action would only embarrass the boy.

IN THE EVENING, THE BRITISH HAULED DOWN THEIR FLAG, leaving the empty rope to snap against the flagpole in the breeze. The sound continued all night, a constant irregular crack that carried on the air, nagging at Jan's nerves. He had heard that the redcoats had to make a flag from soldiers' clothes.[3]

Jan did not care if the Union flag was handmade or straight from the queen's factory. He only cared that it was flying over his land.

"In a few minutes, we will wake them," Abraham nudged Jan with a sharp elbow. "You and me together, eh, Jan?"

"You and me together, Abe. And Mannie," Jan glanced at his brother.

Even though he had been expecting it, the sharp bang of a rifle made Jan start.

"Happy New Year, *Rooinecks!*" Karl shouted in heavily accented English.

"Fire!" Johannes ordered, squeezing the trigger. He was glad the recent raid had replenished the Groenburg Commando's ammunition.

Jan and Mannie aimed at the fort, hearing the fusillade from hundreds of Boers against the small British garrison.

"How many men do we have?" Jan asked.

"Over fifteen hundred!" Johannes told him. "And we have artillery!"

As Johannes spoke, *Ou Greif* fired a nine-pound cannonball at the British fort.

"Do you like our new toy, *Rooinecks?*" Theunis shouted. "Do you like it? We altered it to batter you into submission! Are you glad you came to conquer our republic?"

"Fire!" Johannes ordered. He could not see any soldiers on

THE SOUND OF BOER RIFLES

the wall, so he aimed for the tents, faintly white in the darkness of the fort.

Jan saw that the Burghers surrounded three sides of the British fort, with the constant flare from muzzles and the deep boom of the cannon adding to the confusion. After their initial surprise, the British replied, with the 21st Foot lining the wall and Lieutenant Rundle's artillery firing shrapnel wherever groups of Boers congregated.

Jan felt as if he were somebody else, watching events from above. In his mind's eye, he could see the British fort on its slight rise, with the Burghers in the houses and newly dug trenches and the little men firing amidst the orange flashes and thick smoke. He was not here in this foolish war but at home in Nuwe Hoop Plaas, tending his cattle, working with the servants, and dreaming of Engela. Jan could smell the homely cattle scent and hear the cows bellowing to be milked. Jan smiled, for as an experienced cattleman, he could tell what the herd wanted by the sounds they made.

"This time, we will chase them away," Theunis's grating voice brought Jan to reality. "Get back to London, *Rooinecks!*"

Konrad watched from the back of the room, nodding his head in encouragement.

"Aren't you going to fire, Konrad?" Jan asked him.

"I am a neutral observer," Konrad told him. "The German Empire is not at war with Queen Victoria."

"I thought you were here to help us," Theunis said.

"I can help in ways beyond a single rifle," Konrad replied.

Abraham grunted, brushed back his long hair and fired at the fort. "Watching is not helping," he said.

"Listen!" Jan reloaded his rifle. "The British are singing!" He lifted his head to listen. "I don't know that song."

The words came to the Boers, now distinct, now fading away as the sound of musketry drowned the words.

"By yon bonnie banks and by yon bonnie braes,
Where the sun shines bright on Loch Lomond,
Where me and my true love will never meet again,
On the bonnie, bonnie banks of Loch Lomond."

Jan heard the lighter tones of women as the first verse reached its chorus.

"Oh, you take the high road, and I'll take the low road,
And I'll be in Scotland afore ye,
But me and my true love will never meet again,
On the bonnie, bonnie banks of Loch Lomond."

"Why are they singing? Is that a war song to encourage them to battle?" Jan asked.

Abraham pushed back his hat. "It sounds like a love song."

"Fire, Jan!" Johannes pushed his son's shoulder. "Don't listen to their singing!"

Ou Griet roared again, the sound becoming as regular as the musketry.[4]

The British musketry died away after a few minutes, and only the artillery replied. Johannes borrowed a pair of field glasses and studied the fort. He saw the orange flashes of the nine-pounders and the white smear of tents jerking this way and that as Boer bullets ripped through the canvas.

"The *Rooinecks* are not showing themselves," Johannes said. "How can we shoot them unless they show themselves?"

Theunis fired another shot and reloaded quickly. "Perhaps they've had enough, or they've run out of ammunition."

Jan heard the brassy notes of a bugle sounding above the gunfire and the bark of a sergeant's voice.

"Are they going to storm us?" he asked, looking over his shoulder. Mannie was gasping for breath, holding his rifle in white-knuckled hands. Jan had not seen him fire a single shot.

"I do not know what they are going to do," Johannes said.

"Maybe they think we are going to storm them." He focused his field glasses on the wall. "I can see the reflection of light on bayonets. They are waiting for us."

Jan shivered. "Bayonets are like spears. We do not fight like that."

"The *Rooinecks* do," Karl said. "I saw them charging the Zulus with their bayonets at Khambula. They enjoy stabbing their bayonets into people."

Jan put a hand on Mannie's trembling shoulder.

"Storm them!" Theunis shouted. "Come on, Burghers! Storm!"

"Stay where you are!" Johannes roared as Abraham and a couple of others rose to obey. "The British are waiting for us!"

Jan hugged the wall, fired, and reloaded, thinking of the horror of a British soldier charging at him with a long bayonet. He saw Mannie wipe a tear from his eye.

"It's the smoke," Mannie's voice shook. "The smoke got in my eye."

"Fire your rifle," Jan said urgently. "It will make you feel better." He pushed Mannie to the window, whispering in his ear. "Aim at the fort and fire!"

Sobbing, Mannie obeyed, firing without aiming. He reloaded clumsily, dropping a bullet so the brass cartridge clattered on the wooden floorboards.

"Pick it up!" Jan saw Theunis watching with a sneer on his face. "Come on, Mannie. The sooner we beat the *Rooinecks*, the quicker we can go home." He helped Mannie load his rifle. "Aim and fire; pretend we are hunting on the farm."

Mannie nodded, blinked away another tear, and obeyed.

"Now keep doing that," Jan dropped his voice. "It's all right, Mannie. This war will end soon, and we can go home."

"I want to go home now," Mannie sobbed.

"Soon," Jan said as he fired at the fort. The defenders were keeping under cover, so he aimed at the tents. He fancied he saw his bullet tear through the canvas, grunted, and loaded again. He saw his father crouch beside Mannie and concentrated on the fort, pushing away thoughts of Engela.

At seven in the morning, the Boers' firing stuttered to a halt.

"Have the British surrendered?" Mannie asked hopefully.

"Not yet, Mannie," Johannes replied. He heard the bugle playing defiantly and saw a man hoisting the Union flag back up the pole. "We haven't chased them away yet."

Gunsmoke drifted across Potchefstroom as the sun struggled to light up the scene of the battle.

"Will we ever shift these *Rooinecks*?" Jan asked, lowering his rifle. The barrel was hot to the touch.

"We will," Johannes said.

"When?" Mannie mumbled. "I want to go home."

"So do most of us," Karl said. "We only agreed to a few days away from the farm. I think I'll go back home tomorrow."

Mannie looked at his father hopefully. Johannes shook his head. "We stay here," he said. "Unless the British send an army to invade the republic."

"Then can we go home?" Mannie asked.

"No," Johannes said. "Then we will fight them." He tried to ignore the tears that Mannie dashed from his eyes. *Be brave, Mannie. Nothing lasts forever.*

CHAPTER 9

BRITISH ARMY HEADQUARTERS, NATAL, DECEMBER 1880

Major-General Sir George Pomeroy Colley, the British Governor and Commander in Chief of Natal, had a reputation as one of Britain's foremost soldiers. Like many of Britain's finest warriors, he was an Irishman, coming from Rathangan, County Kildare. Colley shone at Sandhurst, served in South Africa in 1857-58, and fought with the 2nd Foot in the Second Opium War. After spending time in the staff college, he travelled with Wolseley to West Africa, where he participated in the Ashanti War. He returned to South Africa as Wolseley's Chief of Staff, worked in an administrative role in the Second Afghan War, and recrossed the Indian Ocean to become High Commissioner for Southeastern Africa.

Colley occupied the latter role when he faced Andrew across the width of his desk. Tall, bearded, and balding, he looked down his long, straight nose, stroked his whiskers, and nodded.

"Thank you for your report, Captain Baird. I already know about the position in the Transvaal. We currently have less than three thousand men scattered in garrisons throughout a country larger than mainland Great Britain."

Andrew knew that Colley had doubted the Boers would rise against British rule. He drew in his breath. "That's a small number of men to hold down a country," he said.

"It is," Colley agreed. "We also have an unofficial base in Swartspruit far to the west, near the Kalahari Desert."

Andrew frowned. "I don't know that one, sir. I thought I knew the British garrisons in the Transvaal," he said.

Colley tapped delicate fingers on the desk. "Most of our positions, I'd hesitate to call them forts, are more than fifty miles from their neighbour. Some hold irregular colonials rather than regular soldiers and fewer than fifty defenders. Swartspruit has even fewer. Indeed, I doubt it has a dozen men." Colley looked up. "The Boers can isolate our posts and pick them off, one by one."

"I understand that, sir," Andrew agreed. "I know they are blockading Potchefstroom, and Colonel Winsloe hopes somebody will send a relief column. Colonel Bellairs in Pretoria is convinced the Boers will besiege him and also asks for help, sir."

Colley smiled gently. "I haven't forgotten your report, Baird. We have Wakkerstroom and Standerton in the south of the country, Marasastad in the north, and Rustenburg and Potchefstroom in the west." He stepped to a map on the wall and indicated each position. "You have informed me of the state of Potchefstroom and Pretoria. From what little information I can gather, I presume the other forts are similar."

"Yes, sir," Andrew said.

Colley stroked his whiskers again. "We hold our Empire with a skeleton force, Baird, and we can't let other powers call our bluff. To ensure we retain the world's greatest empire, we must maintain our reputation, which means winning all our wars." He paused to fix Andrew with a steady stare. "There are always hyenas baying around the Empire. Some are waiting for scraps we discard, and others hope to replace us as the world's foremost power." His fingers began tapping again. "Do you know who I mean, Baird?"

"Perhaps, sir," Andrew said cautiously. "The major powers are France, Russia, Austria, and now Prussia, although I think Italy may be hoping to join the club."

"France is interested in North and West Africa," Colley said. "Russia is our rival in Central Asia and hopes for a warm water port at the expense of Turkey. Italy is too young to be a threat, which leaves the German Empire."

"Yes, sir." Andrew did not know whether he should mention Konrad Bramigan and decided to keep quiet.

"We must show a bold face to hold them all at bay." Colley moved to the map. "I intend to muster an army, enter the Transvaal, and relieve the garrisons," he said. "If we are lucky, the Boers will stand to fight, and we can smash them in battle."

"They're a formidable people, sir," Andrew said. "I saw them at Potchefstroom and Bronkhorst Spruit when they defeated the 94th. They outmanoeuvred a column of good infantry."

"They vastly outnumber the garrison at Potchefstroom, while at Bronkhorst Spruit, they ambushed a column on the march," Colley countered. "They've declared war on us. Let's see how good they are." He smiled. "Now, Baird, you've witnessed the Boers at first-hand. Tell me everything you can about them."

"They are mobile mounted infantry, sir," Andrew said. "Excellent horsemen and fine shots."

"What weapons do they have?"

Andrew thought for a moment before he replied. "The men I saw carried a variety of rifles, sir. Some had Martinis, Sniders, or Snider-Enfields, and a few older farmers had muzzle-loaders that must be thirty years old."

Colley nodded.

Andrew thought back to the Boers' armaments. "However, most had the Wesley Richards breech-loaders, .45 calibre with percussion caps. I saw a handful with repeating rifles like the American Winchester or the Swiss Vetterli."

Colley scribbled notes. "Wesley Richards breech-loaders," he repeated. "Their weapons are as modern as ours."

"Yes, sir, for the most part," Andrew said.

"You told me that the Boer general, Piet Joubert, and around two thousand men have camped on the far side of the Drakensberg mountains at the pass of Laing's Nek."

"That is my estimate of his numbers, sir," Andrew said. "Boer numbers tend to fluctuate as men decide to join or leave the army."

Colley shook his head. "What a way to run a country. No wonder they needed us to rectify their economy."

"It's certainly not how we would do things," Andrew agreed.

"I intend to meet Joubert in battle," Colley said. "The Boers may be good at ambushing men before they know they're at war, but Joubert is a farmer, and I am a professional soldier. We'll see how the Boers fare against British soldiers with their tails up."

"I am sure you're correct, sir," Andrew said. "I neglected to mention the Boers are excellent at finding cover. At Bronkhorst Spruit, they lay behind boulders or in dead ground to shoot at our men, and most of our shots were too high."

"We found the Ashanti tribesmen were also skilled at hiding when they fired."

"Yes, sir," Andrew replied. "The Ashanti carried old-fashioned Danish muskets that fired slugs with little penetrating power. The Boers do not have that disadvantage."

"I am sure British soldiers can cope, Captain Baird," Colley said. "Thank you for your assistance and advice. You'll want to return to your unit now, Natal Rangers, isn't it?"

"Natal Dragoons, sir," Andrew said. "Before I return, I have another report to deliver."

"To whom?" Colley asked.

"General Hook, sir. It's a verbal report."

Colley gave Andrew a cold stare. "Very well. Do you know where General Hook is based?"

"I know his headquarters is in Newcastle, sir."

"Go to him," Colley allowed.

"Thank you, sir." Andrew left General Colley's office with a feeling of deep foreboding. *That man underestimates the Boers.*

Hook listened to Andrew's report without any change of expression. "You have no doubt it was Konrad Bramigan," he said quietly.

"No doubt at all, sir," Andrew said.

Hook sighed. "I sent to London for any intelligence on that fellow. He's a Prussian aristocrat named Von Bramigan, with large estates in East Prussia. He is close to the Prussian hierarchy and had a reputation as a fire-eater and skilled duellist at university."

Andrew nodded. "I thought the scar on his face was a souvenir of a duel. He's a brave man, then, and perhaps intelligent."

Hook grunted. "Perhaps so. The Prussians use swords with a large guard they call the soup plate of honour and wear protective head and body gear so any wounds will only be superficial. Then they allow the wound to remain open, making the scar more prominent."

Andrew smiled. "No false modesty with the Prussians, then."

"Evidently not," Hook said. "When Bramigan was young, he joined the army and fought in the Franco-Prussian War. He was a junior officer in the Prussian Guards and acquitted himself well, by all accounts. He won a medal or two and followed the rules and traditions of war, Prussian style."

"If he was a Prussian Guardsman, sir, why become a spy in Africa? Is that not beneath a member of the aristocracy?"

Hook nodded. "You hit the nail squarely on its proverbial head, Baird. I also asked myself that question and ordered my people in London and Berlin to investigate further. They discovered that Bramigan had a spectacular fall from grace and all over a woman."

"Ah," Andrew nodded. "The old story, was it?"

"The Prussian newspapers were alive with rumours and speculation," Hook said. "My people found out he seduced the daughter of one of the nobility, even though she was far younger than him and promised to another man. Bramigan challenged the girl's father and her fiancé to a duel, but both refused and instead had him kicked out of the Guards."

Andrew remembered Konrad's arrogant stance. "He wouldn't like that very much."

"Apparently not," Hook agreed. "Bismarck intervened and sent Bramigan to Africa. I don't know the details of his mission, but my people say he will be reinstated in his old regiment if he's successful. If he fails, he may as well not return to Prussia."

Andrew whistled. "He has a strong motivation to succeed."

"And we have a strong motivation to stop him," Hook said. He sighed. "All right, you've been busy and deserve some leave. Take two days to see that woman you rescued; what was her name again?"

"Mariana Maxwell," Andrew reminded.

"Yes, Mariana Maxwell. Take two days with her and then report to the Natal Dragoons. Have them in readiness for the fray."

"Will General Colley invade the Transvaal, sir?"

"The purely military is Colley's domain, Baird. I cannot interfere in his decisions." Hook sorted the papers on his desk with an air of finality. "However, Colley is an ambitious officer, and I am sure he won't allow the Boers to besiege British garrisons without attempting a relief." He paused for a significant moment. "Whatever the Prime Minister wishes. Her Majesty would not approve of inaction."

"No, sir. The Queen is more in touch with the nation's feelings than Gladstone seems to be."

"You'll be glad to return to real soldiering, Baird."

"Yes, sir."

"Your father was always thankful to return to his regiment," Hook said with a dry smile.

"It must be in the blood, sir," Andrew replied.

Andrew was thoughtful as he rode slowly home. It seemed that Konrad Bramigan had a weakness for women. *Is it any woman? Or was he only attracted to one woman in particular?* Andrew shook his head. *I doubt it will make any difference to this war.*

MARIANA WAS HOEING THE FRONT GARDEN WHEN ANDREW dismounted. "Andrew!" She dropped the hoe, lifted her skirt above her ankles and hurried to him. "Andrew! You're back!"

"I am!" It was instinct that made Andrew lift her and whirl her in a circle before placing her back on the ground. "How have you been?" He looked into her eyes, dreading to see the dark shadows that had dominated her since her kidnapping.

She smiled back, evidently happy to see him. "Mr Briggs has been looking after me," Mariana said. "He's been teaching me about the army, and I've been telling him about Natal and how to farm." She grabbed his arm. "Come on in, Andrew, and tell me what you've been doing."

The house looked immaculate, as Andrew had expected, with Briggs standing at attention outside the door. "Welcome home, sir," he said.

"Thank you, Briggs. Anything to report?"

Briggs slid his eyes towards Mariana before he replied. "All's well here, sir."

"Good. I think coffee is in order," Andrew said. "And whatever scoff [1] you can rustle up."

Briggs smiled. "Give me five minutes, sir."

Andrew was unsure what he thought when he looked at Mariana. On one hand, she reminded him of Elaine. On the other, he remembered the bubbly, laughing girl she had been before the renegades captured her and who still occasionally surfaced.

"How have you been, Mariana?" Andrew handed Lancelot's reins to a servant and entered the house.

"I've been well, thank you," Mariana replied.

The house's interior smelled of beeswax polish.

Briggs brought coffee for Andrew and Mariana before retiring to the kitchen, leaving them alone.

"Now," Andrew said. "Tell me all your news."

He listened, smiling, as Mariana related her catalogue of domestic triumphs and disasters, with Andrew watching the play of emotions on her face. Mariana looked up every few seconds, anxious in case Andrew's attention strayed. She smiled to please him whenever her flow of words slowed.

"Carry on," Andrew encouraged.

"I must be boring you," Mariana's words tailed off.

"You're not," Andrew replied, looking into her eyes for the recurring shadows. He grunted in satisfaction when her eyes remained clear. "You're looking a lot better."

"Mr Briggs has been looking after me," Mariana repeated.

"That's good," Andrew approved, unable to recognise the emotion twisting within him. "I am glad you two are friends." He thought for a moment of the impropriety of leaving Mariana alone with a man but dismissed the images that came to mind.

"How long are you here for?" Mariana asked.

"I have to return to the regiment in two days," Andrew told her. He saw the disappointment on her face. "We're in Newcastle," he said, "and I'll be able to see you often unless we're called to the war."

"I hope you're not sent to the war," Mariana said.

"So do I," Andrew replied truthfully.

POTCHEFSTROOM, JANUARY 1881

The church echoed to raised voices as hundreds of besiegers crammed inside. Jan stood at the back, with Mannie at his left. Both had their hats in their left hand as they sang the old familiar hymns.

"This reminds me of Sundays back home," Mannie whispered when the singing died away. "Do you think we'll ever see home again?"

"We'll be home soon," Jan told him. "Mother will be waiting for us at the door, and the table will be filled with food. You can tell her all our adventures."

"I've never been away for so long," Mannie said in a hush punctuated by half a dozen low voices.

"Neither have I," Jan admitted, caught the minister frowning at him, and concentrated on the service.

Silence descended save for the rustle of clothes and the shuffle of booted feet on the floorboards. Sunlight seeped through the plain windows, highlighting a face here and there, casting long shadows and revealing the motes of dust that floated in the air. One sunbeam glinted on the array of rifles beside the door, a reminder that peace was an illusion in this town at war.

Jan did not expect to have to use his rifle today, for both the British and Burghers kept an unofficial truce on the Lord's Day. However, Jan knew it was better to be ready to fight, however genuine his sentiments as he praised his Lord and thought of home and Engela.

They say that absence makes the heart grow fonder. I hope Engela feels the same. He glanced at Mannie and looked away, pretending not to notice the tears that glistened on his brother's cheeks.

As the siege entered its twentieth day, the weather changed. Jan looked up as the first drop of rain fell, heavy with portent. It landed on the street, where the dust soaked it up. A second drop followed, and a third, with a low growl of thunder in the distance.

"We're going to get wet," Jan predicted.

Karl nodded. "I have found that rain often gets men wet," he said solemnly.

"I thought you were returning to your farm, Karl," Johannes said.

Karl shrugged and pulled the collar of his jacket up as more rain followed the first few drops. "No. When Dolinde heard we were at war, she handed me my saddle and rifle. 'Go to war, Karl,' she said. 'I can always get a new husband, but I can never get another free republic.'"

Johannes smiled. He knew Karl's wife and believed the story. "It is the women who are the backbone of our nation. They were the strong ones during the Great Trek, and they will hold out against the *Rooinecks* when we have fired our last bullet."

"Ja. Anyway, I dare not go back until we have won. Dolinde will make my life a misery."

Jan listened with a smile. *Tante* Dolinde had always been kind to him, although he had heard her raging at Karl.

Johannes nodded. "If the women were here with us, we'd have captured this fort by now."

Karl laughed. "If Dolinde led us, we'd be flying our flag above Cape Coast Castle or Queen Victoria's palace in London."

"We'd better bring her, then," Mannie made a rare contribution to the conversation. "Then the war will finish soon." He shifted aside when Johannes ruffled his hair.

The rain increased, hammering on the Boers as they occupied the houses in Potchefstroom and the slowly expanding network of trenches.

"I shot another *Rooineck* today," Jan said. "He was crossing inside the fort, more concerned with avoiding the puddles than our rifles, and I shot him through the shoulder."

Johannes smiled. "You are a warrior, Jan," he said.

"I am not a warrior," Mannie looked at his rifle. "I never will be."

"You are young yet," Johannes reminded him. "Maybe you are too young to be on commando."

"*Oom* Gideon's grandson is younger than me," Mannie said. "He is only eleven, and he has shot three *Rooinecks*."

"*Oom* Gideon's grandson boasts of his deeds," Jan told him

quietly, "but nobody ever sees him shooting soldiers. I do not believe he has shot anybody."

Mannie looked up. "I also hate the rain," he said.

"However wet we are," Karl reminded them. "The *Rooinecks* will be wetter."

Jan wondered how the British were coping inside the open fort, where they had even less shelter and knew any careless movement could bring down accurate Boer fire. He nudged Mannie with a brotherly elbow. "Cheer up, Mannie; maybe the rain will force the *Rooinecks* to surrender."

Mannie nodded miserably as the rain dripped from the brim of his hat. He coughed, covered his mouth, coughed again, and stifled a sneeze.

The Boers were no longer content to contain the British garrison within the fort, snipe at them and have an occasional shooting frenzy. They dug trenches from Dr. Poortman's house towards the town's magazine, partly to deny the contents to the British but mainly to increase their ammunition supply.

"It's our turn in the trenches today," Johannes told the Groenburg Commando as Jan watched the teeming rain.

"I'll come too," Mannie volunteered, desperate to be accepted in the company of men.

"No, Mannie. You're not well," Johannes said. Mannie had developed a hacking cough over the last few days. "Maybe later when you get better."

"I can dig," Mannie said. "I know how to dig."

"Not this time," Johannes repeated more sternly. "Stay under shelter until your cough gets better."

"Yes, Pa," Mannie lowered his eyes, hiding his relief as he sneezed.

"I've also got a cough," Karl said. "Listen!" He forced a dry rasp. "I'll stay behind as well."

"No," Johannes said. "The dampness in the trench will help lubricate your throat."

Jan found working in a wet trench miserable and tedious, but he hefted his spade and hacked at the sodden ground. "I didn't know that going on commando was like this."

Johannes grunted. "We do what we must do to defend our land. Keep down in case a British sentry decides to shoot you."

Jan shovelled wet earth to one side, where his father piled it on the parapet. He had imagined going on commando would be a short and glorious campaign of a week, perhaps two, with the *Rooinecks* running before them. After the victory, he would enjoy a triumphant return to Nuwe Hoop Plaas. Engela would come to greet him, holding her skirt up as she ran and with her bonnet only partially hiding her smile. Jan could smell her already, the homely, welcoming smell of fresh bread, with her blue eyes laughing in her broad, familiar face.

War was not as he imagined, but he would not complain. He was a man among equals, ready to share the hardships and shed his blood. He could endure. He would prove himself worthy to ride on commando with the other men and be a fitting man for Engela.

"Keep digging," Johannes said. "When we reach the magazine, we will ensure the British can't get more ammunition."

"We'll grind them down," Theunis said, grinning.

They worked on, gasping and panting with the effort of shifting wet soil under a constant downpour.

"That's our time finished," Johannes thrust his shovel into the sodden earth under the puddles. "Let's get somewhere dry, Jan, and find a fire, a mug of coffee, and something to eat."

With Engela still dominant in his mind, Jan smiled. "That is a good idea. I do not enjoy digging holes in the ground."

The coffee was hot, strong, and welcome. Jan leaned back, allowing the warmth to return to his body.

"Is that better?" Mannie asked and coughed. He sat with his back to the wall, watching his father and brother through huge eyes.

"Much better," Jan replied. "You make good coffee, Mannie." He closed his eyes, imagining the rain was pattering on the roof of Nuwe Hoop Plaas. If he concentrated, he could smell the crispness of the veld rather than gun smoke and unwashed male bodies and hear the lowing of cattle rather than grumbling men and *Rooinecks'* orders from the fort.

"Alarm!" Karl's roar woke Jan from his dream. "Alarm! The *Rooinecks* are coming!"

Jan heard an urgent spatter of musketry, with the blare of a bugle rising above the town. A distinctively British volley followed, then a rising cheer, with more gunshots.

"Groenburg Commando!" Johannes shouted. "Grab your rifles and follow me!"

Jan dropped his mug, reached for his rifle, and ran for the door to find his father in front of him and Karl disappearing to spread the word.

"Stay here, Mannie!" Johannes ordered. "You are not well."

"But Pa!" Mannie objected.

"That's an order!" Johannes said and dashed outside. Jan followed his father out of the door and into the teeming rain. "What's happened?"

"The British have made a sortie!" Karl spoke from under his dripping hat. "They have broken into the magazine and taken all the ammunition away."

Jan looked over to the magazine, still thirty yards from the edge of the Boer trench. "So, all our digging was for nothing?"

"Ja!" Karl stamped his foot in frustration. "We wasted time and effort, and the *Rooinecks* grabbed everything anyway."

"How much did they get?" Jan asked.

"I'll find out," Johannes strode away to return within half an hour, frowning.

"The British raid was successful," he told his commando. "Their Lieutenant Rundle led a strong patrol into the magazine. They took a ton of gunpowder, over twenty thousand Wesley Richards cartridges and about ten thousand Martini-Henry bullets."

Jan felt instant dismay. "They won't run out of ammunition for a while, then."

"No, but we might," Karl said. He glared at the fort as if he could defeat the defenders by the force of his dislike.

Jan flinched when they heard the explosion half an hour later. "The British are attacking us again!" He reached for his rifle.

"No," Johannes put his hand on Jan's arm. "That will be the British blowing up our ammunition."

Jan lifted his head to examine the fort, where grey smoke battled the falling rain. "Should we not attack them while they are distracted?"

"Stay put and trust in General Cronje," Johannes ordered curtly. "He won't waste lives advancing across open ground against British riflemen."

Konrad had arrived at the Groenburg Commando's house. He grunted. "Sometimes it is necessary to break eggs to make an omelette."

"Prussia may not care if it loses hundreds of men. The Transvaal does," Johannes said.

"The British are digging a trench to the magazine!" Abraham lifted his rifle and fired. "Stop them, everybody!"

Karl swore, following Abraham's lead as he fired, loaded, and fired again. Jan pushed a cartridge into the breech of his rifle and poked his head above the window frame. A bullet crashed into the wood an inch from his face, throwing a wooden splinter into his forehead. He pulled back, unsure what had happened.

"I'm hit!"

Mannie beat Johannes to Jan's side by half a second. "Let me see!"

Jan removed his hand, feeling a trickle of blood down his face.

"It's nothing," Johannes reassured him. "Barely a scratch."

Jan grinned. "I thought a *Rooinek* had killed me."

"They couldn't kill my brother," Mannie said.

"Wash away the blood and get back on duty," Johannes told

him with false severity.

Jan felt sick when he realised the progress the garrison had made. The British had thrust a trench from the fort to the magazine, removed the building's roof and turned it into a strongpoint. With even a handful of riflemen in position, they could hamper the Boers' trench digging.

"Let's push them out!" Theunis shouted and pointed to the enemy trench. "Come on, boys!"

Jan stepped beside Theunis with the sting of his new wound encouraging him to finish the siege as quickly as possible.

"No," Johannes put a hand on Jan's shoulder. "We will not charge into British rifles."

"But," Jan said, "we have to push them out."

"It is not the way we fight," Johannes told him. "Watch and learn, Jan."

A dozen of the younger and more reckless Burghers followed Theunis in a wild charge towards the new British positions. When the men of the 21st opened fire, the Boers realised how exposed they were and quickly threw themselves to the ground.

"Covering fire!" Johannes ordered and aimed toward the British trenches. Jan joined him in an exchange of gunfire as the too-enthusiastic Burghers returned to their starting point. The skirmish ended without casualties but a slightly abashed Theunis.

"Stop firing," Johannes ordered. "We are wasting ammunition. You see?" he said to Jan. "You would have put yourself in danger for no purpose."

"What will we do?" Jan asked. "We are making no progress."

"We'll build more trenches around the fort," Johannes said. "We will fight a patient war." He tapped the butt of his rifle. "The British are an impatient people for whom speed is important. We are farmers and know that nature does things in her own sweet time. It is natural for every nation to be independent. The good Lord will not let us down."

"Amen," Jan replied as Mannie coughed again.

CHAPTER 10

BRITISH ARMY HEADQUARTERS, NATAL, 22ND JANUARY 1881.

Andrew stood at the back of the crowd as Colley spoke to the senior officers. He marvelled at the magnificent display of scarlet tunics and gold braid, with sunlight reflecting on arrays of medal ribbons that told of battles, glory, and hardship across the breadth and length of the Empire. His gaze roved over the faces, pondering the experiences and history of these distinguished officers.

"Who the devil are you?" a gaunt-faced Lieutenant Colonel demanded, staring at Andrew's badges of rank.

"Captain Andrew Baird, sir," Andrew replied evenly.

"This meeting is for senior officers. Good God, man, you're only a captain."

"I know, sir." Andrew did not explain that General Colley had asked him to attend the meeting because of his experience fighting the Boers. He ignored the colonel's frown and faced forward as Colley raised a hand for silence.

"You all know the situation in the Transvaal," Colley began quietly. "The Boers are blockading our garrisons and have set up camp near our border." He paused, allowing his words to sink in. "We must gather our men and defeat what is becoming a nation in arms."

"They don't have an army, sir," the gaunt-faced colonel interjected. "One regiment of British regulars will be sufficient to scatter them. They are only farmers."

Colley lifted his head towards Andrew. "What do you say to that, Baird? You've seen the Boer fighting men first-hand."

"I'd say every Boer is a born light horseman," Andrew replied. "They ride like centaurs and shoot like marksmen. They can vanish behind a rock or into dead ground, fire, and withdraw. We would be foolish to despise them." He felt the poisonous glare of the colonel.

"Forgive Captain Baird's hyperbole," Colley said, faintly smiling. "But he has fought the Boers at Potchefstroom and Bronkhorst Spruit, and his points are well made. Every Boer is a natural warrior. We must show them that even the best warrior will fail against a professional soldier."

"How, sir?" a staff major asked. "They tore us to ribbons at Bronkhorst Spruit."

"How, sir? We gather all our men and face them in open battle, sir," Colley replied. "I will send Piet Joubert an ultimatum, ordering him to disband his men, or he'll face the full force of the British Empire."

"We might raise fifteen hundred men, sir," Andrew's neighbour murmured, "if we strip every garrison to the bone. Let's hope the Basutos and Zulus don't take advantage of our men being tied down in the Transvaal."

Colley nodded. "We can't afford a long war. The Zulus will still be smarting after their recent defeat; the Basutos could strike at any time, and even the Galekas could take advantage of Europeans fighting among themselves."

Andrew said nothing, although he wondered if Colley also considered European powers watching Britain's discomfiture. The British military's reputation suffered considerably when the

Zulus defeated Lord Chelmsford's army at Isandhlwana. Despite the press pushing the defence of Rorke's Drift as a counterweight, the sting remained. A recent reverse at Maiwand in Afghanistan only added to the hurt.[1]

"I'll send the message to Joubert tomorrow," Colley declared. "As well as my threat, I have written this piece for the Boer commander," he held up a sheet of notepaper and read to the silent officers.

"The men who follow you are, many of them, ignorant, and know and understand little of anything outside their own country. But you, who are well-educated and have travelled, cannot but be aware how hopeless is the struggle you have embarked upon, and how little any accidental success gained can affect the ultimate result."

Colley lowered his paper and looked around the officers. "I invite your comments, gentlemen."

The colonel nodded. "That's good, sir. We might tell them their fortunate achievements do not alarm us, and our outposts hold firm."

"Quite so," Colley agreed. "Now, I intend to relieve the closest of our beleaguered garrisons as quickly as possible. Every advance will lift our men, and the addition of even a couple of hundred soldiers will strengthen our force." He glanced at Andrew. "You're dismissed, Baird."

"Yes, sir," Andrew saluted and left the senior officers to discuss their strategy. He hurried to the makeshift barracks where his Natal Dragoons lived, aware he had neglected them for far too long.

WITH GENERAL COLLEY'S ARMY, NATAL-TRANSVAAL BORDER, south of Laing's Nek.

27/28th January 1881.

"Keep up, lads!" Andrew called as his Natal Dragoons rode in file behind him. He surveyed the familiar faces of men he had fought beside through the Zulu War. Middle-aged and bright-eyed, Sergeant Meek wore his array of medals proudly, while Trooper Ogden was a wild drunkard but good in a fight. He carried a bugle at his saddle, looted from a British soldier after Ulundi. Spalding was an intelligent, thoughtful soldier, and Lieutenant Fletcher rode as straight-backed as if he were on parade. Briggs slotted into his place back in the ranks as if he had never left, although Andrew worried whether Mariana would be all right with only a couple of hired servants. He had asked the local doctor to call on her twice weekly and hoped his attentions were sufficient.

"It's not a great force to reconquer a country, sir," Fletcher observed, eyeing the British column that slogged doggedly towards the frontier.

"No, it's not," Andrew agreed.

General Colley's army of 1,200 men marched towards the Transvaal frontier, kicking up dust and grumbling in the manner of soldiers everywhere. Andrew halted to view the column, shaking his head at the general's overconfidence. Five companies of the 60th Rifles and five of the 58th Foot, the Rutlandshire Regiment, comprised the bulk of the column. Even beneath the covering of dust, the scarlet of the 58th's tunics stood out, with blue trousers and red piping moving rhythmically across the hard ground. Their long bayonets bounced on their hips, and the battered sun helmets gleamed like lanterns above each sweating, dusty face.

The Rifles wore their traditional green uniforms and marched with the jaunty swing that had characterised them since their formation.

"They're good fighting men," Andrew approved. *But far too few for the task at hand and insufficiently mobile to face the agile Boer horsemen.*

"The backbone of the army," Fletcher remarked. "If we had a few thousand more, I'd be happier."

Andrew nodded. "We'll work with what we have," he replied.

Augmenting the regular infantry was a squadron of cavalry, in Andrew's eyes, more fit to parade in London's Hyde Park than to fight the rough-riding Boers on their own territory. There were also mounted infantry, some of whom seemed more nervous of their horses than respectful of the enemy, and a Naval Brigade with two seven-pound guns. Andrew had served with seamen before and knew them to be brave, resourceful, and energetic. The Royal Artillery, true to their motto of *ubique*—everywhere—pulled their battery of nine-pounders. Lastly, Colley had recruited local horsemen and the Natal Mounted Police, the latter as tough as the Boers, veterans of wars with the Zulus and Basutos. Beside them, the Natal Dragoons rode in file rather than acting as scouts, which Andrew would have preferred.

Andrew noticed that many recruits rode Cape horses, notoriously hard to handle even when trained. Other horses included a few pensioned-off artillery mounts, quiet, inoffensive beasts that could barely muster a trot even when encouraged with bit, whip, and spurs. Although the horses were of poor quality, Andrew thought the riders were worse, men who would never have passed the most perfunctory medical examination.

"The Boers will laugh this lot to scorn," Fletcher commented. "Then they'll shoot them out of the saddle."

"I suspect you're correct," Andrew checked his men.

The road led from Durban on the Natal coast via Newcastle in Natal to eventually reach Pretoria in the Transvaal. Colley's initial destination was Standerton in the Transvaal, where Major Montague commanded a British garrison of under four hundred men, mainly of the 94th Foot. Although the distance from Newcastle to Standerton was only twenty-five miles, the road crossed the Drakensberg Mountains at a formidable pass known as Laing's Nek.

"If the Boers know their business, they'll have men at the pass," Fletcher said.

"They'll be waiting for us," Andrew replied grimly.

"Who the hell was Laing to have a pass named after him?" Fletcher asked.

Andrew shook his head and passed the question to his Dragoons.

"Henry Laing," Morrison, one of the newer men, replied immediately. "He farmed at the foot of the mountain."

"No," Kerr shook his head. "It was Willie Lang. He farmed the other side of the hill."

"Were they related?" Fletcher asked.

"I doubt it, sir," Kerr replied. "They spelled their names differently."

Leaving his men to bicker happily, Andrew studied the terrain. Laing's Nek was the lowest section of a ridge that extended from the Buffalo River to the prominent eminence of Majuba Hill. From his position, the hills looked steep and difficult to climb, especially for fully laden troops.

A sweating subaltern approached Andrew, gasping from the heat. "General Colley's compliments, sir, and could you join him?"

"Where is he?"

"On that little knoll, sir," the subaltern gestured to a small hill a quarter of a mile from the column's route.

"Take over here, Fletcher," Andrew said.

A knot of officers gathered around the general as he surveyed the hills through field glasses. "My scouts tell me that the Boers hold Laing's Nek," Colley said. "I hope so. If they stand, we will defeat them. Nothing is more certain."

The officers nodded, confident their men could defeat any number of ill-disciplined farmers.

"A solid victory here might be sufficient to convince the Boers they cannot win this war," Colley said. "Better a bloody battle at the outset than a long-drawn-out conflict that will eventually mean many more casualties."

Andrew could see the logic in Colley's strategy while hoping the general would outflank the Boers rather than chance a frontal attack.

"We'll camp here at Mount Prospect for the night and remove the Boers tomorrow," Colley ordered. "Form a wagon laager."

The British camped three miles short of the pass, with the hills looming like a brooding barrier to the Transvaal. Within half an hour, the wagons were in a circle, with the cooks lighting fires as officers and NCOs barked orders and set pickets.

"Water and feed the horses," Andrew ordered the Dragoons, "then grab some scoff yourselves. Kerr, you and Morrison take the first stag. Keep your rifles close by, knee-halter the horses and let them graze."

The Dragoons obeyed, most falling instinctively into the routine of active service after months of garrison duty. Leaving Fletcher and Meek to supervise the men, Andrew lifted his field glasses and studied Laing's Nek. When he saw a flash of sunlight on glass, he guessed that General Joubert would be scrutinising the British camp, making arrangements, working out what Colley intended and planning his counters. Andrew grunted, thinking that war was like chess, with move and countermove, except the pawns were fragile men of flesh, blood, and feelings.

Andrew glanced over the 58th Foot, who appeared relaxed as they raised rows of bell tents. The cooks were already toiling over their fires, with farriers shoeing two horses and sergeants fussing over their charges with hard words and concerned eyes.

Colley called another meeting that evening, sitting at his travelling desk with a map pinned to a wooden framework at his side and the officers grouped before him. Lifting a pointer, he indicated the road ahead. "This is not the easiest route over the Drakensberg," he said, "but it's the most direct to Standerton."

Lieutenant Alan Hill of the 58th nodded. "Yes, sir. We'll shift the Boers, never fear." He glanced at his companion, Lieutenant Lancelot Baillie, and winked. "We're the Steelbacks! The famous 58th!"

Andrew remained silent, wondering what part his Natal Dragoons would play.

Colley continued. "We'll leave two hundred and sixty men and both Gatling guns to defend the laager. The oxen will also stay here, with the Army Hospital Corps and the drivers." Colley indicated Andrew. "I want Lieutenant Fletcher and your Natal Dragoons to remain as a mobile screen, Baird, but I might need your knowledge so you come with the main force."

"Yes, sir," Andrew disliked leaving his men behind but had to obey orders.

Colley groomed his whiskers with an elegant hand and carried on. "We'll bombard the Boer positions with the artillery and rocket tubes to soften them up and then put in a two-pronged attack. The infantry will advance up Table Hill on the left, and the cavalry will take Brownlow's Kop, the hill on the right."

Andrew nodded. Colley had planned a classic attack. He only hoped the Boers would give a classic reaction or, better still, surrender without a fight. He looked up at the ominously steep hills, thought of the determined men waiting at the summit and was suddenly glad his Dragoons were not involved.

I should not think like that! I am a British officer; I should be leading my men forward to glorious victory.

The dawn broke in bands of silver and pink, throwing strange shadows over the terrain and altering the hills to sombre shapes against an ominous sky. Birds filled the air with song, competing with the harsh voices of NCOs berating the infantry. The British were already on the move, with Colley leading the attacking column, a commanding figure with squared shoulders and an air of outstanding confidence.

The men followed, stumbling in the dark, gripping their Martinis and either grumbling or silent. Andrew looked along the lines of young, determined faces under the white sun helmets and wondered what would occupy these men if they were back home. Most had fought the Zulus at Ulundi and knew the reality of war, the smell of raw blood and the courage and comradeship needed to stand in line and face a brave enemy.

"Halt!" Colley ordered. The men stopped, staring at the hills as the rising sun burned away the crisp cold of the night. They formed up on a ridge about two thousand yards from the hills, with the artillery in the centre and the blue-clad gunners fussing over their charges like mothers with newborn children.

The 60th Rifles were on the extreme left, with the blue-jackets from HMS *Dido* and HMS *Boadicea* and the Natal Mounted Police at their side. The scarlet-clad 58th, with the mounted infantry, were on the right, stamping their feet, exchanging black humour, and pulling at their belts.

The ground rose steeply to the broad Table Hill, with a conical spur about fifteen hundred feet distant. Through his field glasses, Andrew could see a strong Boer picket waiting on the spur. He saw the Boers moving seemingly casually, some smoking large pipes, others cleaning their rifles and watching the movement of the colourful British army far below. They looked like men on a grouse shoot rather than warriors preparing to defend their republic.

"It's too nice a day for a battle," Lieutenant Hill said, lighting a cheroot. He looked young and very keen as he surveyed the hill.

Andrew smiled. "Amen to that," he thought. Hill was probably about his age but lacked his experience of hard campaigning.

"Let's hope the Boers stand," Lieutenant Baillie said. "One good victory will settle the issue."

"I doubt they'll fight," Hill said, drawing on his cheroot. "Not when they see we're in earnest."

Andrew recalled the Boers advancing at Bronkhorst Spruit. "They'll fight," he said quietly. "They're a stubborn breed, sure of their cause, and they've already defeated one British column. They won't run from a few hundred redcoats."

"How about green coats?" A Rifles captain asked with a faint smile. "My lads are in this affair as well."

"I served with the Rifles before," Andrew said. "They're a match for anybody."

The captain laughed. "We'll soon see, won't we?"

At half-past nine, all six British guns opened fire with common shell and shrapnel. Andrew saw dust and stones rising around the Boer positions while the orange-yellow flashes of the explosions contrasted with the dull grey-white smoke. Augmenting the artillery, the Navy unleashed their rockets, with the fiery missiles giving a thin hiss as they ripped through the air to land with a bright crash.

"Poor buggers under that," a bearded corporal of the 58th said. "There's nothing worse than being on the wrong end of an artillery barrage. All you can do is hug the ground and pray like hell."

"The Boers started it by rebelling," a thin-faced private replied. "It serves the buggers right."

After ten minutes of furious bombardment, Colley ordered the Naval Brigade and a company of the 60th forward.

"There go the Rifles and bluejackets!" the bearded corporal said. "We'll be next, lads, mark my words."

The Rifles and Naval Brigade moved in good order to a defensive wall, where the seamen again opened fire with their rockets. The hissing projectiles crashed onto the Nek and beyond, where Colley believed the Boer reserves waited.

The Boers retaliated, with riflemen in a patch of forestry targeting the Naval Brigade in an accurate fusillade. The Rifles fired back, with the crackle of musketry adding a background to the more resounding boom of artillery and whoosh of rockets.

"Get ready, lads," the bearded corporal shouted above the hammer of artillery. "Check your rifles. Watch each other's backs when the order comes."

After another twenty minutes of screaming shrapnel and high explosives, Colley gave the order for the main advance.

"Now, Major Hingeson," Colley ordered. "Take your 58th forward and capture the spur. The artillery will cover your advance."

"Here we go, lads!" the corporal said. "They're only farmers, but their bullets can still kill. Keep the line steady and aim low."

When Colley headed up the hill, Andrew followed, whispering encouragement in Lancelot's ear. "Ignore the shine, Lance; we've been through all this before."

The 58th moved slowly and in perfect formation as though they were on a field day at Aldershot. Lieutenant Hill carried the Queen's Colours in the centre of the line, with Lieutenant Baillie holding the Regimental Colours a few yards away. The regiment moved in column of companies up the steep slope, with men peering forward to find the still-invisible enemy.

Andrew watched for a moment, aware he was witnessing history, for British soldiers had advanced into battle in scarlet uniforms with the colours displayed for centuries.

Not for much longer, Andrew told himself. *The army is shifting away from scarlet to khaki now, and with rifles with longer range and better accuracy, regiments won't advance in this manner again.*[2]

On the right, the cavalry eased up Brownlow's Kop. Rather than move quickly, the raw colonials walked their horses, with the riders seemingly more concerned about retaining their seats than Boer musketry. As Andrew watched, a shell landed square in the centre of the bunched riders, fortunately without exploding, although the threat forced the horsemen to open their ranks and increase their speed.

"Our artillery better change their aim," Andrew told a grim-faced Major Hingeson. "They're hitting the colonial horse."

"It might be Boer artillery," Hingeson said, glancing casually at the horsemen.

"The Boers don't have any artillery," Andrew replied.

Hingeson frowned. "It's bad enough getting killed in battle," he said. "It's much worse when your own side fires on you!"

The ground was steeper than it had appeared from Mount

THE SOUND OF BOER RIFLES

Prospect, with men stumbling and gasping under the already hot sun. They slithered on loose stones and swore as they lost their footing, kicked at the long grass that tangled around their boots, and blinked to clear the sweat from their eyes.

"Push on, lads," the sergeants encouraged. "Follow the Colours!"

The 58th moved on, swearing and struggling with the steep hill. As they neared the three-quarters mark, they broke formation on the uneven, rock-strewn ground. At that moment, hidden Boer riflemen opened fire so fast and accurately that the hillside rippled with muzzle flares, and the bullets kicked up little fountains of dust and rattled from the rocks. Red-coated soldiers fell, with officers and NCOs shouting sharp orders. Some men pushed on towards the muzzle flares, others stopped to fire back, and always Hill and Baillie carried the silken Colours at the front.

Andrew suddenly felt conspicuous on Lancelot as bullets zipped past. He felt for his rifle and paused as the musketry ceased.

"They've stopped firing," Hingeson said. "What's happened? Have we chased them away?"

"I hope so," Andrew replied cautiously. "Come on, Lancelot," he urged his horse forward.

The spurt of Boer musketry had ended without a Burgher in sight. As the 58th approached the summit, nobody fired at them, although the horsemen on the neighbouring hill struggled to make any progress. Andrew glanced at Brownlow's Kop, willing the mounted men to advance. He saw a small bugle boy lift his instrument to his lips and sound the first note of the charge, then fall back as a Boer shot him through the head. After that initial shot, the musketry became general as the Boers sprung their ambush.

"They were waiting on the reverse slope!" Andrew said.

Major Hingeson nodded calmly. "The Boers were safe from our artillery. They've taken a leaf out of Wellington's book."

As at Bronkhorst Spruit, the Boers targeted the officers and NCOs, shooting them out of the saddles and killing and wounding the horses and the riders. Above the sound of Boer rifles, Andrew heard the trilling of a cavalry trumpet and the sharp bark of orders.

Andrew looked away; he could not help the cavalry but might be useful with the infantry.

"Where are the Boers?" the thin-faced private asked. "I can't see a single man."

"Maybe they've already run," the bearded corporal replied.

"They're keeping their heads down," another NCO said with great satisfaction. "They haven't faced artillery before."

The 58th Colours hung limp in the clear air, bright against the landscape of duns and browns. Andrew heard continuous firing from Brownlow's Kop and glanced over again. Tired, disorganised, and faced with a half-hidden enemy, the horsemen stood, taking casualties without being able to retaliate. After a few moments, they withdrew, slowly at first, and then faster as survival beckoned with sweetly crooked fingers. They left sixteen dead and wounded men on the rough ground.

"The Boers outmanoeuvred us," Andrew said. "Our artillery didn't even touch them."

That's something to add to my military knowledge, Andrew told himself. *If I ever command men defending a hill, I'll use the reverse slope.*

Despite the cavalry's repulse, Colley allowed the 58th to rest rather than pushing on to the summit of the pass. Some men pulled at water bottles, others exchanged bawdy jokes but most lay on the rough grass, gasping for breath as sweat soaked dark patches in their uniforms.

The thin-faced private wiped perspiration from his face. "Where's the Boers then? They must all be on Brownlow's Kop, facing the cavalry."

"They'll be here," the bearded corporal replied. "If I were General Colley, I'd keep in extended formation."

"You're not in charge here," the private told him, grinning.

"No, but if I were, I'd have the men extend into skirmishing order. Joubert seems to know his stuff." The corporal nodded towards the retiring cavalry on Brownlow's Kop. "He's given the horsey men the right about anyway."

The private grunted. "Since when did cavalry know anything about fighting? The Zulus smashed them at Hlobane, and it took us to finish the job at Ulundi."

Andrew dismounted, gave Lancelot a drink and listened without comment. He agreed with the corporal; Joubert knew what he was doing.

After half an hour's rest, the infantry moved off again, toiling to the summit.

"Extend the front," Major Hingeston ordered. "Watch for a Boer ambush. They're sneaky buggers."

The 58th marched cautiously over the skyline, with Lieutenants Hill and Baillie proudly carrying the Colours and the scarlet jackets and blue trousers of the men bright in the sunshine. When the British were only two hundred yards away and nearly impossible for a marksman to miss, the Boers opened fire. Andrew saw the spurts of smoke a millisecond before he heard the crash of the shots and then the bullets hammered into the advancing infantry. Men fell, some in silence, others with grunts or surprised yells. The thin-faced private grunted, staring at the spreading stain in his stomach and jerked back as a second bullet slammed into him.

"Return fire!" Andrew shouted, dismounting. He pushed Lancelot away, "Run, Lance!"

Once again, the Boers aimed at the officers. Those on horseback were easy targets, and Major Hingeston fell dead, hung from one stirrup for a few seconds before sliding to the ground. Boer bullets crashed into most of the other officers, killing or wounding them.

Andrew swore in frustration. He saw Major Essex from the

75th Foot, an Isandhlwana veteran, shouting orders that the men ignored.

"Push forward!" Andrew wished he had an official position with the regiment. He roared above the crackle of musketry and zip of passing bullets, "B Company! Find cover and fire back! Aim at the smoke! Keep the Boers' heads down! C Company, advance! Charge! The quicker you're there, the fewer casualties you'll take!"

Some privates of the 58th obeyed. Others stood in confusion, waiting for orders from officers of their own regiment.

Colley's aide-de-camp, Lieutenant Elwes of the Grenadier Guards, pushed to the front. Tall, slim, and debonair, he was an ex-Etonian with a loud voice. Noticing Monck, adjutant of the 58th and a fellow Etonian, standing beside his dead horse, he waved a cheerful hand.

"Come along, Monck! *Floreat Etona*! We must be in the front rank!" He pushed forward, only for a Boer rifleman to kill him outright.

Andrew swore again. *You were a brave man, Elwes, but bravery cannot stop a Boer bullet.*

The Boer musketry increased, with the near-invisible riflemen picking off the British infantry. Having repelled the cavalry attack, more Boers came on the flank, enfilading the 58th in a murderous crossfire.

None of the 58th charged forward, although many advanced slowly. Andrew responded to this new Boer threat. "With me, B Company," he shouted. "Move to the right flank and reply to the Boer fire!"

For the first time since the advance began, Andrew saw Colonel Deane of the 58th miraculously still astride his horse. The colonel spurred forward, yelling encouragement. When the Boers shot his horse, he struggled free and ran forward towards the now visible Boer trenches. Half a dozen bullets crashed into him, killing him instantly.

Andrew swore. *The Boers are slaughtering us.*

To the left of the 58th, two companies of the 60th Foot advanced, with the skirmishers firing at the Boers. They ducked, weaved, and fired, shouting encouragement to each other as they aimed at the Boer riflemen.

"We're getting murdered!" The bearded corporal shouted. He organised his section, returning the Boer fire on the flank, loading and firing with mechanical precision.

Andrew fired automatically and looked around. All he could see of the Boers was gun smoke, with the occasional muzzle flare or a bobbing hat. The 58th were falling fast, swearing as they tried to retaliate against men they barely saw. A dozen Boers advanced down the hill, the agile men in slouch hats shooting at the Naval Brigade, then dropped into cover, crouching in dead ground or behind rocks so only the muzzles of their rifles were exposed.

Major Essex had taken command of the rearguard, and together with Andrew's handful of men, they responded to the Boer fire.

"Hot stuff, Captain," Essex said.

"Yes, sir!" Andrew agreed.

The Boer musketry slackened as they rose from cover and advanced against the 58th, moving from cover to cover. With most of the officers and many men down, the British fired back, swearing in frustration.

Andrew did not see who ordered the retire, but when the bugles blared, the men withdrew, cursing as they stumbled back down the hill.

"We had them beat," a man complained. "I tell you, we had them on the run."

The bearded corporal grunted. "On the run? The only running the Boers were doing was chasing us!"

Andrew helped support a wounded man, saw Lieutenant Alan Richard of the 58th aiding another, and wondered how a bunch of farmers could repulse an attack by British regulars. The Boers followed, still firing.

A bullet caught Lieutenant Baillie, knocking him to the ground. He lay, writhing, with the Colours at his side.

"Baillie!" Still miraculously unscathed, Lieutenant Hill dismounted and tried to lift Baillie. "I've got you, man!"

With the Queen's and Regimental Colours in the crook of his right arm, Hill could not help Baillie into the saddle, so he wrapped his left arm around his friend's shoulder and stumbled down the steep hill. He ignored the Boer bullets that zipped past, kicking up small fountains of dirt.

Unable to leave his post, Andrew could only watch as another Boer bullet plunged into the wounded Baillie. He saw the anguish on Hill's face as he lowered Baillie to the ground, handed both the Regimental and Queen's Colour to Sergeant Budstock, and lifted a wounded private.[3]

The bugler repeatedly sounded the retire, blowing hard amidst the chaos of shouts, shots, and screams.

"Pull back, lads," Andrew ordered the men around him. "We're retiring."

"They beat us!" A shocked private said. "They beat us! How could they beat us?"

"We'll be back," Andrew told him. "It's only a temporary setback."

Andrew knew that many British soldiers would ask the same question that night. It was unheard of for untrained farmers armed only with rifles to defeat British regulars with infantry, cavalry, and artillery led by one of the most intellectual generals in the army.

The men staggered back to the foot of the hill with heads down and shoulders slumped. As the infantry counted their casualties and exchanged blasphemy and curses, local Africans helped carry the wounded and dead to the ambulances for the jolting, painful trip back to the hospital at the camp. Some of the less shocked soldiers acknowledged the African help.

"Good lads, these natives," one Geordie voice said. "We

should recruit them against the Boers. They've got a score or two to settle."

"It's a white man's war," a Liverpool man replied. "Why should the Africans get involved? They can stand back and cheer as we and the Burghers shoot each other silly."

"That's a fact," a Bedfordshire man said. "After we kicked the blazes out of the Zulus, why should the natives help us anyway? The Boers are worse; they enslave them."

Andrew listened, watching the infantry retire, some helping the walking wounded, a few turning to shout insults at the Boers, but most were stunned by the defeat.

Lieutenant Richard and Andrew shepherded the last men down the hill, with an occasional defiant private firing at the pursuing Boers. A final bullet pinged off a rock beside Andrew, leaving a distinctive blue-grey smear. When he checked his watch, it was quarter past twelve.

"Reform," the surviving officers shouted, with the bugles reinforcing the order.

Andrew helped, getting the men back into ranks, sending the wounded to the waiting ambulances, and setting a rearguard in case the Boers tried to follow up their victory.

"I'll stay with you, lads," Andrew reassured the rearguard. "Retire slowly and fire if you see a Boer."

The 58th formed up, men straightening their uniforms as the non-commissioned officers roared them into orderly ranks.

"You're soldiers, not blasted scarecrows! Get that button fastened, Burrows! Jones! Stand straight! Just because the Boers repulsed us is no excuse for slouching! Stop bleeding on your tunic, Sinclair! You only bleed when I give you permission!"

The NCO's usual blandishments and a return to normality stiffened the 58th. They checked to see who had survived and marched back to Mount Prospect, three miles to the south. The rhythmic thump of boots on hard ground helped ease the hurt, and after a few moments, a man began to sing, with a few others joining in.

"Oh, a soldier and a sailor were talking one day.
Said the soldier to the sailor, 'Let us kneel down and pray,
And for each thing we pray for may we also have ten,
And at the end of every chorus, we will both sing, Amen!'
Now the first thing we'll pray for, we'll pray for some beer,
And if we only get some it will bring us good cheer,
And if we have one beer, may we also have ten?
'May we have a whole brewery,' said the sailor. 'Amen!'

Now, the next thing we'll pray for, we'll pray for our Queen,
To us, a bloody old bastard she's been,
And if she has one son, may she also have ten,
'May she have a bloody regiment,' said the sailor. 'Amen!'"

When the verses became more obscene, Andrew moved further away. The Boers may have won the battle, but if the British Army could laugh at itself and grumble at its leaders, Britain would survive.

Our army needs to improve, Andrew thought. *Survival alone is not sufficient. That's twice the Boers have defeated us, and this time, one of our best generals had planned the battle. Where are we going wrong?*

CHAPTER 11

BRITISH CAMP, MOUNT PROSPECT, JANUARY 1881.

"The enemy fought well," a plump staff major said. "The Boers are courageous and determined men who showed no fear of our troops."

Andrew nodded. "Our men were courageous, too," he said. "They pressed on as far as they could and fired back until they heard the bugle sound the retire."

The major looked up as if he had not given the other ranks another thought. "Of course, they were. They are British soldiers."

Don't take the men for granted, Major!

"Yes, sir," Andrew agreed.

"I was surprised how tenaciously the Boers acted," the major continued as he poured champagne for the senior officers. "They did not withdraw even when we were close upon them." He mused for a moment. "If we had more men, we could have shifted them."

"We can't allow the Boers to take control of the Transvaal," a burly staff captain announced. "It is a fact that they are too divided amongst themselves to rule a nation effectively. They divide and sub-divide into factions, like the Irish."

Andrew wondered what Irish-born General Colley thought of the major's words.

"Yet the Boers are easily led," the captain continued. "Given good British leaders, we can look forward to a combined South Africa under British rule." He sipped his champagne. "These backveld Boers cannot help their ignorance; they are the product of their environment and upbringing. Take away their archaic ministers and backward schoolteachers, cane them soundly on the battlefield, add powerful treason laws to teach them loyalty to us, and the next generation will be as British as the Canadians or Australians."

Andrew raised his eyebrows, saying nothing.

"Give it twenty years," the captain said smugly. "A good influx of British immigrants will drag the Boers out of the seventeenth century and into the nineteenth." He ordered another drink and sat back, pleased with his philosophy.

Irritated by the captain's words, Andrew had to reply. "We have to defeat them first," he said. "My duty as a soldier is to face the enemy on the field. I'll leave the aftermath to the politicians. I dare say they will make as big a shambles of the Transvaal as they have of Ireland or Britain." He paused to control his temper. "Between the rivalries of Tory and Whig, Disraeli and Gladstone, I don't think we can complain about faction fighting among the Burghers." He closed his mouth, aware that every officer in the Officers' Mess was staring at him.

"We shall defeat them, Baird," the staff captain said confidently.

"I am sure you are correct," Andrew retorted.

When the doctors reported the casualties, the British had lost eighty-three killed, with over seventy coming from the 58th Foot. Augmenting the dead were one hundred and eleven wounded, also mainly from the 58th. Although the British did not yet know it, the Boers had lost fourteen dead and twenty-seven wounded.

"That's another chastening day," a Rifles captain said, reading the casualty list. "We lost too many good men."

"The Boers seem to have our measure," a naval lieutenant replied. "What do you think, Baird?"

"I think we'll have to alter our tactics," Andrew said. "Advancing at a slow walk in broad daylight against concealed riflemen is just presenting our men as living targets."

"General Colley knows what he's doing," the burly staff captain said. "He's one of our best men. He's in the Wolseley ring[1], you know."

"I know," Andrew said. "But he's never faced the Boers before. Nobody in our generation has. Sir Harry Smith was the last British officer to defeat them."

"Ah," the captain said in a tone of triumph. "The Boers have never faced us either."

As evening approached, Colley addressed the men. "We suffered a reverse today, men," the general said. "You have not been beaten; you have simply been repulsed. There is no blame attached to you. You all behaved very well. Any fault lies with me." He waited for a moment. "With the number of troops at my disposal, it is impossible to renew operations, and I must wait for reinforcements. I hope the wounded will do well. I can say no more. I wish you all good night."

The men dispersed, some slope-shouldered and silent, others muttering incoherently, and a few talking loudly. Andrew joined his Dragoons, interested to hear their reactions.

"That was a fiasco," Fletcher said directly. "Did the general not think to scout the enemy positions?"

"Is that what you would have done?" Andrew asked.

"Yes, sir," Fletcher replied. "I'd have sent a couple of good men up first to see where the Boers were rather than advancing in daylight onto hidden positions."

Andrew grunted, thinking Fletcher would make a decent

senior officer if he survived. "Learn everything you can, Fletcher. Make every campaign, every battle, every patrol a learning experience."

"Yes, sir," Fletcher said.

The camp at Mount Prospect was unhappy that night as the British licked their wounds and discussed their defeat. With over a hundred wounded crammed into the hospital tents, Andrew could smell blood wherever he went, despite the best attention of the surgeon and the seamen who acted as orderlies and nurses.

"We suffered a reverse today," Private Burrows repeated the general's words. "Well, Colley, you were in charge. If we suffered a reverse today, it was because you led us into the bloody reverse!"

Andrew sighed. Whatever the senior officers believed, the ordinary British soldier was no fool. He knew and understood what had happened.

POTCHEFSTROOM, JANUARY 1881.

"What's been happening here?" Jan asked as he placed his rifle in a corner of the room and slumped to the floor. Dust had stuck to the sweat on his face, and he smelled of rifle smoke and horses. "Or have you all been smoking quietly while we fought at Laing's Nek?"

Karl shook his head. "I would have been with you had it not been for my aching back. We were also fighting when you were away. Anyway, somebody had to care for your brother."

Jan glanced at the fort, where the makeshift Union flag still hung above the battered camp. "The British are still there, I see."

"Yes, and growing more aggressive," Karl said. "A British raiding party attacked one of our strongholds and fired three volleys at our men. We were not fast enough to catch them."[2]

"They should have surrendered by now," Johannes joined

them, with the lines of responsibility etched deeply on his face. "They must be suffering from the rain." He knelt beside Mannie, lying on the floor in a cocoon of blankets.

"They are," Karl agreed. "They have dysentery in the fort, and we hear them digging at night. The *Rooinecks* are either strengthening their defences or burying their dead."

Johannes spoke to Mannie for a few moments, then lifted his field glasses, cleared raindrops from the lens, and surveyed the fort. "They have raised the walls a fraction," he said. "They are like ant bears, well dug in and refusing to move."

"The British work on the walls every night," Karl said. "We damage them during the day, and they add sandbags at night. It's a little game we play." He looked up as water began to drip through the roof. "Somebody will have to fix that hole before it spreads."

"We'll have to get the British out," Jan said. "We must clear the *Rooinecks* from our land." He hoped that Engela still remembered him.

"We will," Johannes reassured his son. "Be patient." He sat beside Mannie, concerned that the boy barely acknowledged his presence. "Once we win this war, we can all go home."

Theunis looked up. "I have a plan."

"You have a plan?" Johannes repeated.

"I'll see if the general will accept it," Theunis said with a smile.

"What is your plan?" Jan asked.

"To offer the British a way to defeat us," Theunis' smile broadened. He rose, placed his pipe in his mouth, and strode away.

"Theunis has a plan," Johannes said. "Now we shall see if he is as *slim* as he believes."

Jan began to clean his rifle, ignoring the steadily increasing drip of water from the leaking roof. He counted his cartridges, thought of the *Rooinecks* he had shot at Laing's Nek, and dismissed the images. War was war, and the British had invaded his country.

"How are you, Mannie?"

Mannie looked up and tried to smile through a coughing fit.

WITH HIS HAT PULLED LOW OVER HIS HEAD AND RAINWATER dripping onto his face, Johannes raised the white flag and guided his horse to the fort's gate. He felt a curious tingling at the base of his spine, aware that at least half a dozen British soldiers would have their rifles pointed at him.

"Halt!" A British sentry poked a cautious head above the parapet. "I've got you covered, Piet! Who are you, and what do you want?"

Johannes saw more British soldiers appearing, with the constant rain causing the brown stains to run from their sun helmets. Their tunics were no longer scarlet but every shade from a rusty brown to faded pink. "I come under a flag of truce!" he said in his broken English.

"Aye, I see that!" Sergeant Lennox joined the sentry. "What do you want, Piet? Do you want to surrender?"

"No," Johannes shook his head, spraying water around his horse. "I have a message for Colonel Winsloe."

"Have you now?" the sergeant eyed Johannes suspiciously. "What sort of message, Piet?"

"I do not know," Johannes replied. "I have not read it." He lowered the flag and dismounted. "Could you bring him here so I can give him the message?"

"The colonel will not come at the whim of a Boer," Lennox said and relented with a wry smile. "Or at the request of a sergeant. If you give me the message, I'll ensure he gets it."

"No, Sergeant," Johannes shook his head. "The letter says, 'Private and Confidential.' It might be from his wife."

"What's all this?" Lieutenant Rundle bustled up and nodded to Johannes. "Who are you, sir?"

Johannes lifted his hat. "I am Veldcornet Johannes van Collier of the Groenburg Commando," he said. "What is your name, *meneer*?"

"Lieutenant Henry Leslie Rundle of the Royal Artillery at your service, sir," Rundle replied. "I heard you have a message for the colonel."

"I have," Johannes replaced his hat. "If I give it to you, do you promise on your honour as a British gentleman and officer to hand it to him unopened?"

"I do, sir," Rundle replied, smiling faintly.

Johannes nodded and removed a battered and sealed envelope from inside his jacket. "One of my men found this letter on the ground," he said. "We were going to keep it in case it was military information, but not even the British are foolish enough to lose that."

Rundle joined in Johannes's sardonic laughter. He glanced at the outside of the envelope. "It doesn't look like an official message," he said truthfully.

"It may be from the colonel's wife," Johannes said. "Maybe she is ill, or having a baby, or wants him to surrender to get him home quickly."

Rundle smiled again. "Two of your three ideas are possible," he said. "I shall hand this message to the colonel in person, Meneer van Collier."

"Thank you, Lieutenant Rundle," Johannes said. "I trust you not to shoot me as I retire."

"You are safe for five minutes, *meneer*." Rundle saluted. "And when you lose the war, I shall be honoured to meet you as a gentleman and a friend."

"You are also a gentleman, Lieutenant Rundle," Johannes replaced his hat and remounted with effortless grace. He rode away without looking back while Rundle strode inside the fort to Colonel Winsloe's tented headquarters.

"A message?" Winsloe looked at the envelope suspiciously.

"The Boer thought it might be a message from your wife, sir," Rundle suggested.

"Constance?" Winsloe shook his head. "Not her style and not her writing." Breaking the seal, he slit the letter open. "It's in code, damn it! It must be official. How's your Morse code, Rundle?"

"Fair to middling, sir," Rundle replied cautiously.

Winsloe handed over the message. "Read that, then. Just give me the gist of it, not every damned detail."

Rundle scanned the document, borrowed a pen, and scribbled down the message, letter by letter. "It purports to come from Colonel Bellairs in Pretoria, sir. He says he is sending a column to lift the siege."

"Does it, now?" Winsloe said enthusiastically. "That's good news. When can we expect them?"

"In three days' time, sir," Rundle said, frowning as he checked the Morse code. "Sir, there's a passage here that makes no sense. Listen. 'When you hear heavy firing, leave the fort with your party and attack the back.'"

"Attack the back?" Winsloe said immediately. "The back of what?"

"Precisely, sir. Maybe Bellairs means the rear," Rundle said.

"Then why the devil didn't he say so?" Winsloe took the letter from Rundle. "What do you think, Lieutenant?"

Rundle shook his head. "I'm not sure, sir, but I've never known a military message phrased like that."

Winsloe nodded. "Nor have I, Rundle. There's something wrong here." He scanned the lieutenant's translation, sighed, and listened to the rain hammering from the patched canvas above his head.

THE SOUND OF BOER RIFLES

JOHANNES CHECKED THE WATCH HE HAD LOOTED FROM A DEAD British officer at Bronkhorst Spruit and nodded to the waiting commando. "It is time," he said. "Theunis, are the men ready?"

"My men are ready," Theunis confirmed. "Everybody knows what to do. Let's teach the *Rooinecks* how *slim* us stupid Boers can be." Some of his men laughed while others nodded in agreement.

"What if the British see us?" Karl asked. "That will spoil the whole plan."

"They will think we are going to fight the oncoming relief column," Theunis reassured him.

"Come on, Groenburg Commando," Johannes said. "Shoot low and keep under cover." He winked at Jan. "You too, Jan."

Thick clouds concealed any stars, forcing Johannes to ride by memory. He saw the gleam of light from the British fort and knew the British sentries would be sheltering from the constant downpour rather than looking for enemy activity. Sentries were the same the world over.

"No talking," Johannes reminded softly.

The commando plodded on, with the sound of their horses' hooves hollow in the dark. Mud and water splashed the horses' and men's legs while the rain wept onto their bowed shoulders, increasing as they entered the open countryside. When the commando was half a mile from the town, Jan inspected his rifle for the third time.

"Have you checked your rifle already?" Johannes asked quietly.

"Ja," Jan said.

"Was it all right?"

"It was all right," Jan replied.

"Has anybody taken it from you or touched it since then?" Johannes asked.

"No," Jan shook his head.

"Then leave it alone. It will not break in the space of two minutes," Johannes told him. "Concentrate on what will go right and let me think what may go wrong. That is the veldcornet's job." Johannes winked to remove any sting his words held. "You are a man now, Jan."

"Yes, Pa," Jan said, hiding his surge of pride. He straightened his back and rode beside Abraham, thinking of the task ahead.

"Halt here," Johannes stopped the commando. They formed a circle around him, with rainwater dripping from their hats and the horses' coats. Each man held his rifle in his right hand, with the barrel upended to protect the muzzle from the rain. "We gave the British a letter telling them Bellairs in Pretoria was sending a relief column. Our job is to pretend we are that column."

The men nodded and smiled, enjoying the idea of fooling the *Rooinecks*.

"When the British hear the noise we make, Colonel Winsloe will lead his men out of the fort to help the column, and we will have the *Rooinecks* out in the open," Johannes pushed his hands together. "When we hold Winsloe's *Rooinecks*, General Cronje will bring the Burghers out of Potchefstroom, and we'll have the British between two fires. Without their walls to guard them, the *Rooinecks* will be helpless."

Jan nodded. He could visualise the British falling before his rifle, dying like tin soldiers on a tabletop as he fired, with each shot helping cleanse the infestation from his land.

"It will be Bronkhorst Spruit all over again," Johannes said. He suddenly looked very old as the responsibility of command wore him down. "Theunis had the idea. You'll hear some loud explosions soon; that is Theunis." He smiled. "We must sound like British infantry, so we'll fire in volleys, as they do."

Jan looked at the other men in the commando. Individuals to a man, they were not used to firing on the word of command.

Karl nodded. "We will fire on your word," he said. "How will we know?"

Johannes nodded. "I will count to three and say 'fire'," he said. "Aim into the air so we don't shoot each other."

The men raised their rifles, some amused and others irritated at this novel method of fighting. Jan saw his father looking at him and smiled.

Even though he was expecting it, the explosion took Jan by surprise.

"That is Theunis simulating artillery fire," Johannes explained. "The British will believe the relief column is approaching. Ready? One, two, three: fire!"

Jan squeezed the trigger, with the Burghers firing a volley so ragged any self-respecting British sergeant would have turned purple with rage.

"Reload," Johannes ordered.

As Jan thumbed a cartridge into the breech of his rifle, he heard another explosion. To him, it sounded more like a charge of gunpowder than artillery.

"That's Theunis again," Johannes reassured them. "Is everybody loaded?" He waited for the men to nod. "All together this time. One, two, three," Johannes said. "Fire!"

The second volley was more controlled, with only two men later than the others.

"That's better," Johannes said. "Now we'll fire two more volleys and wait for Winsloe to lead his garrison out." He grinned. "If anybody wants to shout like a British sergeant, do so. I hope you can curse in English because their sergeants swear a lot." He waited for the laugh before ordering the next volley.

Jan fired with the rest and waited for any sound from the fort.

"Listen for the bugles," Johannes said as the minutes dragged on with only the steady hammer of the rain around them. The fort remained silent.

Abraham swore softly. "I hope Colonel Winsloe falls for Theunis's plan."

"Shall I go and check on the fort?" Jan volunteered.

"I'll go," Karl said. "An old head is better than youthful eagerness." He grinned. "You'll probably knock on the door and ask if the garrison is ready to come out yet."

Jan smiled, recognising that Karl's humour was not malicious. He saw Abraham laughing and nudged him. "You're not so clever, Abe!"

"Too clever to chase after Engela," Abraham replied. "I know how moody she can be!"

Karl laughed. "All women are moody," he said and rode towards the fort.

"Fire another volley," Johannes suggested. "That might entice the *Rooinecks* out."

Karl returned in ten minutes, shaking his head. "The British are not moving," he said. "Their sentries are in the same place, and they haven't opened the gate."

"The ruse failed," Johannes decided. "Ride to Theunis and tell him we're returning to Potchefstroom." He watched Karl trotting away, with his horse's hooves splashing up mud and water.

"Shall we fire another volley?" Jan asked, impatient to do something.

Johannes shook his head. "We will not waste any more ammunition," he said. "We have not fooled the British this time."

The commando was dejected as it returned to base. Jan was not alone as he glared at the fort, wondering if the *Rooinecks* were laughing at them. He could imagine them with their beery, drunken voices mocking the sodden Burghers riding back with their tails between their legs.

"The British must have found out," Theunis said when they slumped in their quarters. "Maybe somebody told them."

"Maybe they are more *slim* than we think," Johannes said, checking Mannie's condition. His younger son was shivering under his blankets, with his eyes deep sunk in his face.

"Maybe the rain will wash away the fort," Jan glared at the

Union Flag, "and pour the *Rooinecks* back into the sea and back to London".

"Pray to the Lord for heavy rain," Abraham advised solemnly. "I am sure He will listen to you. More than Engela ever will."

The rain continued, hour after hour, day after day, with Jan watching the British soldiers working within the fort, dragging buckets through the flooded interior and emptying them over the walls. The Boers occasionally sniped the toiling men, but mostly, they kept under shelter and watched.

"*Suid Afrika* is drowning them," Theunis said. "The country is fighting for us."

Jan nodded. "It is also keeping Mannie sick," he nodded to his brother, who lay swathed in blankets, tossing and turning in a fever.

"Mannie is strong," Theunis said. "He will recover."

"I think he is getting worse, not better," Jan did not hide his concern.

"He'll get better," Theunis placed a sympathetic hand on Jan's shoulder.

"Look!" Johannes studied the fort through his field glasses. "The British are burning their wagons!"

Theunis took the field glasses. "They must have run out of fuel." He nodded in satisfaction. "Soon, they will want to surrender."

The garrison removed their wagons, one by one, broke them up, and burned the wood. They only kept five, which they added to the wall to strengthen the defences.

"They copied that idea from us," Abraham objected. "We taught them about wagon laagers."

"As long as we don't teach them how to shoot," Johannes said.

"Will they surrender soon?" Jan asked. "We have to get Mannie home."

"I hope so," Johannes replied so quickly that Jan knew he was equally worried about his son. "Maybe you should take Mannie back to Nuwe Hoop Plaas."

"I cannot leave the fight," Jan said. "People would think I am afraid."

"Nobody will think you are afraid," Johannes reassured him. "Everybody in the commando has seen you fighting."

Jan glanced at Konrad, who moved from the Groenburg Commando to General Cronje's staff when he was not seducing young townswomen. "*Meneer* Bramigan will think I ran away."

"Konrad will not believe you ran away," Johannes said. "He knows we are not the Prussian Guards."

"The Prussian Guards would have stormed that little fort weeks ago," Konrad stepped forward, running a finger down his scar.

"And lost many men in doing so," Jan retorted.

"Victory is more important than cost," Konrad replied with a shrug. "I hope to report a Boer victory here, not a prolonged siege with General Colley bringing in a relief column."

"They are holding out longer than I thought," Theunis admitted. "The British are eating raw mealies, and their cooks are only baking bread for the women and sick."

"I thought we allowed the women to leave the fort," Jan sat beneath the window with his loaded rifle in his hand.

"We asked the women to leave," Johannes reminded. "Those that remain are in a shelter in the centre of the fort. Or they hide in the dugout when the serious fighting starts. We wounded two when our artillery hit them, but they survived."

"I don't like making war on women," Jan said.

"Nor do I," Johannes replied. "We will not prevent the women from leaving the fort if they want to."

"Wait!" Theunis held up a hand. "Adriaan Coetzee is coming this way."

"Adriaan is Gideon's son and General Cronje's messenger," Jan reminded. "That might mean trouble."

"Maybe the British have surrendered, and we can go home," Karl sounded hopeful.

A young man with a wispy beard, Adriaan removed his hat

when he approached Theunis and Johannes. "General Joubert wants you to know that the British are sending convoys to Mount Prospect," he said. "The general wants volunteers to disrupt their supply line."

"That's the Groenburg Commando," Theunis said immediately. "The *Rooinecks* fooled us last time. We won't let that happen again."

Johannes glanced at Mannie before he replied. "When are we going?"

CHAPTER 12

BRITISH CAMP, MOUNT PROSPECT, NATAL, 4TH FEBRUARY 188

"Well, Captain Baird," General Hook sat opposite Andrew in the tent, with a cigarette in a long holder curling blue smoke into the air. "I heard you've been busy fighting the Boers."

"We've all been busy, sir," Andrew replied.

"Indeed so." Hook drew on his cigarette and allowed the smoke to trickle from the side of his mouth. "You've been present at one siege and two battles so far. That makes you the most experienced Boer fighter in the army."

Andrew said nothing, wondering where Hook was leading. He allowed his eyes to stray to the map of Southern Africa on a wooden easel. Red pins marked the British garrisons, while blue pins marked the known Boer positions.

Hook let Andrew wait, scrutinising him through narrowed eyes. "The situation in the Transvaal is not as simple as you may imagine," the general said at last. "I have already told you about the German threat."

"Yes, sir," Andrew tried to hurry Hook along.

"Well, there is more to the story."

There always is, Andrew thought.

"You may be aware there is gold in the Transvaal," Hook seemed determined to test Andrew's patience by dragging out the interview.

Andrew nodded. "Yes, sir. People discovered gold a few years ago at the New Caledonian Gold Fields in the eastern Transvaal." He smiled. "Some people called them the Mac-Mac Fields because of all the Scottish diggers."

Hook smiled slowly. "That's correct, Baird, and then a digger named Alexander Patterson, Wheelbarrow Alex, found gold in Pilgrim's Creek, a few miles away."

"Yes, sir," Andrew curbed his impatience, for the story of the gold diggings was well known. "Does Britain want the gold, sir? We moved quickly enough to claim the Griqualand diamonds."

Hook shook his head slowly. "Mac-Mac and Pilgrims Creek are only alluvial gold, Baird. Useful but not necessarily commercial. We had geologists working in the country, and they believe a great amount of gold is sitting under the Witwatersrand, the Ridge of White Waters, and maybe elsewhere."

Andrew realised Hook expected him to say something. "Is there, sir?"

"We know it's there, but we don't want the knowledge to spread yet," Hook told him. "More specifically, we don't want the Germans to know."

"Yes, sir." *What the devil has this to do with me?*

"Naturally, having gold in the Transvaal will revitalise Prussian interest," Hook spoke so slowly that Andrew felt his impatience increasing.

"I understand that, sir," Andrew said.

Hook paused as if pondering how much information he should release. "The longer this war continues," he said at last, "the greater the possibility of Germany becoming involved and gaining a foothold in Southern Africa. We want a short war, whoever wins."

"Whoever wins?" Andrew stared at General Hook, hardly believing what he had heard. "Even if that means the Boers control the Transvaal, sir?"

"I thought that would surprise you, Baird," Hook gave a wry smile. "Sometimes, one must look at the big picture. We don't lose many wars, but occasionally, losing a little war is necessary to stabilise the world. Prussia is the dominant European military power at present, and we are the world's major naval power. Our army, however good the material, is modest compared to the continental powers and trained for small colonial warfare. If we ever war with the Germans, we'll need an ally with a large army, either France or Russia." Hook gave every point slowly, pressing a finger on his desk as he held Andrew's gaze. "We are hostile to Russia with this Afghan business and the last Ottoman nonsense. That leaves France, who has not recovered from its mauling in seventy-one and with whom we have difficulties over Suez."

"Yes, sir," Andrew followed Hook's logic.

"Given the geo-political situation, we must play our cards carefully," General Hook said. He leaned back in his chair. "We'll ensure Germany does not get a foothold in Africa for a few years yet." His eyes were like gimlets. "If that means losing a minor war against the Boers, then by God, we'll take our medicine and correct matters later."

"Yes, sir," Andrew said. "Do you mean we might allow the Boers to win and retake the Transvaal in the future?"

"What Gladstone and the Whigs believe and what the Tories want are two radically different things, Baird. Politicians are strange animals who alter foreign policy to suit their party."

"I don't want anything to do with politicians, sir, of whatever persuasion."

"We are soldiers, Baird. Ultimately, politicians decide our

fate." Hook stood up, a tall, grey figure with great wisdom in his sad eyes. "In the meantime, watch out for Konrad Bramigan. If you find him in your sights, don't hesitate to pull the trigger."

"We're not at war with Prussia, sir."

"No," Hook agreed, "but one death now might stop thousands later."

"Yes, sir," Andrew agreed. "Politics is a dirty business."

Hook sighed. "So is life, Andrew, so is life."

MOUNT PROSPECT, NATAL, 7TH OF FEBRUARY 1881

The horseman came at a gallop, kicking up dust as he rode. When he came closer, Andrew saw his hat was missing, and the horse was lathered with foam and sweat. *This lad's in a hurry.*

"Hold there!" The sentry stepped forward from the closed gate. He raised his hand. "What's your business, friend?"

"Behind me!" the man gasped. "The mail!" He indicated a distant plume of dust. "The convoy! The Boers are attacking the mail!"

Colonel Ashburnham of the Rifles hurried across. "Baird! Go and see what's happening!"

Andrew nodded and ran to the horse lines. "Briggs! Saddle my horse!"

"Yes, sir!" Briggs had anticipated the order and was already saddling Lancelot. "Take care, sir!"

Mounting Lancelot, Andrew shouted for the sentries to open the gate and trotted outside, increasing his speed as he came closer to the dust. Holding his Martini in his right hand, he guided Lancelot with his left, scanning the countryside as he rode, for the Burghers' horsemen could operate close to Mount Prospect.

The land seemed empty except for the rising ribbon of dust. Andrew stopped on a slight rise to check his surroundings.

Behind him was the British camp, a sea of tents and temporary huts, where General Colley was waiting for reinforcements, ammunition, and stores. The tail of the Drakensberg mountains loomed ahead, a natural barrier between Natal and the Transvaal, and to Andrew's right was the curtain of dust raised by the mail coach.

Satisfied no Boers were waiting to ambush him, Andrew pushed on, encouraging Lancelot with soft words. He guided the horse towards the coach, slowing as he came closer. The dozen horsemen who acted as escort lifted their rifles as Andrew halted.

"Halloa there!" Andrew shouted.

The mail coach driver was wild-eyed as he headed toward Mount Prospect, driving his animals with the whip. The escort, a mixture of colonials and British, looked rattled, smeared with dust and sweat. A burly sergeant approached Andrew. "Who are you?"

"Captain Andrew Baird, Natal Dragoons," Andrew said quickly before a nervous trooper shot him. "What happened?"

The driver rattled past without stopping, barely glancing at Andrew.

"Boers!" The sergeant gasped, looking over his shoulder. "We were on our way to Newcastle, and they ambushed us. We barely escaped with our lives!"

"How many?" Andrew asked.

"Dozens of them," the sergeant replied. "They came from nowhere. Maybe fifty or more."

Andrew nodded. He saw a single bullet hole in the canvas cover of the wagon and wondered how many Boers had been present. He doubted it had been a full-scale ambush, or the clumsy wagon with its small escort would not have escaped. The men looked ready to flee or run from shadows.

"Best get into the camp," Andrew advised. The escorts were useless in their present nervous state.

"We will!" the sergeant said, spurring on with his men following in a ragged bunch. Even as Andrew watched, the escort overtook the mail wagon in their eagerness to reach sanctuary.

The Boers have unsettled us, Andrew thought. He remained with the mail wagon until it eased into Mount Prospect, and the sentries shut the gate.

Colley closed his eyes when he heard the news. "Boers ambushing our mail! We can't have that," he said. "We must keep the communications and supplies route open, whatever Brother Boer thinks!" He paced momentarily, pulling at his beard as he considered the situation.

"No, we can't allow this. There's a convoy due here tomorrow with ammunition and stores from Fort Amiel. The Boers are bound to attack."

Andrew knew that the general was not asking his opinion.

"I'll take an escort to guard it," the general decided. "Get your Dragoons ready, Baird," Colley said. "They might be useful."

Andrew nodded. "Yes, sir."

They left camp the following day, the eighth of February 1881, with dawn flushing the horizon pink. Despite their earlier setbacks, the infantry marched confidently from the camp with their heads up and hands gripping their rifles.

Colley had five weak companies of the 60th Rifles, two seven-pounders and two nine-pounders, with a platoon of mounted infantry and a few score colonial horsemen, including Andrew's Natal Dragoons. The mail wagon rumbled between the escort.

"Here we are again, sir," Fletcher glanced over the column. "Three hundred men as a wagon escort for Newcastle."

"Indeed, we are," Andrew replied. "Send out half a dozen scouts and change them every hour."

"Yes, sir," Fletcher said.

When the small convoy reached the Ingogo River drift, close

to their objective, Colley ordered a company of the 60th, plus the seven-pounder mountain guns, onto a hill overlooking the river.

"Cover our crossing," he ordered. Colley waited until the infantry and artillery were in position before he sent the remainder of the force over the river. "I want vedettes in the front and on both flanks. Baird, take your Dragoons and the mounted infantry in front and scout for Boers."

"Yes, sir." Andrew lifted an arm. "Come on, lads!" As the Dragoons splashed over the shallow Ingogo, the sun caught the rising water droplets, creating a miniature rainbow that lasted a few seconds and vanished.

Even in war, there can be beauty.

"Extended order, men," Andrew ordered. The land was undulating on the opposite side of the Ingogo, slowly rising to a range of hills. Andrew rode to a prominent knoll, lifted his field glasses, and scanned the area. In the middle distance, the ground rose to a low plateau and then stretched in a sea of brown-dun grass interspersed with occasional trees and rocky outcrops under the high emptiness of the sky. He paused, refocused, and grunted. Over on the left, he saw a tell-tale ribbon of dust.

"Fletcher!"

"Sir!" Lieutenant Fletcher rode to him.

"Take a section to the northwest and investigate that dust cloud." Andrew watched Fletcher trot away and reported to General Colley. "Somebody's over there, sir, and I doubt they're friendly."

Colley lifted his binoculars to scan the area. "I see you've sent a patrol out."

"Yes, sir."

"When they return, report their findings to me."

"I will, sir," Andrew returned to the Dragoons. "Move out five hundred yards," he ordered. "Form a ring to cover the column as it crosses." He watched his men ride out and returned to his knoll.

Colley supervised his convoy, with the Rifles marching beside

THE SOUND OF BOER RIFLES

the wagons and the sun beating down on them, reflecting from rifle barrels and cap badges.

"Move on," Andrew ordered the Dragoons when the convoy was across, and Colley pushed onto the plateau.

"Wait here until we hear from the scouts," Colley ordered cautiously. The convoy halted, dust settling around the wagons and the men looking around.

Andrew pushed his Dragoons ahead of the column. "Keep your eyes open for signs of Boers. They'll have seen us coming."

Sergeant Meek nodded. "We can't hide a dozen wagons and hundreds of men."

"Not easily," Andrew agreed. He glanced over the column. The veterans were watchful yet relaxed, but some mounted infantry and recruits looked nervous. "Keep alert, boys, and guard each other's backs."

Fletcher returned, galloping the final two hundred yards with his hat bouncing from its chin strap and sweat glistening on his face. "The Boers are waiting ahead, sir!" he shouted.

"How many Boers?" Andrew calmed the lieutenant down. "Report properly; we don't want another Balaclava!"

"Sorry, sir," Fletcher took a deep breath to control his excitement. "The Boers are waiting six hundred yards distant, sir."

"Show me," Andrew ordered, leading Lancelot forward until he saw a long line of horsemen, most with distinctive slouch hats and using long stirrups so they appeared to be leaning back in their saddles.

"They may be friendly, sir," Fletcher said, ducking as the closest Boer lifted his rifle and fired. "No, they're not."

The bullet buzzed past, far over their heads.

Andrew and Fletcher fired back, with no noticeable effect on the enemy.

Andrew pressed another cartridge into his rifle, aimed, and fired. The Boers extended their line and moved forward, with further riders appearing on both flanks. At first, Andrew thought there were a hundred, then saw more in the rear, occupying a ridge slightly lower than their plateau.

"How many do you reckon, sir?" Fletcher asked.

"Hundreds," Andrew replied shortly. "Retire, lads. We can't do anything against these numbers, and we'd better let General Colley know."

"Keep the line, boys," Andrew ordered. "Fletcher, take a section and try to hold the Boers back if they get too close."

"Yes, sir," Fletcher moved forward with ten men as Andrew withdrew the bulk of the Dragoons, passing through the Rifles, who settled behind cover and readied for action.

"You're going the wrong way, Dragoons!" a Rifleman shouted.

Acknowledging the sally with a wave, Andrew approached the waiting general.

"How many Boers are there, do you reckon?" Colley asked.

"A few hundred," Andrew said. "Maybe three hundred." He nodded to the leading Boers, who sat in a loose formation a quarter of a mile from Fletcher's section. "Certainly, no more than four hundred."

"Greer," Colley said to the officer commanding the artillery. "Give them a couple of rounds with your nine-pounders."

Captain Greer grinned and issued a string of orders that saw his men unlimber the guns, train them onto the Boer positions, and hurriedly load. Greer strode across, checked the aim, and nodded.

"Fire!" he ordered quietly.

The guns roared with orange flame and spurts of white smoke. Andrew watched the Boer lines, but both shots passed over the horsemen and exploded in the rear.

Greer's mouth twitched. "Lower the elevation a notch," he said.

Watching through his field glasses, Andrew saw the Boers hastily dismount and run to shelter in a *donga*. As always in these long-distant battles, he found the fighting curiously impersonal. The Boers seemed very far away, the explosions only harmless

THE SOUND OF BOER RIFLES

puffs of smoke and the uniformed soldiers like toys on a tabletop. Men seemed to move in slow motion, speaking with a long drawl as they gave and accepted orders. Something hit the ground between Lancelot's hooves, raising a pretty little fountain of dust that hovered briefly and slowly drifted down.

"They're all around us," a Rifle lieutenant said as Boer bullets sang and whined onto the four-acre plateau.

The movement suddenly speeded up, with men moving quickly, officers giving staccato orders and men ducking and bobbing like fairground mannequins.

The Rifles were returning the Boer fire, and Greer ordered one of his guns to point right and the other left.

"Fire whenever you see a target," Greer commanded.

The gunners responded, aiming where the Boer gun smoke was thickest. The explosions blasted dust and small stones into the air, adding their quota of smoke and noise to the day.

"Who said army life was boring?" the Rifles' lieutenant asked.

"Somebody who had never been to South Africa," Andrew replied. "I've been here less than four years, and this is my third campaign!"

"Lie down!" Colley ordered. "Send the convoy away, and we'll hold the Boers here."

The Riflemen and mounted infantry obeyed, but the gunners needed to stand to fire, making them more vulnerable to Boer musketry.

"Get the horses down," Andrew ordered, thanking Providence his men were well trained. The Natal Dragoons pulled down their mounts, but some of the lesser-trained mounted infantry could not comply, and Boer marksmen targeted their horses. The Riflemen also began to take casualties; although they wore green rather than scarlet, they were still conspicuous against the lighter ground of the plateau.

"Fire if you see a Boer," Andrew ordered. "Otherwise, conserve your bullets."

The Boers kept up a steady fire. Andrew saw one gunner fall

and then another, with bullets pinging and whining from the rocks. Despite their casualties, the artillerymen continued to coolly work the guns. When a bullet hit Greer, spinning him around and knocking him to the ground, Lieutenant Charles Parsons, a veteran of the Zulu War, took charge.

"Case shot," Parsons ordered. "Brother Boer is only five hundred yards away. Let's see how he likes hot steel whirling around his head."

Another gunner grunted and crumpled as a Boer bullet smacked into his chest. Steam rose from the puddles of blood, and flies congregated, buzzing obscenely.

The artillery fired again as Boer bullets continued to hit horses and men. Andrew saw a wounded horse, maddened by pain, whinny, and rise to stagger around the plateau, trampling an injured man, whose screams joined that of the horse.

"Reverted shrapnel," Parsons decided. He did not flinch as a bullet ricocheted from the barrel of the nine-pounder at his side. Another horse screamed and fell as a Boer bullet slammed into it.

Overhead, thunder growled from horizon to horizon, with a heavy sky promising rain. Wounded men lay on the ground, some groaning, others suffering in courageous silence. Horses lay beside them, some still alive and bleeding, others already beginning to swell in the heat. Andrew offered water to one ashen-faced man who lay against the wheels of a gun limber.

"Thanks, mate," the man said, realised Andrew was an officer, and attempted to salute. He died with his hand halfway to his head.

"Rest easy, my friend," Andrew said. He glanced up as rain began slowly and then increased to a torrent that drenched the men on the plateau.

"Who said Africa was always hot and sunny?" the Rifles' lieutenant asked.

"I don't know," Andrew replied.

"If you ever find out," the lieutenant said, "send him to me,

THE SOUND OF BOER RIFLES

and I'll put a flea in his ear!" He ducked as a Boer bullet lifted the hat from his head. "That one was close!"

"Keep firing!" Parsons ordered as another of his men fell, hit simultaneously by two Boer bullets.

"This is getting ridiculous," the Rifles' lieutenant said as he toured his men with encouraging words and cheerful advice. "More Boers are joining all the time."

Andrew agreed. A steady trickle of reinforcements rode to help the Boers, some as individuals and others in small groups.

By half past two, so many gunners were down that Lieutenant Parsons asked for Riflemen to help service the artillery. Despite the obvious danger, there was no shortage of volunteers.

"Good lads, the Rifles," Andrew suggested. *If we lose this battle, it's not through a shortage of courage.*

As the Boers and British continued to exchange fire, the Boers once again proved superior in fighting from cover. The firing increased until about three in the afternoon when the musketry slackened.

"We're firing at ghosts," a Rifleman complained. "I can't see a blessed man."

"I bet they can see you, though, Deas! Keep your head down!"

"Cease fire," Colley ordered. "Conserve our ammunition."

Andrew passed the message on to his men. An eerie hush settled across the battlefield, punctuated by the groans of wounded men and the steady patter of rain.

The rain pressed the gun smoke to the plateau's surface and tormented the suffering wounded. Andrew saw a tearful mounted infantryman shoot his badly injured horse, then bury his head in the animal's neck.

Men peered towards the Boer lines, with the officers cautiously lifting their field glasses and private soldiers narrowing their eyes.

"I can't see anybody," a subaltern said.

"Maybe they've retired," the Rifles' lieutenant said. "We've chased them away."

Rifleman Deas began to cheer until an NCO snarled at him to be quiet.

"The Boers are having a lunch break," Andrew gave his opinion. "Either that or they're replenishing their ammunition. They've fired away plenty."

After ten minutes, the Boers began to fire again, hitting another gunner and a horse.[1]

The British retaliated, aiming at the gun smoke.

"Don't fire unless you see a definite target," Andrew ordered. He studied the Boer lines through his field glasses and, for a second, saw a familiar elderly, bearded man with a leopard skin band around his hat. The Boer fired; the bullet zipped past Andrew before he could move and slammed into the Rifles' lieutenant, blowing his brains out the back of his head.

Andrew dropped his field glasses and grabbed his carbine, but the Boer had vanished, leaving only a small cloud of grey-white smoke to mark his presence.

"Keep down, Lieutenant Parsons," Colley gave belated orders. "Only fire if you have a decent target."

A Rifleman raised a hoarse cry. "Look! The Boers are surrendering!"

Andrew saw a white flag rise above the Boer positions.

"Cease fire!" Colley ordered. "Maybe they want to parley."

As the British fire ceased, the Boers advanced, still firing on the artillery.

"So much for the white flag," Fletcher muttered. "Never trust a Boer."

"They're moving around our rear," Andrew reported to Colley. The plateau was roughly saucer-shaped, with a slight depression in the centre, so the men on the firing line on the rim were more exposed than those in the centre.

"Bring the wounded into the dip," Colley ordered. "They're safer there."

THE SOUND OF BOER RIFLES

Cowering from the lashing rain, men dragged or carried their injured comrades away from the terrible rifle fire and into the depression.

"Another one, Doctor!" Deas supported a wounded colleague.

"Put him down there," Surgeon McGann pointed to a smooth area of ground. Two orderlies helped Deas lower the wounded man as bullets sighed and whined above their heads.

"I wonder what people will call this battle," Fletcher asked as he lay behind a rock, firing his carbine.

"I believe this place is called Schuinschoogte," Andrew replied, "so that will probably be the name." He looked toward the river, wondering if the other company of the 60th and the two seven-pounder mountain guns would come up in support.

Come on, lads. If you come now, you can catch the Boers when they're extended.

The Rifles fired whenever they thought they saw a Boer or the smoke from a Boer rifle, although the shooting eased as the afternoon ground on.

"Are these men deaf?" Fletcher indicated the Rifle company across the river. "They should be over here to roll the Boers up."

Andrew did not answer. He had never heard of a British officer failing to help men in trouble. *The Zulu War began with a defeat and ended in a resounding victory. This war lurches from defeat to disaster.*

Andrew checked his water bottle, had a sip, and allowed a wounded man to finish the final drop. Lifting his field glasses, he focussed on the camp without sighting the seven-pounders or any sign of a relief force. Down below, more Boers rode to join their companions.

"Half the blasted Transvaal is here now," Fletcher said.

"And the other half is probably on its way," Andrew agreed.

Shortly after five, the two seven-pounders beside the river finally opened fire on the Boers, with the rain distorting the sound of the explosions.

"Thank God for small mercies," Parsons said. "They've heard our gunfire at last."

"If they march now, they can still catch the Boers in the rear and roll them up," Fletcher said.

"Do the Boers have a rear?" Andrew asked. "They're all light horsemen and can alter their position in a heartbeat. Our infantry marches too slow to outflank them; we'll have to pin the Boers against a broad river or fight them with more horsemen."

One of Parsons' nine-pounder shells exploded in an area of thick vegetation on the right of the British position, scattering a dozen Boers.

"Oh, good shot, sir!" Surgeon McGann shouted as he looked up from operating on a wounded man.

"Good shot indeed!" Allan McLean of the Transvaal Light Horse echoed. He had been helping McGann treat the wounded, with both exposing themselves to Boer fire.

"Hold on until dark," Colley said. "We'll leave then!"

Andrew hugged a rock, firing at the puffs of smoke, all he could see of the encircling Boers. He heard a scream behind him as a Boer bullet smashed into a private's shoulder, while another man fell without a whisper, shot clean through the head.

As darkness fell, the desultory musketry ended, with men looking around, wondering that they were still alive and checking on their colleagues. Dead and wounded men littered the plateau.

"Collect all the wounded," Colley ordered. "Bring them to the surgeon."

As the darkness grew more intense, men carried their injured comrades to Surgeon McGann.

"Look after him, sir; he's hurt bad."

"Here's Nobby Clark, sir. The Boers put a bullet in his guts, but I don't think it's too serious."

"Could you look after Harry, sir? He's my backmarker."

Andrew stood up cautiously, expecting to hear the whine of a bullet. Peering through the dark, a rare glimpse of moonlight revealed scores of Boers retreating to their camp on Laing's Nek, avoiding the British on the other side of the river. Andrew heard a single rifle shot and saw a spurt of dust and rock splinters as the bullet struck nearby.

"I thought we had stopped fighting," Fletcher said.

"These are not disciplined professional soldiers," Andrew reasoned. "They are farmers, unused to taking orders from anybody."

Their individualism is both their strength and their weakness.

"Don't fire back!" Colley ordered.

The British held their fire, looking cautiously at the Boer positions and keeping low as they carried the wounded to the surgeon. Lieutenant Parsons walked to the nine-pounder on the right, gasped as a Boer bullet nicked his hand, shook off the excess blood and continued to his destination.

As the Boer musketry increased again, the infantry ignored Colley's orders and fired at the muzzle flashes. All the time, the surgeon and McLean tended the wounded as the chaplain, the Reverend Mr Ritchie, gave spiritual comfort to dying men.

The musketry intensified as the surgeon dressed Parsons' wound. Andrew saw little vignettes of the action. He saw the seven-pounders firing as the Boers retreated. He saw Major Brownlow of the mounted infantry moving from man to man, encouraging them. He saw Colonel Ashburnham standing beside the body of Captain MacGregor, the Assistant Military Secretary.

Too many men are dying for no real reason. War is humanity's most obscene creation.

As the wind rose to storm force, the rain hammered down on the plateau, increasing the soldiers' misery. Thunder grumbled and rolled above, split with intermittent lightning flashes that silhouetted the shapes of the hills in the crowding dark.

"The Boers have retreated," Colley said. "We can evacuate the position. Leave the wounded. Chaplain Ritchie will look after them. The Boers are decent chaps who won't abuse injured men, and we don't have sufficient horses to carry them away."

Andrew saw that the general was correct. The battle had left only two horses remaining for each gun and a pair for one of the ammunition limbers. Colley had to abandon the second limber along with the wounded. The most fortunate of the injured lay under blankets; the majority had nothing to shelter them from the teeming rain as the British withdrew. Andrew checked his watch: nine at night. The men moved in silence, unhappy at leaving their wounded behind and the dead unburied. They slogged back through the rain, frustrated and depressed yet aware they had done all they could.

Without using the bugle, Colley's men slipped away from the hill. They moved in a hollow square, watchful for a Boer ambush. Andrew swore when he realised the Boers had shot a third of the Dragoons' horses, although Lancelot was uninjured.

"Baird, use your men and the mounted infantry as a screen. Fend off any Boer attacks."

"Yes, sir." Andrew ordered the dismounted Dragoons to accompany the Rifles and gestured to the rest. "Come on, lads! We're the escorts and shepherds, rounding up stragglers and watching for the enemy."

The Dragoons rode outside the hollow square, plodding through the rain.

"Can you hear that sound, sir?" Fletcher asked. "What is it?"

Andrew was aware of something between a roar and a grumble coming from ahead. "That's the Ingogo River," he said.

The Dragoons stopped when they reached the Ingogo, staring at the rushing brown torrent. In the morning, the infantry waded across with dry knees, but the storm had swollen the river to four times its normal size, and now the water was chest high and powerful, worse because it was dark.

"How the hell are we going to cross that?" Morrison asked.

"God knows!" Ogden replied. "This blasted country is fighting for the Boers."

Andrew peered into the pelting rain. If the Boers had placed an ambush at the drift, the British would be hard-pressed to retaliate. As it was, crossing the Ingogo was as bad as anything else that day.

"Patrol the banks!" Andrew had to shout above the roaring water and the hammer of the rain. "Look for Boers!"

"They've got too much sense to be out on a night like this!" Sergeant Meek replied as he took his section to the right.

"Go to the left, Fletcher!" Andrew ordered. "My section, follow me!" He forced Lancelot into the surging water, gasping at the force of the current. Game as ever, Lancelot thrust his way across the surging river and emerged, dripping, on the far bank. Checking his men were all right, Andrew spread them out.

"You, three, take the right; the rest follow me. If you see any Boers, drive them off!"

The river was still rising, with the ground underfoot soft and slippery. Andrew guided Lancelot away from the treacherous bank, grunted as branches and other pieces of debris rushed past and hoped the Boers had decided to remain under shelter for the night.

"Any Boers?" Andrew shouted through the noise.

"Nothing here, sir!"

"All clear!"

"Nary a one, sir!"

The reports came to Andrew as the first infantry reached the river.

"It's safe to cross!" Andrew called. "Be careful of the current!"

Ordering his Dragoons to help the infantry, Andrew watched the Rifles tentatively step into the water. The first man stumbled and would have been swept downstream if Sergeant Meek had not planted his horse firmly in the way.

"Up you come, lad!" Meek said, hauling the Rifleman upright. "No lying down on the job! Her Majesty paid a good shilling for you, and she won't see her money tossed away in the river."

"Link arms!" Andrew remembered how the natives had

forded the Buffalo during the invasion of Zululand. *Was that two years ago? Time has flown since I arrived in South Africa.* "Link arms and stay together!"

Pushing a reluctant Lancelot into the river, he tried to guide the infantry across, extending a helping hand to the weaker and offering encouragement to the rest. The night became a nightmare of roaring water, hammering rain and the hoarse cries of frightened men.

"Keep together!" Andrew shouted, blinking into the dark. "One step at a time!" He heard a despairing scream and saw one man's upraised hand as the river knocked him off his feet and carried him away. Andrew glimpsed the man's terrified face, and then the river rushed the soldier into the lonely night.[2]

"Get the stragglers over!" Officers shouted. Andrew knew the fording of the Ingogo River in the dark would remain in his memory for a long time, as vivid as leaving the despairing wounded on the bloody plateau.

"Back to camp, lads!" Andrew mustered his Dragoons and counted them anxiously, relieved everybody was present. He did not see General Colley. "We'll act as rearguard in case Brother Boer tries to harass us."

"Harass us?" Fletcher repeated. "The Boers have too much sense to come out in this weather."

"God help sailors, they say," Ogden shouted from the dark. "God help sailors on a night like this, they say. God help bloody dragoons in Africa, I say!"

Andrew rode around the infantry, shepherding them like a sodden collie dog with a flock of swearing sheep. The guns were in the centre of the reformed hollow square, rattling, jolting, and splashing over the uneven ground, with the remaining artillerymen urging their horses on, and Mount Prospect a distant dream. The world consisted of pelting rain, mud, the memory of Boer bullets, and the screams of stricken men and horses.

"March!" the officers ordered. "Keep in step!"

The men marched, stumbled, swore, and continued, an enduring, defiant, and angry army returning to their base.

"What next?" Fletcher asked.

"Try somebody else, for I'm sure I don't know," Andrew replied.

The column arrived back at Mount Prospect at seven the following morning. The skirmish had cost another hundred and thirty-nine officers and men from the already weak British force, and the morale of the survivors plummeted.

"How about the wounded?" a major of the Rifles asked. "We shouldn't have left them behind. They were our men."

"The Boers will look after them," Colley said. "The poor fellows will be all right." He nodded as if in satisfaction. "I think we can consider that operation a success, gentlemen. We pulled the Boers to us, enabled the convoy to get through to Newcastle, and inflicted God knows how many casualties on the enemy. They won't be so keen to face us again."

The major looked at Andrew in disbelief. "That's a quarter of the Field Force General Colley has lost within ten days," he murmured. "If we carry on like this, only you and I will remain to defeat them."

Andrew looked at his Dragoons as they groomed, fed, and watered the horses. In the turmoil of battle, he had nearly forgotten the convoy. "This war is not going according to plan," he said. "It's not finished yet, though."

"We need reinforcements," the major said. "Whenever we face the Boers, they pull men from all over the Transvaal, and we only have a diminishing force of a few hundred to fight them and garrison the country."

"We need more horsemen," Andrew agreed cautiously.

As the Dragoons cared for their horses and Andrew wrote a small letter to assure Mariana she had not been forgotten, General Colley sent a small convoy of wagons under a flag of truce to collect the wounded and dead.

The Rifles watched the wagons splash through the mud, cursed, and kept their rifles dry.

"I hope the bloody Boers don't think we're finished yet," one Rifleman growled. "I want another shot at them. I want them at the end of my sword."

His companion grunted. "You can have them, chum. I want to be in a public in Wandsworth with a pint in my hand and a woman on my knee. They can stick Africa where the sun don't shine and keep it there."

The first Rifleman laughed bitterly. "I'll join you in the public, mate. Bugger Africa. The Boers can keep it."

CHAPTER 13

POTCHEFSTROOM, JANUARY-FEBRUARY 1881

"Will this rain never stop?" Jan looked upwards. "The Lord is weeping to see his children fighting."

"The Lord is weeping to see the *Rooinecks* still in his people's land," Theunis corrected. "But we're wearing them down and forcing them out." He crouched beside Jan and peered over the trench parapet towards the fort.

"You won't see anybody," Jan said. "The British have learned to keep out of sight."

The Groenburg Commando was taking its turn in the trenches. They kept low to avoid any British marksmen, splashed through knee-deep mud, and crouched in misery as the rain continued to hammer down.

"I didn't think war would be like this," Jan removed his hat, shook off the excess water, and thrust it back, still sodden, on his head.

"Did you think it would be glorious?" Theunis asked. "Did you think we'd be wearing scarlet uniforms and charging behind a flag?"

Jan did not reply, aware that Theunis was mocking him.

"We don't see much of that Prussian fellow in the trenches," Karl said. "He prefers the company of pretty women to the grind of the front."

"I thought he was a soldier," Jan replied without much interest.

"He's the kind of soldier who likes the glory and not the hard work," Karl said. "I wonder if even half his stories are genuine."

"He won some medals," Jan said.

"He probably bought them in Cape Town," Karl replied.

"We are the closest Burghers to the British positions," Johannes interrupted their conversation. "We are the men in the front line, the most forward in all the Republic."

"It would be better if we could stop the rain," Karl said.

Jan raised his voice. "I saw movement in the fort," he said.

Theunis eased his head above the sandbagged parapet. The fort was three hundred yards away, sodden under the rain, and with the walls pock-marked with Boer bullets. "I can't see anything."

"Maybe it was just a careless sentry," Jan said. By the third week of January, the novelty of besieging the fort had worn off, and the Burghers no longer fired whenever they saw a British soldier. The cannon loosed an occasional shot, while General Cronje would urge a spasm of activity from time to time. Apart from that, the Boers and British observed a wary watchfulness, neither trusting the other.

"When do we return to the house?" Karl asked.

"We are on duty here until midnight," Johannes told him.

"I wish it were midnight now," Karl said.

Jan nodded silently. He thought of his warm bed in Nuwe Hoop Plaas and vowed never to leave home again. He looked around as Konrad slid into the trench.

"How are you doing?" the Prussian asked, crouching beneath the parapet.

"We are well," Johannes replied. "Have you completed your report to the Chancellor yet?"

Jan listened without interest. He had never taken to Konrad despite the German's friendliness and evident desire for people to admire him. Jan turned away so Konrad would not talk to him.

"General Cronje sent me to ask how you were," Konrad continued.

"Tell the general we are wet, cold, and hungry," Karl replied. "And ask him to come in person if he is interested."

Konrad shook his head. "The general is a busy man," he replied. "He has too much to do."

"And he'll stay nice and dry while he does it," Karl said.

"Movement!" Jan raised his voice. "The British are moving!" He lifted his rifle, ready for a British sortie.

"Where?" Johannes joined his son.

"Over there," Jan pointed to the left of the trench, where a battered group of houses stood between the Boers and the fort. "Something moved."

"I can't see anything," Johannes said. "Pass over the glasses, Theunis!" He scanned the buildings. "If the British are there, they are very still." He raised his voice. "Konrad! What do you think?"

"The German has gone," Abraham said. "He left when Jan told us the British were moving."

Karl gave a bitter laugh. "Maybe our hero is more sensible than I believed."

Johannes concentrated on the houses, reminded Jan to keep under cover, and moved further up the trench. He checked the time when the light died away, saw the watch-fires flicker to life on the fort's walls, and wished he was back with Aletta.

Why don't the British give up? Their infantry tactics consistently fail against us. Why don't they go back to London and leave us in peace?

"*Rooinecks!*" Jan yelled the warning as a British officer led a dozen infantrymen in a sudden charge on the trench. Jan levelled his rifle and fired as the British came closer. The officer was tall and slender, with a drooping moustache and a row of medal ribbons on his chest. Jan saw the soldiers' mouths open in yells and the glitter of their long bayonets, heard their savage battle cries and the officer's barked commands.

"Run!" Karl shouted, jumping from the back of the trench with another man joining him.

Jan hesitated; he knew Karl was no coward, but defending a position to a glorious death was not how the Burghers fought. They preferred to shoot, withdraw, and live to fight another day. Jan saw the first of the Fusiliersh arrive at the trench, plunging his bayonet into the cringing body of Daniel Eloff. He heard screams of pain and fear, saw the officer shoot a man in the chest, and his father fending off a bayonet with the barrel of his rifle.

"Pa!" Jan shouted.

Johannes stepped back as the British soldier withdrew a step and levelled his bayonet. "Run, Jan! Run!"

Jan shook his head and saw his father scramble out of the trench with the soldier five paces behind. He levelled his rifle but snatched at the trigger, causing the bullet to fly wide. The soldier raised his bayonet and leapt at Jan, snarling.

"Run!" Johannes grabbed Jan by the collar, hauled him bodily from the trench, and pushed him towards Potchefstroom. "Run, Jan! Run for your life!"

Jan ran, with his feet slithering and sliding in the mud and the sound of his breathing harsh in his ears. He heard musketry behind him and the sound of British cheers, the pounding of feet, and a man shouting.

The soldiers pursued the Boers for thirty yards until the officer called them back with some shouting taunts that Jan did not understand.

"Jan!" Johannes put a hand on his shoulder as he ran past the first buildings. "We're safe now. They've stopped chasing us."

Jan gulped in air, hearing the pounding of his heart. "I ran away," he said. "I ran away from the *Rooinecks*."

"So did I," Johannes said. "So did Karl. The men who did not run are still in the trench, dead or wounded."

"They fought with spears, like the Kaffirs," Jan found he was trembling. "That is not how civilised men fight."

"War is not civilised," Johannes replied.

Jan nodded as the truth hit him. The *Rooineck* bayonets had frightened his father, a man he had idolised all his life. Jan looked at him, suddenly understanding his father was as vulnerable as anybody else. War was a sordid, disgusting nightmare where men, women, and children were killed or maimed. "There is no glory in war," Jan said. "Do we need to fight?"

"If men did not fight," Johannes said. "The greedy, the evil and the power-hungry politician or king would always triumph."

"Maybe," Jan said. "But the price is high." He remembered Daniel Eloff's scream and knew he would never see him alive again. He farmed twenty miles east of Nuwe Hoop Plaas. How would his wife cope with two young children?

"Ja," Johannes agreed. "The price is always high, and the men who start the wars are seldom the ones to suffer."[1]

Jan looked around at the survivors of the commando. "Am I a coward for running?"

"No, Jan. You are not. Only an idiot stands still to be killed when he can run to fight another day."

"I feel like a coward," Jan said. He saw Mannie lying beneath his blankets, waxen-faced and shivering. Mannie had always looked up to him as a hero, but now Mannie would know he was scared.

"The *Rooinecks* have taken our forward trench," Johannes said. "We'll have to start over again."

Will this war ever end? Jan wondered. *Will Engela remember me?*

The reverse shook the Boers, and Johannes was quiet when the British sent an officer under a flag of truce with an offer to lend the Boers stretchers for the wounded.

"We'd care for them ourselves," the British officer explained, "but we've few facilities in the fort and less medical supplies."

Johannes nodded. "Thank you, *meneer*, we will accept your stretchers."

"I do have one question, sir," the officer said.

Johannes waited.

"Are you using explosive bullets? One of our lads, Private Colvin, was hit in the arm by what seems to be an explosive bullet. It's not the done thing, you know. Not in a civilised society."

Johannes shook his head. "We don't use such things, *meneer*."[2]

The officer nodded. "I didn't think you would. Well, good luck with your wounded." He shook Johannes's hand and returned to the fort.

Can any society be called civilised when it resorts to war to steal somebody else's land? Jan wondered. *And is an exploding bullet any worse than sticking an eighteen-inch bayonet into a man's stomach?*

Half a dozen British soldiers arrived ten minutes later, each man carrying a stretcher. Jan was one of the Boers who met the soldiers.

"Here we go, Piet," a tousle-haired man said with a grin. "It's not much, but better than a poke in the eye with a blunt stick."

"Yes," Jan's limited English could not follow the attempted humour. "Thank you, *meneer*."

The soldier held out his hand. "You take care, Piet. I'll try not to shoot you."

Jan took the man's hand. "I will try not to shoot you also," he said. "How are conditions inside the fort? Are you ready to surrender yet?"

The soldier laughed, shaking his head. "I'll tell you what it's like," he said.

"I spoke to one of the *Rooinecks*," Jan said after he had returned with the empty stretchers. "He was quite friendly and told me quite a lot, probably because he thought I was too young to take note."

"What did he tell you?" Johannes asked.

"He said the surgeons had hardly any supplies left," Jan said. "The men had been on short rations since the middle of December and will be eating mealies rather than biscuits soon."

"We're starving them out," Konrad said, smiling.

"They have bully beef only every third day," Jan continued. He ignored Konrad's gleeful smile, wondering where he had been when the British charged with their bayonets. "The garrison has no tea, sugar, or even tobacco, and the constant rain is making their sacks of corn rot and sprout."

Johannes nodded. "I'll pass that information to General Cronje," he said. "Now, let's get our wounded back."

Jan had never helped with the wounded before and was shocked at how quickly a single bullet or bayonet thrust could reduce strong men. He knew two of the surviving casualties and tried to reassure them they would get better, although it was plain that one would die. Daniel Eloff was already dead, curled into a foetal ball with an ugly bayonet wound in his stomach and congealed blood covering his clothes.

"I knew Daniel well," Abraham said. "He is my mother's cousin, and now he's dead."

"That's right," Theunis said. "He died to keep the Transvaal free."

Abraham stepped away from the house they used as a hospital. "I'd rather have Daniel alive than a free Transvaal."

"Then you are a traitor," Theunis said.

Jan felt sudden tension as Abraham faced Theunis with his fists clenched. Theunis was six inches taller, but Abraham was more pugnacious, standing erect and with his head tilted back so his long blond hair reached down his spine like the mane of an angry lion.

"I am not a traitor," Abraham denied. "If he were alive, Daniel would farm beside Dian, his wife. Now, she must farm alone or find another man. That is not a victory for the Burghers."

"We should all be willing to die for the Transvaal," Theunis said, glowering at the smaller, younger man.

"We'd all prefer to live for it," Johannes stepped between them as Jan clenched his fists, preparing to help Abraham.

"I meant Daniel's sacrifice is not in vain," Theunis said.

"Dian will be pleased to hear that," Abraham said, refusing to back down. He stepped closer to Theunis with his face raised to meet the taller man's gaze.

"That's enough," Johannes pushed Abraham back and watched Theunis walk away, muttering under his breath.

"I'll be glad when Theunis returns to Groenburg," Jan said, unclenching his fists. "I find him disturbing."

Abraham stared at Theunis's retreating figure. "You should have let me hit him, Oom Johannes."

"He is much bigger than you," Johannes pointed out. "And a noted fighter."

Abraham tapped the breech of his rifle. "If he had won, I'd have shot him," he admitted.

"Leave that to the *Rooinecks*," Jan said. "He's not worth hanging for."

When Johannes returned the British stretchers, General Cronje added fruit for the British wounded and carbolic acid for the medical supplies. "We are not savages," he said. "If we must kill each other, let's do it in a civilised manner."

"You are gentlemen," a Fusilier officer said. "You could be British."

"I'd prefer to be a free Burgher," Cronje replied with a smile.

The officer looked confused. In his eyes, telling a foreigner he could be British was the highest honour he could bestow. He did not understand why this farmer was not delighted with the compliment.

Mount Prospect, Natal, February 1881.

"What happens now?" a Rifles' lieutenant asked as he lit a long cheroot.

Andrew shrugged. "Don't ask me," he said. "We try again, I suppose. The Boers are a different kind of enemy from the Galeka or the Zulus, so we'll have to adapt our tactics to suit their style of warfare."

They sat in the large marquee that acted as an Officers' Mess with the rain pattering on the canvas above and the ground below churned into mud.

"Reinforcements are on their way," the lieutenant said. "Some fresh faces and veterans of Afghanistan too. They'll show the Boers what's what."

Andrew nodded. "More men might help. Trying to invade a country with a force of less than fifteen hundred is pointless, especially when every Boer seems to be a crack shot and a superb horseman."

The lieutenant blew smoke into the air. "We'll beat them, sir. We defeat everybody in time." He leaned back in his creaking cane chair and grinned across to Andrew. "That's how we own the largest empire in the world."

"That's reassuring," Andrew said dryly.

"Excuse me, sir," the lieutenant's soldier-servant interrupted. "There's a young lady to see Captain Baird."

"Show her in," Andrew said.

Mariana was dripping wet when she ducked inside the bell tent.

"Hello, Captain Baird."

"Good morning, Mariana," Andrew hid his surprise. "You look wet."

"That would be the rain," Mariana said.

"Well, Mariana," Andrew caught a few disapproving looks from the regular officers. "Ladies aren't allowed in the Mess except on guest nights, so we'd better go elsewhere. My tent is empty." He guided her outside, placed his tunic over her head as a makeshift umbrella, and escorted her to his tent.

"That's better," Andrew said as he opened the flap. "It's not much, but it's the only home I have. Take a pew."

"A pew?"

"A seat. Sit down." Andrew gestured to the only chair. "Tell me what I can do for you and how you got here."

"Thank you," Mariana perched on the edge of the chair. She looked at Andrew, smiled faintly, and then looked away. "When are you coming home?"

"I don't know," Andrew sat on his cot, hearing the structure creak under his weight. "When this campaign is over, I suppose."

"I don't like being alone," Mariana said quietly.

"You have the servants," Andrew spoke more brusquely than he realised.

"It's not the same," Mariana said. She twined her hands together. "It was all right when Mr Briggs was there. Can you send him back?"

"Briggs is a soldier; his duty is with the regiment," Andrew told her. "I'd be breaking all the rules if I posted him away during a war."

Mariana's hands twisted further. "I thought so," she said bravely. "I just wanted to ask."

"I'll be back as soon as possible," Andrew said. "Can you hold out?" He touched her shoulder. "I know it's not easy."

"I'll be alright." Mariana stood up.

"I'll send Briggs to escort you back home," Andrew said. "These roads are not safe with the Boers going about."

"The Boers don't bother me," Mariana said. "It's the nightmares."

Andrew understood. He knew nightmares troubled some Zulu War veterans, while his father, the famous Fighting Jack, often woke in the night with memories of the Indian Mutiny. *Not all war wounds are physical,* he thought. "Come with me. I'll take you to Dr McGann, the surgeon. He may have something to help."

"Yes, Andrew." Mariana hesitated for a moment. "I dream of

what they did to Elaine," she said. "I was there when it happened."

Andrew rose and held her, unable to imagine the horror Mariana had experienced watching the renegades murdering her sister. Yet, he knew that recalling the memory was a step forward. "It's in the past now, Mariana," he said and listened as she told him what had happened.

"We were all in bed," Mariana said. "All sleeping when they came. We didn't have a chance. Father tried to fight, but there were too many of them. I was in Elaine's room when they arrived." She spoke slowly at first, then sped up as though attempting to unburden herself of the memory.

Andrew held her close as she spoke rapidly between the tears, allowing her time to recover.

"When they had killed everybody, they dragged me away." Mariana stopped there, gulping for breath. "They were laughing, boasting about their actions as though they were heroes for murdering unarmed women and men. They rode for days, shooting everybody they saw."

Andrew listened, aware it was cathartic for Mariana to speak about the horrors but sorry she had to relive the experiences. "I've got you," he murmured. "You're safe now."

Andrew did not know how long he held Mariana or how long she spoke of her time as a captive. He listened as she purged the memories while the life of the camp continued outside. He heard the trill of bugles and the crunch of marching boots, and then Fletcher scratched on the fly and poked his head inside the tent.

"Evening, Fletcher," Andrew said.

"It's morning, sir. That was the reveille."

Andrew started. Mariana had talked all night. "Very good. Could you take the parade this morning?"

Fletcher glanced at Mariana, who had continued to talk despite his interruption. "Of course, sir. I'll post a guard outside."

"Post Briggs," Andrew ordered. *Briggs will understand.*

Mariana spoke on, relieving herself of the burden that had haunted her for nearly two years. Andrew held her with his mind busy.

What am I to do with this woman? I wish I knew how to help.

Potchefstroom, February 1881.

"Here we are again," Jan said as he slumped in the bottom of the trench. The weeks of campaigning and fighting had hardened him. He had lost weight, and his face had altered, tightening the skin around his cheekbones and narrowing his eyes.

"Ja, back again," Abraham agreed. "We have defeated the *Rooinecks* in three battles, but we cannot dig them out of this damned fort."

"These are different *Rooinecks*," Jan said. "They refuse to surrender and won't understand that we have beaten them."

Theunis lifted his rifle and fired at the fort.

"Did you see a soldier?" Johannes asked.

"No. I was just letting them know we are here," Theunis replied. He also looked older, with a wild look in his eyes while his unkempt hair tangled across his face.

"What's happened here?" Jan checked his rifle, cleaned a speck of dust from the foresight and aimed at the fort without firing. "Nothing! We sit in the mud, and the British sit in the mud. We shoot at each other and make no progress."

Konrad stood in the deepest section of the trench, an observer rather than a participant. "The siege has progressed slowly. The Burghers captured some traitor Boers led by Pieter Raaf, who had fought with the British against the Zulus. The Burghers executed two of the Boers for treason, but Paul Kruger gave Raaf a reprieve and locked him up at Cronje's headquarters." Konrad shrugged. "I'd have shot them all, but Kruger is too soft to win a war."

"Oom Paul Kruger is a good man," Jan challenged Konrad's words.

"He is a good man," Konrad was placatory. "But not sufficiently severe. In Prussia, we would shoot traitors."

"Raaf had more than three men," Johannes said. "What happened to the others?"

"A court sentenced them to hard labour," Konrad replied. "They are working on the trenches now with some natives." He laughed. "A British shell killed one of them. The Burghers also hold Major Clarke under armed guard at the Royal Hotel."

Jan leaned against the wall. He was not concerned with Raaf, Clarke or any British prisoner. He closed his eyes and thought of Engela. *Konrad calls us the Burghers; he does not say 'we', so he does not see himself as a Boer.*

"Jan!" Abraham sunk beside him. "Are you awake?"

"I am now," Jan said with a faint smile.

"I have a letter from Engela," Abraham said. "I've never had a letter from anybody before." He showed Jan a battered and stained envelope with his name written in flowing script. "You see?"

"I see," Jan reached out, but Abraham pulled the letter away.

"She mentions you," Abraham teased, holding the letter at arm's length.

"What does she say?" Jan was immediately interested, forgetting the mud, the rain and even the British as he thought of Engela.

"Let me see," Abraham opened the envelope and extracted the letter. He read it slowly, mouthing each word as Jan waited impatiently. "Here we are," he said triumphantly. Abraham had never been skilled at reading; he was a man of the open veld, a practical farmer without any need for scholarship.

"Where?" Jan snatched the single sheet. He could see at once that Engela had taken great care creating the letter, with her copperplate writing filling the page without a single blot. Jan scanned the first two paragraphs, then slowed down when he came to his name. He lingered, smiling at the thought of Engela writing about him. If he could, he would have cut the word out and held it close, but Abraham was watching with faint mockery in his smile.

"Tell Jan that I am thinking of him." Jan read out, smiling, and looked up. "Your sister is thinking of me, Abe. May I keep this letter?"

"It's my letter," Abraham said.

"Yes, but my name is in it." Jan reread the passage where Engela mentioned him. He pictured her in his mind with her soft smile, snub nose, and winter blue eyes.

"I may let you have it later," Abraham retrieved his letter, folded it, and replaced it in the envelope. "She's only my sister, not a special woman."

About to say that Engela was special to him, Jan closed his mouth, knowing Abraham would laugh if he revealed his feelings. When Abraham walked away, keeping under the lip of the trench, Jan leaned against the wall and closed his eyes, wishing he was riding over the veld to see Engela.

How long will this war last? When will these Rooinecks surrender and let me go home?

The rain gradually eased away, but the siege continued. Jan was back in the Groenburg Commando's quarters when a rider from Pretoria arrived.

"I have news!" the messenger said as Burghers gathered around.

"What's happening?" Abraham asked.

The messenger explained that Kruger had offered Raaff and Major Clarke in exchange for Boers that the British had captured, but Colonel Bellairs, the British commander in Pretoria, turned him down flat.

"We do not negotiate with rebels," Bellairs said.

"A pity," Johannes said when they returned to their quarters. "Now we have the expense of holding prisoners. An exchange would benefit everybody."

"The British think differently from us," Theunis said, stroking the barrel of his rifle.

"Have you seen this?" Abraham entered the room with a newspaper in his hand. "It is the *Staatscourant,* and it talks about the battle of Laing's Nek." He waved the newspaper around his head. With a wispy blond beard and tired eyes, Jan thought Abraham looked like a dwarf from one of Grimm's fairy tales, except for the rifle slung over his shoulder.

"Does the article mention us?" Jan asked.

"Do you want to be mentioned?" Johannes sounded slightly worried.

"If the paper mentions us, I would let Engela see our names," Jan said.

Johannes smiled, shaking his head. "She will not forget you," he said. Taking the newspaper from Abraham, he handed it to Jan. "See if the paper says you were the man who defeated the British single-handedly."

Jan smiled and slowly read the account. "It does not mention the Groenburg Commando." He looked up. "We should give the British a copy of this paper. It might encourage them to surrender, knowing we defeated their relief column, and they are alone in our land."

"That is a good idea," Theunis approved. "I'll find some copies and hand them to Colonel Winsloe."

However, rather than lowering the garrison's morale, Colonel Winsloe was glad of news from the outside world and asked if the besiegers could supply newspapers on a regular basis.

Johannes shook his head. "Will that man never surrender?"

"You should storm the fort," Konrad said. "Charge down their guns and take it. There are enough of you to accept the casualties for the sake of victory. You are wasting time besieging a handful of the enemy when you could invade Natal and fight the British on their territory."

"How many casualties would you have us accept?" Jan asked. "How many men would we lose capturing a fort held by a hundred and fifty British soldiers? We'd have to cross hundreds of yards of open ground with their rifles and cannon firing at us, then face their bayonets."

Konrad shrugged. "As Bonaparte said, to make an omelette, one must break eggs."

"These eggs are farmers, husbands, sons, and brothers," Jan said. "We have to farm our land when this war is over, and we cannot do that if we are dead."

"A regiment of Prussian Guards would walk over this little fort in half an hour," Konrad boasted.

"There are no Prussian Guards here," Jan said. "We will fight our war our way." He saw Theunis listening intently to Konrad.

"Storming the fort could be the answer," Theunis agreed. "We might lose a few men, but the others would be free to push the British out of the Republic."

"I don't like Theunis," Jan said to his father when Theunis and Konrad left together.

"Theunis only wants what's best for the Transvaal," Johannes replied. "Maybe he's different from us, but he's a dedicated Burgher."

Jan sighed. "We are back in the trenches tomorrow."

"Let's pray for a quiet time," Johannes said. "And hope the British do not try any more bayonet charges."

"Let it please the Lord they remain behind their walls," Jan agreed.

The following day, the British artillery concentrated on *Ou Griet*, smashing the defences the Burghers had erected around the gun.

"Fire at the British guns," Johannes ordered the Groenburg Commando. "Defend *Ou Griet*."

The British had expected the countermove and returned the Boer musketry with interest. Jan aimed at the gunners, fired, and ducked as a British volley hammered at the house, splintering what remained of the window frame and kicking up dust and plaster from the wall at his back.

"Won't these British ever give up?"

"You'll have to storm the fort," Konrad repeated his earlier statement. "It will be quicker than this long siege for a handful of men."

Jan rose to fire a single shot, and both men ducked when the defenders replied with another volley that knocked dust and chips of stone from the house.

"Best get your Prussian Guards, then," Jan said. "I'm not advancing into a Martini volley."

"Nor am I," Karl said. "You go first, Konrad."

The following day, the fort's garrison launched a lightning raid that shook the Burghers. The British grabbed five sheep to augment their rations, attacked the town jail and snatched a Boer prisoner. Before the Boers recovered, the British were back behind their walls, cheering. One man began to sing a bawdy song Jan did not know until an NCO barked for silence.

"These British are not going to surrender," Johannes spoke around the stem of his pipe. "They will be here until the Day of Judgement." He removed the pipe from his mouth and indicated the Union flag still hanging from the flagpole. "Will we ever clear them out of the Transvaal?"

Konrad threw a disdainful look at Johannes. "I have told you what to do."

When Mannie began to cough, Jan moved to his side. "I do not think Mannie should stay here."

Johannes knelt beside his younger son, placing a calloused hand on his forehead. "You are right, Jan. He should be at home. Will you take him?"

Jan thought for a minute, still aware some men would think him a coward for leaving the fighting. "I will take him," he said. He felt Mannie's eyes on him and knew he had made the correct decision.

"Thank you," Mannie whispered and coughed again.

❄

Mount Prospect, Natal, February 1881.

A low hum of conversation filled the temporary Officers' Mess as Andrew ordered a whisky from a stony-faced mess waiter and searched for a chair. Most were occupied, but he found a cane recliner with a long-faced lieutenant sitting nearby, grooming his whiskers with an elegant hand.

"Who are you?" the languid lieutenant asked.

"Captain Andrew Baird, Natal Dragoons," Andrew said.

"Oh, colonial horse. I'm Primrose, 58th Foot. Did you hear the news?" Lieutenant Primrose selected a cheroot from his silver case.

Andrew shook his head. "Probably not. There are so many shaves going around that I've closed my ears to all of them!"

Primrose lit his cheroot, shook out the match, and puffed aromatic smoke into the air. "The Prime Minister has sent Sir Evelyn Wood to the Boers. He wants to seek an honourable peace."

Andrew sipped at his whisky, remembering the shattered dead on the battlefields and the sound of Boer rifles. *Was their sacrifice in vain? Or do men sign their lives away when they don the Queen's scarlet? Once we accept the fatal shilling, our destinies are in the hands of politicians and senior officers, and we become tools of an uncaring government.*

"An honourable peace? That's tantamount to surrender," a lean captain with a bristling moustache said. "It's a disgrace! We've lost nearly every battle. We can't have peace until we've defeated the Boers."

"The government did something similar during the Zulu War," Andrew remembered. "They sent out Sir Garnet Wolseley [3] to replace Chelmsford after Isandhlwana. And what did Chelmsford do? He launched another invasion and smashed the Zulus at Ulundi."

"Were you there?" Primrose looked over lazily. "I seem to remember mention of your unit."

"I was there," Andrew did not give details. "I'll wager Gladstone's news only spurs Colley to try again."

"With more success, hopefully," Primrose said. "Oh, God, how I'd like to get at these blasted farmers. We'd stop shilly-shallying around if I were there, I can tell you."

"Quite right, Primrose," the lean captain agreed, helping himself to a glass of champagne from the silver tray at his side.

Andrew kept quiet, remembering what General Hook had told him. Some things were more important than winning small wars. "Have you gentlemen seen much action?"

"Not much, old boy," the lanky captain agreed. "I was employed in staff duties mostly."

Primrose nodded. "A little in New Zealand and at Ulundi," he said languidly. "We saw off the Zulus, didn't we, Baird?"

"We did," Andrew agreed.

As Andrew had predicted, Colley decided to launch another attack on the Boer positions.

"Sir Evelyn Wood is coming, is he?" Colley growled to his staff. "I want this campaign all wrapped up before he arrives."

On February 12th, 1881, reinforcements marched into Mount Prospect. First to arrive were the 92nd Foot, the Gordon Highlanders, who had won renown in Afghanistan. Unlike most other British regiments in South Africa, the Gordons wore khaki tunics rather than scarlet, and the swing of their green tartan kilts reminded the watchers of their reputation. They swaggered into the British camp with a string of successes under their belts while the skirl of their pipes announced to the world that the Gordons, the Cocks of the North, had arrived, and God help any Boer who got in their way.

As well as veteran infantry, cavalry arrived to bolster Colley's force. The 15th King's Hussars had a history that stretched back to the Battle of Emsdorf in 1760, the Peninsula War, Waterloo, and the less glorious Peterloo Massacre in 1819.

"We're also expecting the 6th Inniskilling Dragoons and the

83rd County of Dublin Regiment, a unit which fought through the Peninsula and during the Indian Mutiny," Fletcher said.

"Colley has decided not to wait for the Inniskillings and the 83rd," Primrose contradicted, pulling at a cheroot. "Sir Evelyn Wood commands them, and our general wants to win the war himself."

Andrew looked around the Mess, crowded with officers from various regiments. "I suppose we'll try the passes again."

"Maybe so," Primrose shrugged. "I hope Colley makes a better job of it this time. Sending a few dozen men against entrenched Boers doesn't seem to be the answer." He stretched on his seat and blew a perfect smoke ring that hovered above his head for a few seconds before gradually dissolving. "Colley had better hurry up, though. Paul Kruger is pushing for a truce, and our government is too weak to disagree."

"The government's talking about withdrawing from the Transvaal." Lieutenant Hamilton of the Gordon Highlanders joined them. "We might have peace before we smash the Boers in battle."

"Colley will attack," Primrose said flatly. "He'll be smarting after his repulses and has to regain his reputation."

"A victory will give us a better position in the peace talks," Hamilton agreed. "If we negotiate without a victory, Kruger will hold all the cards. If we defeat him, we can name the terms."

"How many men will die to satisfy the politicians?" Andrew asked.

"That's a soldier's job," Primrose replied. "We're the final piece in the diplomat's chessboard. When the talking ends, send in the army."

Andrew grunted. "Or when the army fails, send in the diplomats."

CHAPTER 14

BOER CAMP, MAJUBA HILL, FEBRUARY 1881.

A breeze carried the bellowing of trek oxen from two hundred yards away and a distant murmur from the wagon laagers. General Joubert lit his pipe and surveyed the veldcornets who attended his *kriegsraad*, the tactical meeting before an impending battle.

Johannes and Theunis stood with the rest, listening to everybody's opinions. Theunis stroked the barrel of his rifle with almost sensual attention and checked the foresight while Johannes watched, waiting for Joubert to speak. At their side, Konrad studied the unmilitary ranks of the Free Burghers with partially disguised amusement.

"We have defeated the British in three encounters and have their garrisons under siege." Although Joubert spoke quietly, his words carried to every man present. "However, General Colley has gathered reinforcements and is preparing to attack again."

The commandants and veldcornets nodded in agreement. "Then we shall defeat them again," Theunis shouted. "And every time until we have sent them back over the Vaal and out of Africa!"

As some of the commandants and veldcornets voiced their assent, Joubert lifted a hand. Silence descended, broken only by the bellowing of an ox.

"I appreciate your sentiments, *meneer*," Joubert said, "but we'll take this campaign one battle at a time."

Most men laughed at the sally and waited for Joubert to continue.

"General Colley will be seeking revenge," Joubert said. "I know there are peace negotiations and talk of an end to the war, but Colley is an injured lion, and the British do not like to be defeated."

The commandants growled, shaking their heads. Theunis lifted his rifle in the air.

"Only the Lord knows what will happen," Joubert said. "We must pray for victory and peace, but we can help the Lord make up his mind."

A few of the Burghers shook their heads at Joubert's mild blasphemy. When a church minister began to pray, his congregation removed their hats and bowed their heads, begging God to grant them victory.

Joubert waited until the brief prayer finished. "Now, fellow Burghers, some of you are with me at the laager; others are in the various sieges throughout the republic. If General Colley tries to invade our land again to relieve one of our sieges, I will send a runner to call up men to fight. Be prepared to join us."

The men nodded.

"May the Lord bless our endeavours and our republic," Joubert ended and left the Burghers to return to their camps.

"General Colley is a British gentleman," Johannes offered his opinion as the veldcornets of the Groenburg Commando rode slowly back to Potchefstroom. "He will abide by the ceasefire."

Theunis smiled. "You are too trusting, my friend. The British have not won the greatest Empire in the world by being gentlemen but by deviousness, lies, underhanded diplomacy and sending their soldiers to die without thought for the suffering. British gentlemen are the worst of the lot."

Johannes looked away as Konrad barked his distinctive laugh. "British gentlemen live in the eighteenth century," Konrad said. "They hide behind their navy and play games with their little scarlet soldiers. If they cannot defeat a small nation of farmers, how will they fare against the Prussians?"

"The Prussians are not here," Johannes reminded. "We are."

MOUNT PROSPECT, NATAL, 25TH OF FEBRUARY 1881.

"Majuba, the Hill of Doves, is the key," Colley said. "I've been observing it since we arrived. The Boers keep a picket on the summit during the day but withdraw it at night."

The assembled officers nodded, with some smiling at the Boers' perceived amateurism.

"Majuba dominates Laing's Nek and overlooks both our position and the Boers' camp," Colley said. "I saw a working party of Boers on the summit today. If they entrench, they'll be better able to hold us at bay."

The officers waited for the general's next words.

"I plan to occupy Majuba, gentlemen," Colley said and treated them with a benign smile. "We'll take the hill and push off any Boers who attempt to take it from us."

Andrew looked upward, where three vultures circled the camp. *I hope that's not a portent of the future,* he thought. He watched the scavenger birds for a moment, chased away a shudder, and left to get his Dragoons ready to fight.

At half past nine on the evening of the 26th of February 1881, General Colley led his small army out of Mount Prospect. One hundred and eighty men were veterans from the Gordon Highlanders, with a hundred and forty-eight from the 58th, seventy seamen from the Naval Brigade, and a hundred Riflemen of the 60th. Captain Smith commanded the Rifles, Captain Morris the

58th, and Major Hay the Gordons, who brought along Ghazi, their Afghan hound.

"The Gordons look well," Fletcher said as the kilted infantry swung past. "They should give the Boers a fright."

"If they get close to them," Andrew said. "I doubt the Boers will stand still and wait for our bayonets."

Each man carried three days' rations, with seventy rounds of ammunition, a greatcoat, and a waterproof sheet. The Gordons looked confident as if they had no doubts about the outcome of any future battle. The other infantry looked grim-faced, with none of the usual black humour that carried British soldiers through difficult situations.

"How many of us will Colley kill today?" Private Burrows of the 58th asked.

"God knows," Private Jones replied. "If the Boers shoot me, you get my kit."

"And if they kill me," Burrows said. "Write a letter to the missus, will you?"

The Natal Dragoons rode on the flank of the 58th, with outriders scouting for any possible Boer ambush. Andrew recognised some of the 58th from their previous battles.

"How many of us are there?" Burrows asked.

Jones glanced over the column, hardly seen in the dark. "About five hundred," he replied. "Sawnies, Rifles, tarry-arses, and us."

"Has the general learned nothing?" Burrows grumbled. "He's leading a few hundred men to capture an entire country. The Boers will slaughter us! It'll be another Boer trap and another bloody reverse."

Andrew realised the grumbles were not the usual soldiers' grousing but came from men whom the general had led to two defeats within a few days. He glanced at Fletcher, who said nothing as they reached the foot of Majuba Hill, three and a half miles from Mount Prospect. Above, drifting clouds obscured the stars, with the wind whispering across the dark slopes. An unknown animal howled, raising the hairs on the back of Andrew's neck.

"That's a fair lump of a hill," Fletcher looked up at the massive bulk of Majuba.

"It is," Andrew felt a tight knot in his stomach. He sent the Dragoons to form a loose semi-circle on the flank of Colley's army. "Keep alert, but don't fire unless the Boers fire first. We're meant to be in a truce."

"The Boers don't know the meaning of a truce," Ogden said. "We've seen them firing when they fly a white flag."

"We'll keep our word, Ogden," Sergeant Meek said. "No firing unless the Boers fire first."

Colley left two companies of the Rifles and one of the Gordons at a low-level ridge to maintain communications with Mount Prospect Camp. "You're our insurance," Colley said. "If Joubert tries to outflank us, you will see him off."

Andrew grunted. *Joubert's mobile horsemen will ride rings around our slow-moving infantry.*

"We're only three hundred and fifty strong now," Burrows said as the remainder of the infantry began to slog up Majuba. "How many Boers are there?"

Jones shrugged. "I dunno. Thousands, I think. They seem to be everywhere when we fight them."

Burrows hawked and spat. "God, everything tastes of dust. If it's not dry and hot, it's bloody pissing with rain. What a bloody country." He stamped his boots on the ground. "If there are thousands of Boers, we'll have to pretend there are more of us."

"The noise you're bloody making, that won't be hard!" A corporal snarled. "Keep your mouth shut, you blasted idiots!"

"What happens when we get on top?" a diminutive man named Harris asked. "Do we throw stones at the Boers? We've only rifles, not even a seven-pounder mountain gun."

"You obey orders, Harris; that's what happens," the corporal fell back on the tried and trusted reply. "You obey orders."

Behind the 58th, the Gordons climbed slowly, kilts swinging, and Martinis held in brown-tanned fists. They exchanged low-voiced jokes, with a hard-faced sergeant cutting off one man's laughter.

"Keep your bloody voice down! We don't want the Boers to hear!"

"They're only farmers, Sergeant," the man replied. "We sorted the Afghans out; this lot will be easy."

"Easy or not, McGill, keep your voice down."

"Yes, Sergeant," McGill fondled Ghazi and returned his attention to climbing the hill.

Majuba stretched before them, dark, ominous, and steep. Andrew heard the harsh call of a bird and pushed Lancelot up the slope.

"Baird!" Colley ordered. "Leave Lieutenant Fletcher with your Dragoons down here. I want you with me on the summit."

"Yes, sir," Andrew replied as Colley stepped closer.

"You're the only man who can identify this Prussian fellow," Colley reminded.

"Yes, sir," Andrew had nearly forgotten about Konrad Bramigan.

Colley threw Andrew a sidelong look. "General Hook mentioned your expertise."

"I'll do my best, sir," Andrew said.

"Arrange your men, Baird and join us," Colley turned away and pushed uphill.

"You heard the general, Fletcher," Andrew said. "Take charge here." He dismounted and handed Lancelot's reins to Briggs. "Look after my horse, Briggs. I doubt I'll need him up there." Andrew lowered his voice. "If anything happens to me, look after Mariana as best you can."

"I will, sir," Briggs accepted the possibility of Andrew's death with as much composure as he did everything else.

With a final nod, Andrew left his Dragoons and headed for Majuba's summit.

"The Boers better not be waiting on top," Burrows said.

"It's the sort of thing Colley would do," Jones replied. "He'll lead us into another bloody trap."

"We'll have less talking and more climbing," a hard-voiced sergeant snapped. "Get up this blasted hill!"

The slope seemed to stretch forever into the gloom, with only a fading gleam of starlight to guide the infantry. Some parts of the hill were so steep the heavily encumbered men had to use their hands, while other stretches consisted of massive boulders or loose stones that slithered underfoot. Andrew heard the scrape of nailed boots on rock, muttered curses, and an occasional complaint as men fell on the uneven surface.

"Careful up there," a southern accent sounded from below, "you're causing an avalanche on us."

"I can't help it," the Midlands reply came. "These stones move if you just look at them."

"Well, stop looking then! It's too dark to see, anyway."

At four in the morning, the leading files of the 58th staggered to the top, with an ominously red dawn cracking open the sky to the east. Sweat dried in the early morning chill, men crouched on the ground, gasping for breath while NCOs counted their platoons and sections, rounded up stragglers, and put everything in disciplined order.

"Where's the bloody Boers, then?" Private Burrows asked. "No ambush today, Piet? You're slipping!"

It was well after five o'clock when the Gordons reached the summit, with the Naval Brigade last.

"Now let them come," a seaman said.

"Create a breastwork!" his petty officer growled. "Did you think you were finished?"

"No breastworks," a lieutenant said. "General Colley doesn't want breastworks or trenches."

"Yes, sir," the petty officer exchanged wondering looks with a kilted sergeant but did not argue.

Andrew looked around, wondering at the lack of resistance. The British occupied a gently sloping plateau with a circumference of around a thousand yards. In the centre sat a rocky ridge, hard-edged and dominant. Unseen except for their fires, the Boer positions on Laing's Nek were around two thousand feet below and two thousand yards away.

"If we had some artillery, we could spoil the Boers' morning," Lieutenant Hamilton of the Gordons said.

"We'll use what we have," Lieutenant MacDonald growled. Unusually in the British army, Hector MacDonald had risen from the Gordons' ranks after General Roberts had promoted him from sergeant in Afghanistan.

"Spread the men out," Colley ordered.

The Gordons obeyed, with the NCOs placing their men ten paces apart. Andrew watched the kilted figures silhouetted on the lip of the hill with the wind playing around their sun helmets. They looked very martial, he thought, but also very thinly spread. Ghazi, the Afghan hound, moved from man to man, sniffed at a few rocks, and settled down behind McGill.

"If the Boers come up in force, we're in trouble," MacDonald said. "We're not strong enough anywhere to hold them."

Andrew nodded. "We'll need three times as many men to garrison this place effectively."

When the light strengthened, Andrew could see details of the Boers' camp far below, three separate wagon laagers, with tents and horses outside and the minuscule figures of men riding from laager to laager. A faint whiff of smoke from cooking fires drifted to him, reminding him he had not eaten that day. Regular darker lines told of defensive trenches around the laagers to repel any possible British attack, although the sentries seemed lackadaisical.

"A decent cavalry charge would scatter these men," MacDonald scanned the Boer positions through field glasses.

"Hamilton is right; artillery would be useful here," Andrew murmured. "I remember hearing how General Roberts carried mountain guns on the back of elephants in Afghanistan."

"Bobs Roberts is a good general," MacDonald replied without insulting Colley.

"I wish he were here now," Hamilton said.

I'd settle for Redvers Buller, Andrew thought and said nothing.

As the light strengthened, a small group of Gordons stood erect on the skyline, shouting insults at the Boers and waving their fists.

"Come and get us, Piet! Come and try the Gordons!"

"Enough of that!" a sergeant snapped. "Get back into position! You're soldiers, not wee laddies at school."

Andrew looked at the faces and realised that not all the Highlanders were Afghan veterans. The men who stood on the skyline were very young. They also looked very vulnerable as the edges of the plateau sloped down from the central north-south ridge, exposing the defenders to fire from all around.

Colley posted one weak company of the 92nd to cover the north, west, and most of the south, the most dangerous section of Majuba. A company of the 58th occupied the east. A company of each regiment, plus the hospital, sat between the 58th and the central ridge, where the reserve of the Naval Brigade and fifty of the 58th waited. Finally, Colley ordered the men to strengthen two points that overlooked a steep valley on the south.

"We're guarding a circuit of a mile with only three hundred and fifty men," MacDonald said. "Let's hope the Boers don't realise how thinly we're spread."

"What happens now?" Lieutenant Hamilton finished a cigarette and flicked the stub over the edge of the hill.

"Ask the general," MacDonald replied, "for I'm sure I don't know. The Boer camp is out of rifle range, and we've no artillery. I suppose we can join these young soldiers and shout at the Boers."

"Why did they do that?" Andrew asked.

Hamilton lit another cigarette. "Somebody ordered them to let the Boers know we are here."

"General Colley believes the Boers will see British soldiers on the hill and then withdraw," MacDonald told him. "He gave the order for the lads to make themselves known."

Andrew shook his head. "The Boers will not withdraw," he said. "They've defeated us in every encounter so far. They're filled with confidence while our boys doubt Colley's leadership."

"Look," Hamilton said, pointing to the Boer camp. "Maybe General Colley isn't as daft as we believe."

Andrew saw half a dozen Boers rounding up their trek oxen as if they intended to leave the camp. While some glanced backwards at the British soldiers on Majuba's skyline, others hurried to the wagons, preparing to inspan the oxen. One middle-aged man bundled his wife aboard a wagon and drove it slowly away.

"You're right, Hamilton. Some Boers are leaving." Andrew lifted his field glasses as a small group of men cantered into the laager and began to shout at the rest.

"Those lads must be in charge," Andrew said. "That could be Joubert himself." He shook his head. "If we had a battery of mountain guns here, a couple of rounds of shrapnel would solve a great many problems."

The arrival of Joubert and his veldcornets quelled the panic. The withdrawing wagon returned to the laager, and men stepped away from their oxen and horses.

"Damn it," MacDonald said. "We had them on the run for a few minutes. As you said, Baird, a few rounds from a seven-pounder could have broken their resolve."

Hamilton lit a cigarette and grinned. "It looks like General Colley will have his battle after all. Piet's coming to the front door."

With Joubert stopping their retreat, groups of Boer horsemen rode toward Majuba. Some moved in a semi-disciplined formation as though they were commandos; others approached as individuals, although all had the same objective. Within twenty minutes, they formed into three hundred-strong groups and began climbing the hill.

"That's not what the general intended," MacDonald said. "As

you said, Hamilton, we're in for another battle. Best get the men ready."

The Gordons' officers strode to their men, shouting orders. "Watch your front, lads; the Boers are coming up the hill."

"Then we'll send them back down," a voice replied.

"That's the spirit, McGill," Hamilton replied cheerfully. He peered downhill. "I can't see a single Boer, but I know they're there. Number Three section, get down the slope and delay any Boer coming up. Skirmishing formation."

Andrew heard the first rifle crack just before nine in the morning, with the bullet pinging from a rock. Hamilton laughed. "Here they come, boys! Let's give them a Highland welcome."

The Gordons responded with a volley that crashed against the rocks, with bullets ricocheting and whining on the slopes.

"That's for you, Piet!" a man shouted. "There's plenty more if you've a mind to stay!"

Andrew moved to the shelter of a thornbush and stared downhill. He knew the Boers were there but could not see anybody. He jerked back as a bullet buzzed past his shoulder. More shots followed, and Andrew traversed his rifle, seeking a target.

These boys are experts at keeping under cover as they fire. The Gordons are retaliating, but I can't see any Boer bodies.

The Boer fire increased through the morning as they encircled the hill, firing at the desperately thin British line and gradually easing closer to the summit. The Gordons' skirmishers retaliated, only withdrawing when the overwhelming number of Boers outflanked them. Ghazi joined the skirmishers, barking whenever a Boer bullet came close.

"What was the point of climbing up here? It's Schuinschoogte all over again," a long-faced officer said, fired and moved on.

Andrew agreed, saw a flicker of movement beneath and squeezed the trigger of his carbine. Shooting downhill at elusive targets was never easy, especially when under fire. While the musketry continued, rising into crescendos and falling away, the Boers steadily advanced, concentrating on the area Lieutenant Hamilton and his twenty-strong platoon held. The Boers moved from cover to cover, firing whenever they saw an opportunity, so the Gordons were hard-pressed to hold them back.

"I cannae see them," a red-haired Aberdonian growled.

"Wait till they get closer," his rear rank man replied. "We'll give them the bayonet."

"We'll need to," the Aberdonian said. "I've used half my cartridges already."

At noon, after five hours of constant musketry, the Boers were slowly but relentlessly closing.

"Runner!" Andrew sought a subaltern. "Tell General Colley we need more men at this point."

"I can't, sir," the subaltern said. "General Colley is sleeping."

"He's what?" Andrew could not stop his reaction.

"He's sleeping," the subaltern repeated.

"We're in the middle of a bloody battle!" Hamilton strode across, loading his revolver. "Generals don't sleep during a battle!"

"This one does," the subaltern said smugly.

Hamilton rammed his revolver into its holster and strode to the central ridge. Ignoring the sleeping Colley, he raised his voice. "The Boers are massing beneath my position," he reported. "I believe they are going to rush us. Some reinforcements would be welcome."

The staff officers stared at Hamilton as if he were asking them for something unusual. With his message delivered, Hamilton returned to his men at the most dangerous spot on the plateau. Two hundred feet lower down, the half dozen Gordon skirmishers attempted to stem the Boer tide.

"Keep them back, lads!" Hamilton shouted. "Fire away, but be careful not to hit our men!"

Andrew loped towards Hamilton's position as the musketry increased. Hamilton's platoon remained in position, facing what

Andrew estimated to be three hundred Boers. He fired towards the smoke, knowing his chances of hitting a Boer were minimal.

"Here's the general now," MacDonald shouted from further along the lip of the hill.

"I hope he enjoyed his wee nap!" a man said sourly.

"Reinforcements! Go and help Hamilton!" Colley ordered. "Move!" The staff officers gave sharp orders to the companies waiting behind the ridge.

Andrew glanced over his shoulder. For the first time in his experience, British soldiers were reluctant to face the enemy. Perhaps influenced by Colley's previous defeats, they moved slowly, looking at each other for support and reassurance.

"The general's sending us forward to get killed," Jones said.

"While he stands at the back," Burrows agreed.

The sergeants bellowed them forward, pushing the most hesitant to help the hard-pressed Highlanders.

"Come on, you laggards! The Gordons need our help!"

The tunics of the 58th shone scarlet under the sun as they slouched forward. "We done our bit," Burrows said. "Is the general going to send us into battle after battle until we're all dead?"

"You took the Queen's Shilling," a corporal snarled. "Now bloody earn it!"

"Come on, lads," Andrew encouraged. "Show the Boers what the 58th can do!"

Major Fraser, a Royal Engineers staff officer, raised his voice. "Men of the 92nd, don't forget your bayonets!"

"We won't, sir," a bearded private replied. "I'll gut the first Boer I see!"

The Boer musketry increased until the firing sounded like a single peal of thunder. *If you hear the shot, it hasn't killed you,* Andrew reassured himself. *A bullet travels faster than its sound.*

Andrew saw Lieutenant Hamilton encouraging his men, with Hector MacDonald striding from position to position. When a surge of Boers erupted over the lip, a handful of Gordons retired. Others fired, reloaded, and fired again as more Boers emerged, chasing the retiring skirmishers.

"There's hundreds of the bastards!" a man shouted. "Where's the bloody reinforcements?"

"Retire and reform!" another man stepped back.

"Permission to fix bayonets, sir? Sir?" A corporal asked. "Can we fix bayonets and charge them?"

One and then another, Gordon Highlander fell, shot at close range.

Hamilton strode to General Colley. "Sir! Excuse my presumption, sir, but may I have permission to charge with the bayonet? The men cannot stand the fire much longer."

Colley shook his head. "Wait until they come on, Hamilton. We will give them a volley, then charge."

"They can't come much closer, sir!"

More Highlanders echoed Hamilton's words, requesting permission to go forward with the bayonet.

"We're running out of bullets!" a man said, raking a dead man's pouches for ammunition. "Can we use the bayonet, sir?"

At his side, another private threw stones at the Boers, inviting them to come forward and fight like men.

"Come on! Stop skulking like cowards! Face us in the open!"

Andrew saw the Boers hesitate as though refusing to close with the handful of Highlanders.

If we fix bayonets, we could still turn this battle around.

"We're holding them!" MacDonald shouted. "Send them back!" Andrew saw dead and wounded Gordons all around him, with some men glancing over their shoulders towards the relative security of the central ridge.

"Oh, there they are," an anonymous officer shouted, "quite close."

Although Andrew was unsure if the officer was referring to the reinforcements or the Boers, his words affected the infantry, with the reinforcements, both 58th and Gordon Highlanders, turning away in sudden panic.

"Stand and fight!" Andrew roared.

"Fight!" MacDonald shouted, brandishing his revolver. "By God, I'll shoot any man who passes me!"

The fear spread to the Gordon skirmishers, who had contained the Boers for six hours of sniping and fighting. The survivors turned and ran with the rest, pushing each other in their eagerness to escape.

Dear God! I have never seen British veterans run like that. Andrew experienced a revelation that even the best troops could panic. He realised that underneath all the pomp and pageantry, despite the regimental pride and the years of training and hard discipline, soldiers were only men, subject to the same uncertainty and fears as the most softly-bred civilian.

As the British fled, the Boers leapt up and fired into their backs, killing and wounding more than they had in their initial assault. Andrew saw the Highlanders, bearded veterans of Afghanistan, and the red-coated 58th Foot running down the hill with the Boers firing, reloading, and firing again.

"That's the Gordon Highlanders!" An officer stared in disbelief. "The pride of the British army!"

Andrew refined his thoughts. *Men have a limited supply of courage, and when that ends, even the toughest are vulnerable.* He watched for a second, fighting his shock, for he had been brought up to believe that a British soldier never panicked and Highlanders were the cream of the army.

Not all the British ran. A mixture of Gordons, seamen, and men of the 58th gathered defiantly on the central ridge as Boer bullets felled them in ones and twos.

"Fight!" Lieutenant MacDonald roared at the running men. "Come back and fight, you cowards!"

MacDonald wasted his words. Panic is contagious, and men find it hard to rally once broken. The scramble to escape continued with men pushing each other as they fled and the Boers standing at the summit of Majuba, loading and firing at the retreating British.

Andrew fought the urge to join the retreating men. *Stay and fight.* It was not bravery, for he knew he was as scared as anybody else. *Why then? Pride perhaps? A sense of duty? I don't know. I only know I'd be damned if I'll run away; I could not face myself in the shaving mirror again. What would my father say? What would Mariana think?*

Mariana? Why did I think of her?

Climbing up on the central ridge beside the surviving defenders, Andrew began to return fire. The Boers were still elusive, hiding behind cover, appearing only to fire, and dropping away again. The British soldiers had not been trained to fight in such a fashion; they stood in the open to retaliate, and the Boers shot them for their bravery.

"Come on then! Show yourselves, you cowards!" a hard-faced sergeant shouted. Sunlight gleamed on his medal ribbons.

When the Boers appeared in front of the ridge, many defenders stepped forward for a better shot. Boer marksmen on the flanks killed them as they stood.

"Give them the bayonet!" Private McGill shouted.

"Give who the bayonet?" another man asked. "I can't see anybody!" His words ended in a gurgle as a Boer bullet smashed into his side, knocking him to the ground.

"They're on the flanks!" somebody shouted as Boer fire hammered the defenders from every direction. Andrew aimed and fired, trying to control his trembling hands. He heard Hamilton ordering independent fire. Then, a bullet smashed into Hamilton's arm, and he spun around and fell. *Order, counter-order, disorder. Where is General Colley? Why isn't he taking charge?*

As the bulk of the defenders retreated, the Boers followed, firing at the now defenceless men and leaving the ridge as a British island among a rippling ocean of Boers.

"Fight!" Lieutenant MacDonald roared, drawing his broadsword. "We're the Gordons!"

Andrew fired the last of his bullets and stood at MacDonald's side as the Boers surrounded them, pointing rifles from a few feet away.

"Hands up!" a Boer said, indicating the row of rifles aimed at the stubborn, frustrated survivors.

One by one, the British on the ridge threw down their rifles and glared at their captors. MacDonald was last to comply. "You'd better treat the wounded well," he growled. "And look after my men."

Reluctantly but inevitably, Andrew raised his hands. "You have captured me, *meneer*," he said to a young, freckled Boer with a shock of blond hair. "Now, what are you going to do with me?"

"I will take over now," a tall, prematurely aged Burgher said. "Collect the British weapons and see to the wounded." He put a hand on Andrew's shoulder. "I saw you in previous battles, *Rooineck*. Who are you?"

"Captain Andrew Baird of the Natal Dragoons," Andrew said. "And you, sir?"

"I am Johannes van Collier of Nuwe Hoop Plaas and the Groenburg Commando," Johannes introduced himself.

They shook hands as if they were old friends meeting on a city street rather than enemies who had been trying to kill each other a few moments before.

"Will you *Rooinecks* leave our republic now?" Johannes shouldered his rifle and passed his water bottle to his prisoners.

"That's not our decision to make," Andrew said. "Ask the politicians." He saw a wild-eyed man join Johannes and recalled him from Krugersdorp.

"Theunis," Johannes spoke to the newcomer. "See if our prisoners need help. Give the wounded water and make them comfortable." He returned his attention to Andrew. "Come with me, Captain, in case you have any foolish notions of shooting us in the back."

Andrew complied, ignoring Theunis's baleful glare. He saw a Boer lifting the wounded and still smiling Hamilton and knew the Burghers would look after the injured. He looked up, suddenly tired, and saw a tall man at the back of a group of Boer leaders. The broad scar on the man's face was evident, and Andrew felt something lurch inside him.

That's Konrad Bramigan. That's the Prussian agent, and he's seen British soldiers run.

CHAPTER 15

NUWE HOOP PLAAS, WESTERN TRANSVAAL, FEBRUARY 1881.

"Mother!" Jan helped Mannie off his horse outside the familiar farmhouse. Nuwe Hoop Plaas looked smaller than he remembered but with the same smells and feeling of belonging. "Mother!"

Aletta appeared from the dairy, wiping her hands on her apron as she stared at her sons with a combination of elation and fear. "What's wrong, Jan? Where's your father? Is the war over?" She stepped towards her sons, quelling her panic. "Is Mannie hurt?"

"No, Mother," Jan tried to answer Aletta's barrage of questions. "No, the war is not over. Pa is well, but Mannie is sick. He needs you to nurse him."

Aletta enfolded Mannie in her arms. "I knew he was too young to go on commando! Where is your father? Why did he not come as well?"

"Pa is busy fighting the *Rooinecks*," Jan replied.

Aletta felt a mixture of relief her husband was alive, disappointment he had not come and pride that he was doing his duty.

"Let me see you, Mannie," she held her younger son at arm's length. "Yes, you are thin and pale. I'll get you better. Are you staying home, Jan?"

"No," Jan shook his head. "I will head back tomorrow. I only brought Mannie home. The commando needs me."

Aletta closed her eyes to hide her pain at her son returning to the war. She looked at him, seeing the changes. Physically, he had lost weight, and his cheekbones were more pronounced, making him look more mature. He stood differently, too, Aletta saw, and his eyes were harder, yet it was his mouth that revealed more. Jan's mouth was firm, with new lines extending to the side of his nose. *I have a man for a son and a boy who still needs his mother.*

"Are you going to ride over to Engela?" Aletta asked, hoping to entice Jan to remain a little longer. "She will want to hear about her brother. She often mentions you and Abraham."

On the long journey from Potchefstroom to Nuwe Hoop Plaas, Jan had pondered visiting Engela. The temptation had been strong, the idea of seeing Engela's smile and regaling her with his adventures and experiences nearly overpowering. "No, Mother," he said, shaking his head. "I have wasted enough time. I must return to the commando and fight the *Rooinecks*." He pretended not to see the hurt in his mother's face.

Aletta turned away from this grown man who was her son. "Come, Mannie. We'll get you to bed. Jan: find some food. You have lost a lot of weight."

"I will," Jan said. "I will tell you what to say to Engela."

"She would prefer to hear it from you."

"I have to return to Potchefstroom." Jan touched his mother's shoulder. He felt her tremble and shift closer to him for an instant and saw the anguish in her eyes. "I cannot stay home, Mother."

"I know," Aletta replied. *It is a painful thing to raise a boy that turns into a man. It is a hard thing to be a mother.* She raised her chin, knowing that her life had altered forever. "There is food on the table, Jan."

THE SOUND OF BOER RIFLES

MAJUBA, FEBRUARY 1881.

All over Majuba Hill, the Boers were helping the wounded British soldiers, with Dr Mahon giving orders in English and broken Dutch, performing simple operations in the open and moving from soldier to suffering soldier.

"Leave that man," Mahon ordered. "He's past help. Moving him will only increase his pain." He knelt beside a bearded Highlander who was moaning and holding his back. "Take this fellow down the hill. It's all right, my man; I'll soon have you patched up again."

Andrew moved to support an injured redcoat when Theunis jabbed him with his rifle.

"Back, *Rooineck*! You are a prisoner!"

"Back yourself, Burgher!" Andrew snarled. "This man needs help."

Theunis lifted his rifle until the barrel thrust into Andrew's throat.

"Back!"

"No," General Joubert stepped between them. "You are a good fighter, Theunis, but lack diplomacy."

"You two men," General Joubert pointed to Lieutenant MacDonald and Andrew. "You fought to the end. You, sir," he pointed to MacDonald, "may keep your sword." He handed back the weapon. MacDonald nodded his thanks and replaced the sword in its sheath.

"What happens now?" Andrew asked. He saw Konrad talking to Johannes van Collier and wondered what the Prussian was saying.

Joubert smiled. "You are both my prisoners," he said. "No doubt you shall remain so until the war is over."

Andrew sat on a rock, took his pipe from his pocket, and tamped tobacco into the bowl. *When you can do nothing,* he told himself, *have a smoke. It helps to clear the mind. I never wanted to be a soldier anyway.* He stared over the battlefield and wondered what the British public would say when they heard of another defeat.

"Come on, *Rooinecks!*" the freckled Boer guard seemed unsure what to do with his prisoners. "We will take you into the Republic until the war ends."

"Heads up, lads!" The hard-faced sergeant had survived. "Misfortune is part of a soldier's lot. You accept it and wait for better times. Let's be having you!"

"Has anybody seen Ghazi?" McGill asked. "I've not seen him for hours."[1]

The prisoners gathered in an untidy group, bewildered that ragged farmers could defeat professional soldiers. They looked at one another, unsure who to blame.

Andrew saw Johannes talking to Konrad. *How can I inform General Hook that the Prussian is still with the Boers?*

Johannes and the wild-eyed Theunis called out something, and a dozen men clustered around them. "Come on, Groenburg men!" Johannes shouted. "This battle is won. We'll return to Potchefstroom."

That's worth knowing. If one commando moves from place to place, others may do the same.

Andrew watched the Groenburg Commando ride away, a collection of shabby farmers and small-town Burghers who had defeated one of the finest infantry regiments in the world. *They will be proud of their victory,* Andrew thought, *but I'll wager most of them are more concerned about their farms than the war.*

"March," the Boer guards shouted, pushing the British prisoners into an untidy column. "March."

Unarmed and shocked, the British prisoners headed northwards. The British officers moved to the head of the column and tried to raise morale.

"Get your heads up! You're British soldiers!" Andrew snarled.

Twice, Boer guards approached Andrew to look at him curiously.

"Are you a *Rooineck*?" A broad-faced man asked in halting English. "Or are you a Burgher who has joined the enemy?"

"I am Captain Andrew Baird of the Natal Dragoons," Andrew replied.

The Boers poked at him. "You look like a Burgher. Why don't you wear a red coat? Other *Rooinecks* wear a red coat or look like soldiers."

Andrew agreed. The Gordon Highlanders wore khaki tunics above their green tartan kilts but were recognisably soldiers. "We don't all wear scarlet," Andrew said.

The Boer's words remained with Andrew as they marched north into the Transvaal with an escort of mounted Boers and frequent rain showers soaking them. They camped beside a small *spruit*, with now-familiar star formations sprinkling the great arc of the sky.

"We are here for the night, *Rooinecks*," the oldest of the guards told them. "If you try to escape, we will shoot you, or the lions and tigers will get you." He smiled, showing white teeth. "You'd be as well to remain prisoners because the war will be over soon, and you'll go home."

Some Highlanders responded with obscene comments, while most listened without interest. Typical British infantry, they would be mainly recruited from urban streets, and few would attempt to escape into the unknown veld.

Andrew scooped a hole for his hip and lay on his side, listening to the sounds of the night. He worked out the sentries' beats as they walked languidly around the prisoners. After a while, the sentries grew bored and sat on rocks to talk and smoke, with the perfume of their tobacco drifting over the camp. The prisoners settled down, most sleeping, a few stirring restlessly or muttering as memories of the day's events recurred in their dreams.

Andrew rolled over, keeping quiet. He examined the camp and noted the darkest areas where rocks and two thorn trees cast tangled shadows.

That will do.

Keeping low, Andrew crawled towards the thorn trees. The sentries were lax, laughing together and ignoring their charges. Like many countrymen, they would despise the town-bred soldiers for being helpless outdoors. Andrew exploited their prejudice as he eased into the nearest shadow.

When a sentry spoke loudly and stepped away from his companions, Andrew froze, thinking the man had spotted him, but the Boer was only finding some privacy to relieve himself. A jackal called in the dark, the sound a reminder of the dangers beyond the camp perimeter. Andrew waited in the bush's friendly shadow until the sentry rejoined his companions, then crawled beyond the sentinels' beat. He found a patch of dead ground, lay still for a moment, and snaked into the darkness. Andrew knew the Boers were expert trackers but doubted they would spare the manpower to search for a single escaped British prisoner. Lengthening his stride and using the stars as a guide, he headed south, knowing he had not far to travel before he found a British picket.

I must tell General Hook about the Prussian agent.

POTCHEFSTROOM, FEBRUARY 1881.

"We defeated you again!" Theunis roared to the British garrison. "We defeated your General Colley at Majuba!" His voice echoed from the battered walls. "You may as well surrender now and end your suffering! Why are you holding out?"

"We're the 21st Foot!" A lone voice replied. "The Royal Scots Fusiliers! Bugger off, Piet!"

"What does that mean?" Konrad asked. "The Royal Scots Fusiliers. Does that matter?"

"It means they are fighting for the honour of their regiment," Christiaan Niekerf replied. He caressed his rifle as rain dripped from the leopard skin band around his hat. "The British have great fondness for their regiments."

"But they're only an ordinary infantry regiment, not the Guards." Konrad sounded amused. "They are nothing, peasants with rifles, cannon fodder."

Johannes removed the pipe from his mouth. "You can tell them that if you wish, Konrad. I am sure it will persuade them to surrender." He replaced the pipe and watched Konrad for a moment before turning away.

"These *Rooinecks* are strange people, Johannes," Christiaan said. "I heard that while you and I were fighting at Majuba, some of them here at Potchefstroom carried a scarecrow, a model of a woman, near our lines, gave her an umbrella, and returned to the fort."

"Why?" Konrad asked. "How could that help their cause?"

Christiaan considered before replying. "To show us they could come into our lines at will," he said. "And to mock us."

"Mock us?" Konrad gestured towards the British fort. "We have them under siege. We have defeated their best general. How can they mock us?"

Christiaan removed his hat, scratched his head, and smiled. "I do not know, Konrad. I am not a *Rooineck*."

Johannes shook his head. "They are different from us."

"They are foolish," Konrad gave his opinion.

"They are stubborn," Johannes replied. He nodded to the Union Flag. "I will be happier when that flag is down."

"That strongpoint will help," Karl nodded to the Boer's new fortification northwest of the fort. They used native labour and reluctant prisoners of war for the heavy digging and completed the stronghold at the end of February, on the 75th day of the siege.

"Now we have the *Rooinecks* surrounded," Theunis said with satisfaction. "They can either starve or surrender."

"Whatever they choose," Jan said. "I hope they do it soon." He looked up as the fort's gate opened, and a lone officer emerged under a flag of truce. "Maybe they are surrendering now."

Adriaan Coetzee approached the officer, spoke briefly, and returned to Cronje with the news filtering to the Burghers.

"The British request a coffin and a truce," Johannes reported.

"Tell them to bury their dead inside the compound," Theunis said, tossing his hair from his eyes.

"Who has died?" Jan asked. He had missed the victory of Majuba while at Nuve Hoop Plaas and sought to restore himself at the centre of the commando.

"A lady," Johannes told him. "A Mrs Emily Sketchley died of enteric fever."

Jan looked away. "I don't like making war on women."

"Mrs Sketchley's brother also died of the fever," Johannes said. "And at least four of the soldiers." He cleaned out the bowl of his pipe with a knife. "I heard the garrison places patients in holes in the ground to prevent the disease from spreading."

"I hope it does spread," Konrad said, and Theunis nodded.

"The British have scurvy as well," Johannes said. "But they still refuse to surrender."

Konrad shook his head. "Are they crazy?"

"Maybe," Johannes said. "Colonel Windroe knows the British can't force a relief column past General Joubert, yet he still holds on. I don't know why." He glanced at his commando. "I hope Windroe gives up soon while we still have men left to fight."

By now, many of the besiegers had also drifted back to their homes, some because they considered they had done enough for the Republic.

"My wife will miss me," Karl said. "She'll need me on the farm."

"She'll manage better without you," Theunis replied. "We'll have no deserters in the Groenburg Commando."

"He went home!" Karl glared at Jan.

"Jan was escorting a sick man," Theunis said. "And he returned to the fighting. I am not sure you will."

Karl snorted. "Mannie could have ridden home alone."

"We stay here," Johannes gave his decision. "We will see this war to the end."

Jan sighed, thinking of Engela as he tried to ignore Karl's jealousy.

"Engela will wait for you," Abraham read Jan's thoughts. "I know my sister."

The Rooinecks are keeping me from Engela, Jan thought. *I hate the Rooinecks.* He stared at the low walls of the British fort, lifted his rifle, and fired. *I hate the Rooinecks.* He remained low, expecting the British to reply with a volley, but there was no return fire.

Fight us! Jan thought. *Come out and fight! You have made Mannie sick and keep me here.* Jan gave a high-pitched laugh, saw his father looking worried, and took a deep breath. *Things are worse since I've been home. I miss Nuve Hoop Plaas, Mother, and Engela. Once we win this war, I will never leave home and Engela again.*

MOUNT PROSPECT, MARCH 1881.

"Halt!" The British voice was welcome as Andrew walked through the dim. "Who goes there?"

"Friend!" Andrew shouted. "Captain Andrew Baird of the Natal Dragoons."

"The what? Never heard of them, chum," the cheerful reply came. "Advance and be recognised, or I'll shoot you."

Andrew stepped forward with his hands in the air. "Here I am!" He had walked for three days since escaping from the Boers, avoiding farmhouses and the isolated *dorps*, drinking from streams, and eating only the fragment of army-issue bread he had in his pouch.

"You look like something the dog spat out," the sentry said as he examined Andrew. "What did you say your unit was called?"

"The Natal Dragoons," Andrew repeated. The British

outpost was half a mile from the main camp, with the sentries doubled and more nervous than usual.

"I know of them," a second voice sounded from the dim. "They was at Ulundi. In you come, sir."

Andrew could taste the tension in Mount Prospect, with men jumping at any unusual sound and NCOs barking at every fault. The sentries held their rifles in white-knuckled hands, with more men on guard than Andrew had seen since the aftermath of Isandhlwana. One young private swivelled and raised his rifle when Andrew passed.

"A Boer!" he said.

"He's an escaped prisoner!" A colonial pushed the private's rifle down. "Easy there!"

"Morning, Baird," General Hook greeted Andrew as calmly as if they had met in a London club. "Where did you spring from?"

"A hill called Majuba," Andrew said.

They stood in the middle of the camp, with dawn flushing away the dark and men hurrying about their duties. A bugler sounded reveille, with the silver notes ghosting across the camp.

"Majuba, the Hill of Doves," Hook said. "The Boers will be boasting of that little skirmish for years. You heard that General Colley died, I presume?"

"One of the Boers made sure we all knew," Andrew said.

Hook nodded. "Colley was a gentleman. I've requisitioned a tent here, so you'd better come in and tell me what happened." He shook his grey head. "You've as many lives as a black cat, Baird."

The bell tent was crowded with desks and three of Hook's staff. "Clear out," he ordered cheerfully. "See if the garrison needs some trenches dug or the wall repaired. Do something useful for a change."

Used to General Hook's style, the men left without complaint.

"That's better," Hook said. "I don't know why I have so many staff; they can't do anything I can't do myself. Now, sit ye down, Baird, and give me your version of events at Majuba." He listened as Andrew explained what he had seen and experienced, writing a few notes.

"The Boers outfought veteran British soldiers and one of our best generals," Hook confirmed Andrew's words.

"Yes, sir. The men were too thinly spread, and the Burghers used cover and marksmanship again. They outshot us once more."

"A recurring theme," Hook leaned back in his chair, watching Andrew through tired eyes. "You seem to have a knack for surviving battles."

"Yes, sir. What were the casualties at Majuba?" Andrew asked.

Hook did not have to consult any notes before he replied. "We lost ninety-two killed, a hundred and thirty-four wounded, and sixty men captured, including you. Some of the prisoners were wounded, and others had no ammunition or weapons." The general waited for a moment. "What is your opinion of General Colley?"

"Colley was a brave man," Andrew said. "I don't think he was a great general, however intelligent."

Hook did not respond.

"How about the Boers, sir? Did we kill many of them? God knows we tried hard enough."

"The Boers hardly had any casualties. They claim they lost one man killed and six wounded. From the moment they came over the summit, they pushed us off in about thirty minutes."

Andrew remembered the chaos and the carnage. "Yet the men were shooting well and tried to hold on at the ridge. Our marksmanship is terrible."

"What can we do about that?" Hook raised his eyebrows as if a general was seriously asking the opinion of a very junior officer. However, Andrew knew Hook would have an ulterior motive, so he considered his reply.

"Emphasise marksmanship rather than volley fire," Andrew said. "Volleys were fine eighty years ago when we fought Bonaparte and still useful against tribesmen such as the Zulus but useless against the Boers. When an officer orders the men to fire, the Boers dive into cover, and the volley is wasted. Then we stand in the open like scarlet targets. The Boers can't miss."

"Our infantrymen haven't got the brains to fire independently. We sweep them from the gutters of the slums." The general threw forward his hook and waited for Andrew to bite.

Andrew grunted and slammed shut his mouth on the bait. "Then our entire social system is wrong," he said. "Why does Britain, the greatest country in the world, have so many slums and such poverty? Why do we still, in the late nineteenth century, have so many men who can hardly read or write?"

Hook shrugged with his eyes sharp as he probed deeper into Andrew's psyche. "These men probably roamed the streets rather than attending school."

"We should make schools better then," Andrew responded. "Make education interesting rather than an ordeal where teachers use the stick more than the carrot. Our system lets far too many people down."

Hook shrugged again without taking his gaze off Andrew. "The men are immoral, drunken, foul-mouthed blackguards who would not join the army if they could find anything better."

That's one way of inspiring loyalty in the rank and file. "Maybe your men are," Andrew said. "I served with soldiers." He felt his temper rise as he faced General Hook across the width of the travelling desk. He wondered how such a man could profess to be an officer if he did not respect his men.

Hook's grin took Andrew by surprise. "You are more like your father than you know, Baird. He would have reacted in much the same manner, although with more subtlety. Relax, man, I was pushing to find out about you. I've worked with British soldiers all my life, and I know their strengths and weaknesses."

Andrew took a deep breath, still fighting to control his temper. "And what did you find out about me, sir?"

"That you are a man of deep beliefs, Baird, and genuine humanity," Hook leaned back in his chair. "Whether you can combine that successfully with a career as a soldier, I cannot say."

"Were you testing me, sir?"

"Yes," Hook said. "Your father cares for his men, and they respond with loyalty. I suspect you share that trait." His smile failed to conceal the intelligent eyes scrutinising Andrew from head to foot. "Loyalty is important in senior officers, but vital in small units on detached duties."

Andrew waited, wondering where Hook was leading.

"Have you anything else to tell me?" Hook asked.

"Yes, sir," Andrew said. "I saw the Prussian spy with the Groenburg Commando."

"Is he still there?" Hook looked surprised. "He'll have an interesting report to send to the Kaiser." He eyed Andrew for a moment. "I have another task for you, Andrew. Take a few days' leave to recover, and then ensure your men are ready to leave on short notice."

He called me Andrew; that's very informal. What unpleasant task has General Hook planned for the Dragoons?

POTCHEFSTROOM, MARCH 1881.

"Their flag is still flying," Karl said gloomily.

"We should storm them," Konrad reiterated his earlier suggestion. Nobody replied. The besiegers were down to four hundred men, spread thinly around the perimeter. They occupied the trenches and strongpoints, keeping the British trapped by their presence and accurate musketry.

"How many days have the *Rooinecks* held out?" Theunis asked.

"Seventy-eight," Johannes replied. He saw a British sun

helmet bobbing behind the parapet but did not fire. Few Boers bothered taking shots at stray sentries, while the defenders largely ignored single Burghers. The artillery continued a desultory duel, with both sides conserving their limited ammunition.

"They can't have many supplies left inside the fort," Karl said hopefully.

Johannes lifted his field glasses and scanned the fort. "I think they are eating rotten mealies," he said. "We will starve them into submission without losing any more lives."

"General Cronje has called for all the veldcornets," Adriaan Coetzee thrust a weary head inside the house. "You have fifteen minutes."

Johannes sighed. "That sounds like trouble," he glanced at Jan. "Don't take any risks until I get back."

Johannes returned within the hour. "General Cronje wants to storm the fort," he said. "He knows our morale is low and worries we may drift away and leave the fort in British hands."

"Good!" Konrad said with great satisfaction. "Cronje has seen sense at last! The British are weak with disease, and one firm push will defeat them."

"Jan," Johannes took Jan aside. "You have never had to charge a defended position."

"No, Pa," Jan agreed.

"When Cronje gives the order, we will obey, but it will not be like anything else you have done. Don't run forward in a straight line, or the defenders will shoot you. Move in irregular rushes, from cover to cover, and look for dead ground where the *Rooinecks* cannot see you."

"Yes, Pa," Jan wondered how often his father had attacked a fixed British position. He thought it best not to ask.

"The British will fire in volleys," Johannes said. "When you hear the officer shout 'Fire', throw yourself down. Don't care what others think of you; keep alive."

"I will, Pa," Jan said.

"Stand here," Johannes put his hands on Jan's shoulders as he called the Groenburg Commando to listen. "We are attacking that section of the wall." He pointed to the centre of the British fort. "Study the ground carefully and mark in your head where the cover is. When you run forward, head for these places."

Jan nodded, taking his father's advice.

"Don't bunch up," Johannes said. "You may feel more secure with your friends around you, but the British will aim for a group rather than an individual. Keep far apart, and your chance of survival is greater."

The men grunted or nodded, with some noting the best places to shelter from the British fire and others remaining silent as they contemplated advancing over open ground under fire. Only Theunis and Konrad were enthusiastic about the attack. Konrad walked from man to man, telling them how important their victory over the British would prove. "You can push the *Rooinecks* out of the Republic," he said. "It will be a victory to rank with Blood River."[2]

"Are you coming with us?" Abraham asked.

Konrad did not reply for a few moments. "No," he said. "I have a duty to the German Empire. I cannot get killed fighting your war."

"If you are not fighting," Abraham told him. "You have no right to encourage us to get killed."

Konrad glared at Abraham and stalked away.

Abraham scowled at his retreating back and spat on the ground.

As the Burghers waited for the order to go forward, Johannes and Karl wrote letters to their wives. Others did the same, slightly embarrassed. Nobody criticised them. Some men lit their pipes, watching the smoke coil upwards, and a few drank coffee or discussed their farms.

"Abe!" Jan said. "If the *Rooinecks* kill me, tell Engela," he trailed off, unable to complete his sentence.

"I'll tell her," Abraham said. He touched Jan on the arm. "You do the same for me."

Men were unable to share their feelings yet understood each other without speaking. One man tipped his hat forward over his face and fell asleep. Two others hummed hymns and silently prayed for help and guidance. Christiaan Niekerf cleaned his rifle and stared into the sky. He smiled and began to scrape out his pipe.

"I wonder if my dead wives are watching me," he said, lifting the bowl of his pipe in a silent salute before returning the stem to his mouth.

Jan could feel the tension as the Burghers checked their rifles, shook each other's hands, or simply stared towards the fort.

Johannes came close to Jan. "Remember what I told you. Don't be afraid to keep down. You're a farmer first and a soldier second."

"You too, Pa," Jan told him.

"Ten minutes," the word spread around the Burghers' positions. "Ten minutes. Move into the forward trenches."

"Ten minutes to live," Karl said without any humour.

Jan did not reply. He felt his heartbeat increase as he tried to force a smile.

The Groenburg Commando slogged forward, keeping beneath the parapet so the British could not see them. They took up their positions, with Jan crouched between Johannes and Abraham, humming a reassuring hymn.

The minutes ticked slowly past, each one an eternity as Jan thought of Engela and his home. *Thank the Lord Mannie is safely away from the war.*

"Five minutes," Theunis lifted his rifle, tossed the tangled hair back from his face, and glared at the fort. Jan thought he had never seen a man look so much like a wild animal.

Jan saw the strain in his father's face. He looked older, with deeper lines from his nose to his mouth and around his eyes.

"The Lord will look after you, Jan," Johannes said, touching his son's shoulder in unspoken affection.

"Go!" Theunis gave the order. "Storm, Groenburg Commando! Storm!"

The Burghers erupted from their trenches and houses, shouting to hide their fear.

"Now!" Jan heard the crisp command from the fort, and a line of sun helmets appeared above the wall, with a row of levelled Martini-Henry rifles.

"Fire!" the same British voice roared.

Jan dropped to the ground as the first volley crashed out, knocking down three Burghers.

"It's a trap!" Karl shouted. "They are waiting for us!"

Jan clambered to his feet. He felt strangely elated, as though he was not here but inhabited somebody else's body, a stranger advancing into the concentrated musketry of professional soldiers.

"Fire!" The same clipped, unemotional British voice repeated.

The Fusiliers fired again, with bullets crashing into the ground, hissing overhead, and wounding another two Burghers.

"Load!" the unseen officer commanded.

"Back! Get back!" Karl looked around in panic. "It's no good!"

Johannes grabbed Jan's arm. "Get back, Jan!"

Sudden panic enveloped the Burghers as they scrambled back to their positions with bullets kicking up dirt around their legs. Jan ran with the rest, panting in fear as the British fired another volley. He heard somebody screaming, felt the rush of a bullet zipping past his ear, and threw himself into the trench he had left only moments previously. He landed with a painful thump and lay in the trench, gasping, eyes wide open, and his heart hammering inside his chest. "Pa?"

"I'm here," Johannes said, his voice seeming to come from a long distance.

"Are you hurt?"

"No. Are you?"

"No." Johannes closed his eyes. "The British knew we were coming."

"Abe?" Jan said, seeing Abraham a few yards away, his mouth wide and his eyes darting from side to side.

"Get back to the house," Johannes ordered. "We won't be capturing the fort today."

"Load!" the unemotional British voice ordered.

A man was groaning, his voice the only sound between the Boer and British lines.

"They beat you," Konrad said when the shocked survivors returned to their quarters. "You ran away. If you had charged with more conviction, you would have captured the fort."

"I didn't see you advancing," Abraham retorted. "Why don't you return to Prussia and leave us in peace."

"You don't deserve Prussian help," Konrad told him.

Jan watched Konrad march away and looked over the land between the Boer and British lines, where dead and wounded Burghers lay in tattered bundles.

We'll never defeat these Rooinecks.

THE HARSH BARK OF ARTILLERY WOKE JAN FROM A CONFUSED dream. He lay still for a few seconds, thinking he was in his room at Nuwe Hoop Plaas, until he recognised the sound of the guns, and his heart dropped. *I'm still at Potchefstroom.* He struggled to his feet, shaking the sleep from his head.

"What's happening?"

"The *Rooinecks* are firing at *Ou Griet!*" Karl shouted. "All their guns!"

"Shoot them," Theunis ordered, "man the trenches and shoot the British gunners!"

Some Groenburg men rose to obey, but a controlled volley from the fort made the Burghers duck. The British artillery fired again, raising great clouds of mud from around the Boer cannon.

"They must be scared of our gun!" Theunis removed his hat and thrust a tangle of hair from his face. He lifted his rifle, aimed, and fired at the British artillery. "Come on, boys! Make them pay!"

Jan aimed at a now-badly stained British sun helmet, took a deep breath, and squeezed the trigger just as the soldier bobbed away. Jan swore at the waste of another bullet. "The devil is looking after these *Rooineck* soldiers!"

The British artillery barked again, with two shells landing squarely beside the Boer gun. Jan flinched as he saw the explosions lift tons of earth and rock and land them on top of *Ou Griet*.

"The *Rooinecks* have destroyed *Ou Griet*," he said. He heard the British give a thin cheer.

"Now we'll never capture the fort," Karl wailed.

With their task completed, the British artillery fell silent. A few Burghers revealed their frustration by firing at the fort, but the British remained below their parapet.

Jan watched as a breeze stirred the Union Flag, as if the Lord were mocking the Burghers' frustration. He slumped down, looked at Johannes, and shrugged.

"What next, Pa?"

"We put our faith in General Cronje and the Lord," Johannes said, but Jan saw doubt in his eyes.

POTCHEFSTROOM, 12TH OF MARCH 1881.

Jan stood at the back of the crowd, thinking of Engela. He pushed back his hat with a filthy thumb and watched his father and Theunis talking to General Cronje before they shook hands. The hum of conversation ended when the general stepped forward to speak to the Burghers.

"Fellow Burghers of the Zuid-Afrikaansche Republiek," Cronje smiled as he looked around at the besiegers. "Paul

Kruger, the Vice-President of the Triumvirate, has contacted me with good news."

The Burghers remained silent, listening to the general. Karl was breathing heavily, leaning on his rifle. Johannes searched for Jan in the crowd and winked while Theunis stared ahead. Behind the leaders, Konrad stood erect, as pristine as if he were attending a ball in Berlin rather than observing a siege in an obscure Transvaal *dorp*.

Cronje lifted his voice. "*Meneer* Kruger has informed me that Commandant-General Joubert and General Sir Evelyn Wood have agreed to an armistice between us and the British." He waited for the crowd's murmur to subside. "I will read you one paragraph of Kruger's letter. Listen, my friends."

The men listened, some smoking, others holding their rifles in brown hands. Jan thought of his brother, white-faced and sick, lying in his bed at home, and of Engela, who would wonder why he had not visited when he was close.

"*Meneer* Kruger writes: 'It is your duty to notify Major Winsloe of the agreement between Wood and Joubert, but the armistice at Mooiriver is not to commence prior to the arrival of supplies, and the handing over thereof to you. Before such time, be free to continue warfare."

The veldcornets nodded. Any supplies would be welcome.

Cronje noted the approval. "We shall capture this fort, gentlemen, and then tell the British of the armistice."

The Burghers spoke together, some wondering how to capture the fort and others glad of the coming armistice. They had waited patiently and fought too hard to allow politicians to steal their victory.

Theunis smiled triumphantly. "We know the fort is running out of food, and disease is spreading through the garrison."

The Burghers nodded. "These things are well known," one man agreed.

"The British must surrender soon," Theunis continued. "I

have a man inside the fort, a Burgher who pretends to be friendly with the British."

Jan inched closer, desperate for the siege to end.

Theunis continued, brushing the hair from his face. "The British colonel wants an honourable surrender before his rations are finished rather than have us make him surrender unconditionally."

"Any surrender would be better than sitting here while men are killed," Johannes said. "If it comes a week earlier, let the British have their honourable terms."

The Burghers agreed. "Let's finish this siege and return to our farms," Karl said. "I don't care if the British surrender honourably or dishonourably as long as it finishes this damned war."

Jan agreed. "We have been away from home too long," he said. "Speak to the *Rooinecks* and end the siege."

"Do we all agree?" the veldcornets asked their men.

After all the toil and suffering, Jan thought the siege ended with a whimper rather than a bang. *Maybe all wars end like this when men are too weary to continue fighting and lay down their arms through fatigue rather than in a glorious burst of victory.*

Jan acted as sentry as Colonel Winsloe and his officers met Cronje halfway between the town and the fort. He recognised Lieutenant Rundle among the British delegation and held his rifle ready in case the meeting was a British ruse. Fusilier McWilliam stood opposite him, stony-faced, until the officers disappeared inside the tent.

"All right, mate?" McWilliam asked Jan. "Let the ossifers work things out, and then we can all go home, eh?"

The man's accent and language baffled Jan, but he understood the message. "That would be best," he agreed.

He heard raised voices inside when Winsloe asked Cronje why he had not informed him about the armistice.

"The circumstances were beyond my control," Cronje replied.

McWilliam looked gaunt after months on short rations, but his uniform was impeccable, albeit threadbare, and he grinned and winked.

"Better them arguing than us firing at each other, eh?" McWilliam said.

Jan nodded, wondering if this man had shot at him in their late abortive attack. He smiled back, slightly nervous in case the soldier attacked him with his bayonet.

"We'll leave the ossifers to it, eh?" McWilliam said.

Jan smiled again, only understanding a few words. "Ja," he replied.

After an hour, Winsloe left the tent, leaving his junior officers behind.

"They'll be working out the final terms," McWilliam relaxed when his commanding officer stalked away. "You lads fought well, didn't you?"

"We fought well," Jan struggled over the words. "We thought you would surrender weeks ago."

"Not us, chum," McWilliam replied. "We're the Royal Scots Fusiliers, see? We hold on to the last." He grinned without any animosity.

"Don't you hate us?" Jan asked.

"Hate you?" McWilliam seemed confused by the question. "Bless you, no. Why should we hate you?"

"We are your enemy," Jan said slowly.

The Fusilier considered for a moment. "Aye, maybe, but we don't hate you. Fighting's our job, see. It's what we do. We'll try and kill you in the war, but once there's peace, it's all friends again."

"You live by fighting?" It was a concept Jan found strange.

"It's a job," McWilliam was suddenly serious. "It's better than starving on the streets or begging outside publics," he said.

Jan studied the man, seeing his small stature and pinched look of long-term poverty, and wondered that the richest and most powerful Empire in the world should raise such people.

"Anyway," McWilliam said. "You lads are pretty decent to the wounded and the prisoners."

"So are the British," Jan said slowly.

McWilliam grinned, showing discoloured teeth. "From what I've heard," he said, "the Paythans murdered their prisoners slowly. Bloody savages, them." He lifted his head as Jan wondered who the Paythans were. "Watch out, chum. The ossifers are coming out." The Fusilier stiffened to attention, facing his front and with his face expressionless. Jan watched as Lieutenants Rundle and Buskus left the tent.

"You can go now, Jan," Johannes said as the officers dismissed the Fusilier sentry.

"What's happening, Pa?" Jan asked.

"The garrison has surrendered," Johannes said. "We have won."

"Can we go home? Back to Nuwe Hoop Plaas?"

"We can go home," Johannes confirmed. "Engela will be glad to see you."

Jan had expected to feel elation when the Burghers won the war, but instead, it was relief that surged through him. He looked away. "That is good," he said. He did not know why he felt like crying rather than cheering.

Johannes put a hand on Jan's shoulder. "Go back to your quarters, Jan, and tell Abraham. Drink a cup of coffee together."

"Yes, Pa," Jan forced a smile. Abraham was always cheerful company.

POTCHEFSTROOM, 21ST MARCH 1881

Jan stood beside Abraham as the garrison left the fort. A tall officer held the Union Flag at the head of the column, and the red-coated soldiers, haggard and gaunt but still at attention, marched smartly out.

Theunis began to jeer but stopped when nobody joined him.

Konrad stood beside General Cronjé with a slight sneer on his face.

"There are fewer *Rooinecks* than I thought," Abraham said.

Jan agreed. "We can go home now." He watched the women and children at the rear of the British column and wondered how he would feel if his mother or Engela were stuck in a besieged fort for months.

Abraham smiled. "I had cows ready to calve. The calves will be agile when I return."

"We had cows calving as well," Jan said. "It will be good to get back to farming." The fort was empty now, a slice of history that would never return.

I will tell my children of the day we forced the British from Potchefstroom. They will listen to my stories and believe I am a hero. They will not know I was cold, tired, muddy, and afraid. I can never tell them I was afraid.

CHAPTER 16

NEWCASTLE, NATAL, MARCH 1881

"You will remember I said I might have a job for the Natal Dragoons," Hook said, leaning back in his chair.

Andrew nodded. The series of defeats had been a chastening experience, shaking his confidence in British military expertise. "Yes, sir."

"You will also remember that we still have garrisons within the Transvaal."

"I do, sir," Andrew said.

"Swartspruit, in particular, concerns us," Hook said. "The smallest and most remote of all our Transvaal garrisons."

"Why are we concerned, sir?" Andrew asked.

Hook stepped to the large-scale map of Southern Africa on the wall. "Here is the Transvaal," he said. "And here is Swartspruit." He pointed to a point in the northwest, near the ill-defined border. "It is a hot, dry place, only a hundred miles from the Kalahari Desert."

Andrew nodded. "Yes, sir." He eyed the map. "That area

looks very sparsely populated. Why do we have a garrison out there?"

Hook uncharacteristically hesitated before he replied. "We have been using Swartspruit to conduct geological surveys," he said. "You may know we pre-empted the Germans by taking over Walvis Bay a few years ago. It's the most convenient port on the southwest African coast and far better in our hands than in Bismarck's." Hook grimaced.

"Yes, sir," Andrew said.

"We want to ensure there are no more mineralogical surprises in the area," Hook explained. "Hence, we have a geologist working in the area. We must forestall the Germans, as the Prussian chancellor is continental Europe's most powerful and dangerous man."

"The Germans are becoming as troublesome as the French, sir," Andrew said.

"More so," Hook said dryly. "Their industrial strength is growing faster than ours, and their army is the best in the world." He glanced at the door and lowered his voice. "I'll give you a comparison, Baird. General Colley, one of our most intelligent generals, lost three battles to a rag-tag collection of African farmers. Over the last few years, the German Army has defeated both Austria and France, two major powers. Their victory over Austria took a few weeks and over France six months." Hook shook his head in wonder. "Only six months to defeat what was the foremost military nation in the world."

"Yes, sir," Andrew thought it best to change the subject. "I thought the truce with the Transvaal made provisions for the besieged garrisons, sir."

"You won't find Swartspruit mentioned in any document, Baird." Hook gave a wry smile and altered his tone. "We have a man in that little *dorp* that we want safely back. We don't want him to fall into Boer hands, and still less do we want the Boers to give him to the Germans."

"Would the Boers do that, sir?"

"Perhaps." Hook leaned forward. "You are an unconventional soldier, Baird, and the son of an equally unconventional soldier. You have campaigned in Africa for years, ride well, and shoot better than most. I want you to take a group of volunteers, say a dozen men from your Dragoons, break the Boer blockade of Swartspruit and bring this fellow back to British territory."

Andrew drew in his breath. "There are many colonials who know the Transvaal and are more experienced in that sort of warfare than I am, sir."

"I am aware of that," Hook said. "I also know you are very young for the task, but I have chosen you. Buller speaks highly of your abilities, and you have experience fighting the Boers." He held Andrew's gaze before continuing. "I have another order for you, Captain."

"What's that, sir?"

"I want you to ensure the Boers do not capture this man or get their hands on whatever documents he may be carrying."

"Sir?" Andrew did not hide his confusion.

"If it appears the Boers may capture this man, Baird, I want you to kill him." Hook's eyes did not waver.

Andrew was silent for a few moments. "I'm not an assassin, sir."

"Your duty is to the queen and country, Baird."

"Murdering people is not my duty," Andrew said quietly.

"Let's hope it does not come to that," Hook replied.

Andrew stirred restlessly. "Who is this man, sir, and why is he so important?"

Hook waited for a moment. "His name is Charles Abercrombie, but I can't tell you more than that, I'm afraid." He smiled without humour. "It's not as bad as you think, Captain. You won't be entirely alone in the Transvaal. You will lead a fast, very mobile force of horsemen to rescue Mr Abercrombie, but I'll also send a larger force complete with artillery to back you up."

"That's good, sir," Andrew said.

"You'll take a heliograph, and when you pick up Abercrombie

and reach this spot," Hook jabbed his finger onto the map, "you'll send a message south and east. Our men will pick it up and meet you with horse, foot, and guns."

Andrew stepped closer to the map. "Why that spot, sir?"

"It is easily identifiable with two nearly identical *kopjes* standing side by side," Hook said. "Or so my informants tell me. I'll give you the coordinates and a marked map. I'll also send you a fellow named Turner, who could be useful."

Andrew studied the map. "Let me get this clear, sir. You wish me to take a small patrol, ride halfway across Africa to rescue a man I don't know, and be prepared to kill him rather than allow the Boers to capture him. There are an unknown number of angry Boers besieging their position and possibly some Germans, any of whom will kill us without warning or regret."

Hook gave his slow smile, with his eyes crinkling in his head. "Yes, that's about the size of it, Baird. When can you be ready to start?"

"I'll need to speak to my men first," Andrew said. "I'll explain the situation and see if there are any volunteers."

Volunteers? With the war all but over, who the devil will volunteer to go back into danger? And who is this Abercrombie fellow that everybody seems to want?

JAN STOPPED AT THE ENTRANCE TO NUWE HOOP PLAAS. "Home again," he pulled up his horse and looked around. "It seems like we've been away for years. I never want to leave the farm again."

"It's only been a few months," Johannes said. "And you returned with Mannie."

"I only stayed one night," Jan reminded him, smiling as they neared the farmhouse. He knew every tree, every fold of ground, and every rock of this land. Each square yard held memories of boyhood adventures and misadventures. He took a deep breath, savouring his home. His father and grandfather had broken this land from the wilderness, and he would farm it and raise his children here.

Aletta stood at the door with her arms folded and a small smile playing on the edges of her mouth. Mannie stood behind her, still pale and thin but looking better than he had for months.

Aletta held Johannes' gaze for a long moment before switching her attention to her son. "Engela is here, Jan," she said.

Jan tried to appear unconcerned as he dismounted and threw his horse's reins to a servant. Aletta stepped aside as Jan ran into the house.

"We are back, Aletta," Johannes said, "and I have brought guests."

"They are welcome," Aletta said.

"This is Konrad Bramigan, a friend from Prussia," Johannes said. "And this gentleman is Theunis Steenekamp, whose family have been merchants in Groenburg since the Great Trek."

Both men raised their hats to Aletta.

"I know the Steenekamps," Aletta said. "I know your sister Alice, *Meneer* Steenekamp. She often speaks of you."

Theunis raised his hat again.

"I do not know your family, *Meneer* Bramigan," Aletta eyed him. "But I am sure they are respectable people."

Konrad dismounted, clicked his heels together and gave a formal bow. "I assure you, madam, that my family is amongst the finest in Prussia."

Aletta nodded. "I believe you, *meneer*," she said. "Have we defeated the British, Johannes?"

"We have," Johannes replied. "Their Prime Minister has requested a ceasefire and promised they will leave our country."

Aletta nodded. "Dolinde, Karl's wife, will be pleased." She hugged Johannes briefly, aware the visitors were watching. "Coffee?" she asked, "or something stronger for men home from the war?"

"What do you have?" Konrad asked. "Schnapps? Brandy?"

"We have *mampoer*," Aletta told him.

"I shall try some of your *mampoer*," Konrad decided.

Engela met Jan in the kitchen, stepped towards him and stopped, slightly awkward in his company after so many weeks apart.

"Hello, Jan," she said quietly.

Jan echoed her shyness. "Hello, Engela," he replied. They looked at each other for a long moment. "It's good to see you again," Jan said.

"You too. How long are you back for?" Engela frowned as she examined him. "You're very thin."

"It's the war. I'll soon be back to normal," Jan said. "I'm back for good." He struggled for words. "I've missed you."

Engela nodded and stepped aside as Aletta ushered the others into the house.

"This way, gentlemen!"

Mampoer was home-distilled brandy, generally made from peaches, although the van Collier family made theirs from marula, a local wild fruit. The Nuwe Hoop Plaas *mampoer* was infamous across the western Transvaal for its potency, so even Karl, a man known for his drinking ability, called it lethal.

"However bad you feel," Karl had said after drinking a glass of Aletta's mampoer, "this stuff will make you feel worse."

"I am used to schnapps," Konrad said as Aletta poured him a generous measure. "And champagne and fine wine, of course."

"I have never tried schnapps," Aletta said. "We only drink here on special occasions."

Jan watched surreptitiously as Konrad tasted the mampoer. Rather than a cautious sip, he threw the contents back in a dramatic single swallow.

"That is good!" Konrad said and proffered his glass for more. He looked around the simple house. "I thought your farm would be larger," he said. "The house is small."

"It is sufficient for our needs," Aletta said defensively. Nobody had ever criticised her home before.

Jan frowned at Konrad's words. He had never thought of Nuwe Hoop Plaas as anything other than home. Now, he looked at the farmhouse through the eyes of a man who had seen more of the world. Oblong in shape, the house was built of plain, roughly baked bricks with a roof of mixed thatch and corrugated iron. Jan compared his home with some of the houses he had seen in Groenburg and Potchefstroom and realised Nuwe Hoop Plaas was functional without aesthetic beauty. The *stoep* provided shade and a place to sit in the evenings, while a prickly fence contained a handful of fruit trees.

Konrad nodded. "It is suitable for the Transvaal," he agreed. He placed his glass on the simple deal table and smiled at Engela, clicking his heels in a crisp bow. "And the women here are more beautiful than any in Prussia or elsewhere."

Jan looked at the home-made chairs and the shelf with the highly polished warming pans and brass candlesticks. Apart from the beds, a chest, and the leather-bound Bible, that was all the furniture the house possessed. *It is all we need,* Jan told himself. *Lord Jesus did not live in a mansion.* He looked at Konrad, suddenly aware of his home's simplicity.

He saw Engela smiling at Konrad's words and felt a surge of disquiet. Konrad was tall, elegant, wealthy, and refined, a gentleman who had seen half the world.

"I am going to visit Goeie Weiding," Jan announced. "I will take Engela with me." Goeie Weiding was the farm where Engela and Abraham lived with their widowed mother.

Aletta glanced at Johannes, who nodded. "Ja, that is good," Aletta said. Before the war, she would have trusted her son to behave with Engela, but he had returned a man with deep knowledge in his eyes. "Be careful."

"It is all right, *Tante* Aletta," Engela said, touching Aletta's sleeve. She understood Aletta's warning.

"Ja, it will be all right," Aletta agreed. "Take care of him, Engela."

Jan waited until Engela mounted her horse, and they rode over the familiar land. He glanced across to her, aware life was no longer as simple as it had once appeared.

"It is good to be home," Jan said.

Engela smiled. "It is good to have you back," she agreed. "What happened at the war? Did you shoot many *Rooinecks*?"

Jan thought of the things he had seen. "I shot some," he said, remembering the rain, the mud, the horror, and the sudden fear that had unmanned him during the abortive attack on the British fort.

"Tell me your adventures," Engela asked.

Jan rode in silence for a few moments, enjoying the openness of the veld. "We had some battles," he said. He had waited for his time alone with Engela, but now he could not find any words. The memories were too close and too intense to share. How could he talk to gentle Engela about shooting men and watching them die? Or feeling sick with fear when the British shot at him?

"Did you meet any other girls?" Engela asked coyly.

"No," Jan said. "I did not meet any other girls." He remembered the gaunt women who had survived the siege of Potchefstroom with their haunted eyes and sunken faces. He could not tell Engela about them or the desperate prostitute in Potchefstroom who offered her wasted body for bread. Engela would never understand.

"Were you at Majuba?" Engela asked. "I heard we won a great victory at Majuba."

"We won a great victory at Majuba," Jan confirmed. "I was not there."

"Oh?" Engela looked at him with raised eyebrows and a new heat in her eyes. "Where were you?"

Engela knows where I was. "I had to take Mannie home to Nuve Hoop Plaas," Jan said. "He was sick."

"Ah. You were at Nuve Hoop Plaas," Engela said with an

increasingly tight voice. "Did you not think of coming over to see me? It is only an hour's ride."

"I had to return to the commando," Jan explained weakly.

"You did not think I might be worrying about Abraham and you?" Engela asked. "Or don't my feelings matter?"

"Of course, your feelings matter," Jan replied, not understanding why he was on the defensive.

"Not sufficiently, it seems," Engela retorted. Turning her head, she rode slowly away, with Jan half a length behind.

They were both silent when they arrived at Goeie Weiding. Abraham met them at the gate, smiled broadly, glanced at their faces, and withdrew. "I'll leave you two together," he said diplomatically.

Alizea Hertzog, Engela's mother, watched from an inside doorway, raised her eyebrows at the tension and forced a smile. "You are welcome, Jan."

"Thank you, *Tante*," Jan removed his hat and stood in awkward silence.

Alizea looked at her daughter's closed face. "I see you two have something to work out."

"Maybe, Mother," Engela replied stiffly without looking at Jan.

Alizea nodded slowly. "I will leave you with the *opsitker*. I am going to bed now."

The *opsitker* or sit-up-candle was a Boer tradition that regulated how much a young woman liked the man who courted her. The girl's parents retired to bed, leaving the young couple alone in the *voorkamer*, the front room. The girl brought a candle, with the couple left alone until it burned itself out. The better the girl liked the boy, the longer the candle she would provide.

Having dreamed of this moment through the long weeks of campaigning, Jan found his mind empty of everything. He felt he no longer belonged in this peaceful environment where nature regulated the day, and people slept in civilised beds. He should be sleeping in a muddy trench, with British bullets crackling past and desperately wounded men screaming for help.

"Here we are," Jan said at last, pushing away the raw memories.

"Ja," Engela replied. "Here we are."

They looked at each other across the table that seemed to stretch forever. Jan extended a hand, struggling to break through the horrors in his mind. "Engela," he said.

"Ja, I am Engela." Engela's hands remained folded neatly in her lap.

Jan looked away, noting the grain of the wood on the table and the hum of insects. He watched Engela leave the room and return with the stump of a small candle, which she placed firmly in the centre of the table.

"Sit, Jan," Engela lit the wick and the flame wavered.

Jan took a deep breath and sat down. The space between them seemed like a vast chasm, and he was more unhappy than he had ever been during the battles with the British. "It is a short candle."

"It is a short candle," Engela agreed. She held his gaze without helping. The candle flame guttered.

"Maybe I had better leave," Jan said. He could hear rifle fire in his head.

"Leave, then," Engela said and blew out the candle.

Jan stood in the darkened room, grabbed his hat, and left the room. He thought he heard Engela crying as he mounted his horse but could not be sure.

ANDREW STUFFED TOBACCO IN HIS PIPE, SAT ON HIS FAVOURITE knoll with a view to the south, and lit a match. He watched the flame for a second and applied it to the tobacco, puffing until he was satisfied the pipe drew.

"I thought I'd find you here," Mariana said from behind him.

"What's happening?"

"I'm going back to the war," Andrew told her. He exhaled blue smoke as she digested his words.

"Oh." Mariana sat at his side, folding her skirt beneath her. "When?"

"Very soon," Andrew replied without looking at her. "And that leaves me with a problem."

"What's that, Andrew?" Mariana asked.

"My problem is what to do with you," Andrew said. "Last time I was away, you had servants to look after you. The time before, you had Briggs, and prior to that, you ended up in the guardhouse." He looked sideways at her through a cloud of smoke. "Next time, I might find you on Robben Island."

Mariana started. "That's a terrible place," she said.

"So I've heard," Andrew agreed.

They were silent for a while, with Mariana twisting her hands together.

"I can't help it," Mariana said at last. "I have nightmares, and sometimes the memories come to me during the day as well. They're so vivid that I feel I am back there, and I just stand and stare into space."

"I've seen you," Andrew reminded her. "I don't know what's best for you."

"I'll be all right," Mariana said bravely. "But I wish you weren't going."

Andrew nodded slowly. "I'd take you with me if it weren't so dangerous."

"I don't mind the danger," Mariana replied quickly. "Better danger than Robben Island."

"There might be fighting," Andrew added more tobacco to his pipe. He stared over the landscape without seeing the hills, farms, and forests as he wondered what to do with Mariana.

"I won't get in the way," Mariana promised. "Take me with you, Andrew. Please take me with you."

"If I get killed up there," Andrew said, "what will you do?"

"If you get killed up there," Mariana twisted the question, "and I'm down here, what will I do? The authorities will stick me in Robben Island until I rot away of old age or hang myself."

Andrew grunted. He knew Mariana was correct. She was a woman of the outdoors. Born and bred on a farm beside the Tugela River, she lived for the fresh air and sunshine. The few days shut up in Fort Amiel's guardroom had been bad enough; if the authorities locked her in the asylum at Robben Island indefinitely, Andrew doubted her mind could cope.

"Damn it all," Andrew said. "What a bloody, bloody mess everything is."

"I'm causing you complications," Mariana said.

"No," Andrew tried to reassure her. "It's not your fault, Mariana. We'll work something out."

"I'm not going to Robben Island," Mariana said desperately. "I'd rather join Elaine under the ground. Please don't send me there."

Andrew put a hand on her shoulder. "I won't send you to Robben Island," he said. He saw a small vein throbbing in her throat and heard her short, shallow breathing. "That's a promise."

"Where will I go?" Mariana asked. "I can't stay in your house forever; people are already talking."

"We'll work something out," Andrew said. *I have no idea what to do with you, Mariana.*

She edged closer, with the shadows flitting across her eyes as she remembered the horrors from her past. "I don't want you to go back to war."

"I know," Andrew said. He shook his head. "I don't want to go back either."

"Will you leave me with William again?" Mariana asked.

"William?" Andrew repeated the name.

"William Briggs," Mariana explained.

"Oh," Andrew had never considered Briggs having a Christian name. He was only Briggs, the self-contained, efficient servant. Andrew knew nothing about Briggs except his duties. "Yes, I'll probably leave you with William Briggs."

Leaving Mariana in Briggs' care will alleviate one temporary problem, Andrew thought. *It will not solve the long-term worry about what to do with her. I can't look after her forever, although I'll do what I can for Elaine's sake. And for Mariana's.*

"Thank you," Mariana said.

They sat side by side in miserable silence, each lost in their own thoughts.

"Let's go home," Mariana said. "It's getting cold here."

Andrew finished his pipe, tapped out the embers, and ground them beneath his heel. They walked home, with Mariana reaching for Andrew but dropping her hand before making contact. Deep in his worries, Andrew did not notice.

"How was Engela?" Aletta asked when Jan returned. "You were not long."

"No, I was not long," Jan agreed. He was aware of Konrad watching him, with a half-smile hovering on his lips.

"Was she unwell?" Aletta asked.

"She was well," Jan replied.

"Ah," Aletta understood. "You had a disagreement." She touched Jan's shoulder. "That is normal, Jan. You know that your father and I disagree from time to time. It means nothing."

"Yes, Mother," Jan moved away quickly. He did not want to talk about Engela with his mother. He did not want to talk about Engela at all. He wanted to curl up in a ball or ride across the veld or do anything except talk about Engela. He hoped the war would start again so he could forget his troubles by fighting the *Rooinecks*.

"Has she decided you are too young for her?" Konrad asked.

"No," Jan told him angrily. "She did not decide that I was too young." He wished people would leave him alone.

Konrad nodded in false sympathy. "Women are hard to understand, Jan," he said. "It takes years of experience. Some women need a firm hand, others gentleness and encouragement."

"I don't understand what Engela wants," Jan admitted.

Konrad patted his shoulder. "No young man understands what a woman wants." He smiled. "Would you like me to talk to her for you?"

"No," Jan said. "I do not want you to talk to her at all." Lifting his hat from the table, he threw open the door and stormed from the house. Nobody saw the tears he dashed from his eyes as he ran into the veld.

"I WANT VOLUNTEERS FOR A DANGEROUS MISSION," ANDREW announced. The Natal Dragoons stood in a semi-circle around him with a faint breeze stirring the mimosa trees and a korhaan bird scolding them from a topmost branch.

He knew his men by name, character, and habit. They viewed him through cynical eyes in faces burned nut-brown by the sun and wind. Spalding, the most intellectual, listened intently; Morrison chewed a wad of tobacco while Trooper Kerr tamped down the bowl of his pipe. Ogden cleaned his rifle, half-smiling as Sergeant Meek stood at attention, immaculate in everything he did.

"How dangerous, sir?" Kerr asked.

"Suicidal," Andrew replied cheerfully.

"Where are you taking us?"

"I am not allowed to tell you," Andrew replied.

"Why are we going?"

"To relieve a beleaguered British garrison," Andrew told him.

"I thought there was a truce, sir," Sergeant Meek said. "Have the Boers broken their agreement already?"

"There is a truce," Andrew decided to release a little more information. "But some Afrikander Bond Boers are besieging an isolated garrison to capture an important person. We must ride across the Transvaal, relieve the garrison and the personage, and bring everybody back to British territory."

"How many men do you want, sir?" Meek asked.

"A dozen," Andrew said. "That's a handy figure, yet small enough to vanish in the veld."

"When do we leave, sir?" Meek asked.

Andrew smiled. "Are you volunteering, Sergeant?"

"Yes, sir. I think we all are."

"Thank you, gentlemen." The Dragoons' loyalty touched Andrew. "I need men who can ride in all conditions and outshoot the Boers. I also want men capable of shoeing a horse and navigating by the stars out in the bush."

"That's the Dragoons out then, sir," Meek said, "we'd get lost crossing the road on a sunny day," and the men laughed, knowing they were all capable frontiersmen.

"I thought as much," Andrew said. "That's why I'm going to the 15th Hussars next. I've heard they are at least half-decent horsemen." He expected the barrage of abuse and whistles from his loyal men. "We'll start some intensive training tomorrow, lads. You're looking soft and flabby." He grinned at the Dragoons' sudden expressions of dismay.

CHAPTER 17

FORT AMIEL, NEWCASTLE, NATAL

Major Fotheringham leaned back in his cane chair and surveyed Andrew over the rim of his champagne glass. "So, you're Lieutenant Baird of the Natal Dragoons, are you? Captain Baird, now, I hear."

"That's right, sir," Andrew said.

The officers' mess was busy as scarlet-coated men smoothed their whiskers, downed champagne and brandy, and read the newspapers. Mess waiters scurried around busily as the barman poured drinks as if the officers were celebrating a victory rather than living in the wake of a defeat.

Fotheringham nodded. "I've heard some of the men talking about you. They call you Up-and-at-'em because of your exploits against the Zulus."

Andrew did not reply. He had not sought a nickname and had no pleasure in hearing it.

"Well, Up-and-at-'em, let me tell you that I don't listen to the other ranks' gossip. They are only here to obey orders."

"Yes, sir," Andrew had met men like Fotheringham before,

brave, sporting, probably an excellent shot and horseman but without any knowledge of the men he led.

"Were you at Sandhurst, Captain?"

"Briefly, sir," Andrew replied.

"The briefer the better," Fotheringham said. "All that theoretical nonsense is a waste of time. Now, listen to me. I've been serving the queen for thirty years, and I tell you this: Ignore what the other ranks say and ignore any officer who's only served in India. They only know how to fight Indian troops."

"I heard the Afghans and Pashtuns are excellent fighting men, sir," Andrew said.

"Nonsense," Fotheringham barked. "They are not. Now, take our infantry. They sign on for short service, six years, which is hardly long enough to break them in. Yet," Fotheringham lifted a finger as if he were about to reveal some infinite wisdom. "After six years, they can hardly return to civilian life. We have them, Baird. We have them here." He opened his left fist and closed it again. "Keep the men well in hand, Baird. If you give them too much leeway, they'll find a pub and drink themselves into insensibility. Ensure they fire in volleys on the word of command, or they'll fire wildly without aim or direction."

"I see, sir," Andrew said solemnly.

"They're brave enough when officers order them what to do," Fotheringham said, finishing his champagne. "Otherwise, they're emotional, irrational, and lazy." He stood up, hiccupped, and walked unsteadily away, leaving Andrew alone.

God help the army if that's the standard of leadership, Andrew thought. *In the world of the blind, a one-eyed man is king. In the world of British officers, even mediocrity may be seen as genius. No wonder the Boers ran rings around us.*

The trooper approached Andrew as he stepped outside his quarters. "Captain Baird?" He was middle-sized, with a square, sun-darkened face.

"That's me, trooper."

"General Hook sends his compliments sir, and says I have to hand this to you." The trooper passed over a sealed envelope.

"Thank you," Andrew accepted the envelope. "Did the general tell you to wait for a reply?"

"Yes, sir," the trooper said.

"Very well." Andrew broke the seal, opened the envelope, and read the letter.

"Captain Baird,

I suggest you include Trooper Turner, the bearer of this letter, in your expedition. You might find him a useful addition. Turner knows Abercrombie by sight and may help persuade him to accompany you.

Hook."

Andrew grunted. "Welcome to the Natal Dragoons, Turner." A suggestion from a general was tantamount to an order. Only a very foolish junior officer would refuse.

"Thank you, sir," Turner said.

"General Hook says you know Mr Abercrombie."

"Only by sight, sir," Turner said.

"General Hook also said that I might find you useful. What skills do you have?"

Turner was about thirty-three, with nothing distinctive about him except a light of intelligence in his steady eyes and an aura of self-confidence surprising for a typical British trooper. *Who are you? Hook would not send me an ordinary soldier.*

"I rode with Buller in Zululand, sir," Turner said.

"So did I, Turner," Andrew told him. "I can't remember your face."

"I remember yours, sir," Turner replied.

Andrew smiled faintly. "That war already seems long ago. If you rode with Buller, I'm sure you'll fit in."

"Thank you, sir."

"Go and report to Sergeant Meek at the Dragoons' barracks," Andrew ordered. "I am sure he'll find you something to do."

"Yes, sir." Turner gave a smart salute and marched away.

Andrew watched him for a moment, shook his head, and walked to the stables to check the horses. *Turner looks very regimental for one of Redvers' Bullers' boys.*

"A RIDER IS COMING TO THE FARM," ALETTA CALLED FROM THE edge of the field. "One of the native servants told me."

Jan had been working with the cattle, where a cow had a difficult birth. He had spent all morning helping the mother and had no interest in any visitor. He barely glanced up. "Pa can deal with him."

The horseman reined up in front of the house, with dust rising all around and froth and sweat covering the horse. He dismounted immediately, removed his hat to Aletta, and pounded off the dust against his leg.

"Is your husband at home, *vrou*?"

"Ja, *meneer*," Aletta nodded to the north. "You will find him out in the fields. My son Jan will take you."

Jan recognised the rider. "Adriaan Coetzee, wait a minute, *meneer*, and I will fetch my horse."

Adriaan carried himself with a grim self-assurance that he could face anything the world threw at him, and the rifle at his saddle looked well used.

"Why do you want my father, Adriaan?" Jan asked bluntly as they rode away from the farmhouse.

"It is about politics," Adriaan man said. "And war."

"The war is over," Jan replied. "There is my father with the dun cow."

Johannes straightened slowly to greet the visitor. "Many of

my cows are calving," he said. "Good day, Adriaan. You are welcome to our farm."

"Thank you, Johannes," Adriaan took off his hat.

"And what is your business here, Adriaan?" Johannes asked, sweeping his hand around to indicate his cattle. "As you can see, I am busy here. My farm needs me."

"So does the republic, *meneer*," Adriaan told him. "The British have a spy in the western Transvaal."

Johannes wiped the blood from his hands on the seat of his trousers. "What is there to spy on here? A few farms, a lot of empty veld, some native kraals, and too many rocks."

Adriaan ran a critical eye over Johannes' cattle. "Come, Johannes. We have been besieging a British garrison in the west for months without success. The spy is inside the *dorp*."

Johannes shook his head. "We have a truce with the British, Adriaan. There are no more sieges."

"This siege was left out of the truce," Adriaan replied. "We do not know why the British should send a spy, so we shall ask him."

"Then ask him, and don't bother honest men at their work." Johannes returned to his calving cow.

"To ask him first, we have to catch him," Adriaan explained. "He has holed himself into the *dorp* with other British around him."

"Which *dorp*?" Johannes asked with a feeling of resignation. "I do not want to return to war."

"Swartspruit," Adriaan told him. "You know it."

"I know it," Johannes confirmed. "There's nothing much there to besiege."

"I agree," Adriaan said. "That is also suspicious. The Groenburg Commando is closest, and with your help, we can end the siege and find out about this *Rooineck*. Will you come, Johannes?"

Johannes glanced at Jan, who stood nearby. "Did you hear that, Jan? This man wants us to ride to Swartspruit to catch a British spy."

"I heard," Jan replied briefly. "When do we leave?"

"Fetch my horse, Jan; she is knee-haltered a quarter of a mile away."

When Jan left, Johannes spoke to Adriaan. "Do you need me to help you find Swartspruit?"

Adriaan shook his head, smiling faintly. "We need all the local men we can raise, Johannes, and those of the Afrikander Bond who want to ride this far."

Jan brought Johannes' horse. "When are we leaving, Pa?"

"Are you ready to go back on commando so soon?" Johannes asked. "What about Engela?"

"Men go on commando, Pa," Jan said. "Engela is only a woman." *It is better to fight the Rooinecks than wait for a woman who no longer cares for me.*

Johannes nodded. "Do not disregard Engela so easily, Jan. She has not forgotten you."

"When are we leaving, Pa?" Jan repeated.

"We'll tell your mother first," Johannes said, knowing he would not enjoy that duty.

"Ah," Aletta looked at Jan without hiding her anxiety. "It is hard having two men in the house." Neither of them mentioned Mannie. She glanced at Konrad, who had been listening from the corner of the building. "You will be going as well, Konrad."

"In a day or two," Konrad said easily. "I have a report to write."

"To whom?" Aletta asked.

"To my superiors in Berlin," Konrad said. "I have to make a monthly report on my findings in the Zuid-Afrikaanse Republiek to justify my being here."

"I see," Aletta said. "How will you get it to them?"

"You will have heard of the Berlin Missionary Society?" Konrad said.

"I have," Aletta confirmed. "Alexander Merensky is a good man. He stays in Botshabelo, where he tries to Christianise the Sotho tribes."

"That is so," Konrad agreed. "Have you heard of the Wonderdorp Missionary Station?"

"Wonderdorp is in the Western Transvaal," Aletta said. "I know nothing about a missionary there."

"Wonderdorp is not a real missionary station, and the Berlin Missionary Society knows nothing about it," Konrad said. "It is the station where I send my reports, and they forward them to the coast and on to Berlin."

"Does that mean the Germans are already in the Republic?" Aletta asked.

Konrad smiled. "We are here. Soon, we will have colonies all over Africa to challenge the British and French."

"I see," Aletta stepped towards Johannes. "When will you men be riding away?"

"Very soon," Johannes replied.

"I'll make some bread for you," Aletta said.

ALETTA WAS IN THE DAIRY WHEN SHE SAW ENGELA ARRIVE.

"Good morning, Engela," Aletta called. "Come in."

"Abraham has gone back on commando," Engela entered the dairy. "Have your men gone to the wars?"

"Johannes and Jan have gone," Aletta was glad to recognise disappointment in Engela's face. *Good,* she thought. *She is angry with my son, but the true feeling also remains.* "Mannie wants to go, but he is still weak." She jerked her head backwards. "The Prussian is still here."

"Konrad?" Engela said.

"Ja, Konrad," Aletta confirmed.

"I rather liked Konrad," Engela said.

Do not play your games with me, Aletta thought. *I am not Jan.* "He can be very charming," she conceded.

"I thought so, too," Engela smiled as Konrad emerged from the house.

"Good morning, Engela," Konrad clicked his heels and gave a formal bow.

"Good morning, Konrad," Engela returned.

Aletta stepped between them. "Konrad had a very important report to complete," she said. "As soon as he finished, he will join the men." She smiled at the Prussian. "Is that not correct, Konrad?"

"That is correct," Konrad confirmed, his gaze roaming from Engela's head to her feet and back.

"That is good," Engela said. "A man must do his duty."

"If he does not," Aletta said softly. "He is less than a man." She felt Konrad stir behind her and knew her words had been successful. Konrad would leave the farm to join the Groenburg Commando.

ANDREW VIEWED HIS MEN WITH GRIM SATISFACTION. EXCEPT for Turner, all came from the Natal Dragoons, men whom he trusted with his life. He had sent Trooper Spalding for intensive training in the heliograph and knew his men would not let him down.

"All right, lads," Andrew said. "Most of you know me. We've fought together before, but I'll remind you of the rules. I am in charge, and the final decision and responsibility ends with me."

The Dragoons nodded, some smiling and others looking serious.

"This mission is a bit different," Andrew told them. Now, he had gathered his volunteers, he decided to tell them more. "We are riding to a place called Swartspruit in the Western Transvaal. Despite the ceasefire, a strong commando of Boers, members of the Afrikander Bond, are besieging a small British garrison, with some important fellow the Boers want to capture."

The men nodded again. They knew that wars never ended as tidily as politicians and newspapers claimed.

"We will relieve the garrison and bring them safely through the Transvaal to British territory," Andrew said. "Are there any questions?"

"How strong is the garrison, sir?" Sergeant Meek asked.

"We don't know," Andrew replied. "We know there are no regular British troops there, only local volunteers and civilians."

"If there are no soldiers there, sir, why are the Boers besieging it?" Meek asked. "Is it because of this important fellow?"

"I believe so, Sergeant," Andrew said. "But ours is not to reason why; ours is just to do or die."

"Yes, sir," Meek did not question further.

"Sir," Kerr asked, "How many Boers are there?"

"We don't know that either," Andrew replied. "The Boers don't have a command structure like ours. Their men seem to arrive and leave as they please or fight when they choose. They might have a hundred men one day and a thousand the next." He paused for a moment. "One thing is certain. If these are Afrikander Bond Boers, they will be hardy and determined."

"A thousand Afrikander Bond Boers, and how many of us, sir?" Lieutenant Fletcher asked. "Fourteen? That should be a fair match."

Andrew smiled. "I doubt there will be a thousand, Lieutenant. With the current truce, most Boers will be keen to return to their farms. There may be a couple of hundred or even less."

Fletcher gave an ironic smile. "Only about eight-to-one then, sir. That's much better."

Andrew laughed. "I'm glad you think so, Lieutenant! When we relieve the siege, we will head for this point," he showed them the twin kopjes on the map. "Once there, Spalding will heliograph to the east, where a larger British force will be waiting. We'll rendezvous with them and return together. Any questions?"

The men studied the map. "Memorise the details," Andrew

said. "If I fall, any of you might have to take command. Whatever happens, the Boers must never capture the civilian we rescue."

Turner was not alone in nodding solemnly.

"Right, lads," Andrew altered his tone. "Before we begin, let's have a few reminders of the tricks of the trade. Check your horses; I don't want anybody riding a horse of a distinctive colour. That is an invitation to the Boers; some are phenomenal marksmen and will pick off a rider before he hears the shot."

The men agreed.

Andrew continued. "I know you are all aware of such basic details, but I thought I'd remind you."

"Always best, sir," Meek said. "Some of these lads don't have the brains of a turnip."

Andrew grinned. "That would be a small turnip at best. Secondly, don't bunch up if we get into action. Extended order presents a harder target."

The Dragoons nodded. The late war had reinforced their respect for the Boers' marksmanship.

"Thirdly," Andrew said, "if a long-range shot passes close, don't react. If you ignore the long-range shots, the Boer won't know how good he is and hopefully adjust his range to shoot short or over."

A few of the men nodded.

"All right," Andrew said. "Enough theory. Time for some practical training."

After long periods away from his men, Andrew decided to reacquaint himself with the intricacies of command. He had no intention of tormenting the Dragoons with all the formality of British cavalry drill but thought a return to some discipline might benefit them.

For the following two days, Andrew had his men advancing by sections and forming again, wheeling left and right, dismounting and remounting, firing at moving targets and changing front. After the initial sweat, toil, and frustration,

Andrew eased the pressure. His men had lived most of their lives in the saddle, and he surmised that nothing would blunt their individuality more surely than repetitive manoeuvres.

"We all have Martini-Henry carbines," Andrew reminded his Dragoons. "We'll carry seventy rounds in our pouches and wear bandoliers with an extra seventy cartridges. If you want to carry a rifle with a longer range, that's entirely your choice. Likewise, if you wish to carry a revolver, then do so, but remember we're embarking on a long ride, and every ounce of extra weight will tell on the horse."

"Will we take spare horses, sir?" Kerr asked.

"Yes," Andrew replied. "We might need to ride hard." He ordered that each Dragoon carry a cloak, blanket, and rations for himself and his horses.

"We'll pick up food en route," Andrew told his men. "But not from farms. We aim to pass unseen if possible, so fishing and hunting are the order of the day, with packhorses carrying extra food, ammunition, and medical equipment. The Boer commandos travel light, and so will we."

"How about loot, sir?" Ogden asked with a villainous smile. "Are we allowed to relieve the Boers of their excess possessions?"

"No," Andrew shook his head. "We have a truce with the Transvaalers, so they are not our enemy. No looting." He paused for a moment's reflection. "That does not apply to anybody who attacks us. If a Boer fires on us and we kill him, his horse and any valuables on the man's body are ours. We don't touch personal letters and photographs, but we'll take any official documents back to Natal for the experts to analyse."

Andrew gave the Dragoons a moment to consider his words. "All right, gentlemen. Dismissed."

"I've heard that colonials were better irregular horsemen than British soldiers," Andrew said to Fletcher when the troopers had dispersed. "I disagree. Oh, the colonials are better than town-bred men whose experience of fieldcraft is limited to an annual camp on Salisbury Plain. However, Highland ghillies can stalk with the best of them, and given training or working with the colonials, the potential is still there."

"Even untrained colonials are better than the average Tommy," Fletcher disagreed. "They can read the stars and pick their way across trackless terrain, instinctively avoid the skyline and find dead ground and cover as well as any Boer."

Andrew grinned. "You've been watching the men, Fletcher. Good for you. Now, what we must do is train up our homegrown men to have the same skills."

Fletcher nodded. "Yes, sir. How do we do that?"

"We use the best men to teach the others, including you and me."

"We're officers, sir," Fletcher reminded him. "Should other ranks teach officers? Does that not blur the rank differences?"

"It will, and a damned good thing, too," Andrew said. "Any training will have to be hurried, unfortunately, but anything is better than nothing."

"Yes, sir, and a hell of a lot better than acting as baggage guard," Fletcher said.

Baggage guard was the least popular duty for mounted troops. The men rode in files of two beside a convoy of slow-moving wagons, with scouts posted further out to watch for the commandos. The outriders could get lost in the dark or even keep riding when the convoy stopped, while the men in files could fall asleep on the horse if they were working at night, leading to the horse wandering wherever it willed. If the Boers chose to attack, they would select the least defended section of the convoy, strike and vanish before the escort arrived.

"A lot better," Andrew agreed. "Let's get the men trained up."

However dangerous leading a small unit on a deep penetration mission may be, Andrew preferred the freedom of being in command to the stifling frustration of having some unimaginative senior officer in control. He wondered if he would ever fit into the real army, where strict routine reduced the flexibility of thought.

"A five-hour map reading exercise today," Andrew decided, "followed by some firing practice." He grinned. "Time to get to work, Fletcher."

WITH EACH MAN LEADING A SPARE HORSE LOADED WITH EXTRA ammunition and supplies, Andrew's Natal Dragoons rode out of Newcastle for the north. Knowing that the Boers would watch the main passes, Andrew made a wide detour before he entered the Transvaal. The men quickly adapted to active service as Andrew rotated the outriders every two hours, kept them riding at a steady pace, and frequently stopped to water the horses.

Despite his worry for Mariana, Andrew could not deny his satisfaction at leading his Dragoons. He rode in front, glad to escape the back-aching foot soldier's pace and the perpetual grating dust of an infantry column.

Although the landscape did not alter, Andrew detected a subtle shift in the atmosphere immediately after crossing into the Transvaal. *Perhaps that is an instinct I inherited from my father.* He glanced over his shoulder where his men followed in column of twos, riding easily as the miles soothed past. Even with the ubiquitous film of dust over them, Andrew thought they looked professional, men who belonged in their environment rather than European intruders in Africa. He nodded, satisfied, guided Lancelot to a *koppie*, raised his field glasses, and scanned the surrounding terrain.

A small herd of antelope bounded to the east, presumably disturbed by the Dragoons' scouts. Andrew concentrated on the area until he was satisfied there were no Boers. Shifting his focus, he slowly traversed the land, searching for farms to avoid and watercourses for horses and men. Working with the most experienced Dragoon frontiersmen, he had already selected a route that avoided even the smallest *dorp*, but farms were not marked on the map.

THE SOUND OF BOER RIFLES

Checking the flanks, Andrew looked to the rear and grunted when he saw two figures, distorted by heat and distance, and guessed who they were.

Andrew returned to the Dragoons. "Sergeant Meek!"

"Sir!" Meek rode closer. As dependable as always, he viewed Andrew from under the shade of his broad hat.

"Tell the scouts to extend their range, Sergeant. We're in the Transvaal now."

"Yes, sir," Meek replied.

"Extended order!" Andrew commanded, taking his men in a gliding walk under the glowing sun. He enjoyed the freedom of making the decisions, halting when it was best for his Dragoons, not for the slogging infantry or at the whim of a pedantic silver-haired general. Every half hour, he guided Lancelot to the nearest rise, lifted his field glasses, and surveyed the land.

He saw a ribbon of smoke from a lone farmhouse, the dust a herd of impala kicked up, and the endless yellow-brown plain of the veld.

"A man could get to like it here," Andrew said when he rejoined the Dragoons.

"Could he, sir?" Fletcher wrinkled his nose. "There's nothing here."

Andrew thought of the wind-cropped slopes of the Cheviot Hills, a place he considered home, and grinned. "Maybe that's why I like it," he said. He looked over his men, riding easily with their broad hats and bandoliers, looking as much like Boers as the Boers, sun-browned and confident. Even Turner looked competent in the saddle, although Andrew was not yet convinced that he fitted in.

As the Roman centurion in Matthew said, "I am a man under authority, having soldiers under me: and I say to this man, Go, and he goeth; and to another, Come, and he cometh; and to my servant, Do this, and he doeth it."

Do I like the power of command? Andrew asked himself. *Maybe I* do. *Maybe I am not the free thinker I believed I was, or perhaps the wars have changed me.*

At his next halt to survey the surroundings, Andrew checked behind them and again saw the two dots in the far distance, seemingly crawling across the vast landscape, yet he knew they were moving at the same speed as the Dragoons.

When they stopped to eat, Andrew ensured the pickets were alert.

"I know there's an armistice," he told his men, "But the Burghers may not take kindly to a unit of British soldiers crossing their land."

"We don't take kindly to some Boers besieging one of our outposts during a truce," Fletcher replied, and the men gave a deep-throated laugh.

When Andrew stopped to water the horses, he ensured the men filled their canteens upstream of the animals. The old rules applied: horses first, men second, officers last. Whenever Andrew checked the rear, the two figures were still there, retaining the same distance.

That first day in the Transvaal, the Dragoons camped in a small *sluit*, hidden from the never-ending plain above. The surrounding trees provided shade and shelter, as well as a plethora of birds and insects. Andrew saw a thoughtless Dragoon throw the reins of his horse over a thornbush, but before he spoke, Meek grabbed the unfortunate man.

"Does that bush look like a Dragoon, Ogden?"

"No, Sergeant," Ogden replied.

"We have three half-sections," Meek spoke in a forceful whisper. "Every fourth man is a horseholder. When we dismount, we give him the reins, either in action or when we camp. Is that clear?"

"Yes, Sergeant," Ogden agreed.

"It's basic drill," Meek drove his point home. "The horseholder looks after the mounts. If we were in action and you threw the reins over a bush, and the firing began, the horse would panic, and you'd have a hell of a job controlling it. The Boers would pick you off. Understand?"

"Yes, Sergeant," Ogden said.

"Right," Meek glowered at him. "You're on first picket duty tonight, Ogden."

Andrew hid his smile as he walked away. With Meek as his sergeant, sensible army discipline would continue wherever they were.

OUTSIDE SWARTSPRUIT, WESTERN TRANSVAAL, JUNE 1881.

Jan saw the dust from miles off. "A horseman is riding towards us," he said, sitting on the knoll with his rifle in his right hand, his eyes narrowed against the glare.

Johannes joined him, keeping low. He raised his field glasses. "A single rider," he said after a few minutes. "He rides like a Burgher but could be a British colonial. Here." Johannes passed the field glasses to Jan. "Keep an eye on him. When he gets close, let me know."

Jan raised the field glasses and watched, noting the easy way the man rode, the small, sturdy pony, and the long rifle in the bucket holster beside his saddle. "I think he is a Burgher," he said.

When the man was within a mile, Jan mounted his horse and rode to meet him. He lifted a hand in greeting.

"The Lord be with you," Jan recognised the man from the fighting around Potchefstroom.

The rider pulled up, watching Jan from beneath his terai hat. "And with you." He waited until Jan lifted his hat and did likewise. "What is your name?"

Jan noted the length of the man's beard and the leopard skin band around his terai hat. "I am Jan Van Collier of Nuve Hoop Plaas, *meneer*. I have seen you in various places where we fought the British, but we have never spoken. Nor do I know your name; you are?"

"Christiaan Niekerf." The man spoke without moving the pipe from his mouth. A lifetime of smoking had stained the beard around his mouth a dull yellow-brown while the rest was grey as it flowed to his chest. The leopard skin band around his hat was the only brightness in his attire.

"What do you seek, Oom Christiaan?"

Christiaan did not smile. "Johannes van Collier, the *veldcornet* of the Groenburg Commando," he said.

"My father," Jan explained. "Why do you want him?"

"He commands the only commando still fighting the *Rooinecks*," Christiaan explained. "I fought the *Rooinecks* at Boomplats, Laing's Nek, Ingogo River, and Majuba, and I will fight them until we drive them away. Take me to him."

"This way, *Oom* Christiaan," Jan turned his horse to return to the Boer positions. He could sense Christiaan following him and hear the steady plod of his pony's feet.

"Christiaan Niekerf," Johannes shook the elderly man's hand. "I remember you. You were a Voortrekker and fought with us at Potchefstroom."

"That is correct," Christian agreed.

"You are over sixty years old," Johannes said.

Christiaan nodded. "Ja," he said, "and over seventy. I have lived my allotted three score years and ten."

"The Republic does not require you to go on commando when you are over sixty," Johannes reminded him. "You can go home and live in peace."

"What would the Republic have me do? Waste away watching the grass grow?" Christiaan asked. "It is a man's part to defend his beliefs."

"Do you not have a family, Christiaan?" Johannes asked.

"I have buried three wives and two sons," Christiaan replied. "My daughters have their husbands and families to look after. All that remains is this," he tapped the stock of his rifle.

Johannes glanced at Jan, who was listening. "Then you are welcome, Christiaan. A man with your experience will always be useful."

"This may be my last commando," Christiaan said. "Let it be my best."

Jan thought Christiaan's old eyes were as keen as any hawk when he replaced his rifle in its homemade leather bucket.

"Sir," Kerr rode up to Andrew. "There's somebody following us."

"Is there?" Andrew feigned surprise. "Best see who it is, Kerr."

"Yes, sir," Kerr said. "I think you already know, sir. It's Mariana Maxwell and Briggs, your servant."

"Mariana and Briggs!" Andrew repeated. "What the devil are they doing here?"

"Following us, sir, as far as I can make out," Kerr replied. "Do you want me to send them away?" He gave a crooked smile.

"No, Kerr," Andrew shook his head. "I'd better go myself. Lieutenant Fletcher! You're in command. I'll be back within the hour."

"Yes, sir," Fletcher replied.

As he rode back to fetch Mariana and Briggs, Andrew remembered his father telling him he had been campaigning during the Indian Mutiny, and his future wife, Andrew's mother, had joined them on campaign.

Maybe our family is destined to have spirited women, Andrew thought. *Except Mariana's not my woman,* he reminded himself. *I was going to marry her older sister, and I am only keeping a watchful eye on Mariana until she recovers.*

The two riders looked uncertain as Andrew drew closer. Although Briggs gave a nervous grin and saluted, Andrew ignored him to address the more pugnacious Mariana.

"What are you doing here, Mariana?" Andrew asked as he drew Lancelot to a halt.

"I'm coming with you," Mariana said calmly. "You knew I would."

"I told you not to," Andrew replied. "This is a dangerous mission."

"It's better than Robben Island," Mariana said. She smiled. "It would be noble to take me with you, Andrew. As Tennyson said, better not be at all than not be noble."[1]

Andrew hid his smile, for Mariana had been a prolific reader and quoter of Tennyson before the renegades raided Inglenook. Now, the quotes were few but welcome, a reminder of the bright personality bubbling behind her trauma.

"Come on, then," Andrew sighed.

I had sufficient responsibilities before Mariana appeared, but now she's here, I am happy to have her with me. The Boers won't shoot a woman, and I'll keep her well away from any fighting.

The Dragoons had helped rescue Mariana from her captivity at the end of the Zulu War and greeted her cheerfully.

"Welcome back, Miss Maxwell," Kerr said. "We've missed you."

"Thank you, Mark," Mariana replied.

Others waved and smiled as Mariana rode into the unit. Briggs remained at her back until Andrew ordered him to join the ranks.

"Congratulations, Briggs. You've volunteered to join a forlorn hope.[2] Report to Sergeant Meek, and he'll tell you what to do."

Briggs saluted. "Yes, sir."

WITH MARIANA RIDING IN THE MIDDLE OF THE DRAGOONS, Andrew led them deeper into the Transvaal, frequently consulting his map and checking on landmarks.

"Oh, look at that!" Mariana rode towards Andrew and

pointed forward as a herd of a hundred springbok bounded before the dragoons. Andrew stopped to admire the deer he thought were the most beautiful of South African animals. Triple banded in white, brown, and fawn, the males boasted annulated horns for defence or show.

"This land has some truly noble animals, sir," Fletcher said. "It's a sportsman's paradise."

Andrew nodded. "We agree there."

The springbok caught the human scent, with their fluffy tails lifting straight in the air and white ruffs bristling on every sleek back. They bounced away, springing in the air as they crossed the veld in a display of grace and power. Even the most hardened Dragoon paused to watch the sight.

"Now that's something the people back in Britain will never see," Meek said. "It makes soldiering worthwhile, doesn't it, sir?"

Andrew nodded. "We are blessed sometimes," he agreed. "If we had shot one, we could all have feasted tonight." He saw no irony between his two statements.

"Shall I ride forward and bag one, sir?" Fletcher asked.

Andrew shook his head. "They're well away now, Lieutenant, but thank you for the offer."

They camped overnight with stars filling the high arc of the sky and frost crackling their blankets. Andrew listened to the eerie cries of a jackal and hoped such a notorious scavenger did not come near the camp.

With Mariana sleeping near the shaded fire, the safest place in the camp, Andrew was relatively content. He checked the knee-haltered horses and exchanged a few words with the pickets.

"All right, lads?"

"All right, sir," the pickets had chosen spots where they had a good view of the surrounding terrain as the bright stars illuminated the landscape. In the distance, a kopje showed darkly against the grey background.

If war were always this beautiful, I'd have no complaints. How can there be such serenity when we are carrying weapons to kill our fellow men?

Realising the stars had distracted him, Andrew nodded and moved on. He did not have to teach these veterans anything about watching by night. The jackal called again somewhere in the dark, a reminder that men were not the only predators in this land.

CHAPTER 18

BOER CAMP OUTSIDE SWARTSPRUIT, JUNE 1881

Konrad held his stomach and doubled up. "It's the fever," he said. He crouched on the ground, retching.

Behind the Boers, a small ridge overlooked the settlement of Swartspruit, with three sentinels lying behind bushes and examining the British positions beyond.

"Best rest until it passes," Johannes advised. He had seen many men sick with fever in the last few months. Most recovered and returned to duty. Others succumbed, died, and now filled sad graves on the veld.

"I think so," Konrad agreed. "I have an upset stomach, and my head is swimming, making me dizzy."

"That's not good," Johannes said.

Jan smiled as he walked away. He was on duty later that day, watching over Swartspruit. *I hope it's malaria.*

"Are you fit to continue with the siege?" Johannes asked.

"I cannot continue," Konrad said. "I would be a burden to the other men."

"It might pass in a day or two," Johannes told him solemnly.

"No," Konrad shook his head. "It feels more serious than

that. I'd better get away in case I pass it on to everybody. It could be cholera."

"Cholera is a terrible thing," Johannes agreed. "It can kill a man in hours and spreads quickly. What will you do?"

"I will find a quiet place to recover or die without infecting anybody else," Konrad decided. "That is the honourable course as befits a Prussian officer."

Johannes did not object. "If you think that is best," he said. "I hope you get better and return to the commando." Johannes had long given up on Prussian help, and Konrad added nothing to the military power of the besiegers. He watched as Konrad saddled and mounted his horse, riding away without looking back.

We won't see you again, Johannes said to himself.

"Johannes," Karl slid down from his position on the ridge. "The British have added more men to the defences."

"How can they?" Johannes asked. "We have the place surrounded. Are they breeding them inside the *dorp*?" He scrambled up the ridge, lay down, and focused his field glasses. A row of men waited behind a stone-and-mud wall, with what looked like a disguised cannon in an emplacement further back.

"I don't know where they came from," Johannes said.

"We should attack now," Theunis suggested. "Before even more arrive."

"No," Johannes said. "Remember how many men we lost when we charged at Potchefstroom? The British have an open field of fire and a cannon. They will slaughter us."

"We have to capture this spy, this Charles Abercrombie," Theunis said.

"Why?" Johannes asked. "What good is he to us? Can we eat him?"

Theunis shook his head. "No; we can send him to the German Emperor, and then Germany will help us if the *Rooinecks* attack again."

Johannes nodded to the wisp of dust that marked Konrad's

passage. "There goes the emperor's ambassador," he said. "I don't think the Germans will help us."

"I do," Theunis dragged hooked fingers through the tangle of dark hair across his face. "Konrad promised Germany's assistance."

"We'll see," Johannes said. He studied the tiny village again. "I don't know how the British could have passed reinforcements through our patrols without us noticing. I think they are only moving their men from place to place. We'll circle the *dorp* and count the defenders, Karl. You go left, I'll go right, and we'll meet back here to compare figures."

Karl nodded and headed left, dodging from cover to cover as he counted, while Johannes slid in the opposite direction. They met up half an hour later.

"I saw thirty-two," Karl reported.

"Thirty-one," Johannes said. "That's near enough. Did you see anybody at the gun?"

"No," Karl replied. "It's too well covered."

"The British might not always have men there," Johannes said. "We will say at least thirty British defenders. That's thirty rifles waiting for us if we attack, but thinly spread."

Karl nodded. "The *Rooinecks* have about a quarter of a mile of perimeter, but we'll have three hundred yards of open land to cover. The British could gather all their defenders to one spot in minutes."

"They'd knock down too many of our men if we attack," Johannes decided. "We'll remain as we are; keep them under observation and fire when we see a definite target."

"I agree," Karl said.

Theunis shook his head. "I think that will take too long."

"It will save lives," Johannes told him.

Andrew halted beside a Black Karee tree, adjusted his hat to find the maximum of shade, and looked around. The land seemed to stretch forever, limitless, flat, and featureless, save for the scattered *kopjes*. He could taste the Kalahari dust in his mouth as he lifted his field glasses and studied Swartspruit, baking under the eternal sun. The garrison had thrown up a five-foot-high wall with a ditch to defend a dozen flat-roofed houses with a central well.

"Why the devil would anybody want to settle here?" Andrew compared the fertile farms around Berwick-upon-Tweed to this arid, sun-tortured landscape.

"Why indeed?" Fletcher replied, waving his hand in a vain attempt to ward off a score of questing flies.

"Freedom," Mariana had followed them quietly. "These people want to escape civilisation with its boundaries and restrictions. They can live as they please out here on the edge of nowhere."

"It's a hard life they choose," Fletcher said.

"Freedom is sweet," Mariana replied. "That's why the Boers are prepared to fight so tenaciously to retain it."

Andrew traversed his field glasses to survey the Boer positions.

Between five and seven hundred yards outside the British perimeter, the Boers waited in three small wagon laagers, with horsemen riding to and fro and pickets watching Swartspruit. Andrew tried calculating the Boer numbers, checking each section of the besiegers' positions and counting the men he saw.

As Andrew lowered his field glasses, the sun set in a startling blaze of red, orange, and yellow. He watched without expression, aware that the very beauty of the sunset was a reminder that beyond the horizon lay the Kalahari Desert, a vast, thirsty land devoid of water or anything green or growing.

"How many Boers would you say?" Andrew handed the binoculars to Fletcher.

"Not a huge number," Fletcher said. "I doubt there are more than a hundred in total."

"We have fifteen men and one woman," Andrew said. "The Boers outnumber us seven to one, maybe less than that if there are any fighting men inside the British camp." He reclaimed the binoculars. "We'll also have the advantage of surprise, and our men are equal to any Boer." He grinned, remembering Major Fotheringham's advice to keep his men under control. "We're not red-coated infantry trained to march like marionettes and fire volleys at static targets."

"That's right, sir," Fletcher said. "Do you have a plan to get through the Boer defences?"

Andrew nodded. "Go for it bald-headed, like the Marquis of Granby."

"Who, sir?"

"He was a cavalry commander during the Seven Years War," Andrew explained. "He led a charge in a long-forgotten battle, and his wig fell off, giving us the phrase 'to go for it bald-headed.'"[1]

"I see, sir," Fletcher said diplomatically. "Do you mean we'll just charge them?"

"Yes," Andrew replied. "Keep together, hit them as one body, and not as a scatter of men, and we'll punch through their defences."

"What about Mariana, sir? She can't ride like us."

Andrew worried about Mariana. He had the choice to leave her out on the veld with Briggs and pick her up later, or bring her with the Dragoons. If he left her on the veld, the Boers might find her, and there was the danger of wild animals and food to consider. However, if Mariana rode with the main body, a stray bullet could hit her.

"Mariana grew up on a farm on the Natal-Zululand border," Andrew said. "She's been riding horses all her life, and if we place her in the centre of the men, they'll protect her."

"As you wish, sir," Fletcher said stiffly.

"I want two men with spare horses at the rear to pick up any casualties or men who fall from their mounts."

"I'll act as rearguard, sir, and take Kerr."

Andrew nodded. He would have preferred to be in the rear, the position of most danger, but he had to lead his men.

"We'll find where the Boers are weakest," Andrew said. "I want to hit hard, rescue the garrison, including this troublesome civilian, and return to Natal."

"Every Boer commando north of the Vaal will be after us."

"I know," Andrew said. "Thankfully, the truce will mean most men are back on their farms, so hopefully, by the time they've reassembled, we'll be well on our way." He considered for a moment. "All the same, we'll need more than pluck and determination. We'll need some cunning as well."

Fletcher nodded. "You and I must do the thinking," he said solemnly. "The men are decent enough fellows, but they are hardly suited to solving the intricate problems of command."

Andrew grunted. "Did you see some of the decisions the senior officers made in the late war with the Boers? Or with the Zulus?" *I should not criticise senior officers in front of a subaltern, but it's time Fletcher saw things as they are.*

When Fletcher looked uncomfortable, Andrew continued. "The British soldier will do his best. At Potchefstroom, we saw what he is capable of when well-led. The swaddies will do their duty."

Fletcher nodded.

"The British officer is as brave as he's always been, but many don't seem to understand that bravery is insufficient. The Boers have outfought and outgeneralled us. They fight to their strengths and our weaknesses."

"Yes, sir," Fletcher said.

"You and I had better prove the exception to a sad rule, Fletcher. Let's prepare the men to outthink and outmanoeuvre the wily Boer."

THE SOUND OF BOER RIFLES

A HANDFUL OF DRAGOONS AND ONE WOMAN AGAINST A VETERAN Boer commando. Let's see how good we are. Andrew took the men aside, explaining what he required.

"We hit them at night, shoot our way through and enter Swartspruit. I want everyone to make as much noise as possible. Try to sound like the entire Household Cavalry is breaking through their position. Shout, yell, sing songs, play the bugle, fire your rifle, anything you like."

Kerr grinned. "I have heard of people who try to sneak through the enemy positions, sir."

"So have I," Andrew said. "And another time, that would be the best policy. Tonight, I want speed and shock."

"I see, sir," Kerr said.

"We'll do our best, sir," Ogden promised.

"Keep silent until I give the word," Andrew said. "We'll get as close as possible and then make them think General Wood has led half the British army here, with Redvers Buller commanding the other half at his back."

Although some of the men smiled, most looked solemn. An advance through fixed positions held by expert Boer riflemen was not a pleasant prospect.

"Muffle your horse's shoes and ensure the equipment does not rattle," Andrew ordered. "We'll creep up slowly and quietly. I don't want them to hear us until we're close enough to unbutton their coats."

More Dragoons smiled at Andrew's attempted humour. "Will do, sir," Kerr replied.

"Cover anything that might reflect the moonlight," Andrew continued. "We're going to surprise Brother Boer and scare him senseless."

"How about me?" Mariana asked. "Can I have a rifle?"

"No," Andrew shook his head. "You are a civilian. I don't want to give the Boers any excuse to shoot at you. Stay in the middle of the men and concentrate on riding like the devil. Don't look to the left or right, just ride."

Mariana nodded. "Do you want me to make a noise as well?"

"Yes," Andrew decided. "Shout your head off!"

Mariana smiled. "I can do that," she said.

Andrew treasured that rare smile, although he was unsure if it was because Mariana looked more like Elaine when she smiled or for herself. He wrestled with the question for a moment, decided it was unimportant, and concentrated on the matter at hand.

For the remainder of that afternoon, Andrew studied the Boer positions, marking where their pickets were and the numbers of men. He noted the horse lines, their patrol routes, and what routine they adopted. Occasionally, he lifted his field glasses to inspect Swartspruit. Andrew noted the Union Flag hanging limply under the burning sun, the row of riflemen waiting patiently behind the wall, and the barrel of a piece of artillery pointing toward the Boer laagers.

"Swartspruit has a larger garrison than I expected," Andrew told Fletcher. "And artillery as well. At least a nine-pounder by the length of the barrel. General Hook didn't mention that." He lowered his field glasses. "Swartspruit is well capable of defending itself without us."

We're not here to reinforce the garrison. We're here to get Charles Abercrombie to safety before the Boers or the Prussians capture him. That's our only objective.

When the sun set with its usual brilliant display of red and orange, the African night sounds began. Andrew waited an hour, allowing the Boer sentries to lapse into the boredom of watching nothing as the stars gradually filled the sky.

"Right, lads," Andrew whispered. "Follow my lead. Once we're close to Swartspruit, halt and shout who we are, or our own people will fire at us."

Fletcher passed on the order, and Sergeant Meek ensured

everybody understood. When Andrew was sure his men were ready, he lifted a hand and pushed Lancelot forward.

Half a league, half a league, half a league onward,
Into the Valley of Death.

The Dragoons moved off in silence, with pads muffling the soft thud of hooves in sand and cloth shielding every item of equipment. The stars illuminated their road as Andrew felt his heart race. He remembered where the Boers had their outposts and guided his men to the least observed spot. He hoped Mariana kept her head down, wondered if he should have left her, knew it was too late to change his decision, and pushed on, listening for Boer voices.

Somewhere in the dark, a wild dog yapped while the howling of a pack of hyenas lifted the small hairs on the back of Andrew's neck. He smelled a drift of tobacco smoke and heard the low rumble of a man's voice, speaking the *Taal*.

Lancelot stumbled and recovered. Andrew patted his neck and walked on, fighting the urge to increase his speed. The closer the Dragoons came to the Boer positions without being detected, the safer they would be.

"*Wie is daar?* Who is there?"

Andrew heard the challenge from his left.

Here we go! They've seen us!

Lifting his carbine, Andrew fired towards the voice. "Come on the Household Brigade!" he shouted. "Give them hell!"

The Dragoons responded immediately, shouting and roaring, firing their rifles, and with Ogden blowing his bugle like a demented musician. Andrew heard the various slogans yelled behind him.

"Forward the Guards!"

"Blues forever!"

"Everything's Sir Garnet!"

"We're coming for you, Brother Boer!"

"God save the Queen!"

And the last, "Remember Majuba!" shouted out with the final syllable extended until it was like the howl of a wolf.

Andrew had never heard that slogan before but guessed it would resonate across the country. The British Army did not like defeats and used them to spur future success. Andrew wondered if the Boers would live to regret their victory on the steep slopes of the Hill of Doves.[2]

"Come on, lads!" Andrew encouraged, guiding Lancelot with his knees as he pushed his carbine into its bucket and drew his revolver. "Come on, the Natal Dragoons!"

A surprised Boer picket only fired two shots, and then Andrew was past and galloping towards Swartspruit. He holstered his revolver, took the reins in both hands, and spurred forward, enjoying the sensation of speeding through the night. He heard his men behind him, still shouting their slogans with Ogden's bugle blaring brassily. Some men fired their carbines, adding to the confusion. Lights flared ahead as the noise alerted Swartspruit's defenders.

"Halloa!" Andrew shouted. "British cavalry! British cavalry! Halloa there!"

He heard shouts, saw the sudden flare of watchfires and saw a low rampart with a couple of hats silhouetted against the light.

"British cavalry!"

The horses' hooves were hammering behind Andrew as the passage through the Boer positions had loosened or removed their coverings.

I hope Mariana is all right. I can't hear her shouting.

"Halt!" Andrew shouted, holding up a hand. "Halt!" he hoped his men would hear him before a nervous British sentry opened fire. One by one, the Dragoons pulled up, with only Ogden continuing the mad charge before he, too, stopped at the rampart and lowered his bugle.

"Who are you?" A man's voice demanded. Andrew saw his figure silhouetted beside a watch fire, rifle in hand.

THE SOUND OF BOER RIFLES

"Captain Andrew Baird of the Natal Dragoons!" Andrew replied.

"Come to the light, Captain Andrew Baird," the defender told him. "We'll let you in. Any tricks, and there are a hundred rifles pointed at you."

"A hundred rifles be damned," Meek murmured. "If he had a hundred men, he'd chase the Boers back to Pretoria."

Andrew pushed toward the light to see two men waiting at a small gap in the wall. One was middle-aged, with the light reflecting from his bald head. The other was older, with a long hunting rifle in his hands, the muzzle aimed at Andrew's chest.

"How do we know you are British?" the bald man asked.

"If we were Boers, you'd be dead by now!" Andrew saw a long row of rifles on the wall, all pointing towards the Boer positions. The men behind remained still, dark shadows in the night.

"Come in," the bald man invited. "Slowly."

A rifle cracked behind them, a reminder that the Dragoons were caught between two fires. Andrew saw Fletcher and Kerr in the rear, making sure nobody straggled and felt relieved when he saw Mariana riding entirely composed amid the Dragoons.

"After me, boys!" Andrew led his Dragoons through the gap, stepped aside, and counted them all in. Immediately the Dragoons were inside the defences, the two sentries manoeuvred a gate back in position. Heavy with sandbags and topped with spikes, it appeared a formidable obstacle to any attacker.

"Who's in charge here?" Andrew asked. He frowned to see the other defenders had not moved when the Dragoons entered the compound. They remained at the low wall, facing the Boers, who had only fired a few desultory shots.

The two defenders glanced at each other before the older man spoke. "I suppose that must be me," he said. "Bernard Booth at your service, sir. Why are you here?"

"General Hook sent us when he heard the Boers still besieged you," Andrew did not mention Abercrombie. "How many men do you have?" He glanced at the static defenders.

"Seven," Booth said without emotion. "And two women."

Andrew jerked a finger at the dark shadows on the wall. "It looks a lot more than seven to me."

Booth shook his head, ignoring a sudden fusillade of shots from the besiegers. "They're dummies," he said. "To fool the Boers."

Dummies! No wonder they didn't react when we arrived. Booth is keeping back an entire Boer commando with a handful of men and a great deal of bluff.

"Return the Boer fire," Andrew shouted, and his Dragoons ran to the wall, threw themselves down and fired at the muzzle flashes.

"Sir!" Ogden shouted. "Half these men aren't men!"

"They're to fool the Boers!" Andrew said. "Fire!"

"Some of them haven't even got real rifles," Ogden said. "They're just bits of wood!"

Booth ran to a rope that ran through the trigger guards of the dummies' rifles. "Fire a volley!" he shouted, pulling the rope that operated the triggers. Six rifles fired at once.

"How about the nine-pounder?" Andrew asked as Booth grinned at him, and the bald man ran from rifle to rifle, reloading each from a box of cartridges. "It's made of wood," Booth said.

"That's clever," Andrew allowed. "Who thought of that?"

"Our pet geologist," Booth said. "He's a bundle of ideas, that man."

"Is that Charles Abercrombie?" Andrew asked. "Where is he?"

Booth jerked his head toward the main settlement. "I'll take you to him."

"Fletcher!" Andrew shouted. "Take command of the Dragoons." *At last, I'll meet the man who caused all the fuss.*

THE SOUND OF BOER RIFLES

Jan heard the sudden roar from the picket next to his, followed by the abrupt muzzle flare of a rifle. The noise rose, unmistakable British voices mingled with the blare of a bugle.

"Alert!" He shouted. "The British have arrived!" He fired his rifle towards what sounded like hundreds of British cavalrymen crashing through the outer picket line. The British roared as if they believed that noise alone could regain the Transvaal for Queen Victoria. "Alert!"

The racket brought other Boers from their tents and wagons. They ran toward the picket line, thrusting hats on their heads and holding their rifles ready.

"What is happening? Where are the British?"

"It is a major attack! General Wood must have brought his army!"

"Hundreds of them! Where did they come from?"

Some Boers fired towards the noise, while others looked over their shoulders as if preparing to ride away.

"Stand!" Johannes stilled the incipient panic. "We don't know what's happening!" He looked around. "Jan! Where are you?"

"Over here!" Jan ran to his father's side.

"See if there are any casualties!"

Jan nodded and ran towards the break-in point.

Theunis emerged from his tent, rifle in hand and his hair a tangled black mane down his back and across his face. "Send them back!" he shouted. He fired towards the noise, ejected the spent cartridge, and fired again. Before Theunis fired a third time, the noise had subsided, and the British had gone.

"Jan!" Johannes shouted as his son returned to his side.

"They moved fast," Jan said, thumbing a cartridge into the breech of his rifle. "We have no casualties."

"British cavalry," a stunned picket said. "I didn't hear them until they were close."

"They shouted 'The Guards' and 'Blues forever'," another Boer said.

"We are fighting the Brigade of Guards," the first man said.

"Ja," Theunis said. "They have sent their best against us!"

"Why send the Guards to Swartspruit?" Johannes asked. "There is nothing here for them." He shook his head. "That was not the Guards."

"Whoever they were, there were hundreds of them." Jan fired towards the British camp, reloaded, and fired again, ducking when the defenders replied with an ill-aimed volley. "They made as much noise as an army."

Johannes shook his head. "The British can be *slim* sometimes," he said. "Because they made a noise like an army does not mean they were an army. It may mean they want us to believe they are an army." He put a hand on Jan's rifle. "Stop wasting ammunition, Jan. In the morning, we shall see how many *Rooinecks* there were."

As the firing died away, Johannes reorganised the shaken besiegers, doubled the pickets, and ordered the mounted patrols to increase their vigilance.

"There might be more *Rooinecks*," Johannes warned. "If you hear anything, fire!"

"It might be our men," Karl said.

"Our men know to be quiet."

When dawn broke, Johannes accompanied Jan and Theunis to where the British had broken through. The closest sentry lifted his rifle until Johannes reassured him.

"See?" Johannes knelt on the ground, examining the hoofprints. "There were not hundreds of *Rooinecks*." He shook his head. "Look at the spoor, Jan. There are only thirty horses here, perhaps thirty-two or thirty-five." He measured the depth of the prints with an experienced eye. "Some prints are deeper than others, so maybe half the horses bore riders, and the others were spares. I'd say fifteen, sixteen men at most."

"It sounded like hundreds," Jan defended himself.

"The British wanted us to believe there were hundreds," Johannes said. "We are dealing with a *slim* man, Jan. This is a new type of *Rooineck* from the soldiers we defeated at Majuba." He ran a hand over his bearded face. "Who has General Wood sent against us?" He smiled. "Not the Brigade of Guards."

"I don't know," Jan said. "It is not the same redcoats General Colley led. These men are cunning."

"These men are dangerous," Johannes replied. "We've only held them under siege in Swartspruit. We should be more active now and push them harder."

Theunis stamped his feet. "Good," he said. "We'll destroy the *Rooineck* soldiers, capture the spy and hand him over to the Prussians." He tapped his rifle. "We can end this British occupation in a couple of days."

"A RE YOU THE GEOLOGIST?" A NDREW ASKED.

The man was about thirty, with a ready smile on a pleasant, clean-shaven face. "That's me," he extended his hand. "You've had a long ride from Natal to get here."

"That's correct," Andrew said, shaking the man's surprisingly strong hand. "Could you confirm your name, please?"

"Don't you know?" the geologist looked surprised. "I thought my name prompted Shepstone to send a rescue party. It certainly isn't because of my importance." He laughed self-deprecatingly.

"Who are you, sir?" Andrew asked.

"Charles Abercrombie," the geologist said and waited for Andrew's response. "Does that mean anything to you?"

"Not a thing," Andrew admitted cheerfully. "Except you are the fellow we are looking for."

Abercrombie looked disappointed for a moment. "Have you come to rescue us?"

"That's the plan," Andrew told him.

"Jolly good," Abercrombie replied. "How are you going to do that?"

"I'm not sure yet," Andrew confessed. "I'll have to look around the town first."

"I'll accompany you," Abercrombie said. "I could use the exercise and the diversion. There's nothing more tedious than sitting in a besieged village."

The circuit of Swartspruit took only twenty minutes, with Abercrombie pointing out the trenches, walls, and other defensive efforts the tiny garrison had constructed. "Boothie is a good man," he said cheerfully. "He does his best with limited resources, but if the Boers decided to attack in earnest, they'd walk right in. Dummies and bluff won't stop a determined Burgher forever."

Andrew smiled. "You've done splendidly so far." He scanned the Boer lines in the growing light, noting the waiting pickets and slow-riding patrols. "Unfortunately, our arrival has stirred them a little."

"You made enough noise about it," Abercrombie replied.

Andrew grunted. "That was the idea."

Returning to the Dragoons, Andrew drew up a plan of Swartspruit, sketching in the defences and the Boer positions and adding his estimation of the enemy's patrol routes. After consulting with Booth and Abercrombie, he finalised his plans.

"Here's my idea," Andrew addressed the entire garrison of Swartspruit, plus his Dragoons. "We're going to break out of here and head back to Natal, but the Boers will expect that, so we'll have to fool them."

"They're not easily fooled," Booth murmured. "They have a new man in charge, Johannes van Collier of the Groenburg Commando."

"Johannes van Collier?" Andrew said. "We met at Majuba. He's a decent man."

"And a good commander," Booth said.

Andrew nodded. "That's unfortunate. Do you have a farrier in the *dorp*? A blacksmith with a forge?"

Abercrombie shook his head. "We have a forge," he said, "but no farrier."

"It's the forge I want," Andrew confirmed. "All my men can

shoe a horse. I want every horse shoed backwards. I want men to go on patrol tonight unseen but with sufficient noise to let the Boers know they were there."

"Shoe the horses backwards, sir?" Meek's tidy military mind objected to such an idea.

"It's an old Border trick," Andrew said. "I grew up partly on the Scottish-English Border, and the local reiving families were full of guile and trickery. If we shoe the horses back to front and the Boers find the spoor, as they will, they might believe even more reinforcements have arrived."

Abercrombie nodded. "You're a cunning man, Captain."

"I also want patrols day and night around the perimeter. I want the ground churned with so many hoofprints that the Boers won't be able to follow us for a while when we leave."

"That means a lot of work." Booth frowned.

"The Boers won't know if we're coming or going," Andrew explained. "Confusing the enemy is always a small victory."

Fletcher smiled. "Have you ever heard of a man named Fighting Jack Windrush, sir?"

"The name is slightly familiar," Andrew admitted.

"I've heard he was full of tricks, sir," Fletcher said. "I think you must be related."

Andrew did not tell Fletcher that he was Jack Windrush's son. "Right, gentlemen," he said. "I want to leave Swartspruit at night yet make the Boers believe we are still here. By the time they realise we are gone, I want to be miles away. Any ideas?"

"Keep the campfires burning," Fletcher replied immediately.

"That's a start," Andrew agreed. "And Mr Abercrombie's idea of dummy soldiers is also good. I wish we could make them move."

"That might be difficult," Abercrombie said. "Steam power, perhaps?"

"Do we have steam power here?" Andrew asked as some of his men laughed at the ridiculous proposal.

"Not even a little bit," Abercrombie admitted.

"If the dummies are too static," Andrew said, "the Boers will suspect we're up to something and come forward to have a look."

"We can discourage them with tripwires," Kerr said. "Tripwires and pits."

Andrew nodded. "We'll have to set them up at night. Boer marksmen will shoot anybody outside the perimeter during the day."

"How about a distraction, sir?" Sergeant Meek asked. "We can do something to take the Boer's attention from Swartspruit."

"What do you have in mind, Sergeant?"

"I'm not sure, sir, but I heard that the Boers tried to lure the 21st out of Potchefstroom with a false message and explosions like artillery. We could try something similar here."

Andrew nodded, with his mind working busily. "Do you have any gunpowder in Swartspruit?"

"A few pounds," Booth replied cautiously.

"How many pounds?" Andrew asked. "Five? Ten?"

"No, about seventy," Abercrombie told him. "I'm a geologist, remember. I use the gunpowder to blow up rocks to get samples to examine."

"I thought you people used a small hammer," Andrew said.

"Oh no, I can happily blow things up," Abercrombie told him. "We don't mind how large the rocks are. What's in your mind, Captain?"

"Playing brother Boer at his own game," Andrew said. "Now, I'm thinking on my feet here, so if anybody has any ideas or sees flaws in my plans, speak up."

The men nodded, with Fletcher still surprised at Andrew's democratic approach to leadership. The Sandhurst-educated officers of his acquaintance worked in a more authoritarian manner.

"We can use Sergeant Meek's suggestion," Andrew said. "At Potchefstroom, the Boers pretended that a British relief column was coming. We might be able to do the same."

"How, sir?" Fletcher asked.

"If we heliograph in the opposite direction from that we intend to leave, we might make the Boers think a relieving force is approaching."

"The Boers will see there's no answering flashes, sir," Meek said.

"We can try using very short messages at irregular intervals," Andrew replied. "We'll be on and off before the Boers have time to look." He grinned. "Hopefully. Then, if we can use Mr Abercrombie's gunpowder to make an explosion, we can add to the confusion."

The men nodded, with a low murmur of conversation revealing they were discussing Andrew's plan. He gave them a few moments before he continued.

"Are there any other suggestions?"

"I have one," Mariana lifted a hesitant hand.

"What's that, Mariana?" Andrew hid his pleasure that Mariana's mind was working again.

"Can we split the Boers' forces? Can we make some of them look for the relieving column, and the others remain outside the perimeter as if there are still men garrisoning Swartspruit?"

"How?" Fletcher asked.

"I liked the idea of having the dummies move," Mariana spoke slowly, gathering confidence as she realised most Dragoons were paying attention. "I was thinking about how to make that happen, and I thought of using sand or goats."

"Sand or goats?" Andrew silenced Fletcher's snort of contempt with a lift of his palm. "Could you explain further, Mariana?"

"When we had a leopard hunting our livestock at Inglenook," Mariana held Andrew's gaze as she concentrated on her explanation. "We tied up a goat as bait, and when the leopard came to get the goat, Father shot the leopard. Now, the goat was never still. It knew it was in danger and moved all the time." As she warmed to her subject, Mariana's speech quickened. "Maybe we can tie a goat to a couple of the dummies; give it just enough rope to move so it pulls the dummies around as if they were also moving."

Andrew nodded. "That might work," he said. "Would the Boers see them in the dark?"

"They would if you placed the dummies near the firelight," Mariana replied.

Andrew nodded. "We could try that if we had some goats."

"We can get goats," Abercrombie said cheerfully, looking at Mariana. "That's an imaginative idea."

"You also mentioned sand," Andrew reminded.

"It might not work," Mariana said. "But if we fill one of the dummies with sand and make a little hole so the sand leaks out, the dummy will slowly change shape as if it was moving."

"You have more in your mind," Andrew was beginning to understand Mariana's body language.

"Yes," Mariana said. "This is only an idea, but if some of the dummies fired their rifles, would that not make them more realistic?"

"It would," Andrew agreed as Fletcher shook a doubting head at the idea of a dummy firing its rifle.

"We could have a cable through two or three trigger guards," Mariana said, "and two buckets attached to each, with the top bucket full of sand and the lower bucket empty. We make holes in the top bucket, so the sand trickles into the lower bucket at different speeds, and the lower bucket attached to the trigger, so when the lower bucket is full, the weight pulls the trigger, and it fires."

"By God, that's clever," Andrew looked at Mariana with new respect.

"We could have different levels of sand so the rifles fire at different times to keep the Boers busy while we escape at the rear of the *dorp*," Mariana said and trailed away. "It's only an idea."

"And it's a good one!" Andrew said. "We've plenty of sand, but I've no idea about buckets."

"We can find something, surely," Abercrombie said, giving Mariana a hug. "You're a clever lass, aren't you?"

"Well, we have work to do," Andrew said. "Can anybody think how to distract the Boers with an explosion behind their lines? If you do, let me know."

"I could take a barrel into the bush and blow it up," Kerr said.

"That's a dangerous mission," Andrew reminded.

Kerr shrugged. "I've lived and worked in the bush all my life. When do you want me to go?"

"In two nights' time," Andrew knew Kerr was an excellent bushman. "See Mr Abercrombie for the gunpowder. Thank you, Kerr."

Kerr shrugged and lifted a hand to Abercrombie.

That's one problem sorted; now all I need is three or four spare rifles, a couple of goats, and half a dozen empty buckets.

CHAPTER 19

"We should raid them," Theunis said. "Go over at night and kill the British sentries."

Jan nodded. "That is a good idea," he agreed. "We need to take the fight to them." He thought of Engela and pushed her memory away. As she did not want him anymore, only war remained. "Let's attack them, Pa. Let's chase the *Rooinecks* back to London."

"That is not the way," Johannes eyed his son, worried about his new thirst for blood. "We have an armistice with the British except for their spy here at Swartspruit. Once we capture him, we will keep our word. We wanted our republic, and we have it."

"The British still have control over our foreign policy," Theunis said. "We want them gone completely from Africa."

"Ja! Completely!" Jan repeated Theunis's words. "This is our land."

"We have won the war," Johannes said. "Let's finish this last part and return to our farms."

They looked up at the explosion half a mile to the rear. "*Rooinecks!*" Jan shouted. "They are behind us!"

"Gather the commando," Theunis shouted. "The *Rooinecks* are attacking."

THE SOUND OF BOER RIFLES

"Wait!" Johannes said. "Where are they?"

A second explosion followed the first, and then a third, all behind the Boer lines.

"There they are," Theunis pointed at the orange flashes. "They're firing cannon at us."

"Where are the shells landing? Nowhere! Not even the *Rooinecks* are that bad shots," Johannes said, but a dozen men had already rallied to Theunis, gripping their rifles and shouting that the British were attacking.

"Jan! Don't go!"

"I must go, Pa," Jan shouted. "We have to get rid of the *Rooinecks*!"

"Stay with me, Jan!"

Jan hesitated, looking from Johannes to Theunis and back. "Yes, Pa," he said reluctantly.

Only Karl and Jan remained with Johannes when Theunis led the Groenburg Commando towards the explosions.

"See what the British are doing at Swartspruit," Johannes ordered. "I think they're playing games."

Karl edged forward, ducking when one of the defenders fired.

"That was close," he said. "The *Rooinecks'* shooting has improved."

"We've taught them well," Johannes replied as another defender fired, with the bullet rising far above them. "That man didn't pay attention to the lessons."

Jan scanned the darkness behind them. "These explosions have stopped," he said. "But I can't hear any shooting. Theunis hasn't found the *Rooinecks*."

"Unless the British have bayonetted them all," Karl said.

Jan shivered as he remembered the glint of the sun on British bayonets at Potchefstroom. "The good Lord save us from that."

"We'll wait here," Johannes decided. "Things will be clearer in the morning."

Jan lay down and aimed his rifle at the British positions. "Yes,

Pa. If I hear anything, I'll fire towards the sound."

"You do that," Johannes said.

THE DARKNESS EASED INTO AN ORANGE DAWN, WITH THE Dragoons and the tiny Swartspruit garrison riding steadily towards the rising sun. Kerr's explosions had faded into memory, and the intermittent musketry behind them proved that Mariana's sand and goat idea had succeeded.

"Let's hope we've confused the Groenburg Commando," Fletcher said.

"Every hour gives us a better chance," Andrew replied. "If we reach the twin *koppies* and send our helio signal, we're home and dry. We'll rendezvous with the larger force and get back to Natal."

"Three days to the twin *koppies*," Fletcher said.

"Three days, and we have a decent head start and spare horses," Andrew agreed. "With luck, we should make it." He peered into the dark. "Let's hope that Kerr finds us."

Andrew pushed them hard, listened for pursuit, hearing nothing except the normal African night sounds. An hour after dawn, Andrew halted to feed the men and horses, then allowed them two hours' rest before starting again.

"Don't rush," Andrew warned. "We don't want to raise too much dust. Keep it slow and steady." He signalled to Fletcher. "Take over; head for the twin *koppies*."

"Yes, sir. Where are you going?"

"To look for Boers. Johannes van Collier is a capable commander."

Andrew rode to a small ridge and scanned the veld. He saw the smoke of a couple of farms but no Boer commando. Satisfied, he returned to the Dragoons to see Mariana talking to Abercrombie.

"Any sign of Kerr yet, Fletcher?"

"No, sir."

"Keep an eye open. I told him our route, but it's easy to get lost out here."

"Andrew," Mariana pushed her horse beside him as they moved slowly across the baking plain. "I was talking to Charles."

"I noticed," Andrew said. He tried to quell his pang of jealousy, knowing it was a sign of Mariana's recovery that she could talk to people.

"Do you know who he is?"

"He is a geologist," Andrew replied, more abruptly than he intended.

"That's *the* Charles Abercrombie," Mariana lowered her voice as if the veld were listening.

"*The* Charles Abercrombie? I don't know the significance of the name," Andrew admitted.

Mariana shook her head. "I presume you know who William Gladstone is?" She was vaguely mocking, with laughter a welcome addition in her eyes.

"I believe he's the prime minister," Andrew replied. "We haven't rescued him, too, have we?"

"No," Mariana shook her head. "We've rescued his nephew. Charles Abercrombie is the prime minister's nephew."

"Dear God in heaven!" Andrew glanced back at their cheerful companion. "Thank you, Mariana. That explains a lot."

Gladstone's nephew! No wonder General Hook wants him safe. And no wonder the Boers wish to capture him. With a relative of the Prime Minister as a hostage, Kruger could pressure the British government into giving the Transvaal complete independence, including control of their foreign affairs. That might allow the Germans a foothold in the area and threaten British dominance.

"We'd better get a move on," Andrew said, calculating the distance to the twin *kopjes*. *The sooner we rendezvous with the British column, the more secure I'll feel.* He raised his voice. "Pick up the pace a little, boys and girls. I want to make the twin *koppies* in two days."

"They've gone that way," Johannes examined the trail and stood up.

"No," Theunis shook his head. "They came from there. Read the hoofprints!" He pointed to the ground. "Another force of reinforcements made these marks."

"They reversed their horseshoes," Johannes explained. "This *Rooineck* is *slim*. Everything he does is intended to deceive us. How many men did you find when you chased the artillery fire?"

"We found the spoor of one man and lost him when he rode onto some rocky terrain."

"The *Rooineck* fooled us with a diversion, as we attempted at Potchefstroom," Johannes said. "He will not fool us again. Whatever you think you see, believe the opposite."

Theunis tapped his rifle. "This is my cure for the *Rooineck*." He tossed back the tangled hair from his face.

"His tricks have gained him a twenty-hour lead," Johannes said. "We'll need to ride hard to catch him." He looked at the Groenburg Commando as they sat astride their horses, waiting for his orders. "We follow this trail, men, and we ride hard. The *Rooinecks* are a day's ride ahead, but we are faster than them."

The Boers adjusted their hats, patted their horses, and prepared for a hard ride. Above them, two vultures circled, knowing that a gathering of armed horsemen invariably led to violence and fresh meat.

"Trek!" Johannes ordered and led the way.

Behind Johannes, Jan pushed the thought of Engela from his mind. Abraham's sister was not the only girl in the world. Africa was full of women equally as good as Engela, who would want to marry the heir to Nuwe Hoop Plaas.

"You are back early, *Meneer* Konrad," Aletta said.

"Your husband sent me back," Konrad dismounted stiffly, patting the dust from his clothes.

"Why did he do that?" Aletta asked. She stood outside her dairy, peering at Konrad from under the shade of her bonnet.

"He thought there might be a British patrol in the area," Konrad said. "And you might need a man on the farm to protect you."

Aletta nodded slowly. "Mannie is here," she indicated her younger son, who stood in the doorway, silently watching.

"Good," Konrad smiled at Mannie. "He and I will keep you safe."

"I am sure you will," Aletta said.

"Your husband said I should look after Goed Weiding as well, with Abraham on commando and his father dead."

Aletta nodded. "That was thoughtful of Johannes, *Meneer* Konrad. You will need coffee after your long ride."

"Coffee would be welcome," Konrad agreed.

ANDREW HAD BEEN WATCHING THE LONE RIDER APPROACH FOR half an hour before he was sure it was Kerr. Turning Lancelot, he rode to meet him.

"I'm glad you are safe, Kerr. I expected you yesterday."

Kerr reined up in a whirlwind of dust. "I had to make a few detours, sir. The Boers have picked up your trail, and van Collier has scouts everywhere."

"Damn!" Andrew scanned the veld through his field glasses. "That man is clever. How far back is he?"

"Ten hours, sir, at most." Kerr was travel weary, with dark shadows under his eyes and deep lines carved on either side of his mouth. "Whenever I thought I had a clear road, two or three of his riders appeared. He's set a wide net out for you."

"Well, he's not caught us yet," Andrew looked over his unit. Two days of constant movement had wearied the civilians, so they slumped in the saddle. He wondered how long they could continue without a rest. The women were not used to long-distance riding, but Andrew had refused to bring a wagon.

"We need a wagon," Mrs Murphy, red-faced and hollow-eyed, wailed.

"It will slow us down," Andrew replied firmly.

"The Boers don't make war on women," Mrs Murphy insisted. "If Murphy were here, he'd tell you that."

"The ordinary Boers don't," Andrew agreed. "I don't know about the Afrikander Bond, but the Groenburg Commando has a Prussian with them. They can be ruthless."

"I wish Murphy were here," Mrs Murphy had said. "He would not let you treat me like this."

Booth had told Andrew that Murphy had left his wife to try his hand at gold digging and never returned. That had been a full year ago.

"The twin *koppies* are only a few hours' ride," Kerr broke Andrew's train of thought.

Andrew nodded. "Join the men, Kerr, and we'll push on."

With scouts riding all around, Andrew forced the pace, discarding the civilians' complaints.

"Women can't ride as fast as men," Mrs Murphy wailed. "We can't keep this pace."

"Miss Maxwell is keeping up, Mrs Murphy!" Andrew replied sternly. "If she can ride on, then so can you."

I don't want the Army to remember me as the officer who allowed the Boers to capture the Prime Minister's nephew. We've already had too many disasters in South Africa with the defeats at Isandhlwana and Majuba, plus the death of the Prince Imperial of France.[1]

"Ride, boys and girls!" Andrew ordered, aware that the civilians and probably some Dragoons were cursing him. He reasoned they'd be safer once they sent their message from the twin *kopjes*, and he could hand Abercrombie over to a more senior officer.

Moving to the rear of the column, Andrew took the reins of

one of the flagging women. "Come along, Mrs Murphy. You must keep going, you know."

"I'm trying!" Mrs Murphy said.

"I know you are," Andrew agreed. "I know it's hard for you, riding all night and half the day, but I am trying to keep you safe."

Mrs Murphy favoured Andrew with a weary smile that revealed something of the beauty she once possessed. "I know, dear," she said. "I only wish Murphy was here. He might never find me now."

"I'm sure he will," Andrew replied. "Only a fool would not search for a woman like you."

"Oh!" Mrs Murphy smiled again and redoubled her efforts.

The Natal Dragoons reached the base of the two *kopjes* in the early afternoon, with the sun high above and not a whisper of wind.

"Fletcher! Set up camp a hundred feet up the hill beside that *spruit!*" Andrew pointed to a stream that trickled down the hill. "Make a defensive perimeter, send out two-man pickets, water the horses and watch for the Boers. I'm going up with the helio."

"Yes, sir," Fletcher agreed.

"Look after Lancelot," Andrew ordered, passing the reins to Briggs.

The *kopje* was steeper than Andrew had anticipated, with hard-baked ground littered with boulders and cloaked in thorny scrub. He scrambled to the summit with Spalding at his side and Kerr and Ogden as porters.

"How far can that thing be seen?" Andrew asked as Spalding readied the heliograph's tripod.

"I'm not sure, sir," Spalding replied. "I've heard the Seaforth Highlanders used their helio over a distance of seventy-two miles in Afghanistan, but I've never used it over twenty."

Andrew nodded. "Well, I wonder if it can be seen over a hundred miles." From the summit, the veld stretched to a seemingly limitless extent, broken only by *kopjes* and the green curves of river valleys. Using his field glasses, Andrew could see a couple of lonely farms, dwarfed by the brown-yellow expanse of the high veld, but no sign of any British column.

Spalding pursed his lips. "It might, sir. The air is very clear out here."

"There's a British force to the southeast," Andrew said. He glanced at the neighbouring *kopje,* slightly smaller and about a mile distant. "I want you to signal in that direction."

"As you wish, sir," Spalding replied. "What shall I say?"

Andrew had considered his message for every mile since they left Swartspruit. "Signal: Natal Dragoons have secured the package. Require rendezvous coordinates."

Spalding raised his eyebrows. "Yes, sir." He wrote the message in a small notebook. "Thank you, sir. Give me a minute, and I'll set the helio. Give me a hand here, boys!"

Spalding erected the heliograph on its tripod, angling the mirror to catch the sunlight.

Kerr slid into the shelter of a thornbush. "I can see men on the other *kopje,* sir."

"Where?" Andrew turned around, lifted his field glasses, and swore. "You're right, Kerr." *You're too late, van Collier. Once Spalding gets his message away, there's nothing you can do.*

Andrew saw half a dozen Boers moving confidently across the hill. One climbed a slight elevation and lay down. "That fellow is going to fire at us."

Kerr nodded. "He's over a mile away, sir. Not even the Boers can fire at that range."

Andrew nodded. Although he did not want the Boers to see him, sending the message was more important. "Spalding, have you got that message away yet?"

"Not yet, sir," Spalding replied and bent to the heliograph.

"One of the Boers is aiming at us," Kerr said. "The silly bugger's ready to fire."

Nobody flinched, knowing the range was too far for even the most powerful rifle. They saw the puff of white smoke and half a second later heard the report of the rifle, with a corresponding echo slightly later.

"See?" Kerr said. "Nowhere near," and swore as the bullet burrowed into the ground between the legs of the heliograph. "Bloody hell!"

The Boer fired again, with the bullet smashing the lens of the heliograph, sending shards of glass over Spalding and Andrew.

"How the devil did he do that?" Kerr said as he threw himself to the ground.

"What sort of rifle does he have?" Andrew asked as the Boer fired a third time. The bullet kicked up dirt and rocks a foot from his elbow.

"A bloody good one, sir," Kerr replied. Lifting his Martini-Henry, he took quick aim and fired. "He's well out of range, but I may unsettle him."

"Did you get the message away, Spalding?" Andrew asked.

"Only the first part, sir," Spalding replied. "The part about the package." He ducked as the Boer fired again, with the bullet completing the destruction of the heliograph.

"Let's hope that was enough," Andrew said. *Van Collier must have guessed we were sending a message. He had his sharpshooter deliberately smash the heliograph. I'd like to meet that man.*

"Do you want the rifle, sir?" Ogden asked. "We can round him up." He grinned. "I'd like to see what kind of fancy weapon Brother Boer uses."

Andrew considered sending his men to the neighbouring *kopje*. It was tempting to capture the Burgher's rifle, but he knew the time and risk were not worth the prize. "No," he said. "That Boer has smashed the helio, our reason for climbing this hill. Best get back down."[2]

Andrew cursed as he scrambled down the hill. With the heliograph gone, he had no method of contacting the relieving column, and with an unknown number of Boers following him and many more in the country, Andrew knew his Dragoons were in a precarious position.

We'll get out of here, ride on, and hope the column saw our all-too-brief message. If not, we have a long ride to the Natal border and a dangerous enemy far too close behind.

"THANK YOU FOR COMING TO SEE I WAS SAFE, MENEER," Engela said. "It was very kind of you."

"I must look after the most beautiful woman in Africa," Konrad said, bowing. He smiled and fingered the broad scar across his left cheek. "I can see you are curious about my scar."

Engela blushed. "It looks very romantic," she said.

"I got that in a duel," Konrad told her. "In Prussia, gentlemen prove their bravery and honour by fighting duels with swords."

"Do they?" Engela widened her eyes. "Why do they do that?"

"It is the mark of a gentleman to stand up to danger," Konrad told her proudly.

"Are you a gentleman, *meneer*?"

"I am," Konrad favoured her with a smile. "At home, I am Count Konrad von Bramigan, with an estate of thousands of acres in East Prussia."

Engela smiled, reached forward, and touched the broad scar. "Is a count very important in Prussia?"

"A count is fundamental to Prussian society," Konrad told her. "We are the nobility, with pedigrees that stretch back centuries." He smiled. "My ancestors were Teutonic Knights."

Engela did not ask who the Teutonic Knights were. "Why are you in Africa if you have lands to farm?"

Konrad sat beside her at the kitchen table. "The emperor asked me to come," he boasted. "Konrad, he said, Konrad, the German Empire needs your help."

"Did he say that?" Engela asked, widening her eyes.

"He did," Konrad continued. "He said: my friends, the Burghers of the Transvaal Republic are in danger. The British are trying to steal their land. I want you to go over, see what is happening and come back to tell me."

Engela looked at this tall man who was so different from the farmers she knew. "What will you tell the emperor when you see him again?"

"I will tell him that his friends in the Transvaal Republic are fighting hard against the British."

Engela smiled. "Tell him he can visit us whenever he likes," she said. "I've never met a lord before. Is a count the same as a lord?"

"I am of the Junkers class," Konrad told her. "That is higher than a British lord."

"You must feel strange coming to our little farm."

"Your presence would make even a hut feel like a palace," Konrad replied.

When Engela made food for him, sour milk and coffee, rusks, and quinces, he told her about his estate in Prussia and how he had fought in the Prussian Army against the French.

"My brother is also a soldier," Engela said. "You and he are alike."

"We both belong to the brotherhood of the sword," Konrad said. "We shall drink a toast!" Producing a silver flask from his inside pocket, he took a sip and passed it over to Engela. "Drink with me! This flask contains brandy."

"I don't drink," Engela said.

"In Prussia, noble ladies drink equal to the counts," Konrad said, shaking his flask and holding it out again. "Come, my sweet princess; when I take you to visit the palaces of Prussia, you must be able to act like Prussian nobility. Drink!"

Engela smiled and accepted the flask.

"Have you noticed all the wildlife out here?" Mariana asked.

Andrew shook his head. "I saw some antelope and a herd of springbok," he said. "I am a little more concerned about the wild Boers."

"We must have ridden past a hundred lizards," Mariana continued. "And an iguana, hiding in a willow tree. Plenty of bullfrogs, of course; you hear them croaking at night when the jackals are quiet. Sometimes, I hear the grasshoppers."

"Do you like the wildlife?"

"We used to hate it on the farm," Mariana said. "Father hunted the wild animals, partly for sport but mainly because they were rivals for our grazing, particularly in times of drought." She looked away, reliving happier times.

"Did you ever shoot?" Andrew asked, his eyes constantly moving as he scrutinised the landscape for any signs of Boer activity.

"Oh, yes," Mariana replied. "Father taught Elaine and me to shoot when we were quite young. We had to know in case a leopard or snake came." She smiled with memory. "We had a cobra in our tree once, hunting the sparrows. Father killed it because it was dangerous. Elaine wanted to shoot it, but Father said it was too wily an opponent for her."

"Not many women in Britain can shoot," he said. "The aristocracy probably can, and some farmers' wives and daughters." He negotiated an anthill, checked his men were still alert, and signalled to change the scouts. Above them, the great arc of the sky stretched to infinity, unbroken by a single cloud.

Andrew had increased the column's speed, moving steadily while trying to minimise the dust. He continually scanned the veld, searching over the yellow-brown landscape for the splashes of green trees surrounding a Boer's farm. The colours seldom varied; the grass was a dull yellow, as were the *kopjes* when the darting midday haze descended, yet the green of the British countryside was sadly lacking. The *kopje* flanks boasted the *taibosch* – tough bush – an attractive plant tinted in blue, while the aloe hedges that guarded the native kraals were coloured like steel.

"Do you like the veld?" Mariana seemed desperate for conversation.

"I find it fascinating," Andrew replied. "The sheer scale makes one realise how insignificant we are. We believe humans are the lords of creation, yet out here, we could be ants crawling across a playing field."

"Maybe this place is God's playing field, and we are his playthings," Mariana said. "He could be watching us now, deciding on his next move as we plot, scheme and plan our little dreams without real hope of achieving our ant-like ambitions."

Andrew smiled, glad that Mariana was thinking again and enjoying her twists of imagination. "Maybe that's God's idea of giving humanity the veld, to show us how small we are compared to the infinity of nature."

Mariana pointed ahead. "Look over there, Andrew, can you see that green slither? Like a snake coiling across space? It looks like nothing from here, a child's scrawl on a piece of paper, yet when we get close, we'll find a broad river, an obstacle we must cross."

Andrew studied the river through his field glasses. "You're right, Mariana. We'll camp on the bank tonight and cross when we are fresh tomorrow."

They pushed on, with the scouts searching for the searchers and seeking good water for the horses and men. They passed an acre of red conical anthills, three-foot-high mounds of grass and mud, teeming with minuscule life.

Andrew checked to ensure Abercrombie was still with them and thought life could be very pleasant riding with Mariana if the Boers left them alone. No sooner had the idea entered his mind than Sergeant Meek galloped towards him, and Andrew knew his few moments of relaxation had ended.

"Sir!" Meek said. "There might be trouble ahead."

CHAPTER 20

"What is it, Sergeant?"

"I saw a flash from that farmhouse, sir," Meek indicated a distant farm. "It might be innocent, or it might be a Boer watching us through a glass."

"Well done, Sergeant," Andrew said. He pondered for a moment. If he sent a man to scout, any hiding Boer could shoot the lone rider from a distance and gallop away before the Dragoons arrived. On the other hand, if he failed to investigate the farm, a Boer commando could ambush his Dragoons.

"Lieutenant Fletcher," Andrew said formally. "We'll advance in an open line, then split to take the farm in front and rear. You command the right flank, and I'll take the left."

"Yes, sir," Fletcher agreed.

"Sergeant Meek. You and Briggs remain with the civilians." He lowered his voice. "Whatever happens, Sergeant, ensure the Boers don't capture Abercrombie."

"Very good, sir," Meek was too old a soldier to show emotion.

"And Sergeant," Andrew glanced at Mariana.

"I'll look after her, sir," Meek promised. He grinned. "Or Briggs will; he's like a father to Miss Maxwell."

Andrew held Briggs' gaze for a moment. "Did you hear that, Briggs?"

"I did, sir," Briggs replied. "I'll make sure Miss Maxwell is all right."

With a final nod, Andrew turned Lancelot and rode away. The last thing he saw was Mariana waving goodbye.

"No shooting, boys," Andrew said when he joined his Dragoons. "Don't fire unless they fire first. This farmer may be completely innocent."

When Andrew gave the signal, the Dragoons advanced in a sinuous line. Andrew knew it was harder to shoot a moving rather than a stationary target and increased the speed to a canter.

"Sir!" Kerr pointed ahead, where a fold of ground concealed a *spruit* between the Dragoons and the farm.

Too late to stop; we'll have to chance it. "Ride through, boys!"

Willows surrounded the *spruit,* and a small herd of impala scattered in panicked flight as Andrew led from the front, encouraging his Dragoons to follow. Horses' hooves thudded and splashed through the water and up the short, steep slope at the other side. Andrew thrilled to the canter as he signalled for Fletcher to take his section to the right.

"Come on, lads!" Andrew increased his speed.

The Dragoons advanced, hooves pounding, men enjoying the exhilaration of the gallop despite the possible danger; one Dragoon's hat flew off to rise in the air and drop behind the horsemen, drifting in the falling dust.

Every man waited for the double crack of a rifle; every man lifted the Martini-Henry from its bucket and prepared to retaliate, yet they closed on the farmhouse without firing, slowing with as much disappointment as relief. Andrew dismounted first and ran into the steading to see a handful of hens and a middle-aged woman working in the dairy.

The woman looked up in surprise, holding a hand to her chest. "*Meneer?*" She stared at Andrew and spoke in a thick accent he could hardly understand. When more Dragoons burst into her dairy, rifles held ready, she stepped back in genuine alarm.

"It's all right, *tante*," Kerr reassured her. "We mean you no harm."

Andrew pointed to one of the hens that was scratching at the ground. "We would like to purchase some of your chickens," he said. "We'll give you sixpence for every hen."

The woman's eyes narrowed. "Ninepence," she replied.

"Sixpence," Andrew insisted with a smile. "And that's a thief's bargain."

With fresh oat straw for the horses and half a dozen freshly purchased hens to feed the men, Andrew felt the visit was worth the initial excitement as he led his Dragoons away.

The sound of the shot broke Andrew's mood as the bullet whistled past, burrowing into the dirt. "Extended order!" he shouted.

Andrew did not know if a lone Boer had fired the shot or if a commando had caught them. "Ride, boys; Kerr, take the right flank!"

The second double report sounded, with the bullet passing above Andrew's head. "Did anybody see the shooter?"

The Dragoons left the farmhouse at a trot, well spread out, with some men straining to see who was firing at them, while others were only determined to escape. Andrew glanced over his shoulder, counted his men, and saw a faint drift of smoke from the farmhouse, followed by an explosion of horsemen.

Damn! The Groenburg Commando has found us.

"Ride, boys! Ride for your lives!"

"You must have been very brave to be in the Prussian Guard," Engela said.

Konrad tilted his head to one side, a trick he believed made him attractive to women. "No braver than anybody else," he said with mock modesty. "I did earn the Iron Cross at the Battle of Sedan."

"I thought you were brave. Was Sedan a big battle?" Engela did not admit her ignorance about the Iron Cross.

"We had about two hundred thousand men, and the French about a hundred and fifty thousand," Konrad exaggerated the French numbers. "I also fought at Gravelotte, an even larger battle, and the Siege of Paris."

"Oh," Engela could not envision a battle with so many men. She had never seen more than a couple of thousand people gathered at one time. "You have seen some huge battles."

"Battles are the culmination of a soldier's life," Konrad said.

"Were you not afraid?"

"No," Konrad shook his closely cropped head. "I was with the Prussian Guards, the best soldiers in the world."

"Better than the *Rooinecks?*" Engela asked.

"Much better." Konrad showed his teeth in a smile. "It was Blücher's Prussians who won the Battle of Waterloo. If we had not arrived, Bonaparte would have defeated Wellington."

"I see," Engela did not want to admit she had never heard of Waterloo or any battles Konrad had mentioned. She wondered how Konrad had felt when he fought. "It must have been terrible in these wars," she said.

"No," Konrad shook his head. "They were glorious victories, fighting for the Fatherland, defeating an ancient foe, and proving myself as a leader of the Guards."

"What is Prussia like?" Engela asked.

Konrad stepped closer. "It is the most magnificent country anywhere," he said. "We have the bravest soldiers and the best cities." He began to extoll the virtues of Berlin, leading Engela through the cultural delights of Prussia's capital.

Engela listened to Konrad's stories of elegant ladies, fine coaches, great opera houses, restaurants, and balls. Konrad's words transported her to a different world, where she imagined herself far from the farm and everything she knew. She looked down at herself, seeing a plain woman with short fingernails and clumsy shoes, wearing handmade clothes, and wondered what Konrad saw in her.

"I would never belong in Berlin," Engela said sadly.

"You would," Konrad assured her. "You are as beautiful as any woman I have ever seen."

"I am not!" Engela denied, hoping for a rebuttal.

"Oh, you are," Konrad said, smiling with his head on one side. "I can picture you in a silk and satin gown flowing to your ankles, a pearl necklace around your throat, diamond rings on your fingers, and your hair piled up. I would introduce you to the best hairdressers and dressmakers in Berlin, and you would look even more like a princess than you do now." He stood beside her, nearly a foot taller, slim, elegant, and more debonair than any man Engela had met. "Shall we step out of our coach?"

"What is the coach like?" Engela asked. "I've only ever seen a farm cart or the trek wagons."

"Oh, one of our family coaches has tall wheels of bright red," Konrad improvised, "with a dark green body and gold trimmings, deeply padded leather seats, and velvet curtains for the windows. We'll have a team of six matching white horses, a coachman and two servants in livery with my coat of arms – our coat of arms – and a man sounding a horn to clear everybody from the road."

"Do you have a coat of arms?" Engela asked.

"I have, and so will you," Konrad twisted the ring from his middle finger. "There it is."

"Oh," Engela examined the ring. "It's beautiful," she said. "Do you have a castle as well?"

"We have four castles. We live in the largest," Konrad told her, "with grounds and tenants and a host of servants."

"We have servants here," Engela defended her home.

"When I take you to Prussia," Konrad recovered his ring and replaced it on his finger, "I will show you wonders such as you would not believe."

"Will your family not mind that you bring a guest over? It must be very formal to live in a castle," Engela said. "I would not know what to say or how to act."

Konrad laughed. "Oh, you silly little princess," he said, putting his forefinger on her nose. "I would not be bringing you as a guest. I'd be bringing you home as my wife."

"What?" Engela stared at him. "I will probably marry Jan van Collier." She thought of Jan, the hard-working, determined boy she had known all her life, comparing him to Konrad with his elegant manners, wealth, and supreme confidence. Suddenly, Jan looked like a clumsy farm boy without knowledge of the outside world.

"I know Jan well," Konrad said. "He's a decent enough young boy. Honest and brave." He nodded. "Yes, Jan will make a good husband for an ordinary Burgher woman."

Engela frowned. "An ordinary Burgher woman?"

"Yes, but not for you," Konrad said. "You are far from ordinary."

"I am a Boer woman, sir," Engela shook her head. "Your words are weaving a spell around me, but I am no princess to sit on silk cushions and ride in a gold carriage. I have a farm to run."

"I will give you a far better life than anything out here in the wilderness," Konrad said. "I will give you palaces and furs, silks and satins, balls and opera houses, champagne, fine wines and intelligent, influential company."

"I am not suited to that life," Engela protested. "What do I have to give in return?"

When Konrad smiled, his scar puckered into a zigzag. "I am sure you already know what I want, Engela." He stepped towards her with his intentions visibly apparent.

"No!" Engela backed away, half laughing, half alarmed. "Get away!"

Konrad's laughter rose above Engela's sudden fear.

❋

"The Boers are closing, sir," Kerr wiped the sweat from his eyes. "The Groenburg Commando is two miles to our rear, and our scouts report dust in front, a great deal of dust, sir."

Andrew swore. *A great deal of dust means a large commando.* "Johannes van Collier is a good soldier." He looked around, wrestling with their situation. With no possibility of help, he had to rely on guile and determination to escape. "Keep the men moving. Where's Mr Fletcher?"

"Here I am, sir!" Fletcher rode up beside Andrew. His hat was perched on the back of his head, and sweat had created furrows on his dust-coated face. "What do you want me to do?"

"Take a good man and delay the Groenburg Commando. Try and act as though there are ten of you or a hundred. Hold them as long as possible and retire; you know the drill. Take spare horses and try not to get killed."

"Yes, sir," Fletcher said. "What will you do?"

Andrew forced the grin that had earned him his 'Up and at 'em' reputation in the Cape Frontier War. "I'm going to scatter the enemy in front."

"Yes, sir. May I have Kerr?"

Andrew glanced at Kerr, his best man but weary after days of scouting. "Are you fit, Kerr?"

"Yes, sir," Kerr replied immediately.

"Go with Fletcher."

"Yes, sir." Kerr and Fletcher trotted towards the Groenburg Commando.

Andrew returned to his men. Abercrombie was riding beside Mariana, with Sergeant Meek shepherding the Dragoons and civilians like an anxious father.

Meek moderated his habitual roar. "Come on, Mrs Murphy, try to keep up. Mrs Williams, there's no need to panic, even if the Boers catch us, they won't eat you. That's better."

"The Boers are in front and behind," Andrew informed his men. "I've sent Lieutenant Fletcher and Kerr to delay the

Groenburg Commando so we can concentrate on the enemy in front."

The Dragoons listened, immediately understanding their position.

"We're going to show a bold front," Andrew said. "Rather than avoid them, we're going right for their throat."

Meek and Ogden grinned while others nodded grimly or lifted their rifles.

"What about the ladies, sir?" Briggs asked.

Andrew thought for a moment. "You and Booth look after the women and other civilians," Andrew said. "Keep them out of danger."

"Yes, sir." When Briggs hesitated, Andrew knew he would prefer to fight alongside his colleagues.

"That's an order, Briggs."

"Yes, sir," Briggs stiffened his back.

"Keep Abercrombie safe," Andrew lowered his voice. "And Miss Maxwell."

"I will, sir."

General Hook might consider Abercrombie more important than Mariana, but Briggs will put Mariana first, which suits me.

Andrew felt Mariana watching him, so he allowed her a reassuring nod and called the Dragoons together.

"We'll ride forward openly, and when we see the enemy, we charge," Andrew said. "There's a river ahead. If we can trap them between us and the river, we can do some damage and keep them away from the civilians." He thought on his feet, aware his knowledge of the local terrain was imperfect. He nodded to a small ridge where thornbushes crackled under the heat. "I want Brown and Spalding, the best two shots, to lie there and fire at the enemy. We all know a charging man will never hit his target, but a man lying can. If we charge and fire, and the two marksmen bring a Boer or two to the ground, the enemy might believe we're superb shots. Which we are, of course."

The expected ripple of laughter defused some of the tension.

"Are there any questions?" Andrew could see the dust ahead, concealing the second commando that closed the net on the British. They must have superior numbers to advance so openly.

Sergeant Meek shook his head. "No, sir. We'll just follow you."

Andrew hoped he appeared confident. "Keep your heads down, boys and the best of luck to us all."

Charging a more numerous force of expert shots was never easy. Andrew knew his chances of survival were slim.

I hope Briggs looks after Mariana. "Right, lads. Up and at 'em!"

The Dragoons moved forward, each horse kicking up a quota of dust, so they advanced through a choking haze toward the hidden enemy. Andrew heard his two marksmen firing, with the bullets hissing above the Dragoons' heads. Unable to see the Boers through the dust, Andrew could only advance, hoping his Swartspruit tactics worked a second time. He heard Ogden blow on his bugle and felt the shudder of scores of hooves on the hard ground.

"They're on the flanks, sir!" Sergeant Meek shouted.

Andrew glanced to his left, where half a dozen Boers surged from a shallow valley and charged toward them, while another group of riders appeared on their right.

"They'll cut us off from the civilians, sir," Fletcher said.

"Damn it," Andrew replied. "You're right." *Van Collier is after Abercrombie.* "Ogden! Sound the recall!"

Ordering cavalry to charge was one thing; halting them in full flow was completely different. Ogden blew his bugle while Andrew, Fletcher, and Meek roared their loudest, yet still the Dragoons galloped forward. Swearing, Andrew spurred on, turned Lancelot, and lifted his arms. "Retire! Get back to the ridge!"

One by one, the Dragoons halted and turned. Andrew saw angry, surprised faces and men pulling at excited horses.

Where are the Boers? Where are the men we were charging?

When a chance breeze cleared some of the dust, Andrew

only saw two horsemen firing rifles in the air and dragging bushes behind them.

Only two men with bushes creating a dust cloud! Van Collier is using our deception tactics against us.

"Back to the ridge!" Andrew yelled. "Fletcher! Round up the civilians and get them to the ridge!" *Thank God Sergeant Meek saw the men on the flanks before it was too late.*

The Dragoons retired in a confused rush, each rider choosing what he considered the best route. Andrew counted his men, relieved none had fallen.

"Get these civilians onto the ridge," Andrew roared. "Horse holders, take the horses to the middle. The rest form a firing line and prepare to repel boarders." He looked over his men, knowing the Boer commander had outridden and outthought him. "We'll hold on here, lads, and hope the British relieving column finds us."

There is little chance of that in the vastness of the veld unless our gunfire attracts them.

The three groups of Boers merged until the Groenburg Commando came in a single wave of horsemen, shouting and firing as they advanced towards the ridge.

"Fire!" Andrew ordered. "Shoot them flat!" He aimed and fired, wondering which vague shape in the dust was Johannes van Collier. Although he wanted to shoot him for the sake of victory, a small part of him admired the Boer veldcornet.

The Natal Dragoons fired and reloaded, fired, and reloaded, trying to repel the Boers by the sheer volume of musketry. After five minutes of concentrated firing, Andrew saw the Boer line hesitate, with riders dismounting to seek cover and the dust slowly drifting away. The sun reflected from small piles of empty brass cartridge cases.

"Enough! We've stopped them! Don't waste ammunition, boys," Andrew saw Briggs usher the civilians into the safest section of the ridge. "We could be here for some time."

Here we go. How long can we hold out against the Groenburg

Commando and whatever else van Collier throws at us? Unless the relieving column reaches us soon, the Boers will be able to boast of another victory.

"I want you, my little milkmaid," Konrad said. "I'll show you what a Prussian man is like." He slid off his jacket and advanced on Engela. "Once you've experienced me, you'll not want your peasant farm boy again."

"Get away!" Engela shouted, backing against the wall. She looked around frantically for help. Until recently, she had only met close friends and relatives and did not understand a predator like Konrad. "Leave me!"

"You don't mean that!" Konrad stood before Engela, blocking her escape as he removed his shirt. "You find me attractive, Engela, a sophisticated European man, rather than some clumsy boy from nowhere."

"No!" Engela looked for a weapon. "Get away!"

"Look!" Konrad lowered his trousers, grinning.

"No!" Engela shook her head.

"I'm looking," Mannie slid through the door behind Engela. "Leave her alone!"

Konrad hardened his voice. "Go away, boy; this has nothing to do with you."

"Leave her," Mannie stepped closer.

"Get out, boy!" Konrad snapped. "I am a Prussian officer, and I order you to leave. Engela wants me here."

Konrad's tone made Mannie flinch. He stopped, staring at Engela, who shook her head.

"Engela is my brother's girl," Mannie was younger, smaller, and slighter than Konrad and still weak from his recent illness. "Get away from her."

Konrad's backhanded slap knocked Mannie off his feet and slammed him against the wall. Engela screamed as Mannie slid to the floor, leaving a smear of blood down the rough stonework. He lay still, stunned.

"Now, my girl," Konrad said. "There are no more distractions." He grabbed hold of Engela's shoulder. "You're mine."

Engela tried to break free, but Konrad had a powerful grip. He squeezed cruelly, revelling in his strength. "Struggle if you wish, my little Boer milkmaid; I enjoy it when women try to fight back."

"What about the palaces, carriages and opera houses you promised?" Engela asked, wriggling. Konrad blocked her slap, twisted her wrist behind her, and began to rip off her clothes.

"Too good for the likes of a little milkmaid," Konrad responded.

"Leave her!" Mannie pushed himself up, blinking through the blood that covered half his face.

"Get away, boy," Konrad sneered. "Or I'll take a whip to you."

Mannie threw himself forward, using his anger as a weapon. With Konrad partially distracted by holding Engela, Mannie's rush forced him backwards. He swore, released Engela, and recovered.

"I'll take care of you first, boy," Konrad snarled, "and then show the little milkmaid what a Prussian is made of."

Mannie was slight but wiry and angry. His punch landed on Konrad's cheekbone, causing the Prussian to wince.

"I'll kill you for that," Konrad hissed.

Lifting a heavy milking pail, Engela swung it, catching Konrad on the side of his head. "You'll kill nobody!" she screamed. "Get him, Mannie!"

Konrad backed away, staggering as his trousers tangled around his ankles. When he bent down to unholster his pistol, Engela swung the pail again, knocking him onto his face. Konrad hauled out his gun, mouthing threats. He aimed at the advancing Mannie and curled his finger around the trigger.

The roar of the shot echoed around the dairy. The heavy bullet crashed into Konrad's head, smashed his skull, and sent fragments of bone, brain, and blood against the whitewashed wall.

Engela and Mannie stared as Konrad slumped to the floor with the pistol still gripped in his dead hand.

Aletta lowered the rifle. "I knew that Prussian was trouble," she said quietly, with the gun smoke curling around her poke bonnet.

ANDREW CHECKED HIS WATCH. THE SUN WOULD SET IN AN hour, which meant the battle had raged for five hours. Now, the Boers were edging closer, keeping to the dead ground and shelter of rocks and ant hills, ready for a final rush in the dark. Three bodies lay in front of the Dragoons' position, the Boers' casualties from their first abortive advance, with a fur of flies feasting on each man. Two more lay beside rocks on the approach to the ridge. Andrew guessed that van Collier did not wish to risk further casualties from his commando, friends, and neighbours he had probably known all his life. The close-knit companionship was both a strength and a weakness of the commando system.

"They're closing in!" Turner said, aiming and firing. His bullet kicked up a fountain of dirt beside a rock as the empty cartridge added to the brassy pile at his side.

"They're coming for the kill this time," Ogden said. He touched the blood that had dried down the side of his face.

"They'll have to cross the open ground to reach us," Kerr reminded. "The Boers don't like that."

"We can hold them off," Andrew glanced at the civilians, where Mariana stood tall, watching him. "Keep your head down, Mariana! Even an Afrikander Bond Boer won't deliberately harm a woman, but a stray bullet might hit you."

Mariana lifted her chin and gave a brave smile. "I'll be all right," she said. "You look after yourself, Andrew." Her eyes were clear.

If Mariana survives this battle, I think she'll be fine.

Andrew rose to check on his men. The Dragoons were dug into shallow trenches or waiting behind rocks, firing at any Boer who showed himself. They had seen off one impetuous Boer attack and delayed the besiegers' slow advance, but at a prodigious cost in bullets.

My men could do no more. It's unfortunate that we're against such an innovative Boer commander. If only that marksman hadn't destroyed our heliograph, we could have rendezvoused with the relieving force. Now, Van Collier will capture Gladstone's nephew and hand him over to the Prussians. I have failed unless we have some miracle.

With the Dragoons as secure as possible, Andrew moved to the civilians, who huddled in a slight depression in the ridge, holding the horses and acting as bravely as any trained soldier. Booth greeted Andrew with a wave.

"How are we doing, Captain?"

"We're holding our own," Andrew replied. "The Boers can't advance without losing men."

"Good show," Abercrombie was on his hands and knees, examining the rocks. "Tell them to hold off, will you? I might find something interesting here, apart from ants and scorpions."

"You keep safe, Abercrombie," Andrew said. "Are you all right, Mrs Murphy? And you, Mrs Williams?"

"We're just grand," Mrs Murphy replied bravely. "Mr Briggs has been looking after us."

"Briggs is a very capable man," Andrew replied.

"Sir!" Meek shouted. "The Boers are advancing again!"

Andrew lifted his hat. "Excuse me, ladies. Duty calls!" He moved to the firing line, ducking as a Boer bullet hissed overhead.

"They seem serious this time, sir," Fletcher said. "They might charge us in the dark."

"Maybe so," Andrew agreed.

"What's happening?" Abercrombie emerged from the central depression.

"The bloody Boers are happening, you blasted idiot!" Andrew's response revealed the shredded state of his nerves. "Get under cover!"

"Oh, all right!" Abercrombie seemed unconscious of the bullets that zipped and pinged from the British positions.

Turner moved closer to Abercrombie. "You stay with me, Charlie boy. I'll do what's best."

What the devil does that mean? Andrew frowned and realised other matters demanded his attention. The Boers were closing in, firing from cover, and moving forward, nearly invisible against the dun and brown of the veld.

Andrew raised his voice. "How much ammunition do you have left, boys?"

"Five rounds, sir."

"Three rounds, sir."

"Seven rounds, sir."

"Seven? Haven't you been with us, McAlister?"

The laughter was forced but welcome as the Dragoons accepted any excuse to relieve the tension.

"Don't waste what you have," Andrew ordered. He tried to count the Boers, spotting them by a slight movement here, a bird's sudden flight or a puff of falling dust. A bullet plunged into the ground at his side, seemingly intent on hitting him but stopping three inches short of its target.

Half an hour until night, and then Van Collier's men will walk over us.

"Ogden! Blow your bugle! They might think reinforcements are coming."

The bugle sounded above the intermittent crackle of musketry, a defiant sound in the hot African air. When the liquid notes faded away, there was a moment of silence, as if the world waited for a reaction, then a single shot cracked the peace, and reality returned.

Half a dozen vultures circled above, waiting for their opportunity to feast.

Andrew saw the tip of a hat above a rounded rock and aimed his rifle. The man had to move slightly to fire. Andrew waited, saw a flicker of movement, the curve of a hip momentarily exposed and squeezed the trigger. The Boer reared up, reaching behind him, and rolled away, holding his wound. Andrew reloaded quickly, contemplated finishing the man off and decided he was already wounded and out of the fight.

Don't waste ammunition.

The Boer response came immediately, with bullets hammering around Andrew's position. He lay snug behind his rock until the fusillade ended and crawled to a new position.

"Hold on, Dragoons!"

"Sir!" Fletcher shouted. "They're showing a flag of truce."

"Hold your fire, boys!" Andrew shouted. Aware of the renewed hammer of his heart, he took a deep breath and stood up. When nobody fired at him, Andrew released his breath. Two Boers rode towards the ridge, one holding a white flag.

"Are you surrendering, *meneer*?" Andrew asked. He recognised the leading man. "You're Johannes Van Collier, aren't you?"

Johannes lifted his hat. "I am, Captain Baird. And this is my son, Jan."

"What can I do for you, Mr van Collier? I'm afraid I've no facilities to care for prisoners, but if you choose to return to your farm, we won't stop you." Andrew saw two men attending the Boer he had shot.

"We have a proposition for you, Captain," Johannes said.

"What is it, Mr van Collier?" Andrew asked.

"We have five hundred men," Johannes said. "You have about twenty soldiers and three women. We are in our own land, and you are lost in a foreign country. We have you surrounded, and you are short of food and ammunition."

Andrew listened without comment.

Johannes paused momentarily, with a faint breeze stirring the white flag. A fly buzzed around Jan's face, landed on his cheek, and began to drink his sweat. He brushed it away.

"Although we can kill or capture you all," Johannes said, "we will let you return to Natal unharmed, with all your horses, guns, and ammunition. On one condition."

"What is your condition?" Andrew asked.

"Hand over Mr Charles Abercrombie to us," Johannes said. "We will look after him; he will not be harmed."

Andrew held Johannes' gaze, knowing the veldcornet spoke the truth. He did not want any more bloodshed. Andrew shook his head. "Thank you for your offer, Mr van Collier, but we are fine as we are. You do not have five hundred men, although you may have a hundred at the most. We are not lost, but only a short distance from British territory; we expect a large relieving column any minute, and we have sufficient food and ammunition for an army ten times our size." He forced what he hoped was a confident smile. "As for Mr Abercrombie, he remains with us."

Johannes touched his hat. "Is that your last word, Captain?"

"It is, *meneer*," Andrew replied.

"As you wish, Captain," Johannes said. "I will allow you the night to consider my offer. If you have not agreed by the morning, I must regretfully attack and wipe out your handful of men. Good evening to you, Captain Baird." Raising his hat politely, Johannes turned his horse and withdrew. Jan lingered a moment longer, threw a poisonous glare at Andrew, and followed his father.

That lad will be trouble if this war flares up again.

"I could give myself up, Captain," Abercrombie volunteered when the Boers withdrew.

"No," Andrew replied shortly.

"It would end the killing," Abercrombie said. "I'm not really important, you know."

"You're the Prime Minister's nephew," Andrew snarled. "You've no business wandering off into the wilds."

"Would you have me wrap up in cotton wool because of my uncle's position?" Abercrombie asked.

Andrew calmed down. "No," he said. "Of course not. You have as much right to put yourself in danger as anybody has. Did you find gold?"

Abercrombie smiled. "I wasn't looking for gold," he said. "I was looking for diamonds and didn't find them either." His smile widened to a grin. "Either I am not a very good geologist, or there's nothing here except dust and space."

"If that's true," Andrew replied slowly, "it might be a blessing for all concerned. The earth's treasures seem to attract trouble."

"Captain Baird said there was a British column out here," Johannes said. "We had better end this stupidity before they arrive."

"We knew there were more *Rooinecks*," Theunis replied. "That's why Baird was signalling with the heliograph."

"He could have been trying to dupe us," Johannes said. "He is as full of tricks as a troop of monkeys."

"We should attack them now," Theunis looked over at the ridge, where the British campfires flickered through the night. "When they don't expect us."

"I gave my word to wait until morning," Johannes said.

"It was a foolish word to give. The *Rooinecks* think we have a hundred men. How many do we have left?" Theunis began to count, using both hands as he named the members of the commando. "Thirty-one men only."

"Thirty," Johannes corrected. "Karl is wounded and cannot ride."

"That's correct," Theunis said. "All the more reason to attack now. Come, Johannes, or we'll lose more men."

"No!" Johannes refused.

"At least we can take Abercrombie!" Theunis said. "If we

capture him, the *Rooinecks* will have no reason to stay, and we can all go home."

Johannes looked at Theunis, thinking of Aletta and his farm. *Why does the Lord allow wars?*

ANDREW HEARD THE MOVEMENT WHEN HE RETURNED FROM checking the pickets. *Have the Boers launched a night raid?* Holding his carbine, he sank low and listened to locate the source of the noise. His pickets were quiet, watching outward over the dark veld. Behind him, the two campfires crackled and hissed, sending aromatic smoke into the air. The civilians remained close to the heat, for the night on the veld was cold.

The noise came again, a definite rustle and the slight scrape of a boot on rock. Andrew remained still, quartering the camp with his eyes, examining each section before moving to the next. His practised eyes could distinguish the Dragoons by the hard edge of their bush hats or the faint glint of starlight on the barrels of their weapons.

"What?"

Andrew heard the single word, instantly stifled. *That's Charles Abercrombie's voice!* Andrew strode forward. He saw a shrouded figure beside Abercrombie with the glint of a blade.

What the devil? The Boers are trying to kidnap Abercrombie. So much for van Collier's word!

"Halt!" Andrew threw himself forward, crashed into the knifeman, and knocked him sprawling to the ground. "You oath-breaking bastard!" He swung his rifle, aiming for the man's head but hitting his shoulder. "Lie still, you Boer bugger!"

The noise had roused the Dragoons, who grabbed their rifles and glared around, searching for the enemy.

"What's happening?"

"Where are they?"

"I can't see anything."

"Bring a light!" Andrew snarled, and Sergeant Meek lifted a burning log from the Dragoons' fire and hurried across. "Right, my Burgher friend, let's be having you." He turned the attacker around so he lay face up. "Turner! What the hell?"

Meek lifted the makeshift torch with his left hand and jabbed the muzzle of his carbine into Turner's chest with his right. "What's it all about?"

Turner glared up at them, still holding a long-bladed knife.

Abercrombie was standing with his hair a tousled mess and his mouth open in shock. "Turner? Why?"

Andrew stood on Turner's arm and removed the knife. "Get up!"

Turner stood, holding his shoulder. "Orders, sir. I was obeying orders."

"Are you a Boer spy?" Meek asked as the Dragoons and civilians gathered around.

"No," Andrew shook his head. "He's acting for General Hook. Isn't that right, Turner?"

Turner shrugged with a faint smile on his face. "I was obeying orders," he repeated. "I was to ensure the Boers did not capture Abercrombie."

Andrew grunted. "Take this man away, Sergeant, tie him up and put him under armed guard."

"Very good, sir," Meek replied. "Come along, Turner."

Abercrombie dusted himself down. "All this fuss over a failed geologist. I didn't mean to cause any trouble."

"I'm sure you didn't, Abercrombie," Andrew said and raised his voice. "All right, everybody. Excitement over; get back to sleep if you can."

My father once warned me to avoid politicians. I'd add politicians' relatives to the list.

Dawn burst on them with a glorious sunrise and no movement from the Boers.

"Do you think they'll attack, sir?" Fletcher asked.

"They might," Andrew replied. "Or van Collier could be bluffing. I doubt his commando is as strong as he wants us to believe."

The sun rose quickly, spreading light across the veld.

"Dust, sir," Kerr pointed to the horizon.

Andrew lifted his field glasses and studied the land in the direction Kerr pointed. "I see it," he said. "Now, we know a British column is out there somewhere, but there might also be another Boer commando."

"Yes, sir," Kerr said with a tight smile. "The question is, which force is creating that dust; us or the Boers."

The Boers already outnumber us by about six to one, but we're still holding them back. If more Boers arrive, we won't have a chance. However, if that's a British column, the Groenburg Commando will scatter, and we'll get home.

"What do we do, sir?" Fletcher was also studying the dust cloud.

"We continue as we are, Fletcher, and we pray." Andrew saw that Mariana was sitting beside Abercrombie in the centre of the civilians' position, with Turner lying at their side, bound hand and foot. Briggs was watching them, cradling his rifle, and his eyes unreadable. A single vulture flew overhead, circling as it waited for the inevitable casualties.

"Go to your man," Aletta ordered sternly. "He thinks you no longer want him."

Engela looked down at Konrad. "I nearly betrayed him with that thing there."

"It is a long step from nearly to reality," Aletta said. "Do you love my son?"

Engela nodded. "Ja," she said simply.

"Then go and tell him," Aletta advised. "Mannie will take you to the Groenburg Commando."

"Are you fit to ride, Mannie?" Engela asked.

"Ja. I am fit," Mannie ignored the blood drying on his face.

"Come then," Engela raised her chin. "I hope that Jan will take me back."

"That is between you and Jan," Aletta replied sternly. "Tell him how you feel, and let the Lord guide you both." She pushed Engela towards the door. "Go with Mannie." She watched as they rode away, smiling, for her younger son had also proved himself a man.

"That could be the British relief column, or it could be a Burgher commando," Johannes gestured to the rising dust.

"What do we do?" Theunis asked. He swept back his hair and smoothed a hand along the barrel of his rifle.

"Jan!" Johannes snapped. "Ride over and see who is making that dust. If it's the British, come and inform me. Don't do anything to alert them."

"Yes, Pa," Jan replied. Mounting his horse, he kicked in his heels and rode at a steady trot toward the dust. He knew it was some miles away, so there was no point in pushing too hard and tiring his horse. Jan loosened his rifle in its holster, adjusted his hat so it sheltered him from the worst of the sun and prepared for a steady ride.

More men had left the Groenburg Commando to return to their farms, leaving Johannes with less than twenty fighting Burghers. He held the Natal Dragoons by bluff and offensive action, but he would have to withdraw if a larger British force arrived.

"Watch the British positions," Johannes said to the remnants of his commando. "Baird will also have seen the dust. If he sends a rider, I want two men to hunt him down."

Theunis nodded. "I will go."

"Do that. Make sure the *Rooineck* does not hurt my son."

"THE BOERS HAVE SENT A MAN TO GREET THE OTHER COLUMN," Fletcher reported, watching through his field glasses.

Andrew nodded. "Either that or van Collier is checking to see who they are."

"That's possible, sir," Fletcher allowed. "Shall we send a man as well?"

"I can go, sir," Ogden volunteered.

Andrew scanned the Boer positions. Although he could not see them, he knew the Boers were there, remaining behind cover as they held the British on the parched ridge. "Do you think you'd get through their lines, Ogden, and then return with the information? Van Collier is an experienced commander. He'll expect us to try that."

Ogden nodded. "I can try, sir."

"No," Andrew decided. "Stay with us."

"What will we do?" Fletcher asked.

"We'll sit tight," Andrew said. "If that's a relief column, van Collier might try one last rush to capture Abercrombie, and if it's more Boers, well, we're already outnumbered."

Fletcher nodded. "It all depends on what that fellow discovers," he nodded to the thread of dust where the lone Boer rode towards the approaching force.

"It does," Andrew agreed. He glanced towards Abercrombie, but his gaze strayed to Mariana.

The Dragoons waited under the relentless lash of the sun. From their raised position on the ridge, they had a slight advantage over the Boers on the lower ground, watched for any movement and counted their cartridges.

"Fire if you have a definite target," Andrew said. "Make the Boers think we have plenty of ammunition, but don't waste bullets." He glanced upward, where the vultures circled in the vast arc of the sky. That morning, only one bird had watched them; now, half a dozen waited for death to feed them.

"I hate these birds," Fletcher said.

"Nature's cleansers," Andrew replied casually.

"When I die, I don't want one of these things to eat me," Fletcher stared upwards. "The idea of being inside their stomach is horrible."

"You'll be dead at the time," Andrew said. "You won't know anything about it."

"What if I'm only wounded, and they eat me alive," Fletcher said.

"Blow your brains out," Andrew told him. "Or even better, don't allow the Boers to shoot you."

Sergeant Meek raised his voice. "Dust from the west, sir. It looks like a lone rider, or maybe two."

Andrew focused his field glasses. "We know one thing," he said. "There are no British forces in that direction."

Kerr glanced at Meek, raised his eyebrows, and pressed a bullet into the breech of his carbine. He checked his bandoleer, found it empty and plunged a hand inside his ammunition pouch. His fingers scrabbled frantically until they closed on a couple of fat brass cartridges.

Three bullets left, and then it's butts, bayonets, boots, and fists. Kerr stamped his feet on the ground. *On you come, Brother Boers; we're ready.* His smile was self-mocking as he peered over the veld.

CHAPTER 21

Mannie felt his strength draining as he pushed his horse forward. Still not fully recovered from his illness, he found riding day after day across the veld tiring but knew he could not let Jan down. His brother had helped him during the siege of Potchefstroom and had taken him home, missing the victory of Majuba. Mannie wanted to return the kindness, whatever the physical cost. He slumped in the saddle, forcing himself to cover the miles. Whatever happened, Mannie knew he had to ride on. He stared ahead at the endless dun plain, listened to the remorseless hollow thump of his horse's hooves and continued.

I'm coming, Jan. I'm bringing Engela to you. Mannie repeated the exact words until they seemed to echo his horse's hoofprints on the hard ground.

Engela rode at his side, wondering what to say when she met Jan. She hoped he would understand when she told him about Konrad. She knew she would admit everything, for lying was not in her nature.

Oh, dear Lord, please let Jan forgive me. I don't want to lose my man.

"Over there!" Mannie smelled tobacco before he heard anything. He turned his horse and led Engela over the small ridge and down, where a man in a broad-brimmed hat stepped in front of them.

"Mannie!" Johannes lowered his rifle. "What are you doing here?"

"We are looking for Jan," Mannie explained. "Where is he?"

"He's out scouting," Johannes said. "I see you have brought Engela with you."

"Ja," Mannie said. "She wants to see Jan."

They all looked up as firing broke out to the west.

"A British column is coming!" Theunis roared. "Storm the Dragoons! Capture Abercrombie!"

"The Boers are moving," Fletcher reported.

Andrew nodded. "I see them." He raised his voice. "Keep alert, boys, Piet is up to something."

The Dragoons checked their rifles and settled down. Few had more than three rounds of ammunition remaining, some less. Briggs looked from Andrew to Mariana.

"You keep your head down, Miss Maxwell," he advised. "Like the Captain told you, the Boers won't hurt you, but a stray bullet might."

"Thank you, William," Mariana said. "I'll look after myself. You take care of Mrs Murphy; she seems to favour you." She smiled at Briggs' startled expression.

Abercrombie lifted a tired hand. "I'm giving you all an awful lot of trouble," he said. "It might be better if I surrendered, and you could all go home."

"Now, now, Mr Abercrombie," Sergeant Meek rebuked. "We'll have none of that defeatist talk. You obey the captain's orders, and everything will turn out fine."

"Get back down, Mr Abercrombie!" Andrew snarled. "Kerr!"

"Sir!" Kerr hurried across with his carbine at the trail.

"If it looks like the Boers are about to overrun us, I want you to take Mr Abercrombie and break free. Ride like the devil for the border. Natal is only thirty miles or so to the south."

"I don't want to leave you, sir." Kerr protested.

"You'll do as you're damned well told," Andrew said. "You'll keep close to Abercrombie, ignore everybody else and get him to safety."

"What about Miss Maxwell, sir?" Briggs asked, "and the other ladies?"

Andrew realised that every Dragoon was listening to him. "Johannes van Collier is a gentleman," Andrew said. "He won't hurt any of the ladies."

"I wouldn't leave anyway," Mariana lifted her chin. "And you could not make me."

"That's another reason you're not taking Miss Maxwell," Andrew said. "She's as stubborn as a battery mule."

The men's laugh eased the tension. Mariana frowned for an instant, then smiled. "I am glad that's cleared up," she said.

"Keep your head down, Mariana!" Andrew snapped. "Or I'll have Briggs tie you hand and foot and carry you face down over a horse!" he closed his mouth as he realised the strain was affecting him.

Mariana looked sideways at him. "I'll keep my head down," she understood.

"Here they come!" Briggs said and unceremoniously shoved Mariana into her trench.

The Groenburg Commando advanced slowly, with some men firing and the others advancing from cover to cover. Theunis led them with his hair a dark tangle over his shoulders as he encouraged the men.

"Onwards, boys! Send the *Rooinecks* back to London!"

"Only fire when you have a definite target," Andrew reminded. He saw the dust cloud approaching and hoped it hid a British column. If he could hold out for another half hour, he might be safe. But half an hour was a long time when the Groenburg Commando was attacking.

The Dragoons fired slowly and carefully, conserving ammunition as Boer bullets hissed and cracked around them. Kerr shoved Abercrombie into a shallow depression beside a thorn bush, snarled at him to "keep out of the bloody way," and fired. The bullet caught a Boer in the shoulder, spinning him around. Andrew checked on Mariana, saw that Briggs was sheltering beside her trench and knew she was as safe as anybody could be in the middle of a skirmish. Andrew ducked as a Boer bullet knocked the hat from his head, aimed at a darting man and released his finger from the trigger as the man dived into cover.

Concentrate, Andrew. You can't look after everybody and shoot the Boers.

Fletcher gave a little grunt, opened his eyes wide, and rolled over, with blood spreading from his chest.

"The Boers got the lieutenant!" Ogden shouted. "Shoot the bastards!"

"Steady, lads!" Meek sounded as calm as if he were on exercise on Salisbury Plain. "Mark your targets!" He aimed and fired, hitting an advancing Boer in the stomach and doubling him up. "They can't take many more casualties!"

"Ammo!" Ogden shouted. "I've only one cartridge left!" He rolled towards the fallen Fletcher, scrabbled in his ammunition pouch, and removed two bullets. "Mr Fletcher has been hoarding them," he said.

"Throw one this way," McAlister shouted. "I'm out!"

"I've only one left," Morrison yelled. "I'm saving it until they get close."

Sergeant Meek fired again. "That's my last, sir." He lifted a fist-sized rock from the ground. "Boots and bayonets, lads, boots and bayonets!"

"Wait for them to come, now, boys. They don't like the bayonet!" Andrew ordered. He had surrendered at Majuba and was determined never to undergo that humiliation again. "Wait until they come close and attack them. Mariana! Are you all right?"

"Yes!" Mariana shouted.

"Keep down then," Andrew ordered. "Are you ready, Kerr?"

"Ready, sir," Kerr replied.

"When you see a gap, bundle Abercrombie onto a horse and run. Don't look back, and don't stop for anybody."

"Yes, sir," Kerr said.

"Here they come, sir," Meek warned.

JAN BLINKED AWAY THE DUST FROM HIS EYES AS HE GUIDED HIS horse into the shelter of a thorn bush. He saw the men approaching, riding in an untidy formation with dust obscuring them so he could not ascertain their identity. They might be Burghers, or they might be British Colonials.

I only have to identify them, and then I can outride any Rooineck soldier.

Jan watched them for a few moments without making up his mind.

I'll have to move closer.

Jan slid from the shelter of the thorn bush and guided his horse across the rough ground. He had missed the battle on Majuba Hill and hoped the Groenburg Commando would not engage the British without him. He hoped his father was not trying to keep him away from danger.

I am a man; I must fight to defend the Republic. There is nothing else in my life.

The riders were now closer, more easily seen even through the dust screen. Jan saw two men detach themselves from the mass and ride towards him. Both fired their rifles in the air to attract Jan's attention.

Briton or Boer? He would soon find out.

Jan loosened the rifle in its holster, remembered his father's words about not fighting and prepared to run.

"Who are you?" A further two men appeared behind Jan,

both with rifles aimed directly at him. They spoke in English. "Give me your name and unit!"

ANDREW SAW THE BOERS HAD WITHDRAWN NEARLY ALL THEIR pickets to concentrate on the attack, leaving a massive gap in the rear of the ridge. "Kerr!" Andrew roared. "Now!"

He only had time to shout the two words when the Boers were on them, yelling as they climbed the incline. *There are only sixteen of them. We have a chance.*

The British rose, some with clubbed rifles, others with fixed bayonets, and met the attackers face to face.

"Natal Dragoons!" Ogden roared. "Come on, you Boer bastards!"

"Send them back!" Andrew shouted, swinging his carbine at a hirsute man with a terai hat. "Come on, the Natal Dragoons!"

From the side of his eye, Andrew saw Kerr drag Abercrombie away and throw him on his horse. He saw Meek grappling with a young blond Boer, throw him to the ground, and thrust his bayonet into the man's arm. He saw Ogden falling as a Boer shot him from close range, and then the Boers were recoiling, withdrawing down the hill in a retreat that soon became a rout.

"They're running!" Meek shouted.

"They don't like the bayonet," McAlister strode forward. "Come on, lads!"

"Let them go!" Andrew ordered. "It could be an ambush! McAlister! Don't chase them! Are you all right, Mariana?"

Mariana emerged from her trench. "I'm all right." She stepped towards Fletcher. "Is he dead?"

"I think so," Andrew said.

Mariana knelt at Fletcher's side. "He's still breathing."

"Do what you can for him!" Andrew ordered. He saw Mrs. Murphy and Mrs. Williams emerge from shelter to check on Ogden and then concentrated on the battlefield.

Two dead Boers lay on the ground beside the youngster Meek had bayonetted. One dead man's hat had fallen off, revealing a mane of black hair around the bald crown of his head.

That's Theunis Steenekamp. I saw him talk at Krugersdorp. Andrew wondered anew at the terrible futility of war, where brave men and foolish men fought for ideas that would never benefit them and land they would never farm. Men who would be the best of friends in peacetime strove to kill each other because their political leaders disagreed.

"Send the wounded lad back," Andrew ordered. "He's no danger to us. Take his rifle and ammunition."

Andrew watched as the blond Boer limped down the slope, holding his wounded arm. Another Boer rode up under a flag of truce to help his colleague. Andrew recognised Johannes van Collier as the helper and was strangely glad the veldcornet had survived.

"Come, Abraham," Johannes murmured, deep-voiced.

"Good luck, Johannes," Andrew whispered.

As if he had heard, Johannes turned around, and for a moment, his eyes locked with Andrew's.

Andrew lifted a hand in greeting, saw Johannes respond, and turned away. A small ribbon of dust to the south showed where Kerr and Abercrombie were riding towards Natal.

The longer we hold the Boers here, the better chance we give Abercrombie and Kerr.

"Collect any discarded Boer rifles," Andrew ordered. "See what ammunition the dead Burghers had. Every single bullet helps."

"Sir!" Meek said. "Over there! Are they British or Boer?"

Andrew lifted his field glasses as a mass of men approached under the rising dust. "I don't know," he said. "They could be either."

THE SOUND OF BOER RIFLES

JAN STOPPED AS THE TWO MEN HELD HIM AT GUNPOINT. "Who are you?" the leading man asked again, then repeated the words in the Taal.

"I am Jan van Collier of Nuwe Hoop Plaas and the Groenburg Commando under my father, Johannes van Collier and Theunis Steenekamp," Jan replied proudly. He wondered if he could traverse his rifle, shoot both men and escape. "What are you *Rooinecks* doing in our land?"

"We are no *Rooinecks*," the leading man holstered his rifle. "I am Henrick van Renswick of Pretoria, and this is Piet Cloete, second cousin of Karl Cloete of the Groenburg Commando."

"You are Burghers?" Jan asked, unable to stop his smile.

"We are Burghers," Henrick replied. "We heard shooting."

"We have a British force trapped on a ridge," Jan said. "We didn't know if you were Burghers or British."

"That will be Captain Baird's Natal Dragoons," Henrick said. "Come with us and tell the commander."

All three men stopped as they heard renewed firing from the ridge.

"It seems that your father has ordered an attack on the ridge," Henrick said.

"It seems so," Jan replied.

"Here is our commander," Henrick said. "Tell him who you are and why you are here." He smiled faintly. "His name is Paul Kruger."

Jan gasped. "The Vice-President?"

Paul Kruger greeted Jan like an old friend and listened to his story. "Your father has done well, Jan. Lead us," he said, ordering his commando to follow. They were over five hundred men, all well-mounted and armed, veterans of siege and battle.

The ridge rose two hundred feet above the plain, marked by green thorn bushes and gun smoke. Kruger halted the commando as the British repulsed the Groenburg assault.

"Johannes van Collier?" Kruger approached Johannes, who helped a wounded man.

"That's me. Did my son bring you?" Johannes handed Abraham to Kruger's medical team.

"He is over there," Kruger pointed to Jan. "Where is Theunis Steenekamp?"

"Dead," Johannes said shortly. "He led a charge on the British."

Kruger showed no emotion over Theunis's death. He regretted the loss of any Burgher but had come to accept that war had its bitter price.

"We tried to capture the ridge before you arrived," Johannes said. "We thought you might be British."

Kruger looked towards the ridge, seemingly empty but still occupied by the enemy.

"I will talk to Captain Baird," Kruger said. He gave brisk orders that saw his commando surround the ridge, with each man disappearing behind cover. "Nobody will get past my commando."

"They're Boers, sir." Meek scanned the newcomers through Fletcher's field glasses. "Hundreds of them."

"They're Boers," Andrew confirmed. He felt sick when he saw the numbers arrayed against him.

The newcomers spread around the ridge, with the horsemen forming tight little groups at extreme rifle range.

"These lads know their stuff," Meek said. "They're tempting us to fire and waste ammunition while effectively blockading us."

"How many bullets do we have left?"

"Nine from the dead Boers, sir, but they're only suitable for their rifles. Three Martini cartridges. I took the liberty of borrowing Mr. Fletcher's revolver and all his ammunition, which will give us another seven shots, plus whatever you have."

"I've one Martini cartridge and six revolver bullets," Andrew said.

Meek lowered his field glasses. "Not enough to stop these boys. One more attack should be enough." He tapped his water bottle. "We're short of water and *scoff* as well."

Andrew looked around the ridge. Mariana and the two other women were tending to the badly wounded Fletcher while most Dragoons lay on the ground, seeking shade and cover. Ogden was dead. The sentries crouched behind rocks, watching the surrounding enemy.

"Sir!" Briggs said. "A group of Boers is approaching under a flag of truce."

"They do that a lot," Sergeant Meek said. "I've never known men to talk so much as the Boers."

Andrew forced a smile. "Let's see what they have to say."

A sad-faced, bearded man led the mounted group that rode carefully up the ridge. Andrew stepped forward to meet them. "That's far enough!" he cautioned when they came within two hundred yards of his perimeter. "Any closer, and I'll order my men to open fire!"

The Boers obediently halted. "Are you Captain Andrew Baird of the Natal Dragoons?"

"I am," Andrew confirmed. "Who are you, *meneer*?" He already knew the answer.

"Paul Kruger of the *Suid-Afrikaanse Republiek*," the sad-faced man remained on horseback, sitting easily as his companions studied the British positions. "You are outnumbered and surrounded, Captain."

Andrew affected nonchalance. "I see your men," he said. "We have them trapped around us, waiting for a British column to finish you off. We are the anvil, and the column is the hammer."

Kruger smiled. "You are no anvil, my friend. The British column returned to Natal days ago when we informed them we had captured your small party. You have about a dozen Natal Dragoons, six civilians, three women, and a British spy named Charles Abercrombie."

"We have nobody of that name here," Andrew said truthfully.

"Veldcornet Johannes van Collier has seen him," Kruger replied. "He was at Swartspruit when you arrived, and you took him with you."

"And now he is gone," Andrew replied.

Kruger sighed and looked up at the ridge, where the Dragoons waited with empty rifles. "Can you tell me on your honour that Charles Abercrombie is no longer with you?"

"I can tell you that on my honour as an officer and a gentleman," Andrew replied.

Kruger smiled sadly. "And what do you intend now, Captain?"

"That depends on you, *Meneer* Kruger. We could fight you here, or if you ride away, we will return to Natal," Andrew said honestly.

"We could storm the ridge," Kruger reminded.

"Perhaps," Andrew said. "But you would lose many men and make a lot of widows and orphans in the Republic."

Kruger nodded gravely. "Perhaps we would lose fewer men than you suggest," he said. "Why did you invade our land during a time of truce?"

"The Afrikander Bond Boers were blockading the garrison at Swartspruit, contrary to the truce," Andrew said. "I was sent to lift the siege and bring the garrison home."

"Including Mr Abercrombie," Kruger said.

"Including Mr Abercrombie, the geologist," Andrew agreed.

"Mr Abercrombie, the prime minister's nephew," Kruger amended. He stepped his horse closer to Andrew. "You will be aware that a mutual acquaintance of ours was also interested in Mr Abercrombie."

"Konrad Bramigan, the Prussian agent," Andrew said. "Is he with your commando?"

"He does not ride with us," Kruger replied. "Nor will we listen to his blandishments and exchange one foreign invader for another."

"Thank you for the information, sir," Andrew said.

"I take it you have no further reason to remain in our land?"

"I intend to leave as soon as my way is clear," Andrew replied.

"We shall not delay you," Kruger replied. "There has been enough killing in our Republic." He touched a hand to his hat. "I wish you a good day, Captain Baird."

"Thank you, sir," Andrew replied. "Please give my regards to Johannes van Collier."

Kruger nodded. "I shall," he said.

Andrew watched as the Boers withdrew from the ridge to form up half a mile away.

"Right, lads," Andrew said. "Mount up; we're going home! Column of twos, with the civilians in the rear." He heard Meek hector the Dragoons into formation, ensured Mariana was safe and led them towards Natal.

"Jan!" Mannie shouted. "Jan!"

"Mannie!" Jan felt a mixture of pleasure and apprehension when he saw his younger brother approach. "What are you doing here?"

"Engela wanted to see you," Mannie explained, stepping aside to reveal Engela standing nervously behind him.

"Hello, Jan," Engela did not smile. "How are you?"

"Engela?" Jan stared at her for a few seconds while all his doubts and anger faded.

Mannie smiled as Jan shouldered his rifle, extended his arms, and brought Engela close.

Christiaan Niekerf watched the British ride to the south with the women at the rear and their rifles in their bucket holsters.

"Are the *Rooinecks* returning to their own land?"

"Ja, Christiaan," Johannes replied.

"Is the war over?" Christiaan asked.

"It is over," Johannes said. "We have defeated the *Rooinecks*. They will leave us alone now."

Christian carefully placed his rifle in its holster and watched the retreating British column. Johannes could not read the expression on his face. "I do not trust the *Rooinecks*. I'll follow them as far as the border."

Johannes nodded. "That is a wise plan," he said. "Do not trust any foreign nation that says they are here to help us."

Christiaan patted his horse. "The Lord gave us Africa as the Promised Land. We tamed it from the wilderness, and we will hold it. It is our land." He tapped the butt of his rifle. "I will follow the *Rooinecks* back to Natal, and in time, we shall drive them over the sea."

Johannes smiled. "I hope we are both alive to see that day, Oom Christiaan."

Christiaan examined Johannes with his old, terrible eyes. "You are of good blood, Johannes van Collier. I hope to ride beside you again." Turning his horse, he followed the British, riding slowly.

"How old is that man?" Jan joined Johannes, with Engela and Abraham at his side. Abraham was pale, with his left arm in a sling.

"Christiaan was a Voortrekker back in the Great Trek of thirty-five," Johannes said. "The Zulus murdered his wife and children at Weenen,[1] so he was a grown man then, forty-three years ago. He must be in his eighties now." They watched Christiaan ride away, an indomitable old man who symbolised the spirit of the Voortrekkers.

"The Voortrekkers were men," Jan said.

Johannes looked at his son with a smile. "You are also a man," he said.

THE SOUND OF BOER RIFLES

Cape Town, November 1881.

General Hook looked across the width of his desk at Andrew. "You got Abercrombie out safely and avoided a diplomatic spat, Baird. That was probably the only positive to come from this sorry affair, and we can't tell the papers."

"We lost some good men, sir," Andrew reminded.

"We always do," Hook agreed, pouring brandy into two glasses and handing one to Andrew. "And if you had killed Turner, we would have lost one more."

"Turner was a lucky man," Andrew said.

Hook nodded. "He was an insurance policy, nothing else." He changed the subject. "The peace treaty gives the Transvaal self-government in all internal matters, while Britain controls their foreign affairs."

"That should keep Germany out," Andrew said.

"That may be the idea," Hook agreed. "The treaty has not pleased everybody. There has been an exodus of British residents from the Transvaal. They've given up their homes and businesses rather than live under an oligarchical Boer government."

Andrew sipped at his Cape-distilled brandy and looked out of Hook's office window, where a crowd shouted their dislike of Gladstone and the government in London. One howling group set fire to Gladstone's effigy, while another mob mocked a model of the British lion, calling it a toothless remnant of the past. "Mr. Gladstone doesn't seem very popular here," Andrew said.

"He's not," Hook confirmed. "Many people see him as pusillanimous, refusing to perform his duty to the British. The British of Cape Colony and Natal think the Boers are a threat on their borders, much as they viewed the Zulus." The general shrugged. "Opinions are, as always, divided. Many others, particularly in Great Britain, see the treaty as the magnanimous action of a power that does not have to prove its strength by squashing a small nation. They believe Gladstone has shown that Britain is willing to aid a struggling country."

Andrew tried more brandy. "I doubt the Boers see things in that light."

"President Johannes Brand of the Orange Free State said the treaty was the noblest act England has ever done." Hook grunted. "He means Britain rather than England, but one must forgive these people their occasional lapses into ignorance."

"Yes, sir," Andrew agreed. "Miscalling Britain as England is a foolish mistake many people make."

Hook nodded. "Foolish indeed. However, the Boers of the Transvaal believe the treaty directly resulted from the skirmishes they won. They think Britain was scared to fight them."

"Gladstone has his own agenda," Andrew said.

"Don't all politicians? Many soldiers believe the government betrayed the army." He threw Andrew a sharp look. "You were present at Laing's Nek and Majuba. In fact, you saw most of our defeats."

"Yes, sir," Andrew agreed.

"How did it happen?" Hook asked. "How did a collection of semi-educated farmers defeat a modern European army? We already discussed your thoughts. Have you more to add?"

Andrew considered before he replied. "May I be frank, sir?"

"I wish somebody would be frank rather than soothing me with platitudes!" Hook said.

"Very well, sir. The trouble starts at the top. I think some officers are deficient in intelligence. The cleverest boys in school don't enter the army but find more lucrative employment in the professions or industry. We'll have to increase pay to attract a better-quality officer. At present, many Officers' Messes are little more than social clubs for gentlemen, with sport and hunting more important than soldiering. In the so-called smart regiments, only the rich and well-connected become officers. They are charming fellows, no doubt, but not always the most intelligent of leaders."

Hook nodded grimly. "Are you saying that many officers see the army as a glorified social club?"

"Yes, sir," Andrew said grimly. "If we hope to improve the army, we must end the system where money, titles, and old school connections ensure near-automatic selection and promotion."

"That would be a monumental alteration," Hook responded.

"Maybe every officer should serve at least a year in the ranks," Andrew continued. "Let them see what the men are like before they condemn them with brainless decisions."

"Anything else?" Hook asked.

"Training," Andrew said. "Standing men in line to fire volleys does not work against an enemy as wily as the Boers, who have weapons as good as ours. We must train our men to fire from behind cover and advance as the Boers do. We also need to improve our soldiers' marksmanship."

Hook scribbled notes. "You've given this some thought, Baird. Anything else?"

"Mobility," Andrew said. "The Boer commando could move from battle to siege and back at a speed we cannot emulate."

"Are you proposing we mount every British soldier on a horse?"

Andrew shook his head. "That would be ideal, if hardly practical, sir," he replied. "I would suggest more mounted infantry and less rigidity in drill."

"These are major proposals, Baird," Hook said.

"Yes, sir," Andrew agreed, "but in the eyes of the world, the Boers have defeated us, and it's a defeat that will rankle in the army."

"It's a defeat we may yet avenge," Hook said softly. "Although not if Gladstone is in office. Well, thank you, Captain. I have asked the opinion of several officers who served in the war. I'll add your ideas, create a file, and send it to the appropriate government minister."

"Thank you, sir," Andrew said. "Do you think he will listen?"

Hook shrugged weary shoulders. "That's in the lap of the Gods, Baird. Who knows the workings of a politician's mind?"

He finished his brandy. "Now the fighting is over; what do you intend to do? Will you remain with the Natal Dragoons?"

"I don't know, sir," Andrew thought of Mariana. "I haven't decided yet."

"Keep in touch, Baird; I anticipate trouble in Suez next." Hook grinned. "Not your bailiwick, eh? You'd better get back to your Dragoons and that young lady of yours." He held out his hand.

"Yes, sir." Andrew shook the general's hand and left the office.

MARIANA STOOD AT THE DOOR OF THE HOUSE AS ANDREW dismounted. "What did the general say?"

"I don't think he's optimistic that our army will reform," Andrew patted Lancelot and handed him to Briggs. "How are you?"

"Fine," Mariana told him. She held out her arms. "Will the peace last?"

"For the time being," Andrew held her, looking into her eyes without seeing any shadows. "Many in the army will seek another round with Brother Boer, mainly men who have never met him. The papers will stir up discontent and print all sorts of nonsense."

"The papers often do," Mariana said. She slid her arms around his shoulders, examining him as minutely as he studied her. "You look tired."

"You look well," Andrew countered. "Better than you've done since..."

"Since the day the renegades came," Mariana said levelly.

"Since the day the renegades came," Andrew agreed, searching for the shadow's return. Mariana's eyes remained clear, with a sparkle he had not seen for over two years.

"I love you," Mariana said suddenly, with a slight lift of her chin. "I have always loved you."

Andrew felt his heartbeat increase. He instinctively held tighter.

"I know you always loved Elaine better than me," Mariana said without breaking eye contact. "But can you love me just a little bit?"

Andrew felt something twist inside him. He was unsure how he felt for this girl, no, this *woman* now; her experiences had altered Mariana, so her girlish years were behind her. He thought of the promise he had made at Elaine's grave to always look after her sister. "More than a little bit," Andrew said softly, unsure how much truth was in his words.

"More than a little bit?" For a moment, Mariana looked very vulnerable, and then she smiled. "For my sake or Elaine's?"

About to reply, "For both," Andrew changed his mind. "For yours," he said and saw Mariana's eyes widen.

"Will Elaine mind you loving me more than a little bit?" Mariana asked.

"No," Andrew told her. "Elaine won't mind in the slightest." He could picture Elaine standing in the room with her so-sensible smile as she watched them.

They entered the immaculate house, which smelled of beeswax polish and cleanliness. "You've got the place looking lovely," Andrew said.

"Elaine would like it this way."

Andrew shook his head. "This house is about Mariana and Andrew," he assured her.

When Mariana smiled, Andrew knew he had said the right thing. Mariana closed the door. "I've made coffee," she said and placed a possessive hand on his arm.

Aletta looked up from the table where she was making bread. *Ja,* she thought, *I have my men back. They have gone to war, and all have returned to me. Johannes has new grey hairs on his head, and the lines on his face have deepened. Working on the farm for a few weeks will not remove the grey, but it will smooth his face. Jan is a man now, with iron inside him. He will never tell me what he has seen and done, but he is now ready to take Engela to wife, and she is prepared for him.*

She kneaded the dough with her strong hands, allowing the rhythm of the work to ease some of her worries.

Mannie is the most affected. He left as a boy and returned as a boy, and then something happened, and he became a man. She nodded. *I could not have asked for more. A good man for a husband and two brave men for sons. The Lord has blessed me.*

"Aletta!" Johannes stepped into the room. He paused for a moment to wrap his arms around her. "I am going to check the cattle. I don't know how many we've lost to wild animals since the war started."

"You do that," Aletta agreed. "Take Jan with you. And Mannie, if he will go."

"They are both already outside," Johannes told her.

"That is good," Aletta said. She stepped to the door and watched her family ride away. *Life is as it should be,* she told herself as her men shrank with distance. *They'll be hungry when they return. My men are always hungry when they return from work.* Smiling, Aletta stepped back into the kitchen, humming a quiet song as the chickens scrabbled noisily outside.

ABOUT THE AUTHOR

Born in Edinburgh, Scotland and educated at the University of Dundee, Malcolm Archibald has written in a variety of genres, from academic history to folklore, historical novels to fantasy. He won the Dundee International Book Prize with *Whales for the Wizard* in 2005 and the Society of Army Historical Research prize for Historical Military Fiction with *Blood Oath* in 2021.

Happily married for over 42 years, Malcolm has three grown children and lives outside Dundee in Scotland.

To learn more about Malcolm Archibald and discover more Next Chapter authors, visit our website at www.nextchapter.pub.

NOTES

CHAPTER 1

1. See 'The Noise of Zulu Battle' by Malcolm Archibald, published by Next Chapter in May 2023.

CHAPTER 2

1. Redvers Buller was one of the foremost British soldiers in the closing decades of the Nineteenth century. Andrew fought beside him during the Zulu War.

CHAPTER 5

1. Sandwala: a slang term for Isandhlwana, where the Zulus defeated a British army in January 1879.
2. A Commandant Robertse, of the besieging Boers, was wounded in this opening skirmish of the war.

CHAPTER 6

1. The Siege of Lucknow during the Indian Mutiny (1857).

CHAPTER 7

1. The ambush at Bronkhorst Spruit lasted fifteen minutes and cost the British 56 men killed and 92 wounded. Colonel Anstruther later died of his wounds. The Boers lost two dead and five wounded, with most of the British fire going above the Boers' heads. Conductor Egerton of the Commissariat and Transport Department and Sergeant Bradley smuggled the Colours to safety. Three soldiers' wives were awarded the Royal Red Cross for their courage and for attending to the wounded.

NOTES

CHAPTER 8

1. The Battle of Boomplats was fought on 29th August 1848 between a British force led by Sir Harry Smith and Commandant General Andreas Pretorius. The British won the skirmish and later annexed territory to the British Empire.
2. Kriegsraad – a pre-battle meeting to discuss tactics.
3. The flag above the fort was homemade. Lieutenant Rundle of the Royal Artillery provided a cloak, with Lieutenant Lindsell a coat and an unnamed sergeant his scarlet tunic. The flag remained in place for the duration of the siege. In 1912, Rundle, then General Sir Leslie Rundle, presented the flag to the 2nd Battalion Royal Scots Fusiliers.
4. Nine of Ou Griet's balls either hit the walls of the fort or landed inside in the attack on the First of January 1881. They did some minor damage without killing or injuring a single soldier. During the entire siege, Ou Griet was accredited with killing one man and wounding five others. The other cannonballs passed over the fort. Private Dobbs of the 21st Foot was killed during this attack.

CHAPTER 9

1. Scoff or skoff became accepted as a slang word for food after the Second Boer War of 1899-1902, but British soldiers based in South Africa would have added it to their vocabulary in the late 1870s or early 1880s.

CHAPTER 10

1. The Battle of Maiwand, fought on the 27th of July 1880, was an Afghan victory over a British army.
2. The Battle of Laing's Nek was the last occasion British redcoats marched to battle with the colours displayed.
3. Lieutenant Hill gained the Victoria Cross for rescuing wounded men under fire during the action at Laing's Nek.

CHAPTER 11

1. Wolseley Ring: General Sir Garnet Wolseley formed a group of the brightest and best officers known as the Wolseley Ring. They included Colley, Redvers Buller and other prominent late Nineteenth century officers.
2. Lieutenant Lindsell led this all-volunteer party on the 7th of January 1881.

NOTES

CHAPTER 12

1. Out of a total strength of twenty-seven officers and men, the Royal Artillery lost thirteen killed and wounded in the battle of Schuinschoogte. Lieutenant Parsons was one of the wounded.
2. The Ingogo claimed three men that night, and one more next day when Captain Wilkinson of the Rifles drowned trying to bring medical help to the wounded.

CHAPTER 13

1. On the 22nd of January, 1881, Lieutenant Dalrymple-Hay of the 21st Foot, the Royal Scots Fusiliers, won the DCM for leading twelve men to clear a Boer trench. He rose to become a major, and his son, John Dalrymple-Hay of the Gordon Highlanders, died of enteric fever in the Second Boer War.
2. The wound to Private Colvin created an exchange of letters between Colonel Winsloe and General Cronje. The missile may have been a bullet fired by an 8-bore elephant gun.
3. Sir Garnet Wolseley was one of Britain's foremost soldiers of the period. Sir Evelyn Wood was another distinguished officer and a favourite of Queen Victoria.

CHAPTER 15

1. The Gordons recruited Ghazi, an Afghan hound in Afghanistan. The dog was wounded at Majuba but made it home. He kept regular watch with the men, drew his rations and guarded the other regimental pets.
2. The Battle of Blood River was fought on the 16th of December 1838, when a few hundred Boer Voortrekkers defeated a Zulu impi at least fifteen thousand strong.

CHAPTER 17

1. Alfred, Lord Tennyson: *The Princess*.
2. Forlorn Hope: a near suicide mission.

CHAPTER 18

1. This incident occurred at the Battle of Warburg, 31st of July 1760.
2. "Remember Majuba" became a common war cry during the Second Boer War of 1899 to 1902.

NOTES

CHAPTER 19

1. When the Zulus killed Louis Napoleon, Prince Imperial of France, during the Zulu War, the Bonaparte dynasty ended. Some people in France thought the British had allowed the Zulus to kill him, or French Republicans or even Queen Victoria.
2. This incident was based on a similar event during the Second Boer War, 1899-1902, when a Boer marksman fired at them from a range Captain Doyle of Doyle's Australian Scouts calculated at 2300 yards. The rifle was an 1877 Steyr with a drop-block breech and a .303 bore. The marksman was an old man with a long beard. Captain Doyle's son, the late Douglas Doyle, informed me of the encounter.

CHAPTER 21

1. Weenen: The Place of Weeping, where the Zulus massacred many Boer settlers.

Printed in Dunstable, United Kingdom